His Lady Bride

Brothers in Arms, Book 1

Shayla Black
writing as Shelley Bradley

His Lady Bride
Published by Shelley Bradley LLC
Copyright © 2000 Shelley Bradley LLC
Edited by Amy Knupp

Print ISBN 978-1-936596-24-9

PROLOGUE

November 1484

The princes were dead. Children, both of them, slaughtered by Richard III, their own uncle, for the power and wealth that came with England's throne.

And only a handful of people in all of England, including Aric Neville, knew for certain.

He bid Godspeed to the spy he had paid handsomely for information about the boys' mysterious disappearance, then rubbed numb fingers over the sockets of his dry, sleep-deprived eyes. It brought no relief. He wished the informant had a reason to lie, but the brave man had risked life and limb to come here and spill the truth.

From the keep's arrow-slit window, Aric cast his weary gaze over the moonlit Yorkshire hills surrounding Hartwich Hall. 'Twas the home of his mentor, Guilford, Earl of Rothgate—and a second home to Aric. Yet for the first time since he had come to this castle at age seven to receive his knight's training, the familiar place brought him no solace.

Nothing would comfort him now that he had no hope of finding the princes alive. While most of England still prayed for the best, Aric knew only guilt and grief, for he had played a role in bringing about the demise of the younger royal child. Jesu, the boy had been but ten!

With mechanical precision, Aric secured the last of his armor, the greaves about his shins and the poleyns over his knees. This day would see another battle fought. More bloodshed. More men wasted.

For this, he had trained his whole life.

He let loose an angry oath. Since coming to Hartwich, he had been blessed to make friends with two of Guilford's other pupils, both closer to him than brothers. His mentor had certainly been more like a father than his own. But over that span of years, Aric had also earned his fierce reputation as the White Lion, ever ready to kill for the House of York.

God, he'd been an ambitious fool, so eager to win back the earldom of Warwick after his uncle had lost it supporting the Lancastrians more than a decade ago.

His ambition had abetted the murder of a child.

"The Campbells are below and ready for battle," one of his good friends, Drake MacDougall, murmured from behind.

Aric turned. Drake stood in the arched door, dark hair swept back, battle gear in place. The Scotsman was no ordinary knight, and on another day, Aric would be proud to have Drake fighting by his side. Over the course of their training, Guilford had made them the best.

"Will the Campbells never cease these petty squabbles with the MacDougalls? They should have understood long ago that your mother's marriage to your father was not an act of aggression."

"Aye, 'twas naught but a mistake." Drake sighed. "Let us fight them once more."

His friend's grim tones sounded rife with pain—and no wonder, given Drake's unfortunate past. 'Twould seem they both dealt with some disquieting problems this day.

"I'll be below shortly."

Drake hesitated. "Did you receive word, then?"

"Aye." Aric swallowed past a raw throat. "As I feared, they are dead. Suffocated September last in the Tower."

Drake crossed the room, his well-oiled armor clinking, and clasped Aric's arm. 'Tis a grievous day, indeed. I am sorry for England's loss."

"My thanks." Aric nodded, unable to confess his guilt even to his closest of friends. This shame was his to bear alone. Instead, he changed the subject. "Has Kieran arrived?"

"Aye, last night after you were abed."

"How is our Irish friend? As reckless as ever?" Aric asked,

eager for a change in subject.

"Of course." The man in question grinned from the doorway.

Drake and Aric whirled to the sound of Kieran Broderick's voice, their expressions surely a mirror of welcome and reprimand at once.

Kieran sauntered into the room with a jaunty wink and a loose-hipped gait. Candlelight danced in his chestnut hair, which had obviously been arranged by a haphazard wind, not any intention with a brush.

"Zounds, the two of you look as happy as mutts that lost their meals." He frowned. "Good to see you, too."

"Aye, 'tis good," Drake assured. "We simply would prefer to keep seeing you in one piece."

Before Kieran could defend his wanderlust with a typical pithy reply, the battle readied on the open field just outside the window. The horses pawed the mist-hung earth restlessly, their breaths white with chill, stark against the blue-black of the predawn sky. Troops formed. Over one hundred men unsheathed weapons.

The trio of knights vaulted down the stairs and left the castle to join the impending fray. Aric knotted inside with foreboding. Drake, as always, would serve Guilford with an abiding sense of duty. And Kieran...well, the youngest of the three always followed his thirst for adventure, often at great peril, until it was momentarily quenched.

With all the enthusiasm of a condemned traitor on execution day, Aric mounted his gray steed, the creak of his saddle echoing the ache in his heart. Sighing heavily, he unsheathed his sword and waited, wishing this battle gone and the warring Campbells back to Scotland.

Aric had not long to wait. The battle began with a shout in the dark morn. The clash of swords declared the fighting underway.

Reluctantly, he urged his mount into the melee, his weapon ready.

Opponents came at him one after the other, sometimes in pairs. All seemed eager to test England's White Lion, the symbol emblazoned on the breastplate of his armor.

Feint. Thrust. Parry. Kill.

Feint. Thrust. Parry. Kill.

The motions were automatic and unchanged, as were the results.

The metallic scent of blood tinged the air, along with the smells of
damp earth and dewy grass. The thud of metal upon bone mixed
with the cries of anguish and the laments of death. The greedy soil
drank in the liquid carnage as the battle continued all around him,
unabated. Still, the sun hid slyly behind the winter-bare hills, as if
concealing the utter brutalities of war.

But Aric knew them all too well. He'd known naught else since
youth. His uncle Warwick had made sure of that.

And all of this waste of human life for what? Another parcel of
land? Another territorial right? The squabble the Campbells had with
Guilford now seemed petty and ancient. Years ago, the Scots had
become Guilford's foes once his daughter, Drake's mother, had wed
Drake's father, an enemy MacDougall. The union, broken by
betrayal and death, still angered them.

Several paces away, Aric caught sight of Drake, who was
outnumbered. Three of the Campbells hovered about his friend.
Drake dispatched one of his enemies with a broadsword to the side,
then gave a vicious yank to extricate his blade.

A Campbell lifted his ax to Drake. Aric knew his friend would
not be able to turn in time to fend off the blow. Without another
thought, Aric hurled a lance across the space between them. It
landed in the Campbell soldier's back a moment before he slumped
forward on his mount.

Drake nodded his thanks. Aric did not answer in kind, just urged
his mount toward the dead Scot and retrieved his lance from the
corpse.

A Campbell, thinking to take them by surprise, charged them
from Aric's side. Drake tensed. But Aric saw the cur studying them.
With a mighty swing of his arm, he cut the Campbell soldier nearly
in two.

The dying man screamed in agony before terrible silence fell.
Aric ignored the sound.

"Watch yourself, friend," he said to Drake, pushing strands of
his tawny hair from his sweat-slick face.

He then made his way down the hill, farther into the grunting,
bleeding crowd. Someone had set fire to the cottages of Guilford's
crofters. Rage thundered through him for that slight, King Richard's
machinations, and the ill-fated choices that had led him here. Soon,
Aric's sword was slippery and red, fresh blood mingling with the

rotting, illuminated by the eerie orange flow of the fires all around him. Only his calluses saved him from losing his grip on the weapon.

His knee ached where a Campbell mace had glanced it. A cut above his eye bled. Still, Aric slashed his way through the crowd until the Campbells were outnumbered and retreating.

Behind him, Kieran hollered in triumph. Though relieved his friend was alive, Aric could not spare the energy to lecture him on caution. 'Twould fall on deaf ears, anyway. At least the battle was over.

Tiredly, he dismounted, looking for Drake and the old earl. At the top of the next rise, he spotted his friend nearly surrounded by his fellow Scotsmen as he knelt with bloody hands next to a fallen man. Aric peered out at the warrior lying upon the earth—Lochlan MacDougall, Drake's father.

"Traitor! Murderer!" one of the Scotsmen yelled at Drake.

Think they that Drake killed his own father?

As Aric raced to his friend's side, he heard not his clansmen's accusations or Drake's protestations.

"Drake is innocent." Aric dismounted with a scowl. "His love for his sire is well known by you all."

His words affected none of the Clan MacDougall. Hunger for blood was running high amongst the men now that the cowardly Campbells had thwarted everyone's feast before they could finish gorging. Bile rose in Aric's throat as a pair of men grabbed Drake and shoved him roughly to his feet.

"Pea-witted fools, he would never kill Lochlan!" Kieran dashed to Drake's side, eyes blazing.

The Scotsmen still paid no heed.

Suddenly, the crowd parted to admit Guilford. The old earl's shock of white hair stood out against the dismal dark gray sky. "Release him. Drake murdered no one, least of all his own father."

Still, a Scotsman named Duff refused. "The Clan MacDougall maun judge him now…" Aric heard before the voice faded away, drowned out by the sounds of crows above the scene. He despaired. If the powerful Earl of Rothgate could not help Drake, he feared no one could.

Would he lose a friend this day, too, along with his honor?

Drake struggled, but the MacDougalls contained him. All too quickly, Drake was taken away. Kieran raised his sword, ready to fight. Guilford stayed him with a calming hand. Aric looked on with gritty, aching eyes until the Scotsmen disappeared.

He turned to Guilford with a questioning glance.

"Let the hotheads work this foolishness out of their blood," the earl advised. "They will soon see their words as senseless and release him."

"I would rather fight!" Kieran objected.

"Of that, I have no doubt," Guilford answered wryly.

"They cannot imprison an innocent man so unjustly!"

"And so they shall not, Kieran. Leave this to me. You, too, Aric." The aging man shot him a sharp, blue-eyed gaze.

"Aye," Aric replied automatically, though he liked it not.

The crowd began to disperse as morning finally burst over the craggy Yorkshire hills. Men pilfered the fresh corpses on the battlefield, gathering valuable weapons, armor, and boots. Aric turned his back on the customary gruesome scene with a curse.

"Aric?" Kieran questioned, his deep voice laced with a concern the glib man did not often exhibit. Beside him, Guilford looked on.

Uncertain what to say, Aric remained silent. How could he reconcile the murders of two royal children by means so foul, the loss of his honor, the death of his ambition? How could he reply to the peril in which one of his oldest friends now found himself, knowing all the while he could do nothing to stop it?

Gripping his broadsword in his tense, throbbing fingers, he looked at Kieran, then at his mentor. His mind felt slow, almost numb. His heart felt only rage for the injustice, the inhumanity of this bloody power struggle for the throne, these dangerous times in which a man could make a healthy living by killing.

No more.

Aric glared down at the heavy sword in his hand. This weapon, this instrument of death, had cost many men their lives. He had wielded it to uphold a prosperous England he had believed in. 'Twas all a lie. A giant hoax revealed.

He refused to take part in it any longer.

With a mighty thrust, Aric cast his sword into the ground and left the battlefield behind.

CHAPTER ONE

April 1485

Sitting in the shadows, Aric carved on the block of half-shaped wood in his hand as dusk settled over the tranquil, spring-shaded forest in greens, blues, and pinks.

Here lay peace, endless days of it, uninterrupted by greed, ambition, or war. Here he would remain, unfettered by the world.

"Damn you! Dagbert, where do you take me?"

Aric stilled his knife and lifted his head to peer into the surrounding forest, where the unseen woman had screeched into his prized tranquility. Dare he hope that if he ignored the loud wench and her unwanted companion, they would leave him be?

The woman shouted her protest again, closer this time. Uneasiness skittered through him. He set the wood aside, clutched his knife, and rose. Scowling, Aric felt the resurgence of his battle instincts.

From between a pair of giant, eons-old oak trees, a diverse party emerged. A servant, a soldier, and a holy man marched directly toward him, holding a fetching female captive beside them. He studied each face, feeling his scowl deepen.

Aye, this group intended to shatter his peace with their demands, so said the bearing of all. Except one.

The maiden, dressed a trifle more finely than the soldier, shouted and kicked like a wild thing as two men gripped her fragile wrists and dragged her toward him like some virgin sacrifice to a pagan altar.

The woman was clad in striking crimson and gold that stretched tautly across her young breasts. Her glossy black hair shone in the sun as she struggled. For the first time since leaving politics, battle, and women behind, Aric felt intrigued.

He cursed the intruders—and himself.

She shouted, "A pox upon you all, you hen-brained fools!"

Clearly, the beauty had no trouble finding her tongue.

"Release me now," she continued loudly, "for I will not be subject—"

"Aye, ye will, Lady Gwenyth," the soldier interrupted, grunting as they dragged her ever closer. "Or the baron says we all could die."

"Die? What foolishness do you speak, you maggot pie? My uncle will know of this scheme!"

"'Twas Lord Capshaw's own idea to wed you off to yon sorcerer as an offering to stop the drought."

Yon sorcerer. Aric knew they described him, and he had done nothing to dispel the untruth. The rumor had bought him six months of peace—at least until today.

Before he could protest, the woman looked at him, her eyes large and furious and fearful. And blue, so blue he'd ne'er seen a color so rich, so deep and fine, so striking against the pale roses of her skin. An instant image of her as she lay beneath him, those brilliant eyes liquid with languid passion, assailed him.

He frowned. Nay, he wanted nothing to do with anyone, even such a comely wench as this. His existence was a solitary one, and he had never been happier since leaving court intrigues and Northwell Castle behind and coming to this tiny cottage.

"Wed *him*? Have you gone daft?"

The woman's gaze snapped over him like blue flames, flashing with contempt—and that same hint of fear.

"Dagbert, I will not marry this…hermit," she insisted.

Aric gave the ebony-haired beauty a sharp glare. Hermit? He lived comfortably, with an abundance of candles and plenty to eat. The roof over his head kept him dry, while his bed kept him warm from the night's chill. What more could a man want?

Certainly not a woman who, by all appearances, was a sharp-tongued shrew—albeit a lovely one, with a full pink mouth that made him recall the joy of kissing. But she was a shrew all the same.

One he had no wish to marry.

As Aric prepared to tell the castlefolk to leave him in peace—and take his bride with them—Dagbert looked at Lady Gwenyth with wicked glee. "If ye refuse to wed the warlock, we've been told to kill ye in offering."

Kill her? Shock vibrated through each bone and muscle of Aric's body. She was but a woman, whose only crime appeared to be a lamentable freeness with her words. Surely they could not be serious.

The soldier pressed his blade against Lady Gwenyth's throat, his grin broadening. Aric knew they would indeed kill her, without haste or remorse.

More senseless death was not something he could tolerate.

"Do not touch her." As his fist tightened about the hilt of his knife, Aric leveled a glare at Dagbert.

"What say you, sorcerer?" Dagbert asked, easing his knife from the arched expanse of Lady Gwenyth's throat.

She trembled, Aric saw. And she fought it, if the strain in her arms and face was any indication. Somehow the thought of the black-toothed ruffian causing her fear angered Aric as nothing had in his blissful months alone.

"I say you release her now and leave my sight."

"And ye will take 'er to wife and stop the drought plaguing Lord Capshaw?" asked Dagbert.

He could no more stop a drought than he could predict the rain. "Nay, this is foolishness."

Dagbert scratched his head. "Does she displease ye?"

Lady Gwenyth's startled gaze flew to his face. Silently she pleaded with him, though he sensed she rarely pleaded for anything. That square chin told the story of her stubborn nature—that and those vivid, keen eyes.

"She's the comeliest wench at Penhurst Castle," Dagbert added.

That he could believe, but it did not change his answer. "I've no wish for a wife."

With a shrug, Dagbert brought the knife back to the frightened lady's pale neck. Her pulse raced beneath the sharp steel, and Aric's own heartbeat quickened.

"If she ain't well-pleasing enough to take to wife, then we'll see 'er dead. The Lord Capshaw asks only that ye end the drought in return."

Lord Capshaw apparently was a superstitious baron, willing to sacrifice his own niece to bring prosperity back to the castle. The baron was also willing to kill her if she failed to win the sorcerer's favor and end the drought. Aric wondered how he could possibly respond to such idiocy.

"Leave her here with me and be gone with you."

"Ye accept her, then, as Lord Capshaw's offerin'? Dagbert lowered his knife a fraction, his hand hovering somewhere around Lady Gwenyth's breast. Those blue eyes of hers colored with indignation.

"Aye. Leave her to me." Aric gritted his teeth in irritation.

What he would do with her once Dagbert and the baron's other cowards left was anyone's guess. He could solve only one problem at a time.

"Nay, I must see ye wed all proper-like. Lord Capshaw insisted."

Aric found his patience thinning. "I told you, I have no wish for a wife."

"The baron gave me but two options, a wife or a corpse. 'Tis for ye to decide, but I'll not risk me arse in crossing a man like Lord Capshaw."

"So you would rather cross a sorcerer?" Aric raised a brow in question.

Dagbert lifted the slabs of his shoulders in disdain. "I don't believe in your rabble-rubble."

"Don't you? How do you explain the dog?"

At Aric's shrill whistle, the half dog, half wolf emerged from the cottage's shadows, his gray-brown ears up on end, his sharp teeth bared. The small crowd drew back at the animal's approach, their expressions ranging from piqued interest to panic as the animal padded beyond a cluster of flowered toadflax and across the soft dirt to heel at Aric's side.

The dog growled, and the priest crossed himself. The servant pointed, his eyes wide with fear. Dagbert's face gave away little, except that he turned a shade paler.

To Aric's surprise, Lady Gwenyth's face held almost no fear. Did she sense the animal's goodness, or did she not know the beast had once ravaged the countryside?

"He tamed the devil's own and took him for a pet, a sure sign of evil," the holy man claimed.

"The dog, he might be from the devil," Dagbert conceded, casting furtive glances at the mutt, "but ye don't have any more powers than me. 'Tis a sense for these things I have. Now take the wench to wife, or I kill her."

Aric looked about for another means of thwarting Dagbert. The servant, pitifully dressed, did no more than clutch Lady Gwenyth's wrist and stare at the ground. If he was not mistaken, the beefy man was the one the castlefolk called Mute. Aric assumed the man could not speak. Little help there. The holy man merely clutched his Bible to his chest, wearing an expression of outraged righteousness. Aric sighed. He had to try, anyway.

"Good Father, would you wed two unwilling people to each other?"

The priest puffed out his thin chest. "Lady Gwenyth can rid you of Satan's evil with her purity. It is my duty and God's will."

"And what if I should place a hex on you?" Aric crossed his arms over his chest in what had always been a most intimidating stance.

If possible, the little man puffed out further. "God will protect me from evil like you."

Christ's blood! Now what?

Dagbert snickered. Aric speared the odious man with a lethal glare but found his gaze ensnared by Lady Gwenyth, instead. Her heated eyes, her soft mouth, the tempting curve of her breast—and her sharp tongue. Lord, he hated to think of that.

"Well," Dagbert prompted, "shall I see her wed or dead this day?"

Why did the world have to intrude upon his peace now, just when the nightmares were beginning to abate?

Aric sighed. "You shall see her wed."

* * * *

It seemed to Gwenyth as if the whole matter ended in moments. No matter how she'd protested to the tops of the oak and alder trees above or kicked the gluttons beside her, Mute and that wretched cur Dagbert had held tight.

The towering, thick-chested stranger was now her husband, his

13

thatch-roofed shanty her home.

With the vows now spoken, Dagbert sneered at her. "Don't ye come back to Penhurst, or the baron says he'll kill ye himself."

With that, Dagbert and the others retreated back into the forest, leaving her alone with the imposing sorcerer.

The golden-maned man the Church saw as her husband turned his broad frame about and headed toward his tiny dwelling, his feet falling silently on the soft spring earth. Gwenyth stared, openmouthed, at his retreat. Had he nothing to say to her? Nothing at all?

She could not remember a time she had been more scared—or more angry.

"Could you not have done something to stop Dagbert's madness?" she ranted, following the silent stranger. "Why did you allow this foolish wedding to happen?"

He turned back and stared at her, his strong, wide face sharp with question, his icy gray eyes challenging.

The silence dragged on. And on. Gwenyth gritted her teeth, and her nails dug into the callused flesh of her palms. She had never been one to keep her patience or hold her tongue. And at the moment, restraining either seemed impossible.

"Well, say something, you fen-sucked lout!"

Surprise crossed his chiseled tawny features. "Fen-sucked?"

Was that all he had to say? He had married her against her will. God's nightgown, it seemed he had married her against his own will! And he spoke first of her choice of insults, instead of their preposterous exchange of vows? The man hadn't seemed shy of wits earlier. Why wouldn't the coxcomb make sense now?

"Aye, fen-sucked, fly-bitten, and beef-brained. Why did you wed me?"

Turning away, he flung the door to his shanty open and ducked to step inside. "Should I have seen you dead?"

"Of course not, you tottering horn-beast," she shouted at his back. "You should have talked them out of this fool-born idea, promised to lift the drought, or fought your way out."

"I tried to reason with them, if you recall," he said through clenched teeth, his voice deep and tight.

Oh, and was he angry now? 'Twas a state he should finally reach, her having arrived long before! "Tried? Is that what you call it? My cousin's unborn babe could have said more to stop this farce."

He whirled on her again, hovering just inside the doorway, the simple green tunic covering his massive chest mere inches from her face. His eyes resembled angry storm clouds as he stared down at her. "And what did you try?"

"I-I told them I wanted this not. I kicked, railed, I screamed—"

"Aye, and everyone between here and London heard you."

Gwenyth gasped, and the beast turned away with a smile, evidenced by a flash of surprisingly straight teeth and the curve of his wide mouth, before retreating inside the little cottage. With much foot stomping, she followed. The oaf would feel the full measure of her fury!

At the door, she stopped as her gaze fell upon the dwelling's interior. A ramshackle bed sat upon the dirt floor next to a blackened pit of a hearth. A pair of his braies lay strewn across the single chair, and a tiny table with a teetering leg and a pitcher with a broken handle filled the rest of the small space. The lone window had no glass. Nay! Gwenyth closed her eyes in despair.

For half her life, she had lain upon the cold stone floor every night at Penhurst and wished to reclaim her position as lady of the castle, of the fine home she'd been born to. Most of all, she yearned for a place where she belonged, where the people within saw her as a prize, not a burden, something her Uncle Bardrick had taken great pains to remind her she was.

She'd always known he much enjoyed being Lord Capshaw and showing his two daughters off as great ladies. Still, she had imagined he would see his brother's only child well wed. Hadn't he brought the exceedingly handsome Sir Penley Fairfax to the keep for just that cause?

She had thought so for the past fortnight. Now she knew better, damn Uncle Bardrick's eyes!

Instead, he had married her off to the only man within twenty miles who frightened everyone, even Sir Penley. He had married her to a pauper of reputedly dark powers.

Gwenyth shivered as her memory dredged up the tales of his powers. His taming of the wild dog that had slaughtered pigs, chickens, and even cows all over the village had started the rumors of his magical abilities. That alone made people suspicious. Uncle

Bardrick's cook had exchanged cross words with the lone warlock over the purchase of food, then promptly died the next day. The castlefolk thought that all too eerie. And then the drought started soon thereafter, and had not been eased by blessed rain in nearly six months. That convinced everyone the hermit was a sorcerer. 'Twas likely true, she acknowledged with a sigh.

Bristling braies, had she been hasty-witted in insulting him? What would he do to her now?

"Well, do you plan to stand in the door all night or come inside?" asked the stranger.

What choice did she have? 'Twas either die by Uncle Bardrick's hand or test fate with the sorcerer. "I shall come in, but do not assume I mean to be your wife."

With tiny steps, Gwenyth made her way into the dwelling, treading on the tips of her toes through the dirt to the room's lone chair. She stared at the seat, currently occupied by his undergarments, wondering how she could stay with the man for even one night. This was—indeed, *he* was—everything she did not want, even if he was handsome in that overpoweringly male way.

The man did nothing to move his undergarments from the chair. Weary and impatient, Gwenyth tapped her toes against the earthen floor and waited. Finally, he heaved a giant sigh and crossed the room to retrieve his braies. She sat.

"As you can see, I did not expect a lady."

"Are you certain?" She needled. "Your paltry protests against this union make me think you lie, hermit."

He stretched his solid length out on the small bed, nearly engulfing the mattress. His long, muscled legs, encased in clean brown hose, were mere inches from her knee. Gwenyth swallowed. The man was certainly big enough and likely strong, too. Would he expect her to do her wifely duty by him on that small, no doubt flea-ridden bed?

"Actually, my lady, I wanted no one here, least of all someone so free with her tongue. But what is done, is done."

Gwenyth's mouth fell open at his insult. "If you wanted your peace, you should have fought for it! Instead, you showed all the mettle of a posy. And should you think—"

The sorcerer was off the bed and across the floor before she could blink. He stood in front of her chair, grabbed both her arms, and hauled her to her feet, flush against him.

My, he was certainly showing his mettle now. Those gray eyes of his were dark as charcoal, menacing in his golden face.

"You have insulted me and my home at every turn. I wanted neither you nor your tireless mouth here in my shelter. I tried to reason with your fine friend Dagbert to no avail. I surrendered my bachelor state to save your pretty neck, and you yell at me? God, woman! Has no one told you what a harpy harridan you are?"

Uncle Bardrick had told her that nearly every day since coming to Penhurst ten summers ago to bury her father and assume the castle's duties. "Why can you not be more like your cousins Nellwyn and Lyssa?" he would ask. She could not be such a paragon of demure virtue, no matter how she tried. Pleasing Uncle Bardrick and his vain wife, Welsa, without her temper showing seemed impossible. She'd given up trying long ago.

"I humbly beg your pardon, kind sir."

Her attempt at a decorous tone sounded more acidic than modest as she leaned into him and unleashed her temper. Gwenyth hardly cared if the sorcerer could turn her into a toad. It could not be worse than the position she now found herself in.

"In the last hour, I have been threatened, unwillingly wed, and insulted. Pray forgive me if that makes me a trifle irritable, you ass."

The tawny-haired hulk shook his head, grunted, and turned away without another word.

"What mean you by that? That grunt?"

The man to whom she found herself married said nothing. Indeed, he glanced not her way at all, but trod to the charred hearth, started a fire, and set a beaten kettle above it.

Moments later, the rich aroma of warming broth invaded her senses. Gwenyth ignored the fact the air was tinged with not just the familiar scent but also with something woodsy and earthy that could belong only to him. She focused on her anger instead.

"My life is in complete disarray, and you mean to make broth?"

He spared her but a glance over his shoulder, his brow lifted in irritation, before he turned his attention back to the kettle.

Argh! She had been much yelled at within Penhurst's walls. Even the cook's spoon across her hands she had learned to tolerate. But she hated to be ignored.

"Have you gone mute now? Grim only begins to describe the

trying state of our affairs. Of our very lives! At a time like this, you find nothing more pressing than to make broth whilst you grunt? Have I wed something better suited to the barn?"

Still, he said nothing, did not even bother himself with a glare in her direction. Gwenyth fisted her hands at her sides and stomped across the cottage toward him, venting a measure of her frustration.

She spoke to the imposing width of his tight-muscled back. "Can you not hear I am speaking to you, or are you always this crude in your manners? 'Twould explain why you are unmarried, despite being past your youth." She threw her arms up. "Well, that and this dwelling. Have you no rushes for the floor? No servant about to see to your comforts?" Silence. "Can you even speak the king's English?"

The blasted slow-wit still said nothing. Lord, how she wanted to kick his shin, step on his toes, beat some sense into his thick skull.

Still, 'twas not a good plan. Not only was she unlikely to cause him much pain, but the remembrance that many thought him a sorcerer stayed her—barely. She drew in a deep, calming breath, knowing she must try to reason with him somehow.

Behind him, Gwenyth cleared her throat, then touched a hand to his arm. "Clearly, you see I do not belong here. What comforts can you provide a lady? My…good man—"

"Aric," he said finally, his teeth gritted.

"What say you?"

Aric turned to face his new bride, who he had known for less than an hour, a bride who had not known his name until moments ago. The lithe length of her body was tense with fury, her brow furrowed with confusion. Her full, extraordinary mouth turned down in a frown.

By the saints, what was he to do with the woman?

She talked more than any female he'd ever known, few of her words something other than an insult or curse. She thought him and his home beneath her and wanted nothing more than to be gone. What would the luscious, shrewish Lady Gwenyth say if she knew he had just made her the Countess of Belford?

Clearly, she needed time to adjust to wedded life. 'Twas to be expected, he supposed. Still, Aric found it disconcerting that his ignorance about the flavor of her opulent mouth tugged at him almost as much as the fact she was now his wife—a very spirited one who thought him a fen-sucked barn animal.

As he turned away from her to pour his broth, Aric grimaced, wondering what the night would bring.

* * * *

The cheeky wench—his wife, Aric amended—could sleep anywhere. He envied her that. Oh, she had struggled to stay awake, but once the rhythm of slumber had overtaken her, she had scarcely stirred.

Trying to adjust his numb backside on the hard wooden chair to a more comfortable position, he eyed the woman he had wed hours ago. She lay in his bed on her stomach, her arms sprawled about her head, her fingers tangled in her thick, dark tresses. She looked peaceful, but not angelic. Never that.

The slash of her bold raven brows and the sensual mouth would never bespeak innocence. Her square jaw and surprising height merely added to her fierce image. The softly rounded curve of her buttocks, lifting slightly as she moved in her sleep, also reminded him she was far indeed from being a child.

Aric cursed, then shifted again to accommodate the expanding front of his hose.

She could not stay here. No matter that he found his blood heating for her now. He craved peace, which, Lord knew, he would never find with her impudent mouth constantly achatter and her feminine allure close at hand.

Yet he could not force her to return to Penhurst Castle, where her uncle, the superstitious baron, might well see her life ended. Though the saucy lady had both rankled and scorned him, he could not wish death upon her. His life had been filled with too much of that.

He thought back to his first battle—Tewkesbury, the bloodiest battle England had yet seen. A boy of twelve, he'd stood anxiously back from the battlefield's edge, watching the bloodied knights fall. Friends of his father and his uncle had lost their lives that day, men he had known from the cradle. Men he had respected were gone forever, but the succession of England's throne remained precarious despite their sacrifices.

His last battle, that with the Campbells of Scotland, had felt little different. Too much spilled blood for very little reason.

He would not have Lady Gwenyth's blood on his hands as well.

Aric sighed and rose as night grayed toward a new dawn. Should he send her to Northwell to stay with his younger brother, Stephen? Nay, his she-devil of a stepmother, Rowena, remained there.

And Gwenyth's words bothered him. 'Twas clear she had expected better of a home. Her expressive face had revealed her deep disappointment when she had first set eyes on his cottage. He had seen the yearning in her eyes for more, recalled with clarity that she thought him a mere hermit, worthy of her contempt.

Ambition in a woman had poisoned him since Rowena, once his betrothed. She had married his father for power and wealth. What would Lady Gwenyth do with the knowledge he had both in plenty now that his father was gone?

Aric had no intention of sharing that information. She and her displeasure might remain here out of necessity, at least until he could send her elsewhere. Before that day came, he would simply ignore her and her unforgettable mouth…somehow.

CHAPTER TWO

By midmorning, Gwenyth noted her host—the term she preferred over husband—looked bleary-eyed. Guilt needled her for taking his bed last eve, until she remembered she would not have taken it at all had he but fought this cursed union.

As the sun inched up in the sky, Aldrich—no, Aric he had called himself—lay down on the surprisingly comfortable bed and drifted off to sleep.

Gwenyth stared at the hulking man in repose. He should have looked relaxed in slumber but did not. 'Twas something of a puzzle, along with his use of well-born English. How had a peasant learned to speak so well?

Neither was of import, really. Her life had taken a terrible, unexpected turn, and during the wee hours, she had realized she must remedy the problem by seeking an annulment to this marriage. Sir Penley would take her to wife. Then she could have her own grand home where people welcomed her, accepted her. Sir Penley would smile at her, as he'd done from the moment they had met. He would hire poets to write flowering stanzas explaining why he needed her so.

None of those dreams could come true without the handsome hermit's help.

Gwenyth perched on the edge of the rickety chair and wondered how to proceed. To gain an annulment, Aric had to say they had not shared a bed. Aye, they had, but not at the same time, so she supposed that was different. The marriage was not consummated, not that she would allow him to poke her with his shaft. 'Twould end her hopes with Sir Penley, and it sounded most unpleasant besides.

While her husband slept, she would sneak back to Penhurst to reason with Uncle Bardrick, if such a thing were possible. She could creep back to the keep without Aric's knowledge. After all, he had told Dagbert he had no want of a wife. If he wished to remain in the thick of the forest with a wild dog his only friend, she would oblige him with pleasure. She wanted to avoid those piercing gray eyes and the sculpted magnificence of his face. He made her tingle in a most unusual way. Sir Penley never had such an ill effect upon her, thank goodness.

As she turned away to braid the dark mass of her hair, Aric groaned. Gwenyth whirled around to him and noticed sweat filming his face. His large fists bit into the mattress. She frowned.

His body jerked, and he groaned again. Gwenyth leaned closer in concern. Why did he rest so unwell? 'Twould seem nightmares troubled him. Did he dream of his black magic, or was he no sorcerer at all?

Suddenly, Aric lunged up, grabbed her arms, and threw her to the bed below. His large, hot body pinned her to the mattress; his strong grip made escape impossible.

In shock, Gwenyth stared at the half-wild man above her. His eyes closed, he snarled fiercely as his fingers crushed her throat. Gasping, she choked in a breath of air. Sweet Mary, did he mean to kill her?

Panic assailed her, and Gwenyth kicked and lashed out.

She could not budge him.

Spots danced before her eyes, but she managed to scream. Suddenly, Aric snapped upright at her side, his hands whipping away from her throat. His eyes opened wide.

Gwenyth sat up and backed away on the bed, clutching her abused neck. Horror flashed across Aric's face before he turned away and raked a tense hand through his long tawny hair.

"You wed me to slay me?"

"I am sorry," he mumbled as his taut back filled her gaze. "I...I but dreamed."

"Of killing me?" she questioned.

"Nay," he replied, breathing harsh.

"Of what, then?"

"Of hell." His voice sounded like desolation itself.

Knowing somehow he would reveal no more, she frowned. "'Tis just as well I am returning to Penhurst. Uncle Bardrick is not likely to kill me himself."

"Are you certain?" He whirled, his face now without expression. "Dagbert seemed certain last eve your uncle would indeed end your life."

Gwenyth bit the inside of her lip. Aric spoke true. Would her own uncle put an end to her? For what purpose?

Nay, 'twas all foolishness. Dagbert had never liked her. She, the daughter of a dead baron, would always be a dunderhead in the kitchens and a burden to the current baron. Dagbert had reminded her of that irritating truth often indeed. So had her uncle. Even so, would he truly see her dead?

"Uncle Bardrick will see reason. He cannot turn family away thus." She brushed Aric's words aside with a flip of her hand.

His skeptical expression bespoke much. "If Dagbert followed Lord Capshaw's orders, why did the baron send you to wed me? Why not one of his own daughters, if he feared the drought so?"

Gwenyth knew why. Uncle Bardrick had never wanted her there. He found her presence too distracting from his own two daughters, around whom the sun revolved, should one ask him. He would never offer up one of his precious girls to a man of dark powers.

The dead baron's daughter, who had been little better than a servant for some years, however, was of no import. She was a fitting sacrifice—young, untouched, and unnecessary. And Gwenyth would gladly choke on her pride before she would make the husband she wanted not aware of her sorrow and shame.

"He lies about my uncle. Dagbert is naught more than a droning hedge pig filled with hot air," she said, ruffled. "What does he, a mere foot soldier, know of a baron's mind?"

Aric's thoughtful gray gaze touched Gwenyth and lingered. Bristling braies, why did the man always make her shiver?

"He did not seem confused about your uncle's orders," Aric pointed out. "What shall you do if Dagbert spoke true?"

Gwenyth, refusing to consider that, waved his words away. "My uncle would not dare harm me! No uncle would."

Her host's lean face tensed until it appeared carved from granite. Pain, sadness eve, clouded his eyes before he turned away.

"Anything is possible."

She glared at his broad back as he rested his large fists on his narrow hips. She would not believe his doomsday view. Aye, Uncle Bardrick had never thought much of her, but he had never wanted to see her blood spilled, either.

"Such is possible only in your lunatic mind. Is that not grounds for annulment, your madness?"

Aric turned to face her, crossing his thick arms over his chest. His face had hardened with vexation. "You cannot prove I am mad, Lady Gwenyth."

"But you do not deny it."

He released a long-suffering sigh. "I will deny that foolery until my last breath. You shall have to think of some other way to rid yourself of me."

"I shall cry male impotency, then. That will relieve me of you."

Aric cocked his head to one side, his arms crossed over a chest that should have been a warrior's. A more potent-looking man she had ne'er seen.

Gwenyth swallowed hard as he dropped his arms to his side and made his way toward her slowly. His massive, muscled frame blotted out the light and the view of her surroundings as he came closer. Gwenyth bit her lip as she glimpsed the hot challenge in his stare.

"I shall be happy to prove you wrong." His whisper sounded low and not well pleased.

Gwenyth resisted the urge to back away. Had she pushed him too far? After all, he was her husband—for now—and well within his rights to demand she share his bed. She had no doubt he could fill every inch of that duty.

"Nay." She curled her shaking fingers into fists. "I shall have to be a maiden still for this marriage to end."

"True. But should you stay long as my wife, dragon-tongued or nay, do not expect you will remain untouched."

"You would have me unwillingly?" she challenged him.

"I would not."

"Then you would not have me at all."

"Wrong," he whispered, reaching out to capture her arms and bring her flush against the heated, rigid length of his body.

As Gwenyth gasped with both fear and shock, Aric closed his

mouth over her own.

A thousand sensations assailed her at once—the feel of him close to her, his solid, strong hands as they slid around her shoulders and down her back. The rasp of stubble on his cheeks as he dipped his head to place another hard kiss across her tingling mouth. The smells of rich earth, midnight rain, and aroused male blended to an intoxicating elixir that blotted out all thought.

The taste of him clung to her lips as he parted them and found his way inside without haste, swirling, dipping, tasting, until Gwenyth could not find her next breath, until honeyed fire flowed within her. Then his groan reached her, vibrated inside her, echoed in the pit of her stomach and lower.

He lifted his head and spoke. "Stay here long at all, and we will share that bed."

Gwenyth raised a trembling hand to her lips. Why did she feel so alive? Why did pulses and tingles skip and hum inside her? That sensation he roused by looking at her had multiplied tenfold. She actually wanted the recluse to kiss her again. And again. Had he worked sorcery upon her?

Taking a deep, steadying breath, she vowed she would not remain here to find out.

"Then I shall depart this moment, for I've no intent to share your bed."

Aric said nothing to stop her as she walked out of the shanty and emerged into the noonday sun. Not a single word of farewell! She walked briskly across the clay-soiled hills, listening to the chirping of birds, determined to put her temporary husband from her mind.

'Twasn't as if she truly cared that he did not speak to her, but could he simply dismiss her after such a kiss? Forget such oddly pleasurable sensations? The roguish sheep-biting buffoon! She had not given the lewdster permission to touch her, nor had she wished to feel any pleasure at his kiss. Certain she could not get away from him quickly enough, Gwenyth made haste through the forest.

She reached Penhurst so soon, she was near startled. The swaying leaves parted, some dropping to the ground in a green cascade, as the castle came into view and stole her breath.

The round turret and the battlement were as familiar to her as her own heartbeat. This was home, the place of her memories of a laughing papa and a tender mama. She had missed being here in the past days, even if Penhurst's current inhabitants had not missed her.

The portcullis was lowered against intruders. Against her.

Inside, she heard the bustle of the castlefolk, the blacksmith, the apothecary, the soldiers training. Animals bleated and lowed as the sun rose to its zenith. Gwenyth so longed to be a part of it all again that she ached.

Gazing into the turret, she motioned to the lookout, a scrawny lad named Hamlin, to let her inside.

The boy shook his head. "Lady Gwenyth, milord said ye ain't to come in."

Mortification blazed through her entire body. Hamlin had spoken loudly enough for the whole of the castle to hear she was not wanted. 'Twas likely he had yelled loudly enough for Aric to hear. Heaven forbid!

Drawing in a deep breath, Gwenyth calmed. Uncle Bardrick could not be so cruel as to cast her out of his life completely, without a single word in the doing. Mayhap Hamlin was to open the portcullis to no one.

No matter, she decided. The ancestor who had built Penhurst had also built tunnels beneath, in case of a siege. She had played in the tunnels as a child and knew they would take her near enough to the solar.

She made her way around the outer curtain of walls surrounding the castle. Just within a cluster of brambles and bluebells lay the opening to the tunnel, covered now by twigs and rocks and leaves.

Sweeping the impediments aside, Gwenyth lowered her feet into the opening and slid down into the narrow red-brown passage until her feet touched the ground. Cool, dark, and musty—just as she remembered—the tunnel soon became narrow and short, forcing her to crawl. Firm damp earth filtered through her fingers and no doubt soiled the knees of yesterday's gown. Goodness, she would look a fright when she saw her uncle, which would no doubt displease him.

At the tunnel's end, Gwenyth found herself behind the chapel. The stairs to her right would lead her to the solar and her uncle.

Dusting herself off as best she could, Gwenyth turned to the stairs, only to find Sir Penley striding toward her, his face a mask of surprise. His sandy, shorn hair was unmoving in the breeze, which she knew would lift the glinting strands of Aric's golden mane.

Nay! Now was not the time to think of her surly husband.

"My Lady Gwenyth." He took her hands in his, concern furrowing his pleasing features. "You have returned, and worse for the wear," he said, frowning at her tousled appearance. "Lord Capshaw told me you had gone away to wed. Is that so?"

Certainty that her uncle had indeed ordered her gone muted the joy of Sir Penley's concern. But she would fix it, by the moon and the stars!

"I but went away to visit a…friend. An ailing friend. I'm up to see my uncle now."

Relief crossed Sir Penley's smooth features. "Joyous news. Not that your friend is ailing, of course, but that you have come back. I will see you later?"

Gwenyth's heart sighed. Sir Penley was so eager to see her, so tender with his words. He had actually been worried about her wedding another. 'Twas a good sign, so long as she could rid herself of the roughhewn hermit she had wed.

"I vow you shall see me the moment I am done with my uncle."

Sir Penley smiled. "After you, I shall speak to him, so that I may talk to you of a very important matter."

Gwenyth knew what those words meant. He wanted to marry her! Of that she was certain. Though she was no longer the baron's daughter, Sir Penley had chosen *her*. Joyous news, indeed! Now she must see her uncle and convince him to help her have this marriage annulled.

"Then I shall return with all haste," she vowed.

"And I shall count the moments." His soft blue eyes probed hers as he lifted her hands to his mouth. Upon seeing the dirt there, however, he merely smiled and released her. "I await you."

Nodding, Gwenyth dashed to the stairs and rushed up to the solar door. There she took a deep breath to still the trembling of her stomach, then pushed her way inside.

In a chair beside the window, her uncle sat drinking from a tankard of ale. At her entrance, he glanced up from the account books before him. His eyes narrowed in anger when he saw her hovering just inside the door.

"I thought I made it clear you are no longer welcome at Penhurst."

Gwenyth closed her eyes for a moment, fighting a wave of grief. She had always known that Uncle Bardrick had little heart, but to cast her from the only home she had ever known without so much as a word… She battled tears.

"Why?" She hated the fact her voice shook. "I have always done as you asked, worked in the kitchens, slept in the straw. I endeavored never to be in your way."

Bardrick stood to his full height—five inches over five feet—and settled his arms across his round stomach. "Gwenyth, my brother and his slut of a wife spoiled you, gave you the finest clothes, the finest home, and educated you, though for what purpose I cannot fathom. You are willful, too spirited by half. Opinions fly unheeded from your mind to your mouth. And 'tis a foul mouth, full of naught but curses and slurs."

The aging man turned his back to her and cast his gaze out the window to the inner bailey below. "I could find clever enough ways to ignore you until Sir Penley came. He would be Lyssa's husband, but she does not have your beauty or wit."

Gwenyth gasped. Nay! Her future, her dreams, given to her timid younger cousin?

"But 'tis me Sir Penley wants!"

Her uncle turned to spear her with an ugly stare. "Aye, and well I know it. I have seen the lust in his eyes when he looks upon you. Think you I don't know he plans to ask me for your hand?"

"But you cannot alter the course of love," she blurted.

Bardrick's mouth turned up in a sneer. "I already have."

Icy fingers of anguish squeezed Gwenyth's heart. She wanted to ask if her uncle could indeed be so cruel, but she knew the answer. This was the man she had seen starve a headstrong servant near to death, the man who had ordered a starving poacher to be rendered sightless for his thieving.

This was the man who had stripped her of everything dear.

"Go home to your husband. Warm his bed and keep your viper tongue in your head. If the drought ends, I shall be pleased enough to allow you to visit. If not, expect never to see Penhurst again."

"But—"

"Get out of my sight, girl. And do not come back, for I will see you dead."

"But—"

"Out!" he roared.

Tears stinging her eyes, Gwenyth ran out the door, down the

28

stairs, and into the inner bailey. She darted behind the chapel as tears ran down her face unchecked.

Spotting the tunnel entrance, Gwenyth hunched down to wriggle inside. Ten feet away stood Sir Penley looking tall and elegant in his finery. His light brown hair gleamed in the sun, and his straight, thin nose was perfectly in profile. She would miss his tender heart, his smile. She began to cry harder.

Bristling braies, what was she to do now? Her love was lost to her, and she was wed to a sullen eremite who might well practice the devil's work instead of God's! She was chained by the bonds of marriage to a man who could never give her the home and family of her dreams.

* * * *

At the crackle of leaves beneath quick feet, Aric rose and peered out the window. His wife had returned quickly from Penhurst and, judging by her red, swollen eyes, none too happily.

Christ's blood, female tears. He who had made war all his life— and made a name for himself doing it—felt uncertain at the sight of her tears. He sighed, trying to decide what Drake or Kieran would do, besides laugh until their man parts turned blue at his discomfort.

Lady Gwenyth trounced through the door and slammed it behind her. Without a glance in his direction, she sat on the edge of the bed, her back toward him. He watched her shoulders shake, though she made no sound. Aric frowned. No wails, no catching of breath?

He leaned to the side in order to catch a glimpse of the outline of her face. Gwenyth's milk-smooth cheeks were splotchy and mottled red. Her small square chin quivered. She was indeed crying.

Backing away, Aric turned and made his way to the door. Outside, he settled himself in a chair under the cottage's thatched eaves. He retrieved his half-formed wooden carving from beside the chair and his knife from his belt.

Whittling absently, he let her cry alone. She needed privacy to battle her uncle's ill-treatment of her and time to conquer her sorrow. Who knew better than he that such feeling was best harnessed alone?

Still, her sobs, which had grown louder, disquieted him. Why he could not say. He turned his attention back to his carving.

Minutes later, he realized all was silent once more and rose to peer inside the dwelling's window. She had flung herself across the tidy bed in his absence. His pillow was quite wet, his bedcovers tousled. But her still body and occasional indrawn breath told him the crying had stopped.

Aric entered the domain to fetch her a cup of water from the bucket and a cloth from the table. He returned to Gwenyth's side and paused. Part of him felt an inexplicable urge to touch her, though he knew she would not welcome it.

Frowning, he cleared his throat. "Water?"

She jerked upright and whirled to face him. Strands of her long chestnut hair clung to her wet, spiked lashes, to her moist, red mouth. By God, she looked beautiful with her hair a wild tangle and her blue eyes raging. Nothing cool or controlled about Lady Gwenyth. Unlike Rowena, his wife had no passion lacking in her blood.

The very thought heated him. Gripping the cloth in his hand, he stifled a staggering urge to brush the soft strands of hair from her face and kiss her senseless.

"Tha-thank you," she replied finally, taking the cup from his hand.

As their fingers brushed, Aric's skin burned and desire poured through him. Stunned, he jerked his hand away.

Lady Gwenyth gazed at him with red-rimmed, cautious eyes, then lifted the cup to her mouth. Closing her eyes, she drank deeply. Aric could scarcely lift his gaze from her beautiful face, red nose and all.

Finally, she took the cup away from her wide mouth and held it between tense fingers. "I do not understand how he could do this. I am family."

For a long moment, Aric said nothing. He did not want to become embroiled in her problems. He cared nothing for the petty baron's machinations.

But Gwenyth's beseeching eyes made it impossible to remain mute. "As I told you, I feared he would not welcome you back."

"Aye, you did," she said, fresh tears flooding her eyes. "I never believed my own uncle would threaten to kill me."

Since Aric knew all too painfully the lengths a man would go to further his own ends, family be damned, he was not surprised in the least. But with that thought, came a disturbing certainty: Lady Gwenyth had nowhere else to go. She, along with her passions, her prejudices, and her pulchritude, was here to stay. His new bride certainly did not want to hear that truth any more than he wanted to think it.

"I know," he said softly. "Lord Capshaw is a fen-sucked varlet, and I am surprised you have not mentioned such as yet."

Gwenyth bit her lip, but a smile crept up her cheeks, until each dimpled most charmingly. Finally, she let out a small laugh that had him smiling in return. "Aye, fen-sucked for sure."

CHAPTER THREE

A silent evening gave way to a troubled night. Come the bright spring morn, Gwenyth began plotting ways to persuade Aric into lifting the drought. If he had such power, she must cajole him to use it so she might visit Penhurst and win Sir Penley and perhaps even her uncle's approval. No method came immediately to mind.

At a sudden, cheerful "hello" from outside the shanty's window, Gwenyth paused. The greeting had come from a female voice she had not expected to hear again for a long while—if ever.

Gwenyth rose from her cross-legged position on the little bed and gazed out the window—and into the round face of her cousin Nellwyn.

Dashing across the room to admit uncle Bardrick's elder daughter, Gwenyth prayed the woman had some good tidings from Penhurst. Hopeful, she opened the door.

Nellwyn entered the cottage with a quick glance about. A stilted smile followed. Her cousin's gown was of the finest silk, though Nellwyn would soon outgrow it because of the babe due three months hence. As she crossed the room, she lifted her skirts so they would not touch the dirt floor.

Her cousin looked radiant, nearly glowing. Her light brown hair was swept up in curls that framed her pleasant face and pale blue eyes. Gwenyth's own dress was little better than a dirt-stained rag. She had no others with which to replace it, and Aric did not appear to have the funds to rectify that.

Then there was Aric himself, a vital flesh-and-blood reminder she held little value to the people of Penhurst. Now that Nellwyn had come, she felt suddenly glad Aric had wandered into the forest, as he often did.

As was her cousin's wont, Nellwyn greeted her with a hug. "Oh, Gwenyth, how good it is to see you! My dear husband and I have come to visit on our way to London. Can you imagine? I have never been there, and I think I shall faint from the excitement. We are to stay for Parliament! My dear Sir Rankin says there is much Lancastrian intrigue swirling about the Yorkist crown, and that is why we travel, but who cares when there is so much entertainment to enjoy?" She laughed.

Gwenyth did her best to smile. While she wished good fortune for her cousin, she could not deny she wanted some of it for herself.

"But you—" Nellwyn broke into her thoughts. "Father tells me you have a new husband. Where, pray tell is he?

Reeling with the news that her cousin would take a coveted journey to London, Gwenyth merely shrugged. How she had always longed to visit that place of excitement, see the mass of people, take in the court intrigues. Perhaps Sir Penley would take her someday— if she could become his wife.

"Is he not here?" Nellwyn asked, wearing a puzzled frown.

"Nay, he often…" *Disappears* would have been the truth, though she was loath to say it. Nellwyn's life was so clearly perfect, while her own might never be more than misery. "He often hunts."

"Oh, a sporting man, I see. Well, I shall probably come back to Penhurst on our journey home. Perhaps I will meet him then. What manner of man is he?"

Though she felt certain her uncle had told her cousin all the details of this ridiculous marriage, she refused to admit Bardrick had bartered her to a sorcerer to ease the drought. Gwenyth hated her embarrassment and vowed Nellwyn would never see it.

"He is a…quiet man. And so far, a kind one."

"Wonderful! You shall do all the speaking and be allowed anything you desire." Nellwyn giggled.

Despite her melancholy, Gwenyth could not help but laugh in return. "Exactly as I plan."

After seating her cousin on the room's lone chair, Gwenyth sat atop the bed. Outside, she heard Aric's footsteps and prayed he had not heard her conversation. She prayed even harder he would leave again. She did not want Nellwyn to meet her silent husband. Though he was disturbingly handsome, gruffly gentle, and well spoken, his position was a lowly one. This marriage was but one more reason for Nellwyn to pity her.

Thankfully, her cousin remained oblivious to Aric's presence under the eaves.

"Well, as you can see"—Nellwyn's hands cupped her rounding stomach—"the babe is growing. I'm certain it will be a son, and my dear Sir Rankin is beside himself. He's been the most indulgent husband during this time. I fear I shall grow quite used to it and become spoiled. What kind of wife will I be to him then? Certainly not a useful one!" Nellwyn smiled cheerfully.

"Indeed. But should you grow useless and fat, he will have no one to blame but himself," Gwenyth teased.

"You are right!" Nellwyn giggled, then grabbed Gwenyth's hands in a rush of excitement. "Though we have oft discussed names for the babe, we have not decided upon one. I feel so fortunate that Sir Rankin allows for my opinion. Indeed, he even seeks it in this matter."

Holding in a sigh, Gwenyth regarded her cousin. She yearned so deeply for a caring husband and the return of the world into which she was born that an ache pulsed within her.

"Of course," Nellwyn continued, "we shall have to determine a name all too soon. By the saints, I can hardly let Sir Rankin's heir go nameless, at least not for too long."

"That is true," Gwenyth agreed as her cousin smiled widely.

"And I did not tell you of the king's gift," Nellwyn said, changing subjects. "King Richard himself gave my husband another castle! Is that not exciting? 'Tis our third one now, and I know not how we will keep up with everything. As it is, we already have more land than Sir Rankin can oversee. I should be thankful, I suppose, for that means we shall never go hungry—though certainly I have more servants than I can direct in a day. I can scarcely remember their names, much less all their duties. And with this growing babe, I have felt naught but weariness. I am overwrought, I tell you."

Gwenyth struggled to hide her envy at Nellwyn's good fortune. Could her cousin not see her misery? Could Nellwyn not understand Gwenyth would give nearly anything to possess those same challenges?

Though she felt certain Nellwyn made no attempt to dishearten her, just listening to her cousin's chatter made her heart feel as low as if it rested between her feet.

"Anyway," Nellwyn said after gathering another breath, "Sir Rankin says we will visit this Corbridge Castle come autumn. I can only pray the resident steward is competent.

"Oh, and I'm to meet the king whilst we are in London, as well as his queen, Anne. Sir Rankin believes we may even sup with them. I vow I shall faint!"

"Would he expect different from a breeding woman?"

Nellwyn glanced at her with smiling reproach. "I'm told he is quite somber and would disapprove. If I embarrassed Sir Rankin in such a manner, I do not know that he would forgive me—at least, not in the first ten minutes."

As her cousin laughed, Gwenyth smiled, even as sadness pervaded her. 'Twas not that she disliked Nellwyn or wanted to see her unhappy. Nay. She simply wished she could have a similar life, respected in a grand castle, a chatelaine everyone looked to for comfort and direction. She yearned to be respected and doted on by a husband.

As it was now, she had only Aric, who seemed happier ignoring her for most of the day. She had no servants to lead, no tapestries to see hung, and no hope of returning to Penhurst unless she could persuade Aric to make rain.

Nellwyn sighed, looking quite serious for the first time in Gwenyth's memory. "Of course, Sir Rankin tells me there is a rumor about court that Queen Anne suffers from ill health and may not live long. Certainly she will have no more heirs. My husband frets about who shall rule England if King Richard does not remarry and have a son, for that upstart Henry Tudor is ever keen to gain the throne. But I always remind Sir Rankin that such is unlikely to happen. There is much time for the king to get a new wife breeding. He is not an old man. And even if he does not produce a new heir, a new king would certainly value a man as brave and loyal as Sir Rankin."

Gwenyth nodded, wondering why Nellwyn had come to visit. True, she alone had been compassionate in the last ten years. Now she questioned whether the woman's benevolence was designed to please others or to recollect her own good fortune.

That could not be so, Gwenyth mentally chastised herself. Nellwyn had oft helped her with household chores in the past and had given her leftover scraps of food and nearly new dresses. Still, her cousin's presence made her feel out of sorts.

She rose, desperately wanting her cousin—Gwenyth's biggest reminder of her poor fate—gone. "You're looking tired, Nellwyn. Perhaps you should return to Penhurst for a rest." At the least, she should give her mouth a rest, Gwenyth thought unkindly, then rebuked herself silently. What ill humor ailed her?

Nellwyn stood and smiled, though Gwenyth could see she had piqued the other woman. Guilt needled her.

"Perhaps you are right. The midwife has told me too much dirt in the air is not good for the babe."

Shame and anger blazed through Gwenyth at her cousin's intimation that her home was not good enough. It wasn't, but 'twas not Nellwyn's place to say so. Still, the innocent insult gave Gwenyth an idea.

"If you're going to remain at Penhurst for a time, perhaps I could visit you there on the morrow, since the dirt is harmful."

The smile fell from Nellwyn's face. "Oh, I should love that, but Sir Rankin has made plans that we should leave before the dawn. London awaits, after all."

Gwenyth resisted an urge to close her eyes in misery and cry again. Not before Nellwyn. Never before perfect, blessed Nellwyn!

"Of course," she said finally. "Perhaps I should visit you at Penhurst when you make your way back from London."

Her cousin shrugged, her smile stiff. "Perhaps. Well, I am off. Wish me luck in London!"

Before Gwenyth could reply, Nellwyn had exited the cottage, mounted her dappled gray, and set off for Penhurst with a foot soldier behind her.

Gwenyth closed the door, turned to the bed, and plopped down onto the straw mattress. She would not cry. Not again. These two days past had seen too much of that. If her tears flowed as freely as a river, Aric might well oust her from his presence, as well. Somehow, the thought dismayed her.

* * * *

After the chatty female visitor departed, Aric entered the cottage, uncertain what he might find. A morose Gwenyth somehow surprised him. She would let that boasting sow dishearten her?

With a frown, Aric sat in the room's sole chair, directly across from his wife, who had her unhappy face resting in her hands. Her expression changed to something blank but tense when he caught her gaze. Gwenyth's expressive eyes, however, told him she was truly upset.

Aric battled with himself. 'Twas true he had no wish for, no use for, a wife in his solitary life. Having her here disrupted his peace in a manner no one ever had, yet he did not mind her beneath his roof—except at night.

The torment of his nightmares had been compounded by the torment of his unexpected desire for her. Aye, he wanted her something fierce. The thought of surrounding himself with all that fire, getting this passionate woman to yield herself to him, made his blood run hot.

The fervor with which she approached people fascinated him. Guessing her feelings was never a feat, for she seemed to have no thought of hiding them, as did nearly everyone else he'd ever known.

It seemed impossible to deny her comfort. Aric sighed.

"Who was she?" he asked.

She dropped her hands to her sides. "Nellwyn. My Uncle Bardrick's elder daughter."

"And she finds herself well pleased to be wedded, breeding, and traveling to London, from what I heard."

Gwenyth bit her bottom lip, then said, "Aye. And why should she not?"

He paused. "Not everything is always as it seems, Gwenyth."

"How can you say thus? 'Tis clear how lucky she is—an adoring husband, not one grand castle but three, and a babe on the way!"

He could hardly tell her Sir Rankin loved a good wench—sometimes several at once—or that Corbridge Castle was little more than rubble next to a dried-up river on inhospitable lands near the Scottish border. He could say none of those things without revealing himself. He would never expose his past and his life to Gwenyth, since he meant never to return to Northwell, Richard's murdering machinations, and Rowena's scheming.

Instead, he said, "Your lady cousin is too chatty by far and possesses a backside larger than Penhurst's barn. Perhaps she is envious of you."

"Of me?" Shock overtook Gwenyth's face. "Whatever on earth for?"

"Your beauty. Your quick wit," he offered.

She shrugged, though her cheeks flushed pink. "Your thoughts are kind indeed, but Nellwyn has a wonderful life, one I so want. One I might have had if Uncle Bardrick had allowed me to wed Sir Penley."

"Sir Penley?" he asked, suspicion taking hold.

"Aye, Sir Penley Fairfax from—"

Aric laughed. His uncontained mirth spilled forth before Gwenyth could finish her sentence. She had hoped to wed cowardly, sniveling Sir Penley?

Rising, Gwenyth angrily placed her fists on her hips. "And just why is Sir Penley funny?"

Aric stopped chuckling long enough to say, "The man hardly knows what to do with the sword in his hand, much less the one between his legs."

The latest in court gossip slipped out before Aric remembered that Gwenyth was unstudied in the ways of sensuality. Yet he was sure his passionate, exquisite wife would have been wasted on such an oaf.

"That is unbearably crude. What do you know of Sir Penley? Nothing, I am sure, you pig-bottomed dolt!"

Aric pictured the fop's appalled reaction to Gwenyth's inventive oaths and kept laughing.

Gwenyth's cheeks turned red. "And in case you did not know, women are interested in a man's heart and affections, not his…sword."

Wearing an indignant frown, Gwenyth crossed her arms over her chest. Aric laughed even harder.

"Sweeting, sooner or later a woman is always interested. You are just too innocent to know such."

"I am not a child! I am a woman grown, and I tell you I've no interest whatsoever in your sword."

Smiling, he touched a hand to her soft pink cheek. "God willing, you will."

* * * *

"Do you plan ever to fix this infernal table leg?" Gwenyth shouted out the window to Aric the following afternoon. "'Tis clear it has been broken for some time."

When he did not respond, she poked her head out the window to glare at her temporary husband. He sat under the cottage's shady eaves, whittling again on the damnable block of wood in his hands. Whatever he carved, it enthralled him far more than conversation, she thought irritably.

"I am speaking to you," she called again.

As if startled, he whipped his gaze to her, then slid the wood onto the ground and covered it with a cloth. "What say you?"

She heaved an irritated sigh. "The leg to this table. 'Tis broken, and I have tripped upon it twice."

With a shrug, he eased out of the chair beneath the eaves. "Step carefully."

Gwenyth stomped to the door. 'Twas a simple enough task she asked, and he clearly had some talent with wood. Why should he tease her so?

She yanked the door open. "I want you—"

Aric stood directly on the threshold, his body inches from her own. The words on the tip of her tongue died. Of a sudden, her heart began beating so quickly 'twas like the thunder of racing horses in her ears.

He seemed as one with the out of doors, for his scent always reflected something of night's mist, fertile soil, some unnamable wood, and always that subtle hint of something that was Aric's alone. Something that made her stomach dance.

"You want me?" His smile beguiled Gwenyth.

Her palms began to sweat.

"'Tis a wondrous change from yesterday, my lady."

Frowning, Gwenyth wondered what she had wanted of Aric, besides his mouth on hers again. Nay! She wanted Sir Penley, stately keeps, and castlefolk who valued her. She wanted her rightful place in the world.

So why could she not forget the hermit's kiss?

He inched past her to enter the cottage, smiling as if he could read her mind. God's nightgown, she prayed not. Such thoughts about a husband she had no wish to keep did not make sense. He was a recluse, perhaps even a sorcerer.

Yet he had been kind in the face of her tears, opened his home to her when her own family had thrown her out, married her to save her life. Not the sort of evil she might have imagined from the man the village children oft called the Wizard of the Woods.

In fact, nothing about him was as she expected.

She turned, watching as he bent to the table leg and examined it. Gwenyth found her gaze fastened upon the powerful width of his shoulders and the capability of his large hands, browned by the sun. Without explanation, she shivered.

Aric stood and faced her. "I will fix this, so you need not glare at my back anymore, little dragon."

Dragon? "And are you so pleasant that crowds gather round you?

"Nay, but you will recall that, until you, I lived here alone. By design."

Gwenyth's mouth gaped open as fury overtook her. "Think you I want to be here?"

A smile crept its way up his lean, brown face. "You have made your preferences for Sir Penley clear."

She snorted. "At least he would not speak to me of...swords."

"Nay. As I said, he knows not how to use one."

Her hands on her hips, she cast him a contemptuous glare. "You, I assume, are an expert?"

Aric lifted a wide shoulder, that challenging grin dominating his full mouth and glinting in his gray eyes. "My lady, I should be happy indeed to let you determine that."

Her belly flipped over at his suggestion. Heat followed, warming her face, nearly melting her resolve.

Finally, when he rose and moved toward her, Gwenyth came to her senses. Her future with Sir Penley was at stake. She could not give the recluse her maidenhead, no matter how handsome his face or how kind his heart.

"The devil plague you," she murmured, then darted out of the house, hearing his laughter behind her.

Aric should not have this effect upon her. He could help her with her dreams in no way except by leaving her untouched and allowing her to seek an annulment.

Unless he could be persuaded to make rain.

Aye, that might bring an end to her plight. If 'twould only rain, Uncle Bardrick might welcome her back to Penhurst. Sir Penley might still be waiting for her.

She dismissed the notion he knew not what to do with a woman. The hermit could know naught of such an esteemed man as Sir Penley.

But how to persuade Aric to end the drought? Gwenyth wondered if he could accomplish such a feat. Was he truly a wizard of black powers or simply an ordinary man?

She frowned and plopped into his chair under the eaves. Certainly if he had no powers, he would correct the castlefolk and defend his goodness. Aye, so he must have some magic.

How did he conjure up his powers?

Gwenyth had never heard him utter any incantations. In her two days at the tiny cottage, she had seen nothing that resembled a book of spells. He was possessed of no crystals and had not looked upon his reflection in the nearby river. Tapping her toe impatiently against the soft earth, Gwenyth vowed she would solve this mystery somehow.

Then her foot struck something solid.

She peered down and found a faded blue cloth covering Aric's whittled block of wood. Was this the magic? 'Twould explain why it held him so enthralled.

Biting her lip, Gwenyth lifted the cloth and grabbed the wood. Raising it to her gaze, she peered at it, realizing 'twas not a mystical symbol or figure but a naked woman. The exquisite carving was long of leg, full of breast, curved at the waist and hip. The woman's hair was long, and the impassioned face—

Was her own.

Gwenyth gasped. The carving's square chin and round nose were like hers. The hair touched to the curve of her elbow, as her own did. The too-generous mouth could belong to no other.

He had spent nearly every moment of their few days together carving an image of her nakedness?

From inside, Gwenyth heard Aric curse. The sound startled her back to attention. Lest she be caught, she put the carving on the soft earth again and covered it with the cloth.

He had thought of her naked. Often, 'twould seem. Gwenyth

rose from the chair, feeling a fine sheen of sweat cover her. Aric had pictured how she would look with one leg curled beneath her and an arm wrapped coyly about her waist whilst exposing the rest of her body in complete abandon.

At once, she felt flattered, uncertain, and utterly afraid to be alone with him for the seemingly endless days and weeks stretching out before them.

Merciful heaven, what should she do?

"'Tis fixed, I think," Aric called from the doorway.

Dazed, Gwenyth stared at him. His black boots were made large to accommodate his size and extended to the knee. His gray hose made prominent the thick muscles running the length of his thighs—and emphasized his generous manly endowments.

God's nightgown, he thought that should fit inside her? Gwenyth jerked her gaze away to the faded wooden door beside him. Suddenly, being here alone with Aric seemed unwise. Though he was considered her husband, he was still a stranger.

"My lady?"

Gwenyth's startled gaze flew to his. "Fixed?"

"Aye, the table you wanted repaired." Scowling, he slid his stare from her face to the carving upon the ground, then back to her face once more. "Why do your cheeks turn red, Gwenyth?"

No reason, except that she saw now that he was powerfully built all over, and he apparently wanted her in his bed.

How had Aric known her dimensions and carved her so exactly? Since he had not seen her without clothes, she could only surmise he wanted her greatly to spend such energy in the carving of her likeness. Certainly she had not removed her gown whilst here, though she had yearned to do so long enough to wash the garment.

Gwenyth rose cautiously. 'Twould seem he wanted to bed her more than any man had. Even Sir Penley, who had sought her as a wife, had never once hinted he wanted her betwixt his sheets. If the speed with which he had carved her image was any indication, Aric had seemingly thought of little else since they had wed. The realization aroused and frightened her at once. Certainly she could not deny he had been kinder than her remaining family.

Tumult and confusion wound through her. Ruthlessly, Gwenyth suppressed it. She could not lie with Aric and yield her body, no matter that her stomach jumped at the thought. Her future would be sacrificed if she gave in to him. She would be here forever in this shanty, more than like wondering whence the funds for taxes and clothing would come. Her circumstances would become more desperate than they ever had under Uncle Bardrick and Aunt Welsa's care. She would be an outcast forever as a sorcerer's wife.

Yet was she not an outcast already?

Aye, but she wanted it changed, everything changed. She wanted the life Sir Penley could give her.

Yet she could not cease wondering if Aric could make ardent magic in his bed—if he could, as her husband, make her feel this wanted always. If so, would the passion be worth the price?

CHAPTER FOUR

Gwenyth was staring at him—and had been since last eve—with a mixture of hesitancy and curiosity. Aric met her gaze, and she slammed her eyes shut, feigning sleep.

As night had fallen, he had noticed the speculation in her entrancing blue eyes. By God's teeth, he had even once seen her gaze fixed on his manhood. Now, as then, he hardened at the thought of having her. Lest the front of his hose expand noticeably again, he looked away from her supine form as she lay tossing upon his bed in search of sleep.

Between the linens, Gwenyth would be no passive wench. This wife of his would loose her passion and make him a very contented man—with the right encouragement. Since they were bound by law, Aric saw no reason not to give her every encouragement and bind them in flesh—and quickly.

He considered her attachment to that milksop, Sir Penley, and frowned. Such an excuse for a man would never touch Aric's wife. No man would. In fact, the very thought of it disturbed him, oddly enough. Aye, a seduction was indeed in order.

He looked forward to the event with great anticipation.

Yet since the moon's last rising, she had become noticeably silent. Aric thought he would find the quiet welcome, but he knew that with it came Gwenyth's uneasiness, perhaps even her fear. Somehow, he missed her pointed remarks. Aye, even her insults. 'Twas as if she no longer cared that he occupied the same home at all.

It would not do, he decided. He had charmed a wench or two in his twenty-six years. He could do so again.

"Gwenyth?" he whispered.

She did not open her eyes. "Aye?"

"Have you seen Dog?"

"Dog?" She frowned, eyes still closed against him and the light of the single candle.

"Aye, Dog. When I found him, I knew not if he had a name, so I simply called him Dog."

"Ah."

"Have you seen him?" he asked again.

"Nay."

Her response did not give him cause to hope. But he knew enough of Gwenyth to realize she liked to talk. He changed tactics.

He touched her shoulder, lightly wrapping his fingers about her arm. Aye, there. Now she opened her eyes. Warily, of course, but he had her attention.

"Today, I found Dog in the forest doing something so uncommon I could not cease my laughter."

"Did you?" Gwenyth sat up, breaking their contact.

Resolved, Aric tried again and brushed his fingers across her knee, pulling away before she could protest. Her cheeks flushed a fetching rosy pink.

"I did," he said. "Dog had found a rabbit, you see. He stood over the creature barking so loud he no doubt rose the dead for nigh on twenty leagues."

"I see."

"But what I saw next was even more unusual." He smoothed a stray lock of her glossy black hair away from her shoulder, retreating when she fixed a narrow-eyed gaze upon him.

"Now, Dog is something of a manly dog," he went on. "I have seen he is fierce in the hunt and in his pride. Yet he stood before this hare, so much smaller than himself, barked his terror, and emptied his bladder like the veriest of infants." Aric clapped a firm hand around her back when she smiled. "Is that not odd?"

"I cannot picture Dog so." She smiled skeptically.

"'Tis true, I vow. I laughed heartily."

Gwenyth nodded, her full mouth upturned. Her skin shone so radiant in the candle's glow, her hair so lustrous. Aric's urge to touch her grew. He gave in to it, reaching for her hand.

45

Shayla Black

"You know," he began, "you have not insulted me for the whole of the day. Does that mean I have succeeded in not rising your ire, little dragon, or have you run out of spirited slurs?"

At his suggestion, Gwenyth raised the dark arches of her brows and yanked her hand from his. "I shall always have a slur for you, you reeky ratsbane."

"I should be surprised if you did not. I suspect your dolt of an uncle knew not how to handle that unruly tongue."

For a heartbeat, Gwenyth said and did nothing. Aric wondered if 'twas a mistake to bring up the family who had shown her such grievous disregard. For all that he and his own father had rarely spoken of more than matters of war and politics, Aric had never suffered anything close to contempt from his father. Then Gwenyth smiled, that mischievous little grin that brightened her face and made his blood run hot.

"Aye, Uncle Bardrick and I have quarreled a time or two over my words."

Aric reached out to nudge her side. As his fingers closed about the soft curve of her waist, he felt his desire rise again. The thought of her bare skin gleaming beneath his hands, her passionate whisper in her ear confirming her desire...such made a man eager indeed.

"Give over. What did you say?" he asked, turning his attention back to the moment at hand.

Gwenyth's smile became a sparkling laugh. "Once, about two years past, my uncle decided he needed to raise an army and join the Yorkists in their fight for the throne. Those were hard times at Penhurst, for the winter before had been very long, and our foodstuffs were nearly gone. Uncle Bardrick invited some important lords to Penhurst for a feast. I don't recall who. I do recall, though, my great anger that he would take food from the very mouths of babes to further his ambition.

"When the guests arrived, he ordered me to serve them mulled wine, which I did—along with an herbal sleeping draught. When all of his guests began snoring at his table, Bardrick roared at me. Everyone in the castle watched. Before I could stop myself, I called him a beslubbering boil-brained dimwit. I spent two days in the pantry for the misdeed, but 'twas worth it to hear the laughter of the others. Even better, uncle Bardrick's guests left for fear he'd tried to poison them, so the feast he had planned never took place."

Aric laughed. That spectacle he would have enjoyed immensely. But he expected such spirit from Gwenyth. Though she had known the half-witted baron would punish her, Gwenyth had fought her battle in the only way she could and had won. She was clever, his wife.

She was also weary, he thought, watching her yawn.

"Sleepy, are you?" he asked

"Aye. The nights are still cool. I did not rest well last eve."

Aric who had been awake half the night fighting his bloody nightmares, doubted she had suffered much, but he would not quibble with her. Instead, he cast a glance at the meager blanket on his bed and realized she might indeed have been chilled. He held in a grimace.

From years of battle, he was accustomed to sleeping in the out of doors, oft without any cover at all. Gwenyth was unused to such. For all her durable façade, his wife was tender in years and experience and so required certain comforts.

He rose to retrieve his robe from the chest in the corner. When he returned to her side, he curled his hands about her shoulders and urged her to lie back upon the fragrant mattress. Gwenyth obeyed his silent command, though she remained stiff, her eyes guarded.

When she lay upon her back, Aric draped the fur-trimmed robe over her prone form and tucked it, along with his blanket, beneath her chin.

Their faces lay mere inches apart. Aric saw her mouth quiver below his, and he ached to taste her once more, to remind himself of her honeyed flavor. Still, he had made progress this night, and shattering this cozy mood by demanding more than she wished to give would gain him naught.

Sighing, he brushed her cheek with a slow stroke of his thumb. "Try to rest well tonight. Tomorrow we will set the bed to rights."

Her eyes wide, Gwenyth nodded. Aric turned away with a smile. Aye, he had her attention now.

* * * *

When Aric had promised her the night before they would set the bed to rights this day, then caressed her face with that warm, tender touch that could melt metal, she had no notion he meant to take her into the village.

As they stood on the outskirts of the little town, Gwenyth held back. How would people receive her now that she was wed to Aric?

Seemingly unaware of her trepidation, Aric grabbed her hand in his much larger one and pulled her into the melee.

Dust rose in a thin, brown haze around the small gathering of humanity. The pungent scents of animals and people mixed into something familiar and not altogether pleasant.

Children scampered ahead of them, chasing a yapping mutt. At Aric's side, Dog tensed. Aric stayed the animal with a curt word, and Dog fell into step beside his master once again. Gwenyth marveled at his command of the half-wild animal.

She noticed the village was more crowded than usual. Women bustled about, spreading gossip and cheer. Newly arrived merchants in their long black capuchins were setting up booths and displaying their wares for the Mayday festival two days hence. The air tingled with excitement. Gwenyth could almost hear the revelers singing now.

"Cor, 'tis the sorcerer!" shouted a dirty-faced boy ahead of them.

Villagers began turning about slowly. The gossip and good cheer ceased, quickly replaced by a rumble of anxious murmurs that disturbed the cool breeze.

Determined to ignore them, Gwenyth spotted the smithy's wife, Ilda, standing beneath an ancient willow, her infant son in her arms. A smile spread across Gwenyth's face as she left Aric to approach the young woman. She had not seen Ilda since helping the woman tend her children when Ilda's ankle had pained her a month ago. 'Twould be good to see a friend and make sure all was well once more.

As Gwenyth reached Ilda's side, the thin woman peered at her through wide, startled eyes and began backing away.

Was the woman ill? Frowning with concern, Gwenyth reached out to touch the woman. The smithy's wife jerked away and stepped back.

"Ilda, fear not. 'Tis only me, Gwenyth. I came to ask about your ankle and little James. Is all well?"

Ilda did not answer. Instead, her eyes widened more. Something akin to terror tempered with pity filled the pale depths. What could the woman be frightened of?

"Ilda?"

The woman's pale complexion turned completely ashen. She gripped her babe to her chest, her stare directed somewhere just past Gwenyth's shoulder.

Gwenyth glanced back to find Aric standing a few feet behind her, his jaw locked. A glance back at Ilda showed the woman deep in dismay, panic racing across her chalky face.

The villagers feared Aric's reputation as a man of the dark arts—including Ilda, it seemed. Did she fear Gwenyth had succumbed to something unholy by wedding Aric? 'Twas ridiculous—completely!

Gwenyth opened her mouth to say so when Ilda turned and fled with little James tucked tight against her. Tears sprang to Gwenyth's eyes as she bunched her fists in her skirt. She and Ilda had always been friends. Why could the woman not see she had changed little, if any, since her marriage?

A glance around her proved other villagers—the smithy, a kitchen maid, and one of Penhurst's weaving women—were all backing away with wary eyes as well.

Nay! These people had known her most of her life, and she had ever helped them when she could. Could no one see she was not a witch? Would no one greet her now?

Gwenyth bit her lip to hold in her tears. Except for Aric, it seemed she was now truly alone in this world. Aye, her life had not been the kindest before, but never had she been shunned so completely by so many people, people to whom she had always tried to be kind.

Grief pushed in on her, even as impotent fury beat in her chest. Aric remained beside her, utterly still. He had endured this kind of treatment repeatedly, without a word of complaint. Yet such must hurt him, at least a little.

Gwenyth turned to Aric. "I am sorry. Ilda…the villagers, they do not—"

"'Tis the Wizard of the Woods," one young girl began to sing as she jumped behind Aric, who spun about to face the child. Soon, three others joined in, clapping their filthy hands. "He brings much evil and no good. He claims the devil as his sire and sleeps upon a bed of fire. Beware the beast and his dog or 'tis certain they'll make you a frog!"

Gwenyth gasped in shock at the bratlings' mean ditty, while their mothers snatched them away from Aric with an admonishing word to take heed of the evil man. Did they not think Aric was a man with feelings? That they could sing and talk about him in whatever manner they liked, without regard for his suffering? Ilda had been ignorantly fearful. The other villagers had been needlessly cruel.

"'Twas foolish of these peasants! They taunted him from gossip alone and knew nothing of the man himself. She had seen no evidence that he claimed Satan as his sire, and she doubted such was true. Nor did he sleep upon a bed of fire.

In truth, he had spent the last three nights uncomfortably, crouched in a chair with his feet propped upon the narrow bed. In all that time, he had not hurt her, not even when she had called him the most vile names she could think of. If he had the magical ability to turn people into frogs at whim, she had most certainly given him ample cause to use it. Instead, he had given her only understanding and kindness, despite their hasty marriage. Could the simpletons of this village not see what she saw so easily?

She wondered how Aric could live knowing all who saw him bore him malice and ill will. Gwenyth peered up into the angles of his profile. His expression remained unchanged, appearing as rugged and as reticent as always. How could he care so little when her own heart ached for him?

"'Tis terrible, the manner in which they treat you!" she cried.

Aric merely shrugged.

"Has it been so always?"

"Since I tamed Dog, aye. Worry not, little dragon. Such suits me."

Incredulity furrowed her brow. "To be abhorred?"

"To be left alone. Come." He clasped her hand tightly. "Here is a peddler with cloth."

Gwenyth frowned in confusion as Aric led her to an old man with an array of fabrics. The merchant shot them a stiff, toothless smirk. "Good day."

"How much for that?" Aric pointed to a serviceable woolen in gray.

As the merchant haggled with her husband, Gwenyth found her gaze wandering through all the material. She gazed upon woolens, silks, and even a velvet or two, all of good quality. The thought of new dresses, fine enough to take on a trip to London like Cousin Nellwyn, made her sigh.

Then she caught sight of a beautiful silk in the deepest red, its surface glossy. What a magnificent dress this would make! She would look a lady indeed were she to wear something in this majestic shade. Aye, she could near picture herself now in a fine castle, surrounded by vassals and villagers, lords and ladies alike, beside a tender husband who always had a smile for her...

"How much for this?" Gwenyth asked the merchant impulsively.

He rattled off an amount that had Aric's brows rising and her own stomach plummeting.

"'Tis unnecessary," said her husband curtly.

"But I need new dresses." She gestured to the stained woolen garment covering her body. "Can you not see that?"

"Aye. That is why I have procured these fabrics." Aric held up more of the gray woolen, as well as similar fabrics in an ordinary blue and an exceedingly dull brown. "These will serve you well and last long."

And make her look every inch a woman of no importance to anyone. She grimaced.

"I find those disagreeable." Ugly was a more appropriate word, but she couldn't well say that to him. 'Twas unlikely he could afford better, though his robe last night had been expensively trimmed in fur. An indulgence, mayhap?

With a shrug, she turned to the peddler. "My good man, mayhap we can work out a trade of some sort. I own several books."

The merchant scratched his graying head. "I cannot read."

Gwenyth bit her lip, her thoughts racing. All too soon, she realized she had nothing of consequence to offer the little man. She turned away, downcast. The picture of her future looked bleak indeed.

"These fabrics are practical, Gwenyth. Come."

Aric settled with the old merchant, who smiled and pocketed the coin. Her husband nodded, as if pleased with the trade.

Once again, no one cared that she was ill pleased. She had been twice a fool for hoping otherwise. No one since her parents had ever really cared. It seemed no one ever would.

* * * *

The following morning, Gwenyth looked about the untidy cottage as Aric attempted to set it to rights. Most of the mess had been her doing. Her shoes lay discarded in the middle of the floor. The bit of her evening meal she had not finished sat upon the little table near the hearth, gathering flies. The bed remained unmade, and the linens needed airing besides.

Surprised that Aric had not demanded her assistance, she joined his efforts to restore the little place, somehow confused and grateful at once for his hush.

Without a word, he handed her the straw broom that occupied one corner. As she grabbed the handle, Gwenyth raised her eyes to meet his. His very closeness made her feel flushed all over. Did he still work on the carving he had of her? Or did he merely stare at it and wonder how correctly he had guessed?

She stared back. Then, unusually timid, she looked away to tend the floor. She swept the twigs and the last of winter's brown leaves that littered the floor into a corner, aware all the while of her silent husband tidying the hearth.

Did he watch her? Gwenyth could near feel his stare upon her back, caressing the curve of her waist, the arch of her backside. Purposely dropping the broom, Gwenyth bent to retrieve it and glanced over her shoulder. Aric did indeed watch her, and with an intense, soundless appraisal that made her tingle of a sudden. She whirled about and began fidgeting nervously with the broom.

Had he been watching her thus all day? Why did he seem to want her so? And why did the realization he did make her unwisely pleased?

"You cannot sweep the very dirt off the floors, Gwenyth," he said suddenly, mere inches behind her.

Gwenyth felt his warm breath against her neck, could almost feel his chest pressing against her back. Would he touch her now, as he had been since telling her the tale of Dog and his hare? That woodsy, musky scent of his she smelled each night on the bed linens rushed up to taunt her as she waited, holding her breath.

Aric looked the kind of man every woman wanted in her bed. Suddenly, she feared she was no exception. An odd disappointment filled her when he stepped back.

She swallowed against the erratic racing of her heart. "Aye, I think 'tis done."

With a gentle clasp of his fingers over hers upon the handle, he removed the broom from her grip. She started at his touch and felt her breathing go shallow from its effect as he raked the leaves onto an old cloth and tossed them outside.

God's nightgown, she must cease this foolish behavior. Why did he sway her senses so fiercely? She must remember Sir Penley and her future.

She must have rain, and if Aric could make it, he must— quickly. Somehow, she had to gently goad him to action or lose her chance at a secure future. 'Twould not do to delay the rain further by annoying the man.

"We've been long months now without rain," she said to his back as he left the cottage with the refuse.

"So I hear." He grunted as he tossed more leaves outside.

"Such will make for a warm summer, do you not agree?"

He shrugged as he reentered the cottage. "As I hail from the north, this southern clime always seems warm to me."

"Do you not miss the rain, though? That gentle patter of water upon the earth, letting trees and flowers and crops grow, always cheers me. I fear the land turned quite brown well before autumn last year. Such a shame, for I care not for brown grass and hillsides. Do you?"

Placing his massive fists on his lean hips, Aric scowled. "I do not think overmuch about the rain. Neither should you."

'Twas clear he saw through her ruse. Knowing she must drop the matter for now, Gwenyth smiled at him. "Nay, I am but making conversation. Since we live here alone, we must talk."

"Not always." He stepped closer and whispered, "At the moment, the bed linens need our attention."

Though he certainly meant they needed airing, the suggestion in his voice hinted at something warm and new, something she felt herself reaching for, despite her better judgment. Gwenyth shivered and prayed Aric had not noticed.

He left her to walk to one side of the bed. Feeling somehow aware and dazed at once, she moved to the other side and began removing the linens with his help.

At one corner, their fingers met. She started, her gaze flying to the masculine splendor of Aric's face. A smile crept over his mouth, something rich with promise, something that made her melt when he laced his fingers with hers and squeezed.

No one had ever touched her so. She felt as if her heart might jump out of her chest.

Gwenyth drew in one deep breath, then another. Her sanity seemed to return, although her senses remained clouded by his evocative scent, his low voice.

"Are you well?" he asked, his tone concerned.

"Aye. 'Tis the heat, I am certain," she lied.

Aric nodded and scooped the bed linens up in his arms. "Take these outside. The air there may help you."

"A good idea."

Slowly, Aric stepped around the bed toward her. The heels of his soft boots reminded her he moved closer, ever closer. His grin returned, stirring her stomach into a new frenzy.

He stopped inches away. Barely a breath separated them as he placed the sheets into her arms. As he released the bed linens, he stroked the length of her arms and fingers with his palms before stepping away. Gwenyth balled her fists, fighting the insane urge to drop the rumpled linens and demand Aric kiss her again.

Both stood still, Aric watching her, Gwenyth drowning in the mysterious depths of his hot gray eyes. 'Twas clear he wanted her. Why did he do nothing more about it?

Why did she want him to so badly?

Gwenyth cleared her throat. "I shall go outside with these."

His smile broadened as he gestured to her to lead the path to the door. Forcing her gaze away from him, she marched outside.

The crisp morning air was beginning to give way to the promise of the afternoon's warmth. Birds sang amid the leaves covering the tree branches, and a squirrel scurried into a fragrant bunch of wild hyacinths, sending their sweet scent into the air.

Gwenyth inhaled deeply. Certainly such pleasant smells were found nowhere near Penhurst. Animal droppings and unwashed bodies filled the air there. And 'twas so quiet here, she thought, as she hung the bed linens on a low tree branch. She could almost hear time pass, almost feel the whisper of God's hand moving in the swaying trees.

If Aric had chosen to remain here for the peace of this place, he had indeed found a wondrous spot.

Thwack! The noise rent the peace of the day. Gwenyth turned to the sound, only to hear another *thwack* coming from the side of the house.

That man! The first moment of peace she had known since their disastrous marriage, and he seemed bent on ruining it. The odd clamor came again. The mangy mongrel. Gritting her teeth, Gwenyth lifted her skirts and hurried to the source.

As she rounded the corner, a tongue-lashing ready to spring from her mouth, she stopped short. There Aric stood, an ax in one enormous hand, eyeing a fallen log before him.

He was completely naked from the waist up.

Gwenyth drew in a shaky breath at the sight. Whatever she had been about to say fled, forgotten at the sight of his male body. Taut golden skin stretched over a chest seemingly fashioned of steel. Hard ridges covered his belly as he drew a deep breath. Curves formed beneath his flat brown nipples as he grabbed the ax and lifted it. Swells of sinew protruded from his shoulders and arms as he swung it down to split the log. If she had half as much talent with a knife and wood as Aric, she would be tempted to carve a likeness of his form for herself.

Dear Lord, her mouth went dry just looking at him.

"Bring that basket to me," he said suddenly between swings of his heavy blade.

Gwenyth only half heard him. "Basket?"

His taut cheeks looked as though he repressed a smile. "Aye, the basket under the eaves, beside the door."

Nodding, she reluctantly looked away from her husband and drew in a calming breath. Why did her heart race merely from looking at the man? 'Twas not a good sign, she felt sure.

She retrieved the large basket, noting its woodsy smell and the wood chips lingering in the bottom. He was beginning to store wood for the next winter, giving it ample time to cure. Such made sense, and he certainly seemed fit to do so. Still, watching him—in his state of near undress—complete the mundane chore was not wise. She must deliver the basket and go inside until he finished.

But when Gwenyth reached Aric again, her eyes simply would not heed good sense. They led her gaze up the firm length of his calves and the muscle-hardened span of his thighs as she stood before him. His brown hose conformed to the heavy bulge of his man's staff.

Swallowing hard against a rising tide of tingling heat, Gwenyth let her gaze wander up to his unyielding stomach and hard chest. He watched her in silence, his eyes veiling his thoughts. Did this magnificent man truly think her as beautiful as the carving suggested? Warmth surrounded her, whether from the sun or Aric's proximity, she could not say.

"Set the basket down, Gwenyth."

Nodding, she did as he bid, then found her gaze attached to him again. He released the ax and stepped near her.

She was close enough now to see the light thatch of pale hair between his tight nipples and the myriad scars that covered him. A faded gash that began beneath his left nipple and ended near his waist had once been a wicked wound. Nicks and slices, old now, also dotted the sleek surface of his arms and shoulders.

He looked like a hardened battle warrior, no stranger to the lift of a lance and the thrust of a blade. Was it possible? What of his magical ways? He looked like no soft mystic who sat about all day turning children into chickens.

Without thought, she traced the long gash dividing his stomach with her fingers. He sucked in a breath but did not move. Gwenyth jerked her hand away from the warmth of his skin and glanced into his guarded expression.

"How did you come by that scar? And all the others?"

He lifted a tawny brow in question. "Do they bother you?"

Gwenyth frowned. He cared what she thought of his appearance? Or did he mock her?

"Nay," she answered finally. "'Tis surprised I am, is all. I did not imagine that…" *a sorcerer would have such warlike scars*, she started to say. But his reply to that would tell her nothing.

"Whence came you?" she queried instead.

He hesitated. "Yorkshire."

Recognition flashed through her. "Aye, 'tis in your voice, that northern slur. But what manner of man are you? A sorcerer, truly?"

"What do you believe?"

What indeed? "I cannot credit a man of the black arts with a warrior's wounds."

Again, a pause that told her Aric was measuring his words carefully. "I have known battle."

"More than once, 'twould appear. Yet you battle no more. Did you leave a baron's service?"

"Nay." He crossed his strong arms over the width of his chest.

"Were you trained for battle?"

Once more, a pause. "Aye."

Gwenyth peered at her husband, her frustration rising. He answered her questions, yet managed to give her little information. "You were a mercenary, then? And left behind your means?"

"Nay."

She balled her fists in frustration. "Might I have an answer of more than one word, you ruttish varlet?"

Suddenly, Aric turned away and retrieved the ax. "Gwenyth, it matters not about my past, for that is done. You and I are wed, and we will stay wed. I'll not be accused of madness or impotence. The past is a place I can never return, and I prefer to live my life here."

His answer gave her pause, not only because of the implacable tone, but the ease with which he had read her thoughts. Those words, coupled with his nightmares, told her something was unwell in his past. Had he run from someone? Something?

"Here, in a shanty? You have talent as a warrior, yet you choose to live like a pauper? Such makes no sense! Have you always lived thus?"

Aric locked his jaw, anger tightening his features. "Nay."

His reply filled her with surprise and hope. "You have lived in a castle?"

"Aye."

Renewed vexation swept her. "Are we back to a single word again, as if you have no more word-stock than a child? If you mean to stay married to me and can take me from this terrible place, can we not go? Half my days I have dreamed of my own castle and my own lands. Servants and villagers who need me, as does my husband, to oversee it all. You look strong enough for battle, and if you have been trained, I could help you—"

"Nay. Everything comes with a price, Gwenyth. Some are too high. Here we stay."

With his harsh, disheartening words, he threw the ax to the ground and disappeared into the forest.

CHAPTER FIVE

For many long hours, Aric stayed away from their cottage, and Gwenyth could hardly contain her fury. How could the hugger-mugger announce his intent to keep her here, trapped in obscure poverty, then saunter away, only to return in the depths of night as she tossed and turned in his bed? Did he not realize he threatened her dreams of a future as a respected lady, dreams that included a loving husband and giggling children with plenty to eat?

Shortly after dawn, Gwenyth glared at her husband—the man she swore would not have a permanent place in her life—as he calmly ate a hunk of dark, dry bread, then sipped some wine. Did he mean to say nothing of his absence? His declaration?

Aric turned his attention to a small slab of cheese, seemingly impervious to her glare. That gorbellied gudgeon!

Marching to the hearth, Gwenyth resolved he would listen well and grant her an annulment. He would release her this very day!

"Hear me, you surly urchin-snouted scut. You may mean to remain here for the rest of your fruitless days, aspiring to naught, but do not think you will keep me here to sink into nothingness with you! I came into this world a baron's daughter, and I will not waste my life on a man who strives to be no more than an outcast."

Aric took a swallow of beans and again sipped his wine, then fastened his unreadable gaze upon her. Setting his cup aside, he regarded her with thoughtful eyes. "Gwenyth, you must accept what you cannot change. We are bound. This is our home."

"Only because you bind me here to you. England is a large land. If you are a well-trained foot soldier, there is money to be made, perhaps a knightship—"

"Nay."

"Then release me! Choose a hellish life if you wish, but do not make me live in this terrible nether realm with you."

Aric sighed. "Your Uncle Bardrick wants you not at Penhurst. You have nowhere else to go and no one to take you in."

Gwenyth stepped closer, willing Aric to understand her needs, her desperation. "That is where you are wrong. When I was at Penhurst last, Sir Penley all but told me he wished to wed me and—"

"Nay!" Aric stood, abandoning his breakfast to glower at her. "You are my wife. We will have no more talk of annulments or of Sir Penley the buffoon."

"You know him not," Gwenyth insisted hotly.

Aric raised a challenging brow in answer but said nothing, giving her no reason, no hope for her tomorrows.

Tears stung her eyes. "Why punish me for a marriage I wanted not?"

He frowned, concern softening his hard features. "I seek not to punish you but to help you understand fate has chosen this path for us. Now we must walk it. All will be well, I vow."

"I despise it here," she sobbed, turning away from him and lowering her face into her hands.

Her life was ruined, all because of Aric's stubborn nature and her uncle's ambition for Lyssa. 'Twas not fair she should be denied everything—a castle, gracious servants, a place at court, her family, and most of all a husband who understood her and cared. The husband Uncle Bardrick had chosen for her angered, comforted, and confused her at once. What was she to do?

Aric said nothing, merely stepped behind her and put his arms around her. Somehow his solace only made her hurt worse, for he meant nothing by the gesture except to cease her tears, she was sure. Still, he stroked a gentle hand down the tangled length of her hair and whispered softly, "Easy now. The sun will still rise on the morrow, and we will live as well as needed here."

As well as *he* needed or as well as she? Gwenyth wondered, hot tears spilling down her cheeks.

Aric held her tighter. The solid feel of his arms about her, of his beating heart at her shoulder, distracted her worried mind. The rhythm of his breathing, the cadence of his hand stroking her hair slowly soothed her.

Gwenyth turned to him, wet-eyed and confused.

"Cry not," he said softly. "You will be safe here, and if it pleases you, you may cast any slur upon my head you desire."

Despite her tears, Gwenyth smiled. The corners of his mouth lifted in return, even as the warm breadth of his hands continued to caress her hair.

"There, a smile. Much better, for you would not want everyone to see you saddened at the Mayday festival."

Surprise jolted her. "The festival? You would take me, though everyone there despises and fears you?"

Aric shrugged. "Their opinions matter not. If going to the festival will please you, then go we shall."

Mayday was her favorite time of year, from the weather to the joy of the festival's merchants, visitors, and excitement. Gwenyth saw no reason to refuse Aric's offer. Though the difficulties of this curious marriage would be here still upon their return, she could not resist the urge to be gone from this shanty and her husband's unsettling proximity.

"It pleases me much. Thank you."

Aric nodded and assisted her outside. In the morning sunshine, he clasped her hand in his own large one and led her toward the village.

They walked in quiet broken only by their breathing, an occasional bird, and the movement of soft earth beneath their feet. Determined to do nothing more than enjoy this day, Gwenyth felt a peculiar peace settle over her as they made their way toward the village. She did not question why, but she felt safe and somewhat understood, for Aric seemed to know she wished to attend the Mayday festival. Was it his black magic or his occasionally kind heart that told him so? Who was Aric?

By the time they arrived, the revelry was well underway. Merchants shouted through the dust at passing customers, trying to lure them closer. Parents showed their children the maypole, which declared to one and all the location of the festival. The scents of roasting meat hung in the air like a promise of good tidings to come. Gwenyth felt her excitement bubbling, and she turned to Aric and smiled.

His gaze touched her face and lowered to her mouth. The gray of his eyes darkened like storm-filled clouds. Her heart struck her chest with the force of a battering ram, and Gwenyth knew it had naught to do with the excitement of the gathering.

Why did some foolish part of her want to be his wife in every way, despite the fact she would be miserable sharing the life and home he had chosen?

Suddenly, Aric released her hand and retrieved several coins from a pouch hidden inside his tunic. "Buy us some of the sweetmeats over there."

Gwenyth took the coins but frowned. Certainly reading her expression, he added, "I've a bit of business to attend to, but I will meet you here directly. And see if the old woman sells wine as well."

At her nod, Aric turned away into the crowd, which parted on either side of him, giving him a wide berth. As usual, her husband seemed completely oblivious to the stir he caused and the whispers behind his back.

Shrugging, Gwenyth did as Aric had bid and bit into her own sweetmeat. The succulent flavor burst into her mouth, reminding her how hungry she had indeed been.

About her, people began to dance when a lute player struck up a light tune. Soon, someone joined in with words that were too far away to hear but drew a bawdy laugh from the surrounding crowd. Quickly, another of the jongleurs shook a shiny set of bells, while a third lifted a double flute to his mouth and released a merry melody.

Swaying with the music, Gwenyth looked about for Aric, wishing he would return. She loved to dance, loved to feel the music within her, guiding her foot to its rhythm.

As if thought of him conjured him up, the crowd scrambled about, and Aric strode between the villagers with a long-legged gait, a smile, and a wreath of greenery in his hands. The spring breeze lifted the tawny strands of his hair and whipped them about his wide shoulders. Those gray eyes she was beginning to know well seemed fixed on her alone, as if no one else at the festival existed. She found herself smiling in return.

Then he placed the wreath upon her head. The ivy and ribbons cascaded down past her shoulders.

"For me?"

"Pray tell me you did not think *I* would wear it."

Gwenyth laughed. "Nay."

"And a good thing," he insisted, sending her a teasing grin that made her belly turn over in flops.

"Did you get a sweetmeat for me?" he asked.

"Aye." Flustered, Gwenyth held it out to him. Instead of taking it from her grip, he bent and took a bite. His tongue grazed one of her fingers and she shivered.

"And wine?" he asked after swallowing the bite.

"Oh, aye."

Nearly having forgotten the brew, she retrieved it from the peddler and gave it to Aric. He finished the goblet with a toss of his head and several long swallows. Gwenyth watched the broad column of his throat working. The sinew roping the sides of his neck told a tale of strength she well knew extended down his arms, his chest, his belly…and lower. Flushing at her own thoughts, she turned away.

Aric plucked the sweetmeat out of her hand and finished it hastily. Then he surprised her by grabbing her hand. "Come. Let us dance. The music is merry."

Gwenyth smiled again even more brightly. Once more, he understood and granted her wishes, more than her own aunt and uncle ever had. Such courtesy made her feel warm all over when he led her to the dancing crowd. The other revelers made a broad path between themselves and Aric. Before it could anger her, Aric moved her into the steps of a ductia. As he twirled her about, she laughed and marveled that a man so tall and formidable could move with such fluid grace.

The musicians played on. She and Aric danced through the afternoon, taking only a brief respite for more wine, along with a hearty serving of roast goose. He seemed to know every dance. Whether round, line, or for couples, he was well versed in all the steps. Where had this hermit learned such? Indeed, where had he learned to speak and do battle as well?

Before she could ask, another song came to an end. His face slick with sweat, Aric raked the hair from his eyes, then urged her off the floor.

"Have you danced enough, my lady?"

Near breathless, she nodded, clutching the wreath to her head. "Should I dance more, I fear my feet will fall off."

He laughed, a sound so deep and bounteous Gwenyth felt it

vibrate deep within her. Still, she could feel his hand upon her waist guiding her, his other hand enclosing her own. His touch made her quiver.

"Since you will need your feet for another day," he said, "we should indeed stop dancing."

"Aye."

"Come, then." He grabbed her hand again and pulled her to his side.

The musk of his skin, so close now, eclipsed all the other smells. She could detect nothing but the leather of his boots and the bedeviling scent of woodsy, earthy man. Indeed, she could seem to see nothing but the rise and fall of his massive chest, covered only by a white tunic.

"I have something for you," Aric said, leading her away from the revelers and back toward the merchants.

Gwenyth followed along in the waning afternoon sun, her anticipation building. Laughter echoed from the shadows of ancient trees as children played. Men gathered about in a circle, cheering on two others locked in a battle of fists.

Gwenyth grimaced and looked away, only to find Aric standing before the fabric peddler from whom he had purchased the woolens only two days past. Had he forgotten something?

The old merchant, reserved in his demeanor before, now regarded Aric with a wide, welcoming smile. Gwenyth took it in with a frown until the man handed her husband a shiny red bundle. She peered at it in confusion. Then recognition dawned.

The scarlet silk!

She turned to Aric, wide-eyed and breathless, as he handed her the cloth. "You bought this for me?"

He smiled at her whisper. "Aye, for you. I expect you to begin sewing soon."

"On the morrow," she agreed. "How did you afford—"

"Nay." He halted her with a gesture of his hand. "Do not question, simply enjoy."

Gwenyth swallowed a lump of pleasure and launched herself into his arms. "Thank you."

Aric held her against him, only the crush of the silk between them. In that moment, she enjoyed the strength of his embrace nearly as much as she enjoyed his gift. He grasped her tightly, his hands spread wide across her back, his chin upon her shoulder. Beneath her hands, his arms felt tense, and she wondered if he had thought of kissing her again.

She could think of little else.

* * * *

Three mornings later, Gwenyth's fleshy cousin Nellwyn emerged from the forest on a fine dappled gray, with a foot soldier in tow.

Hearing their clatter, Aric looked up from his carving of Gwenyth naked and swore. It had been a fine morning to commune with his thoughts, decide how best to win his wife's charms, and listen to her hum excitedly as she sewed upon her red silk.

Now, as he watched her expectant cousin-by-marriage dismount her horse and settle the folds of her green silk gown about her, he felt certain she would only bring trouble.

She eyed him with open curiosity, as if any objection he might have to such scrutiny was of no import. With a sharp smile, he stood, rising to his full height. Taken aback, the lady placed a fluttering hand to her chest as her eyes widened.

"Oh, my," she whispered.

Her pale blue gaze lingered on his shoulders, then flitted down to his belly and legs, as she assessed him like any fruit in a marketplace.

"Do I meet with your disapproval, my lady?"

Clearly jolted by his words, Nellwyn jerked her gaze back to his face. "Nay, good sir. I but seek my cousin Gwenyth. You must be her new husband," she said and extended her hand.

Hiding his irritation, Aric reached for her fingers and brought them a breath short of his lips. If she noticed the slight, she said nothing, did nothing, except stare. "I am Aric."

"Merely Aric?" She frowned. "No surname at all?"

Aric rolled his eyes. As if he would tell the ambitious woman he was the Earl of Belford and a Neville, as well. She would keep company with his wife for an altogether different reason if she knew that.

He held in a sneer. "Merely Aric."

"I see. Well, I am Lady Nellwyn Brinkley," she said with great pride.

Clearly, the woman expected some exaltation for her rank. Aric simply nodded. 'Twas clear from her scowl he had earned Lady Nellwyn's pique. The thought made him smile.

"Gwenyth is inside," he said instead.

As the woman moved toward the cottage door, she insisted, "You are fortunate to have her for a wife, you know. She is hardworking, possessed of a sharp mind, and of excellent breeding, as well."

Aric stared at the woman without comment. It was hardly his wife's breeding that impressed him. After all, he could not confess he had scarce heard of Lord Capshaw or this obscure little barony before moving here. But Gwenyth herself pleased him, and, wretched family or no, he knew Guilford would approve as well. Since he had ever sought his mentor's good opinion, Guilford's approval would please him indeed. As well, Drake would like her lively conversation, while Kieran would drool over her beauty like a mutt with a fresh bone.

He smiled. "Since Gwenyth is easily the most beautiful, spirited lady for at least fifty leagues, I feel fortunate."

Nellwyn nodded, then scowled. Aye, she had finally realized his slight of her charms, meager as they were. In truth, he found Gwenyth's cousin quite plain and unkind besides. 'Twas past time someone reminded her of her own faults.

Aric opened the cottage door for Nellwyn and hustled her inside.

Inside, Gwenyth rose to greet her cousin before he closed the door on them. And though he knew 'twas unfair, he sat beneath the eaves and listened, somehow vaguely concerned for Gwenyth.

"Nellwyn, I am surprised! Why are you not in London?"

"Those were our plans, but now I have the most wonderful news for you! Once I remembered you were but a short ride away, I rushed here to tell you!"

"What? Tell me."

Aric grimaced at the excitement in Gwenyth's voice. Did she still want to return to Penhurst, where her uncle treated her so ill? Did she believe that would change? Nay, and any good news Nellwyn brought Gwenyth 'twas, he feared, likely to be bad tidings for his wife.

"Well, the morn we meant to leave for London, my father rushed outside to stop us and insisted we celebrate. 'Celebrate what?' I asked, but he would not answer. When I dashed back into the keep—as much as this active babe allows me to dash—I found our little Lyssa smiling so brightly I thought 'twould blind me."

"Lyssa?"

Hearing the confusion in Gwenyth's voice, Aric swore. Clearly, she believed this overlong tale had something to do with her return to Penhurst.

"Aye, you silly goose. Lyssa! Oh, and now I shall cry, I am certain. Each time I think upon it—why, I am so happy I feel tears. And I should *not* cry, because Sir Rankin does tease me so mercilessly about my red nose when I do."

"Lyssa makes you cry?" Impatience sounded in Gwenyth's voice.

"Of course! 'Tis all we hoped for her. My sister is quite happy, and I daresay father is, as well. Mother is already planning—"

"Planning what?" his wife prodded.

"Oh, how foolish of me. Lyssa and Sir Penley are to be wed—and in London, no less!"

Even from outside, Aric felt Gwenyth's silent shock deep in his bones. She had set her cap for the fop Sir Penley, hoping he would give her the kind of life her cousin Nellwyn led. Now she truly had nowhere to belong, except by his own side. While a part of him reveled in that fact for a reason he could not explain, another part felt guilt. To keep his sanity intact, he could never tell her of his past, of the family, wealth, and power he'd left behind, though 'twas her heart's desire.

"Wonderful." Gwenyth's voice shook. "Wh-when?"

"Since the king has already sanctioned the match, I should think no later than St. Swithin's Day. What troubles you, cousin? I should think you would be happy for my sister."

Gwenyth paused. Aric could almost feel her gathering her resolve. "I wish her nothing but joy. 'Tis simply that I feel unwell today."

A lie, Aric knew. Gwenyth had felt fine enough this morn to sew nearly half a gown from the scarlet silk. Indeed, she sounded much troubled.

"Oh, unwell? Perhaps, then, I should be away. Sir Rankin is

forever warning me about all manner of ill that could befall his son. And as he ever reminds me, I must heed a man so important and wise."

Aric wanted to vomit. Never did the woman miss an opportunity to mention the consequences of her husband and family, paltry as it was. The wench had not even inquired after Gwenyth's health.

"Indeed," agreed Gwenyth.

As Aric heard steps approaching the door, he stood. Soon the two women emerged, Nellwyn wearing a proud smile. Gwenyth's shaken demeanor made him bite back a curse.

The vicious bitch. How he would love to see Nellwyn's face if she could know the cousin she considered lesser had wed into the Neville family.

But that would never come to pass, Aric vowed, this time with a tinge of regret.

Within moments, Nellwyn was away with a smile and a jaunty wave. Gwenyth stared after her cousin, her face drawn, her eyes listless and unsettled.

Once the pregnant woman and her soldier disappeared into the forest, Gwenyth turned to him. The eaves cast a gentle shadow on her otherwise unhappy face. Her lips pursed, her cheeks taut beneath her blazing deep blue eyes, she turned to the cottage, entered, and slammed the door behind her.

Aric thought to follow until one of her shoes came flying out the window.

"That miserable wretch!" she yelled as one of his boots soared out the window as well, narrowly missing him.

"Gwenyth?" he inquired, peeking in the window and hoping none of their footwear would find the side of his head.

"Sir Penley is naught but a paunchy milk-livered maggot!" Aric heard his cup strike the cottage wall and grimaced.

She was more than a trifle angry.

He made for the door and opened it. "Gwenyth..."

"I have a very important question to ask you." She imitated a man's voice he could only assume was intended to be Sir Penley's. "I wonder now what that spleeny idle-headed miscreant sought to ask. How best to earn my contempt for eternity?"

She picked up a pitcher of water from beside the little table he had recently repaired and sent it sailing into the wall. It crashed with a great clatter. Soon the pungent stench of wet thatch filled the room. Aric had known for some time his bride was a firebrand. Today, she showed it beyond his expectations.

"'I shall count the moments.'" She again aped Sir Penley. "No doubt the whey-faced fool-licker counted the moments until I was well and truly gone so he could ask for my cousin's hand in marriage." She stomped her feet in fury. "I hope the match brings him—all of them—naught but misery!"

Gwenyth whirled and reached for the table itself, then lifted it above her head. Aric stepped in front of her and jerked the table from her grasp.

"Enough, Gwenyth. Penley is a coxcomb, and you are better off without him."

The laugh she gave him lay somewhere between contemptuous and hysterical. "Aye, 'tis better off I am here, where I shall meet no one, go nowhere, and have no home or servants of my own."

"This is your home," he reminded her. Would the wench never accept that fact?

"All this? A woman could scarcely hope for more." She flung her arms wide, gesturing to the four walls about them.

Aric found his ire rising. Her continued insults of the home he had built for solace and shelter irked him nearly beyond words. Why had fate not blessed him with a less clamorous wife? And why did she continue to refuse to accept the fact they were man and wife in all ways except one?

He planned to change that soon.

"Stop this foolish chatter—"

"You." She turned narrowed eyes upon him. "The fault lies with you, as well. You could have refused to wed me."

"I should have let them murder you at my feet?"

"You should have insisted returning me to Penhurst and wedding me to Sir Penley would appease you enough to make rain."

"Gwenyth, that is utter witlessness."

"So now you call me witless? And why not? 'Twould seem I am everyone's whipping boy today. Of course you should join the others in their unkindness."

Aric had heard enough. The wench had insulted him with her words before. Likening him to Sir Penley and her family was enough to send his temper upward.

"When was I unkind to you, my lady?"

He advanced on her. Her hands on her hips, she squared her shoulders and stood directly in his path.

"Was I unkind to you when I wed you, rather than see you dead?" he asked, his silent steps taking him ever closer to her challenging glare.

"Was I unkind when I gave up my bed for your comfort? Or when I danced with you?"

Gwenyth only glared at him, and somehow that made him angrier. As he reached her, he clasped his hands about her shoulders.

"Have you nothing to say to your husband?" he goaded.

"Piss off!" she shot back, tossing her black hair.

Aric restrained his anger—barely. "I think not. Here we will stay until you remember 'tis who you spoke vows with, until you forget that weakling Sir Penley and accept me."

"Be prepared to wait until old age sets in."

"I think not." He jerked her close, then cupped her jaw with his hands. "I think you shall start now."

He sought and covered her lips with his own. Her damp mouth met his with a catch of breath, a parting of lips. Aric pressed his advantage with the reckless urging of his tongue against her own.

She tasted better than he remembered, like purity and wine, sunshine and vivid red passion. And he wanted her, every smoldering, temperamental, provocative inch of her. A fierce, ravenous hunger seized him, plunging him into a primitive impulse to possess.

Her tongue began to mate with his, uncertainly at first. Aric spurred her closer, against his rising arousal, and stroked her mouth again. Gwenyth responded in a rush, nipping with her teeth, her lips answering his pursuit until their kisses melded in a demanding union. She moaned, inching up on the tips of her toes to meet him.

Burying his fingers in the thick silk of her dark hair, Aric again positioned her lush mouth beneath his own, then angled his head to reap her warm taste to the fullest. Need gripped him with such force he hardly remembered wanting so keenly. He fed himself on her sweet lips, his pleasure spiraling as he locked her within his arms, a tempest of desire raging.

He had to taste her skin. The craving surged within him, possessed him. Aric lifted his mouth from hers and laved her neck with kisses in a blind haze of need. Gwenyth gasped when his teeth found her earlobe and drew it into his mouth for a teasing pull.

As his appetite for her inciting mouth returned, Aric reached for her again. He found naught but air.

Slowly, he opened his eyes. His wife stood across the room, her chest heaving, her eyes fearful and accusing at once.

"I did not tell you to touch me," she whispered.

Her stricken expression told Aric his kiss, given in anger, had been a tactical mistake, for it had done little except raise her guard again. Gritting his teeth, he called, "Gwenyth—"

"Nay! Say nothing. Why keep me here? Make rain and let me be."

"We have discussed this. You have nowhere to go. We have spoken vows. I am sorry that displeases you, but it changes naught, Gwenyth. *I* can change naught. Sir Penley will wed Lady Lyssa and make her a miserable husband. Lady Nellwyn will continue to flaunt her good fortune at every opportunity. But know this: Lyssa will soon seek lovers, and Nellwyn will someday learn of her husband's bad nature.

"Do you not see your life could be worse? I have not beaten you, demanded hard labor, or pressed my rights as a husband to share your bed. I have done my best to see to your comfort. Hell, I have even cooked for you! If you can find nothing good in any of that, you are a foolish woman indeed."

CHAPTER SIX

Gwenyth sat upon the hill behind Aric's cottage, watching the sun set and the stars rise. The moon appeared, glowing with the brilliance of a hundred candles. Cool wind struck her face, bringing with it the scents of grass and wildflowers, of fresh leaves and the nearby forest.

She cared for none of nature's beauty now.

For hours, Gwenyth had been sitting, thinking of all Aric had said earlier. She came to the ugly, unfortunate conclusion he was right. She had nowhere to go now that Sir Penley had asked Lyssa to wife. Gwenyth also could not deny she and Aric had spoken vows. As for Lyssa's soon seeking lovers and Nellwyn's discovering some terrible nature of Sir Rankin's, Gwenyth could only hope Aric was wrong. Though she envied her cousins, she did want them happy and well settled with the best of men, despite what she might have said in anger.

The rest of Aric's angry speech could not be denied, either. He could indeed have been much harder on her, raping her to obtain his husbandly rights, beating her for her lamentable lack of cooking skills. Certainly she had fared well during her teary times. Bardrick had always laughed scornfully at a woman's tears. Aric, at least, had understood—aye, even been gentle.

In truth, everything about the man this far had pleased her—except his lack of concern about security and future. And though she did not seek money for itself, she wanted to reclaim her position as a lady. She wanted the kind of life her cousins led, the life that would have been hers had her parents not perished. And she wanted family, secure in both love and home. Raising babes in a dirt cottage, with seemingly few funds and a father giving no thought to the future, was unthinkable.

Of a sudden, Gwenyth heard footsteps behind her, firm and heavy and unhurried. Aric. She was not surprised when he sat beside her, his knees bent and spread wide, and began plucking at the green grass between his feet.

"You have been gone a long time, Gwenyth. Night has fallen, and you have not supped."

Was he concerned about her, or merely seeing after what he regarded as his? "I do not hunger."

He nodded, then gazed up at the moon. "Nellwyn upset you."

Pausing, Gwenyth considered his words. "Nay, just her news. Until this morn, I believed for years Uncle Bardrick would see me well wed to a good, kind knight or baron and restored to my rank as a lady, despite the fact he treated me as a servant more oft than not. I am his only niece."

"Your beauty was at odds with his ambitions for his very plain daughters, so he wed you away. Can you not see he banished you not out of spite but fear?"

"Nellwyn and Lyssa are not plain," Gwenyth defended. "Besides, you have not seen Lyssa."

Aric sent her a skeptical stare, visible in the golden moonlight. "Aye, little dragon, Nellwyn is plain, and if her sister looks anything like her, neither has much hope of ensnaring a man with her charms whilst you are about."

Gwenyth frowned at him, determined not to be swayed by his praise. "Do you insult my cousins in one breath and flatter me in the next?"

"I but speak the truth. Nellwyn knows she possesses not one tenth of your beauty. 'Tis why she comes to torment you with her good fortune."

Gwenyth regarded him with outrage. "What rot! She alone has been kind to me in the years since my parents died."

"Kind for her own purposes. Besides, Nellwyn's chattering mouth alone could drive a man to flee his castle and country. 'Tis no wonder Sir Rankin has so many lemans."

"How would you know such?" Gwenyth stared at Aric, uncertainty spilling within her. He had spoken before as if he knew

Sir Rankin. Certainly he claimed to know Sir Penley. Who was
Aric? Who had he been in the past?

He grimaced. "Gossip, little dragon. Naught more. But if Lady
Lyssa can talk at the same speed as her sister, Sir Penley may soon
find the war between the Yorks and the Lancasters less active than
the war at home."

Somehow Aric's explanation regarding his knowledge did not
ring true, but she also knew he would tell her naught else. "Lyssa
speaks sparingly."

With a grin, Aric turned to her. "And why should she not?
Nellwyn can say enough for both of them and still keep talking."

Gwenyth gave him a mock punch in the arm. "Stop. You are
terrible to speak so of my only family. And should I ever meet your
family, what would you say if I were to speak so terribly of them?"

Aric paused, his silence so long Gwenyth thought he might not
answer her at all. Wind swept the hill as crickets chirped, frogs
croaked, and stars twinkled. Still, her husband picked at the grass
beneath them. Then he sighed.

"My parents are gone and I have no sisters. If you knew my
younger brother, you would soon see any pestering he receives is
much needed."

Never had Aric shared anything about himself with her. The fact
he had told her this warmed some place inside her she could not
quite name.

"I should like to meet your brother."

Without pause, he shook his head. "That day will never come,
Gwenyth. As I've said, the past is in the past."

Aye, he had said that, but she could scarce believe he intended
never to see his only family again. "Do you not miss your brother?"

Aric cocked his head in apparent consideration. "He
is…younger and given to foolish fits of temper. We have little in
common."

"But he is family!"

With a shrug, Aric returned her stare. "I have friends for whom I
have great affection. They are like family."

"And yet you plan never to see them again?" She pointed out his
illogic. "Surely you miss them?"

A musing smile flitted across his mouth, and something warmed
his stone-colored eyes to a soft gray. "Aye, that I do. But what of

you?" He turned to her quickly. "'Tis clear you miss your parents still."

A pang of emptiness settled in her belly when she thought of their ten-year absence in her life. "I miss them each day."

Aric nodded and reached for her hand, lacing her fingers between his larger, warmer ones. "Tell me of your life with them."

Did he really wish to know? Gwenyth peered into his hawkish face. The warrior countenance she could scarce credit on a sorcerer appeared attentive and curious.

"Life as a child was…free of cares. There was laughter, little war, and festivals aplenty. The serfs had much to eat and decent homes. My father would not tolerate cruelty to anyone." She smiled, even as tears gathered in her eyes. "And he could always spare a moment for me."

"And your mother?" Aric prompted.

"My mother taught me to sew and keep a castle in order. She and my father taught me to read and cipher. Often, they would let me sleep between them and would kiss me awake."

"What happened?" Aric's gentle voice encouraged her to go on.

"When I was eight years, Mother died trying to bring a son into the world. She had never had good fortune in birthing. All died within a week, except me. The last one took my mother with him."

Again, Gwenyth could feel the pain of her father's saying her mother was no more. She had run screaming toward the solar, only to be barred by her father and the midwife. Never had she seen her mother again. Ten years later, her tears still came easily.

She sniffed and continued. "My father went to London soon after that. We received word within a fortnight that he began drinking ale one eve and ne'er stopped."

Warm tears rolled down her cheeks.

"Then your uncle came to Penhurst?"

Gwenyth swiped her tears aside. "Aye. Uncle Bardrick and Aunt Welsa came and brought Nellwyn and Lyssa with them. I had never met them. I believed they would treat me as family, though life without my parents frightened me. 'Twas only the thought I was not completely alone that saved me in the weeks before their arrival. But when they came, I wished with all my might they would leave."

"They were cruel?" Aric's sharp tone took her aback.

"Only to the serfs, many of whom have starved in the last few years. To me, they were indifferent. Other than the fact they gave my chamber to Nellwyn and Lyssa and assigned me kitchen duties, they took little notice of me at all—at least until Sir Penley came."

"Your uncle invited him to Penhurst?"

"Aye, with the purpose of luring him to wed Lyssa, I see now. I stood in his way."

Aric squeezed her hand gently. "You did, little dragon. But you must not fear. I will make certain you are fed and clothed and have a warm, dry bed. I can even tend the cooking, though you must never tell anyone."

She smiled, despite her sad remembrances. "Would no one fear the sorcerer then?"

With a laugh, he rubbed her sensitive palm with his thumb. "Something like that. Can I bribe you for silence with a rabbit stew and warm bread?"

In mock seriousness, she considered it. "For now, I suppose. But you shall have to bribe me often and well."

Chuckling, he raised her hand to his mouth and kissed her fingertips. Her skin began to tingle.

"Always, little dragon," he vowed, rising to his feet. "Always."

Gwenyth followed Aric back to their shanty somehow more at peace than she had been in years.

* * * *

Midnight settled inside the cottage. Slouched uncomfortably in the hard wooden chair, Aric propped his feet up on the bed and watched Gwenyth sleep.

His wife looked peaceful with her dark lashes resting against the pale beauty of her cheeks. Her mahogany hair spread all about her in a dark, glossy sheen, hinting at the tempestuous nature that so intrigued him. The blankets she had recently sewn covered the rest, but his imagination had shown him her naked form many, many times.

But 'twas not that which disturbed him this night.

Rolling his shoulders to ease tension, he considered their earlier conversation. Not only did she put too much faith in the goodness of her cousins, she had a blind devotion to family, despite their ill-treatment of her, something he did not understand.

What he understood less, however, was why he had revealed anything about himself. Gwenyth should know nothing of him. He should have remained mute on the subject of family. Though he had not called his brother, Stephen, by name, revealing details of his past could only lead Gwenyth to want more knowledge—to expect it, even. Worse, he had barely restrained the urge to tell her of Guilford, his wise teacher, Drake and his friend's trouble with his father's murder, as well as Kieran's pranking, devil-may-care nature that hid terrible pain.

As Gwenyth had spoken of her mother and father, some part of him had yearned to tell her of the blood oath he and Drake and Kieran shared to always protect one another. Lately, Aric had done naught to honor that vow. Still, he felt solace at knowing if he was truly needed, Guilford would send word.

And in the future, he must watch his tongue around sweet Gwenyth or find all his secrets revealed.

That decided, Aric closed his eyes. For once, sleep came easily. So did the nightmares.

The sun shone high in the sky. In the distance, London was abuzz with news of the impending coronation. On a hillside, Aric sat on the early autumn grass. Bees buzzed from blossom to blossom. Birds chimed happily in harmony with children's laughter.

Scampering from behind the swaying trees, two golden-haired boys ran, chasing one another across the landscape—young Edward, soon to be England's next king, and his younger brother, Richard, Duke of York.

Their joyful, excited voices carried in muted whispers on the breeze, punctuated by an occasional giggle or shriek. Aric waved. The boy Richard waved in return, then resumed his play.

The Tower of London soared into the sky behind them, looking clean and stately in the brilliant sunshine.

As he stared at the sky, a black cloud enveloped the sun. 'Twas clear rain threatened. Within moments, silence descended. The birds' cheerful songs ceased. The breeze stilled. The bees fled.

Aric looked about the shadowed hillside for Edward and Richard to warn them of the bad weather.

They had vanished.

Around him, grass had died, trees rotted. The Tower of London appeared suddenly red and ominous. The city behind the grand tower was hushed, as if shocked into muteness. And the silence ate at him. Where were those boys? What had ceased their laughter?

Aric woke with a start, gasping. Wiping the sweat from his face, he rose and answered his own question. Murder had stopped the boys' laughter. Their own uncle, Richard, Duke of Gloucester, had arranged for their murders through an ambitious knave named Sir James Tyrell, so he might seek the crown for himself, and seek it he did. Richard wore it even now.

Sighing, Aric stood and cursed. He had pleaded with Sir Thomas More to discover the truth that all London—indeed, all England—sought in vain. But he had not known the truth could be so painful. How could he ever have believed King Richard's lies?

Stifled by the humid air within the small dwelling, Aric left Gwenyth sleeping peacefully and retreated to his chair beneath the cottage eaves. As the night wind washed over him, his thoughts continued to race.

He could not, now or ever, return to Northwell, to Richard's court, to politics and war and ambition. It all came to naught and resulted in senseless death. Aric wanted no part of any of that again.

Resolved, he stood and ambled toward the cottage window. Aric peered inside at his wife and wrestled with the one truth he could not escape: He could give Gwenyth the life she sought—indeed, a life beyond her dreams.

The Nevilles had castles, servants, money, and power aplenty. He himself had a fortune, three titles, and a small army. If he brought her home, Gwenyth would indeed be important, very much needed. Nellwyn would have nothing to lord over her younger cousin, her Uncle Bardrick would kick himself for not forcing Lyssa to become the sorcerer's wife, and Gwenyth would certainly be glad she had seen the last of sniveling Sir Penley.

The thought made him smile, but the smile faded quickly beneath the crushing weight of fact.

If he wanted to maintain his soundness of mind, such as it was, he could not return to his former life. Not for Gwenyth. Not ever.

* * * *

The next morn, Gwenyth completed the touches on her scarlet silk dress. Aric marveled at her tiny, perfect stitches, the simple but elegant gown of her creation. Although ladies learned young the skills of sewing, such patience and talent always surprised him.

Gwenyth would make a fine chatelaine. She knew her role and would be firm when needed, but she also had heart. The people of Northwell would respond to her with great favor.

Cease! He reminded himself. He could never take Gwenyth to his home, for all the reasons he had already considered.

Sighing, Aric wandered out into the midday sun and sat in his chair beneath the eaves. He could not deny Gwenyth had suffered greatly of late in her family's and friends' rejections. Nor could he deny she deserved better. He simply could not give it to her.

As a husband, he could provide her protection, shelter, and food, along with an occasional gift. But the funds he had received from the sale of his armor were dwindling. Soon he would have to find a way to earn a wage, for returning to battle was no option. Still, he would provide for his wife.

He frowned. The past few days had taken a toll on Gwenyth. The fiery wench with whom he had spoken vows had grown increasingly quiet. Her melancholy on the hill last eve gave him pause. 'Twould not do at all.

Seized by an idea, Aric wandered into the cottage and rummaged through a pile of his belongings. When he found the object he sought, he enclosed it in his palm, its cool surface soon warming in his grasp.

Aye, Gwenyth, his wife, was worthy of this token. She would value it. God willing, 'twould make her happy for a time.

He turned about in search of her. Everything—his breathing, his very heartbeat—ceased when he saw her.

Gwenyth rounded the corner wearing her new red gown. The garment hugged her full breasts, dipped with the sharp curve of her small waist, and flared out over the lush swell of her hips. The vivid color made her skin seem brighter, clearer, her eyes a more stunning shade of blue. Aye, and her lips—how very red and moist and full they looked. And Aric felt with every muscle in his being how badly he wanted to taste her mouth again.

Dragging in a draught of air, he noted she had brushed her hair to a dark, silky gloss, and it lay in a straight sheen to her hips. 'Twas all he could do to remember the token in his hand, not throw it aside in favor of seducing her.

"Do you like it?" she asked quietly.

He paused, openmouthed, clearly stunned. "Aye, you look...beautiful."

Aric appeared at a loss for words. Gwenyth bit her lip to hold in a smile. He liked it! Perhaps he even thought she looked well in it. Though she wasn't certain why his opinion was important, she found it was.

"Thank you. The fabric is the—"

"Nay," he interrupted, stepping closer. His warm gray gaze caressed her. "You give the gown light."

Gwenyth could not restrain her smile at his compliment.

"Yet I know how it could shine more."

More? She frowned at him. She had only a simple white chemise, lacking any ruffle, to give her sleeves. The material required for the gown had left none for the headdress. And her sewing could always be improved...

"'Tis the best I can do," she admitted finally.

"And well you have done, Gwenyth. Now it is my turn."

With those intriguing words, he stepped to her, so close she could see the thick muscles of his arms and the pulse beating at his throat. From his fist he unfurled something shiny and silver.

When she caught sight of it, she gasped. "Sweet Mary."

'Twas a pendant of a small sundial with a shimmering ruby in its center, suspended from a silver chain. Did he mean to give such a gift to her?

Holding her breath, Gwenyth waited as Aric leaned in and lifted the stunning amulet above her head. The moment she bowed her head, he placed it around her neck. The cool silver settled on her skin and nestled just above the valley between her breasts, exposed now by the low, square neckline of her gown. The red of the stone and the red of the gown were nearly identical, as if they had been made for one another. Shock nearly silenced her.

"'Tis most beautiful, Aric," she vowed, raising her gaze to him. "I scarce know what to say. Thank you."

His smile softened his angled warrior's face. "If it pleases you, you need say nothing."

"Indeed! I shall want to wear it every day."

No one since her parents had given her a gift of any kind, for any reason. Aye, Nellwyn had given her cast-off clothing and trinkets, but never anything that was all hers—and never anything so valuable.

Whence did Aric come by such a costly item? She frowned. Had he stolen it from someone at the Mayday festival? Nay. No one there would own such an expensive trinket except Nellwyn or Aunt Welsa, and neither owned such. She would know.

So where had Aric found such an item? And why had he chosen to give it to her now?

Lost in her ruminations, it took Gwenyth a moment to realize Aric had paused, his brow furrowed, his expression seeking.

"My mother wore it nearly each day as well," he said, as if knowing her questions. "After God took her back into His keeping, I carried it with me always."

Gwenyth stared at him, again in shock. This costly pendant had been his mother's. Was such possible?

Allowing her gaze to roam his face for any sign of falsehood, Gwenyth could not help but remember other contradictions about her hermit husband. The well-spoken English, his air of quiet but unyielding command, the combat scars coupled with his admission of receiving some battle training. Had he perhaps been trained as a knight? Mayhap come from such a family, who had since lost castle or fortune? 'Twas certainly possible.

"Your mother must have received great joy from such an item," Gwenyth fished, hoping Aric would reveal more.

Again, he paused. Gwenyth's heart leaped, for he always paused before revealing anything of import.

"This pendant was her favorite," he said slowly. "Though I know not if 'twas because she found it lovely or because my father gave it to her."

His father. Gwenyth nodded, her mind racing. Perhaps his father had once been an important knight or lord. Had Aric's mother the man's leman? 'Twould explain more of Aric's circumstances and the appearance of such a gift. Still, curiosity ate at her. She wanted to know more about her husband. But she also knew she must word her questions with care, else Aric would not answer.

"Why did your father give your mother this gift?"

His gaze wandered to someplace far away, and a frown settled over his features. "I know not. My mother told me he gave it to her so she might know what time each day to meet him for their trysts."

Aye, Gwenyth decided, Aric's mother had been a nobleman's leman. But whose? And for how long? Had Aric known his father well? The questions gnawed at Gwenyth, piling her frustration into a mountain of inquisitiveness.

"Did your mother and father love well?" she asked carefully.

Would he answer or refuse her questions? Gwenyth bit her lip as she waited through long moments of silence.

"Aye. After my mother's death, even after he took a young wife, my father spoke often of her with fondness."

The strong tones of his voice gentled as he spoke of his parents' love for one another. Gwenyth felt tears sting her eyes. She wanted such a love for herself. Did Aric seek that kind of bond, too?

Placing her palm over the warm ruby, Gwenyth regarded Aric with a mixture of hope and fear she could not quite understand. "Why did you give such a gift to me?"

Aric scowled. "Do you not like it?"

"I like it," she assured. "Never have I seen anything so lovely. 'Tis simply that...well, the pendant was your mother's, of import to her—and of import to you. Why share it with me?"

His lips curling upward, Aric reached for her and placed his hand at the back of her neck. His warm fingers settled against her skin, attuning her senses to his scent, his heartbeat. The pad of his thumb caressed her cheek and left tingles in its wake.

"You are my wife, and I vowed to share all I have with you when we wed."

Gwenyth's heart warmed. Though Aric had little of value to give her, he had gifted her with one of his most precious possessions. That fact lay in his eyes.

"Thank you," she said again, feeling suddenly warmed.

He nodded. Then his smile turned mischievous. "And if you would like to remember what time to meet me for a tryst or two, I would have no complaints."

"Aric..." Heat spiked within her. Her warning sounded more like a breathy plea.

His intimate whisper became a breath as he bent closer, closer, until his mouth was a moment away from hers. Gwenyth's hands shook as she raised them to his shoulders, whether to ward him off or pull him closer, she wasn't sure.

She did neither. Time passed in moments registered by her

unsteady heartbeat. As he loomed above her, Aric's eyes darkened, seeming without beginning and without end. Her world became a swirl of misty, mesmerizing gray.

Then he inched closer again, and his lips covered hers, a mere shimmer of breaths. Beguiled by his touch, her lashes fluttered shut as his mouth slid across hers, nibbled and teased, warmed as he sampled her slowly, as if he were a man with infinite patience. Gwenyth swayed against the solid breadth of his chest, her limbs suddenly heavy, her thoughts receding.

Again, his mouth covered hers, sensitizing her to the feel of his touch, to his rich scent surrounding her. His other hand joined the first at the back of her neck until he cupped her jaw and gently brought her lips more firmly beneath his.

Her pulse skipped a beat as he made her mouth his gentle captive again. Gwenyth strained closer, utterly willing. Some distant part of her warned she could not remain here with Aric, but another insisted on allowing the indulgence of his exploring lips as he parted hers and eased his way inside.

The small fire his touch had started flickered and fanned into something stronger as his tongue circled about her own, then drifted away to leave a warm, damp trail to the base of her throat.

He murmured something—what, she knew not. Sighing her answer, Gwenyth reached out to him and pulled him closer, reeling with a surprising need to feel his kiss again. Aric obliged her, feathering his silky mouth over hers once more as he eased her down to sit upon his narrow bed. For a moment, she thought to protest. An endless, needy kiss quelled anything she had been about to say.

Fluid pleasure filled her when his hands left her face to skim her shoulders and the curve of her waist, his thumb barely brushing her breast on its descent.

Tingles spread across her skin, dug deep into her bones. She gasped at the sensations, uncertain of this new magic he gave her. As she looped her arms about his neck and arched toward him, Aric met her hungrily, his mouth angling over hers once more for another drugging kiss that left her feeling limp and enlivened at once.

When he lowered her to the mattress, she wallowed in the feel of him, so substantial and strong, above her. At that moment, he seemed her entire world, her very own champion. She felt dizzied by his unwavering mouth, hazed by his warmth and need. To him, she gave all his kiss sought, eager to please.

Moments later, she felt his hand at her back while he nipped his way down her jaw. Suddenly, the cool air hit her shoulders and the swells of her breasts. Gwenyth opened her eyes in time to see Aric tug the gown down to her waist and his mouth envelop the hardened peak of her breast. A jolt of pure pleasure pulsed within her at the feel of his lips and tongue teasing her nipple through her thin chemise. She moaned, grabbing his shoulders more tightly.

With his hand beneath her back, Aric encouraged her to arch into him. As she did, he turned his attentions to her other breast, even as she felt his hands at her waist, her hips.

She could not think, could scarce breathe, for the feel of his mouth over her breast, laving, suckling, gently demanding. Her groan became a moan.

'Twas something of a shock to feel cool air upon her bare calves and thighs moments later. As if looking through fog, Gwenyth saw Aric's large bronzed hands raising her chemise to her hips, felt his firm, callused hands skimming her flesh. At his feet lay her silken red dress. How had he undressed her without her awareness?

Before she could sort through her muddled thoughts or find a protest, Aric ran a light, teasing finger from the inside of her knee up toward the joining of her legs. She gasped as his touch climbed higher, then stopped a mere inch before the apex. But her pleasure kept peaking, and she realized with a wild rush that some part of her wanted his touch there.

Then his thumb slid over her, a mere brush. Her hips lurched off the bed at the unaccustomed touch, the spiraling delight. The gentle feel of his mouth on her bare stomach, a whisper below her navel, sent her need soaring higher.

Threading her hands through his thick, golden hair, Gwenyth pulled Aric closer, wanting these feelings to go on, for they were like bright colors, vivid and undeniable. Aye, she had seen Penhurst's servants mating deep in the night on the floor of the great hall. Always she had thought their grunting gyrations crude and suffocating. She had not considered the wanting, the slow rush of desire that wound through the veins like the headiest of mulled wines.

When Aric's impatient fingers pushed aside her chemise, she welcomed the sensations of cool air and his hot gaze upon her. Then the damp heat of his mouth closed over her bare breast. She gasped. As the silken tip of Aric's tongue flicked over the hard peak of her nipple, her eyes flew open at riotous sensations pounding within her.

Her gaze locked with the seemingly uncomprehending depths of Dog's eyes. The animal sat a mere foot away at the side of Aric's small bed, watching intently and flapping his tail against the cottage's dirt floor. She stiffened, realizing that engaging in this lovemaking with Aric was not only unwise, but, with their canine audience, it was discomfiting.

"Aric," she whispered.

His answer was an unintelligible moan as he lifted his mouth from her breast and started toward the other. Gwenyth stopped him with a hearty push at his shoulders.

"What?" he scowled.

"The dog," she said simply.

With a laugh, Aric sat up beside her. "So I have a modest little dragon, eh? I can put Dog out."

"Nay. 'Tis more than Dog. We simply…cannot."

Aric sighed, then curled a tender hand about her shoulder. "We can, Gwenyth. You are my wife. 'Tis time we sealed our union, as God intended."

"But we… I…" she stuttered, hopelessly mired in a tangle of desire, regret, and apprehension. Why should her flesh desire a man who could not provide the future her heart needed? "We cannot."

Anger hardened his features as he stood beside the bed and tossed her red gown over her meagerly clad body. "As you wish. But someday you must accept marriage to me, hermit or not. The law, the church, and the world already have."

Before Gwenyth could protest that she had not meant to hurt him, Aric whistled to Dog, who followed him out the door. As she watched from the window while the mutt and his master disappeared into the ancient, shadowed forest, tears stung Gwenyth's eyes.

CHAPTER SEVEN

Nearly a week had passed, largely wordless, between Aric and Gwenyth. In that week, he had tried to forget the feel of her beneath him, the taste of her skin, the beauty of her form by candlelight, the snap of her intelligent mind, as well as the sharp wit of her tongue. 'Twas impossible, he knew now, for he thought of little else.

Until the summons came.

From his chair beneath the eaves, Aric watched a man on horseback approach. The gentle rain falling across the misty green land obscured his vision. But as the rider drew closer, Aric caught sight of a crest on the man's tunic. The Neville crest.

He closed his eyes in cold dread, one realization swirling in his head: Someone had sent for him.

God's blood! Aric clutched the wooden carving of his naked wife in his suddenly damp palms and rose with a whispered curse. 'Twas no mistaking the other man's demeanor, for his carriage was straight with purpose as he approached the cottage.

Despite the cool winds, sweat broke out across Aric's chest and back, on his neck and face. He gripped the wooden carving between suddenly unsteady hands. Fear combined with anger and apprehension. What in hell's realm did this herald want? And what of Gwenyth?

With a glance over his shoulder, Aric had his worst fear confirmed. She had heard the approaching horse and even now stared out the window, her expressive face rife with puzzlement. Lord help him. How would he explain the reason Northwell's herald sought him?

"Stay inside, Gwenyth," he instructed her softly.

"But who—"

"Inside," he repeated with quiet force, then turned his attention back to the rider, now mere feet away.

Rather than invite the man into the cottage's shelter, Aric went out into the soft rain, the chill of it drenching him. Surely only that caused him to shiver.

As Aric met the rider, he grabbed the horse's bridle. "Halt. What business have you here?"

The rider dismounted and bowed, his Adam's apple bobbing nervously beneath his oily young face. "My lord, I have a missive for you from your esteemed brother."

Stephen. Aric sighed, raking tense fingers through his damp hair. The whelp had always sought power at Northwell. Certainly he would not wish the return of the elder brother who could take that away from him. He breathed a sigh of relief.

"Where is this missive?" Aric asked finally.

The herald patted his dusty, damp tunic. "'Tis safe in here."

"Let me see it."

"But, my lord, the rain will destroy—"

"Let me see it," he demanded, his patience short.

With obvious reluctance, the young nobleman withdrew the parchment from his red tunic and handed it to Aric.

Settling beneath the relative dryness of a nearby elm that towered above him in sweeping green strokes, Aric tucked the carving of Gwenyth into the crook of his arm and opened the missive.

My brother,

Turmoil is afoot. Gossip says the Lancastrians are plotting to overthrow King Richard and place ignoble Henry Tudor upon his throne. Richard seeks your vow to fight in his favor. You must return home and gather a larger army.

Stephen

Fury washed through Aric. How like Stephen to desire the power of being Northwell's lord whilst being negligent of its responsibilities. Come home to raise an army for the defense of a man capable of murdering children? Return to the woman who had betrayed him by marrying his own father, to the keep which had brought him little but misery?

Nay, Stephen wanted to be the lord of Northwell, so he would have all of its duties.

Nor could Aric deny that for a moment he wished the note had come from Guilford, or even Kieran or Drake. He'd begun to miss them more and more of late, and blast Gwenyth for reminding him of their absence days ago.

With a bitter grunt, Aric tossed the missive to the ground and watched with grim satisfaction as the fat drops of rain struck the parchment with plunk after plunk, and the ink began to blur.

The herald let out a horrified gasp and lunged for the missive. Aric stayed him with a raised hand.

"But, my lord—" His pale, earnest eyes pleaded.

"Leave it."

"What message shall I return to my lord Stephen?" the herald asked.

A glance at the missive proved the rain had blurred the ink upon the page to little more than watery black streaks.

"Tell him I send no message," Aric replied finally.

He felt Gwenyth's gaze upon him, steady and questioning, from her perch just inside the window. Aric prayed the rider would not seek to break his journey inside the cottage. Little hope would he have then of keeping his past from his wife. The other man's livery and his consistent use of "my lord" would no doubt give her broad hints regarding his secret.

After a long pause, the herald sighed and reached for his mount. "As you wish, my lord."

"'Tis exactly as I wish," he vowed, finding his next breath came more easily than the last. "Now be off with you. And do not return."

His frown puzzled, the rider yanked on his mount's reins, turned about, and disappeared into the rain.

Irritation and dread picked at Aric's gut like a vulture upon a carcass, one painful nibble at a time. He pivoted slowly toward the cottage. As he suspected, Gwenyth stood in the portal, her bright blue gaze filled with speculation.

"Not now, Gwenyth." He took long strides toward her, hoping he could pass her without another word between them.

His foolish hope died a quick death.

"Not now? 'Tis never with you, you infernal pig-minded droll. You tell me naught!"

"I have nothing to tell," he lied.

She glared at him, her cheeks flushed with anger, her arms crossed beneath her breasts. The fact she looked like a passionate temptress offering her charms—if he ignored her scowl—only served to annoy him more. Why did he want her in a way he could never remember wanting any woman, even when she called him foul names and did her best to dig up his dishonorable past?

"Who was that man?" Gwenyth demanded, hanging on to the subject like a determined dog with a bone. "What did that missive say?"

"He came collecting taxes I refused to pay," he improvised smoothly.

"Nay. I know all of Uncle Bardrick's retainers and stewards. He is not among them, nor is that my uncle's coat of arms."

"How do you know he was not one of the king's men?"

The glare she shot him told Aric once and for all he could not treat her as if she had the intellect of a child. "He wore no royal markings. And he bowed to you. Why?"

Aric sighed. He had to give Gwenyth credit. She missed very little.

"The man mistook me for someone else, and when I could not solve his problem, I asked him to leave."

Gwenyth's honeyed complexion only flushed with more color. "Were that true, you would not have so wantonly destroyed another's missive. But since you are disinclined to tell me aught, I am disinclined to live here with you and accept you as a husband."

"A threat?" he whispered, fighting a vague sense of panic that tightened his belly. Then he calmed himself with the reminder she had nowhere to go.

"Nay, a statement. Why should I wish to stay wed to a man I know not, who refuses any honest discourse?"

Though her words infuriated him, Aric saw her logic. Still, it changed naught. "You know the man I am today. It matters not who I was last month or last year. That man is gone, never to return."

"Pity," she shot back at him. "I'm certain he was more forthright and had a better disposition than a dead tree. I would have liked him better."

She whirled around and darted into the cottage, shutting the door in Aric's face.

Aric nearly ripped the door open and reminded her she seemed to like him well enough last week when he had her naked on his bed, but he bit the words back. A man experienced in the ways of sex could easily overwhelm an innocent like Gwenyth. Their near lovemaking had nothing to do with her possibly liking him.

For some reason, that fact irritated him. Why couldn't the stubborn wench enjoy the indefinable flame that lay between them without probing into his past? And what the hell was he going to do about her?

* * * *

Four days later, birds sang a cheerful tune as Gwenyth hung clean clothes over nearby willow branches. She tried to disguise her shift, worn as it was, from her husband's silent gaze, not that such mattered anymore. Where once he might have teased her about it, even whispered in that seductive timbre of his, he now ignored it—and her.

Adjusting the new gray dress about her shoulders, she reached for the brown woolen rag she could scarce call a gown anymore and draped it over the next branch.

Zounds, that man was stubborn, always insisting the past mattered not. 'Twas clear that herald had been no tax collector, no misdirected servant. He had sought Aric, more than like out of his past. Aric had turned the man away and been withdrawn since.

Calling the lout names did little, as he refused to rise to that bait. Traipsing about the house in her red dress, which she knew had once enticed him, earned her plenty of heated stares, which made something inside her ache. But still he refused to talk.

What in his past could be so awful, so sinful, that he refused to face it?

Gwenyth knew so little of what Arid hid so well that her speculation could go on for hours without bearing fruit.

Again, she sighed. For the past four days and nights, she had done her best to draw him into conversation, into her confidence. No more. If he could not see fit to speak to her like a human being, like a wife, then she had naught to say to the coxcomb.

She bit her lip. It could take him days, perhaps weeks, before he might notice her quiet. Already the air between them vibrated with sheer silence. Much more of it would surely unnerve her.

She stole a glance at her husband, only to find he held that infernal wooden carving of her nakedness between his powerful hands. Heat crept up her face until she realized he stared not at her bare likeness but over the tree-lined horizon as if it were endless and wise in its age. Like the walls of Penhurst had been a hundred years past, Aric's expression appeared impenetrable. Gwenyth feared she would have to lay siege to him before he would ever notice her own withdrawal.

That meant she must continue to endure his silence, as well as the unfathomable energy between them.

Frowning, Gwenyth considered Aric and his unending stare across the damp-scented land. 'Twas as if he waited for something. His grim expression seemed to portend disaster.

Shaking her head, Gwenyth returned her attention to the laundry. His problem was not hers, since he had expressly chosen not to share it with her. Until he did, she would not show interest in him whatsoever.

* * * *

More than a week later, day dawned without fanfare, the sunrise obscured by haze and fog. Aric watched it from the hillside where he and Gwenyth had once talked of family and hopes, past and present, while saying naught of the future.

A future he would have to shape someday soon.

Beside Aric, Dog panted and whined, begging for his master's attention. Absently, Aric stroked his coarse gray-brown fun. At his side, Dog settled, resting his canine jaw upon Aric's thigh.

Sighing, Aric peered at the landscape around him. Fresh, damp grass carrying the scent of spring surrounded eons-old oaks that swept and swayed against the metallic sky, heavy with impending rain. He had come to know these lands as well as he had once known the hilt of his sword, every gentle swell and enticing valley memorized.

For months, the land had soothed him. Always, the view here had brought him peace, reminding him his life would hereafter consist of more than war and strife. As he had yearned for during the long winter, blossoms the yellow of pure sunshine colored the land like a banner of happiness and hope. Mingled with those blooms were some the blue-purple of a brilliant sky at dawn and a rare few the come-hither red of Gwenyth's lush mouth.

Today, Aric felt only turmoil, its talons reaching into the present to snatch him back into the past.

Suddenly, Dog tensed and raised his head toward the cottage. Aric glanced over his shoulder to find Gwenyth climbing up the hillside toward him. He cursed. His little dragon would want to fight. For days now, she had been itching to say something, to scream at him, he was certain. But she had remained damnably mute, until Aric himself had wanted to rail at the silence. Unhappily, he wondered when being alone had ceased to hold appeal for him.

Before he could say aught to Gwenyth, he saw another figure emerge over the top of the hill, that of a man, lean and striding with great purpose.

Kieran!

Surprised joy spiked within Aric. He had missed his friend—all of his friends—during his retreat. 'Twould be good indeed to see a man he thought of as brother, even if Guilford had sent the scamp to retrieve him.

A wry smile curved his lips. Kieran was likely to be annoyed, for Aric knew he had not made himself terribly easy to find. Nor would his friend find him willing to return to his old life.

Rising to his feet, Aric made his way toward Kieran, noting some changes in his friend. His shoulders seemed broader, his waist leaner. For a man who had oft prided himself on his appearance, 'twas a shock to see Kieran's brown-red hair in desperate need of a blade and a fresh scar beneath his ear, skipping along the curve of his jaw.

Before Aric could comment, Kieran drew him into a brotherly embrace.

"Aric, 'tis good to see you."

In returning the embrace, Aric was struck by a sense of belonging and connection, of having something precious lost, then suddenly found.

"'Tis good to see you, as well," he said finally, then stepped back. "Though I daresay I've scarce seen you look so…rugged."

He shrugged. "The war in Spain has been a fervent one."

Aric felt ten times the displeasure he allowed to show upon his face. "Aye, one likely to see you dead."

Kieran shrugged. "I cannot let the world pass me by because I fear such—though I do heartily regret this moment of carelessness," he said, fingering the scar. "It may bode ill for my chances with the ladies."

Mocking and teasing even the most sacred of subjects. Such was Kieran's way. Still, Aric wished, as did Guilford and Drake, that the brother of his spirit would treat his life with more care.

"Aric?" Gwenyth's voice sounded quietly behind him.

He whirled at the sound of his name and found Gwenyth there, the black silk of her hair sweeping with the wild wind about her shoulders and waist. Those entrancing blue-velvet eyes reflected a trace of irritation, uncertainty, and hurt.

With a curse, he resisted the tug of that bright stare. Aric dreaded introducing his past to his present. He took in the measure of her expectancy, knowing he had little choice.

"Gwenyth, meet my good friend, Kieran Broderick."

Shifting his gaze to Kieran to complete the introduction, Aric noticed his friend's mischievous blue-green eyes drift over Gwenyth with something more than idle curiosity.

Glaring at Kieran, Aric stepped toward Gwenyth and placed a possessive hand at her waist. Kieran raised an amused brow at the gesture. Aric gritted his teeth.

"You may stop staring at my wife," he ground out.

Aric could find no reason for his unaccountable irritation. Kieran, though a rogue as lucky with the ladies as he himself was with a sword, had never used his significant charm to win a female either Aric or Drake had fancied. Why did he suddenly feel the need to bind his wife in a habit and send her to a nunnery until Kieran left his cottage?

All pretense of charm fled Kieran's face, replaced by thunderstruck shock. "Your wife?"

"Aye."

"As in vows spoken in a church binding you for an eternity wife?"

Well, not in a church, but by a priest just the same. "Aye."

Suddenly, Kieran smiled and leaned in to give Aric a hearty slap to his shoulder. "And all this time we feared for your sanity, when you merely wanted your bride to yourself. I can see why, for her beauty would make slaves of kings and sultans the world over."

Aric sent Kieran another warning glare. "I know you mean that as no more than harmless tribute."

Kieran smiled broadly. "Naturally."

"As I know neither of you bray-butted imbeciles mean to discuss me as if I weren't standing at your very feet," Gwenyth interjected with heat.

Kieran's smile became a full-blown laugh. Aric resisted the urge to grimace.

"Not a woman of shy virtue, are you?"

Gwenyth's reply was a snort of disgust.

"My humblest apologies, my lady. I had no intent to offend such a lovely damsel." Kieran's apology flowed smoothly from his lips.

Aric gritted his teeth again. He had meant to apologize and wanted to in so gallant a fashion, but Kieran had ever been better with words, which had never come as easily to Aric, particularly not with Gwenyth's distracting beauty and cutting wit.

"What brings you here?" Aric asked into the still hush.

Kieran turned his full attention to Aric, who found his friend's face a sudden study of unaccustomed sobriety. "You must come home."

"Home?" Gwenyth questioned. "Where is your home?"

With a sharp glance, Kieran questioned him silently. Aric answered with a near imperceptible shake of his head. A flash of disapproval lit his friend's blue-green eyes.

"My home is here now," Aric said finally, feeling Gwenyth's curious gaze upon his profile as he returned his friend's stare. "There is naught I seek I cannot have here."

Kieran nodded his acknowledgement, regret crossing his features. "'Tis something I see well," he said, glancing at Gwenyth. "But others need you."

Aric stared at his friend uneasily. Kieran had been sent to find him. Duty tugged at him, and he tried to ignore its pull.

"Your cousin Anne is dead," Kieran said softly.

Shock washed through Aric as dismay jerked at his heart. The sweetest of his cousins gone? 'Twas incomprehensible. England's Queen, Richard's Neville bride, dead? His late Uncle Warwick, the kingmaker, had fought hard for that match. Now she was no more.

At his side, Gwenyth gasped, placing a comforting hand upon his sleeve. "I am sorry."

Wading through his shock, he whispered, "How?"

"She had been ill for some months." Kieran shrugged. But something on the man's handsome face registered suspicion.

"Yet you suspect foul play?"

Kieran's stare was measuring. "Some say she was poisoned."

Poisoned by whom? The answer dawned with awful certainty. If Richard was ruthless enough to kill children, why let a little thing like a sickly wife prevent him and his line from ruling the kingdom forever? But he required heirs, which Anne had been too aged and infirm to give him since the recent death of their only son.

He sighed deeply, feeling suddenly tired and overcome. "By God, she wanted other sons. She would have had them if she could."

"Aye," agreed Kieran sadly.

"That is barbaric, to kill a woman simply because she can no longer breed! What manner of man would do such a thing?" Gwenyth demanded.

Damn, they had said too much. Gwenyth didn't need to know everything—or even anything. Such knowledge was too dangerous, and he was not going back to Northwell.

"Gwenyth," Aric said with a calm he was far from feeling, "leave us, please."

His fiery wife anchored small fists upon her hips and stared at him in indignation. "I will not. You have hidden some terrible truth from me since we wed. If I am to stay by your side, I deserve to know something!"

"I agree completely, my lady," Kieran said, casting a challenging stare at Aric.

"Traitor," he grumbled.

Kieran ignored him and offered, "Richard seeks you."

The man was skirting dangerous topics. Though Aric knew of King Richard's summons already, Kieran should not mention such in front of Gwenyth. Anger began to pound at his temples.

"My brother can handle that now."

"Can he?" Kieran's gaze was filled with skeptical challenge.

"'Tis as he desired," Aric reminded.

"Foolish men always desire what they should not have."

It was Aric's turn to shrug. "His foolishness is no longer my concern. I will not return."

"'Twas not on those grounds that I asked. I must call upon your oath as a blood brother."

Aric closed his eyes as his heart stopped. Dread slid to his stomach, embedding itself into his gut. As a boy of nine, he had made a vow to Kieran and to Drake, as they had made in return to each other, to protect as need be, as any brother of birth should do.

"If we do not come, Drake will be unjustly hanged for his father's murder."

Alarm coursed through Aric as he whipped his sharp gaze to Kieran. "He's been in Murdoch's dungeon these seven months?"

"Aye, and every effort Guilford made to win his release was brutally refused."

"That is terrible!" Gwenyth blurted. "Can nothing be done?"

Stunned, Aric swallowed hard. Emotions, almost too fast to decipher, assailed him at once—fear, fury, reluctance…acceptance.

"Aye, it can, lady." Kieran turned his attention back to Aric. "Guilford thinks that, together, you and I can do what needs to see Drake free."

"He is right." The hoarseness of his own reply shocked Aric, but Kieran said nothing of it. "We shall leave here for Scotland immediately."

"Have you a steed, armor?"

"Nay," Aric admitted with reluctance.

"Would you leave lovely Lady Gwenyth out in the wilds by herself?"

Normally, with family close by, it would present no problem. But Gwenyth's selfish family had never cared one whit for her. 'Twas a fool's notion to think they would start now.

He sighed heavily. "Nay."

"Then you must return home first and take her with you."

"What of Hartwich Hall? We could gather supplies there and—"

Kieran shook his head. "Aric, Hartwich is too far west. It will waste too much time that may be vital to Drake's life."

The truth of that burned in Aric's mind, in his very gut, along with a realization that he had always known, somewhere deep, he could not run away from his past forever.

Yet Gwenyth would now know the secrets he never intended to

share. For the rest of her life, she would have the chance to play grand chatelaine while the forces of greed and war sucked his soul back into oblivion. He held no illusions that after she stayed at Northwell, basked in its wealth and charmed its people, she would return here, willingly or otherwise.

In little more than ten minutes, he had lost the peace that had taken him months to build. Aric frowned against the blade-sharp sense of loss and pain.

Bleakness pervading him, he said finally, "Aye. I will return home."

CHAPTER EIGHT

"I shall not pack a single garment and follow you until I know where you plan to take me." Gwenyth planted her feet stubbornly on the cottage's dirt floor and glared at her husband.

Gritting his teeth, Aric cursed under his breath but said naught else. Kieran stood in the corner, offering no more than a smile in response to her demand.

Rotted swine suckers, both of them! 'Twould fit that such stubborn men would be friends. Gwenyth moved to sit in the room's lone chair and refused to look at either one of them—no small feat, considering the smallness of the cottage and the breadth of the men. Instead, she directed her stare to her small-heeled slippers and frowned. They were badly in need of repair.

"What do you stare at, Gwenyth?" Aric asked with labored patience as he approached.

"My worn shoes, not that you can be bothered to care. After all, if you will not share your plans or your true home with me, why should a pair of slippers signify?"

Aric gnashed his teeth again. From the corner, Kieran chuckled.

Still, she was no closer to understanding what had happened these past few days. 'Twas clear someone wanted Aric to return to his past life. Had Kieran sent the summons a fortnight ago? Aric's face, though pensive, held no anger for his friend, so Gwenyth supposed someone else had written the missive. But who wanted Aric so badly? And why?

After heaving a great sigh, he knelt beside Gwenyth. "We return to my home in the north of England. I am needed there to guide my brother and aid my good friend Drake."

Though Gwenyth knew Aric had just offered more information in a single sentence than he ever had at once, somehow it was not enough.

"Does this home have a name? A village?"

"Gwenyth…" Aric reached for her with a shake of his tawny head, as if seeking patience. "It matters not. Please trust me and do not ask questions. You cannot remain here without me. 'Twould not be safe."

She jerked away, making an unladylike sound. "Last time I trusted you, I found myself unwillingly wed. Nay, I shall remain here as I please. If you deem me paltry enough that I should not know the name of my new home, then I must decide I am paltry enough to leave behind."

Again, Kieran's deep laugh resounded from the corner. "You cannot argue with such logic, my friend."

Aric rose to his full, towering height and glared at Kieran. "You are lending no aid to my cause."

"On the contrary. I seek marital harmony so we might be on the road come morn," Kieran returned.

Ignoring his friend's response, Aric turned back to Gwenyth. "Damnation, woman! Pack your belongings, or I shall pack them for you."

The surly simpleton thought throwing a few of her gowns in a bag would force her to journey to a place unknown? Aric had no idea how mistaken he was.

"Pack them, then. Once you are through, I shall take them to London. I could mayhap entice a gentleman of chivalry to lend me some assistance." Her threat was a hollow one, but he need not know that.

Aric flashed her a steely stare through eyes of molten metal. "No London fop will touch you, let alone lend you any assistance. Your wedded vows bind you to follow me—or do you forget you promised to obey me?"

Obey? Ugh, surely no worse word had ever been invented. "You cannot expect me to keep a vow made under threat of death."

"A threat of death?" Kieran's shocked voice rose from the corner. Gwenyth looked up to find his relaxed posture gone and a scowl replacing his usual sprightly expression. "Aric, what the hell—"

"Later, Kieran," he interrupted. "Right now, I mean to make Gwenyth understand it matters not why she said her wedded vows, simply that she did. I will keep mine, so I expect the same of her."

An angry flush crept through Gwenyth, heating her cheeks. How could the man speak to her so meanly, as if she were naught more than his property? How could a man who had cared so for her tears suddenly treat her so ill?

"Your man parts will rot and fall off before I will leave here without the truth."

Again, Kieran laughed.

Aric pounded his sizable fist on the table at her side. "Damnation, you are the most stubborn woman I have ever had the misfortune to encounter."

"Tell me what I wish to know and you shall find I can be surprisingly sweet of temper." She flashed him a falsely honeyed smile.

"Aye, your sweetness of temper matches that of a mule."

Gwenyth's mouth fell open in ire. *That man!* He was naught more than a…well, a— "'Tis a mite better to be a mule than a strutting cock."

"Strutting?" Aric braced his broad arms upon his lean hips and leaned into the fight. "I do not strut, an—"

"Children!" Kieran broke into the fray. "Be silent for a moment. Now, Gwenyth"—he directed a glare at her—"certainly you see if Aric must go, you should stay at his side for protection, if naught else. Vagabonds and worse roam the country looking for sweet morsels like you."

Then Kieran turned to Aric. "And you must see she deserves the truth. If you wish Gwenyth to live with you as your wife, you cannot deny all you were born to. This foolish bickering must cease. Drake is waiting."

The reminder of his friend's peril seemed to sap the anger from Aric in an instant. He turned to her, the wide square of his face somber. "If you will come with me, Gwenyth, I will tell you all."

She paused, considering. Kieran was right; vagabonds and worse did roam the country between here and London. Without protection, any manner of ill might befall her. Staying here proved no option, either. Who would cook? Chop wood? How would she explain to all at Penhurst why her husband had left her behind?

Given those questions, Gwenyth realized quickly she had little choice but to accept his compromise.

"I will go," she muttered and rose as regally as a queen.

Because she had few belongings to pack, they were mounted on the horse Kieran had brought and were heading down the road within minutes, Dog trotting behind them. The cottage had scarcely passed from view before Gwenyth turned to her husband with a prompting stare.

"God's blood, little dragon! Must it be now?"

"Best to end the torment of waiting," Kieran agreed, then spurred his horse ahead, away from the two of them.

Gwenyth watched Aric's friend disappear between a green sweep of towering oaks and blooming rhododendrons. She near held her breath, waiting for her husband to speak. What explanation he would provide, however, she had no idea. Again, she heard Kieran's voice in her head. *You cannot deny all you were born to.* What in God's creation did such mean?

Beside her, Aric rode a fine chestnut with an unconscious grace. The explanation, though, appeared not to come as easily. His face showed his struggle as he grappled for the right words. Gwenyth pursed her lips together to prevent the escape of an impatient demand.

"My name is Aric Neville, Earl of Belford. I hale from Northwell Castle in Northumberland, below the Scottish border." He paused. "Earl Warwick, the kingmaker, was my uncle."

Shock drained the blood from Gwenyth's face. Certainly she had not heard him correctly. Impossible! Aric, an earl? And the once-powerful Warwick's nephew? Nay, her hearing was suddenly fuzzy. Only that could make her think her hermit husband had told her he was a man of such consequence.

Still, his explanation would account for his well-born English, his battle scars, the funds he had used to purchase her red silk…and the pendant that had once belonged to his mother. Fingering the red ruby and the warm silver against her skin, Gwenyth's mind raced. Bristling braies, had he perhaps spoken true?

"Ea-Earl of Belford? Warwick's nephew?"

Aric regarded her, his face bleak, his eyes the color of cold stone in a harsh winter. "Aye."

She had heard him correctly. By the moon and the stars! "Then…you have had your knight's training?"

Slowly, he nodded, "I have been called the White Lion."

"You are he?" Gwenyth had heard of this brave warrior, his prowess and cunning, his strength and bravery. All of England had.

"I am."

Though Aric's tone was not welcoming, Gwenyth pressed on, nearly unable to comprehend all he said. Until a new realization dawned…

"Your recently departed cousin Anne—you mean the queen of England!"

He grimaced. "I do."

"And the Richard who has summoned you? *King* Richard?"

After a brief hesitation, he gave in. "Aye."

Gwenyth felt a sudden need to lie down, for her head seemed to spin. Her strong, sensual husband was an earl? Not a sorcerer but an intelligent man who could provide a secure future for her—indeed, in grand style? 'Twas near certain their children would never starve and that she would not worry about having a roof over their heads. Part of her rejoiced.

The rest of her was too furious to care!

"When, pray tell, had you planned on sharing this truth with me? Upon the birth of our first child?"

"Gwenyth." He turned to her with an agitated scowl. "To have a first child, we would have to share a bed."

That she ignored. "Or perhaps upon my deathbed. Aye, when I would no longer have the strength to care for Penhurst's villagers' rebuffs and Nellwyn's bragging. When it would no longer matter who Sir Penley wed. Or perhaps not even then. Isn't that right, *my lord*?" she sneered.

Aric looked away from her. Had she imagined the flash of guilt upon his face? She hoped not. She wanted the devious pox-ridden mongrel to suffer and rot!

"As I have told you more than once, I consider that part of my life over. I saw no reason before now to tell you of a life I planned never to return to. 'Twas not done to anger you but to help me find peace."

"Peace? What drivel is this? Warriors and earls know battle and leadership."

"And that is why I left. I had experienced both war and power before. I wanted no more of either."

"You *left* of your own will? Are you mad—or merely senseless?"

Aric blasted her with a warning glare from a face suddenly ruddy with emotion. She heeded it not.

Gwenyth tossed up her hands. "You planned to keep this all from me forever so I might never have a choice. So I would be forced to endure the life you wanted, never mind what my heard desired."

"'Twas not my intent, little dragon."

She grunted her disbelief. "You thought of me not at all and apparently never will."

Before he could reply, Gwenyth set her mare at a gallop and left Aric behind, almost wishing it could be forever.

* * * *

Staring at her husband's back as he swayed in the saddle with irritating grace, Gwenyth resisted the urge to stick her tongue out at him. She was weary and hot after four days of constant travel north, too much so to take careful note of the changing countryside. More, she was tired of Aric's completely ignoring her, while Kieran chattered away about nothing important. She was afraid of what lay ahead.

Most of all, she was afraid of the reason she could not bring herself to hate Aric completely for his duplicity.

During the journey, Aric had said precious little else about his home, Northwell. In fact, the closer they drew, the less he said. Still, knowing 'twas home to a part of the great Neville family made the castle sound grand indeed. But part of Gwenyth wondered if Aric would continue to withdraw as they drew closer to his past. Would they ever recapture the closeness they had shared at the cottage that had so warmed her heart? Would he ever want to touch her again, as she still longed to feel him?

The fact he seemed wholly disinterested in both made her heart ache and her fears multiply. She had every reason to be angry with *him*, so why was he not speaking to *her*?

"Spring has never been so lovely," Kieran said as he rode up beside her. "Do you not agree?"

She shot him a withering stare. "If I could but rest for a moment to enjoy it, I might."

Kieran laughed. "Do you always speak your mind so plainly?"

Before Gwenyth could reply, Aric did so as he rode ahead of them. "Always."

Scowling at Aric's back, she declared, "I see no reason to behave as though I have not a thought or opinion of my own, even if others do."

Aric stiffened. Without a glance in her direction, he rode ahead, Dog following obediently, leaving her to Kieran's dubious mercy.

"'Tis certain you are in no danger of that, good lady," Kieran returned, gently teasing.

Gwenyth leaned toward him on her saddle. "What of you? Do you see any reason to submit to silence when your thought might be of import?"

With a considering stare, Kieran appeared to mull over her question before he finally shook his head. "I suppose not."

"Unlike our friend"—she gestured toward Aric, riding much ahead of them now—"you see the need to voice your opinions and hear those of others. A more pig-brained, mulish varlet I have yet to meet."

Kieran shook his head, wearing an amused grimace. "Well, no one ever said wedded life was naught but bliss."

She snorted. "A husband would, at least, have to speak to his wife to have a blissful marriage."

"True enough," Kieran admitted, then hesitated, his smile fading. "But Aric… He has had much disappointment of late. I gather your sudden marriage was not a simple one."

Truer words had ne'er been spoken. She stated the obvious anyway. "'Twould appear that is no secret."

Shrugging, Kieran went on. "There is much of Aric you do not know—"

"Because he does not tell me."

"Aye, but he would be agreeable to any kindness you can give him. Honestly."

Though the anger in her wanted to fling the words back in his face, her curiosity wanted more information. "This difficulty you speak of… Is that why he chose to leave a home of such importance and exaltation?"

He responded with a stare that held restraint and chiding at once. "That truth must be borne between you two."

From that, Gwenyth feared Kieran's revelations, slight as they were, had ended—unless she could think of another manner to promote his unwitting confidences.

"Of course," she assured him. "And someday soon, I hope Aric will tell me all." Gwenyth smiled brightly, nearly certain that day would never come. "Until them, tell me of you. Do you hail from the north of England as well?"

"Nay, good lady. I spent my young years in Ireland learnin' to be a scamp and a rogue." He dipped into a brogue, but the smile she expected never came. Pain flashed across his features, then disappeared. "After eight summers, my mother brought me to the Earl of Rothgate and bid the good man to train me as a knight."

"For whom do you fight?"

"For whomever offers the most exciting battle." A glowing grin punctuated his strange reply.

Battle, exciting?

"Sir, I do not understand. In what way does battle excite you?"

Kieran looked at her as if she'd grown a second head. "In every way. A man must keep his wits about him during the whirl of activity. It requires strength and speed. Each battle seems to test a knight more than the last. The heady rush of emotion and fervor—"

"And you enjoy this?" She frowned, uncomprehending.

"Aye. Nothing like the freedom and discipline combined to set a man's heart soaring."

A man's heart soaring? Gwenyth bit her lip as a terrible thought occurred to her. "All men feel as you do?"

"Oh, nay. Yon husband there"—he gestured toward Aric, still riding ahead—"would now rather spend his time engaged in other activities. He battles well, better than most every man in England, and once, he seemed to enjoy the fight." Kieran paused as if seeking an answer. He shrugged. "But no more."

Breathing a sigh of relief, Gwenyth asked, "Did you meet Aric while aiding him to wage war on his enemies?"

"Such imagination," he teased. "Nay, Aric and I, along with Drake, trained together as knights with the Earl of Rothgate. We've been close, like brothers, since."

"Is that why he will leave his solitude so he might help Drake?"

Kieran lifted a shoulder in response. "Again, you shall have to ask him."

Gwenyth wanted to tell Kieran he was proving to be of little help in her quest for information, but she knew that was his purpose. Still, it did not stop her frustration from climbing.

She chose another topic. "Who else lives at his castle?"

After a pause, Kieran supplied, "His brother, Stephen. And his…stepmother, Rowena."

"He told me once he and Stephen have little in common."

Kieran's blue eyes flashed with surprise. "Indeed. Stephen is a fool. Young. He has much to learn, though he sees this not."

"And Rowena? Are she and Aric civil to one another?"

"At times."

Gwenyth nodded. Such made sense. The woman who had sought to take his mother's place would not be welcomed, particularly since his parents had loved so well.

Had her father wed again after her mother's terrible death, it would have angered her more like than not.

When she turned to say such to Kieran, he looked as though he wanted to say something more, then decided against it. She clenched her fists in frustration as he said, "That is enough for now. Since you believe Aric must talk to you to make your marriage one of bliss, I should think you might spend your time asking *him* questions, rather than me."

With a mocking nod, he urged his mount forward to Aric's side.

* * * *

After a fortnight's journey, the familiar walls of Northwell came into view, jutting up from the edge of a windswept cliff. The castle sprawled across a strip of land, seeming to defy the mighty sea directly at its back while lording over the village below. Twilight bathed the massive towers and outer walls in a vivid orange, flushing the stones with soft color. Flags with the Neville coat of arms, held stiff by the breeze, flew from the east and west turret towers.

At the sight of his ancestral home, Aric waited for pride or gladness. Instead, he felt nothing except a pang of dread. He had never meant to return to this world where fathers betrayed sons, where greed usurped goodness, where a man killed his young nephews and seized the crown for himself—and no one stopped him.

For the dozenth time in nearly as many days, Aric asked himself why he had come. His answer was always the same: Drake. For the man who was more like a brother, Aric would see his blood oath upheld, would walk through wind, rain, fire. Drake would do no less for him.

At his side, Aric caught sight of Gwenyth. Her bowed pink mouth hung open in awe as she stared at Northwell. She would be happy here. The people would come to like and respect her forthright manner, despite the fact their first glimpse of their new mistress would be with windblown hair and a much-rumpled red silk dress.

That rapt look on her face shredded his gut. Aye, he wanted Gwenyth provided for, and somewhere in the past few weeks, her happiness had become absurdly important to him.

But, damnation, he did not want to be back at Northwell.

Within moments, he and Kieran and Gwenyth were spotted by sentries. A shout resounded before a small party met them at the gatehouse entrance. Dog growled in warning, and Aric stayed the mutt with a soothing whisper.

Apprehension biting into his stomach, Aric watched Stephen approach, looking as young and lanky as ever with his shaggy sandy hair and mischievous brown eyes. Rowena stood at his side, her hand upon his arm, slender, regal, ethereal as always, her smooth face unreadable. Reginald, the elderly steward, and Baswain, the rotund porter, stood abreast of Stephen and Rowena, who wore disapproving scowls, which Aric avoided.

In silence, Aric brought his horse to a halt, casting his gaze about the garrison. Naught within this part of the castle had changed. The soldiers standing about the lower bailey clutched mugs of ale and reveled in their laughter. They had grown round bellies in his absence. He scowled.

"Aric, you've returned!" said his brother. "'Tis good to see you again."

"Stephen," he greeted coolly, then turned to help Gwenyth dismount.

His brother seemed to notice nothing amiss in the indifferent greeting. Nor did Aric expect he would. 'Twas simply Stephen's way.

"Sir Kieran," he heard Stephen say next. "Good to see you, as well."

His friend nodded. "Young Stephen. You've grown quite tall since I last saw you three…perhaps four years ago."

As Aric turned with Gwenyth's hand in his, he saw Stephen square his spindly shoulders and puff out his lean chest. "I am twenty years now."

"My, that old? 'Tis certain such advanced age will bring on infirmity at any moment," Kieran teased.

Stephen laughed. Then silence fell over the gathering. To Aric's surprise, Rowena filled it.

"Sir Kieran," she greeted, the breeze lifting the golden hair about her shoulders, "I trust all is well with you."

"If I were any happier the king would surely grow suspicious."

Her wan smile showed little appreciation for his friend's humor. But then Rowena had never thought life something to laugh at. She had little appreciation for much beyond money and power. Her final act of betrayal had proven that.

"Aric," she acknowledged, her cool, pale eyes assessing him.

Her gaze might have been avaricious or aloof. The woman's expressions had ever been a mystery to him. Mayhap that explained why he so appreciated Gwenyth's readable countenance. He never had to guess long to know what she thought, and she never hid from him.

His former betrothed was like a pond. The surface remained placid, but beneath the still, murky waters lay a life the mere observer could scarce comprehend. Gwenyth, on the other hand, was like the sea—stormy, ever-changing, rarely leaving one to guess what took place within her depths.

Suddenly, he felt very glad for their differences.

"Rowena." He returned her greeting with even less warmth.

He had always suspected she would stay within the circle of his powerful family even after the death of her husband, Aric's own father. To be proven correct, as evidenced by the fact she clung to his younger brother with a possessive air, only annoyed him more. Then he noted the way she was staring at Gwenyth, civil but not welcoming, with a hint of disdain thrown in.

"Who is your…companion, Aric? Will you not introduce us to her?"

Aric was not fooled by Rowena's cordial request. She was unhappy he had come home with a woman in tow. He was not certain why. More than like because Gwenyth was worthy competition for her beauty. Rowena never liked that.

"Stephen, Rowena, this is Lady Gwenyth, late of Penhurst Castle."

Urging her closer to the remnants of his family, Aric paused with great intentions. Let Stephen wonder and Rowena stew. 'Twas no less than either of them deserved, Stephen for his irresponsibility and Rowena for her superiority.

He watched their rapt faces. *Good*, he thought, eager to deliver the shock that would change both their lives.

Finally, he smiled. "Gwenyth is my wife."

Stephen's eyes near popped from his head. Rowena gasped, then recovered herself. Watching them both, Aric could see understanding dawn: Stephen wondering if Aric, with a wife in tow, was likely here to stay and resume his role as lord of Northwell, and Rowena probably seeing Gwenyth as a new chatelaine, eager to assume Rowena's duties. And as Gwenyth currently occupied Aric's life and most likely his bed, Aric would have no need of any offer Rowena might make to warm his sheets so she might retain control of the keep and servants.

The terrible anguish he felt about coming here again, living here once more, dissipated for a brief moment as he drank in the possibilities.

At the very least, he could make their lives a walking hell upon earth. The thought made him smile.

Until something on Rowena's countenance changed. Her nearly colorless blue gaze swept over Gwenyth with a mixture of fear, contempt, and malice. Her small mouth pursed with determination.

At his side, Gwenyth gazed about at the keep, never noticing Rowena's expression. Aric slipped his arm quietly around her waist, glowered at Rowena, and felt a heated stir of determination to protect his wife.

CHAPTER NINE

For two days, they remained at Northwell without incident, Aric and Kieran awaiting men and supplies so they might rescue Drake from Murdoch MacDougall's dungeon. Then a royal page arrived, bearing Richard III's coat of arms.

The young man left the castle's great hall immediately after he sought Aric and delivered the missive from his master.

Gwenyth held her breath, not believing for an instant her husband's reaction would be pleasant. She knew better. Since they had arrived, his expression had been surly, his mood sour, his demeanor utterly silent. He had not slept in their chamber more than a brief hour or two, much less than the scant amount he slept at the cottage.

Without asking, she knew he did not wish to be here at Northwell. Another summons from the king, whom he seemed to hold in oddly marked contempt, was not likely to improve his manner.

"What does it say?" Stephen asked, lounging on a gleaming bench by a blazing fire, a mug of ale cupped in one hand.

When Aric looked up from the summons, his eyes were as flat and bleak as she had ever seen them. His usually mobile mouth was set in stiff lines, as were his shoulders. Without knowing why, exactly, Gwenyth's heart ached for him.

"He wants an army at the ready for the next battle."

"'Tis as his last note says, I think he fears Henry Tudor is gaining some support," Kieran added from his chair on the dais. He eyed a passing kitchen wench, who smiled in return.

"Aye," added Stephen. "You are far superior at war and such, Aric, so I sent for you."

Ah, so Stephen had sent the missive Aric had allowed the rain to destroy. From the annoyance stamped on her husband's lean features, she could tell he wished the foolish boy had not sent for him at all.

"I have no intent to amass an army for Richard," Aric said finally. "We will not reply."

"Not reply! Aric, Richard is our king. We have ever been loyal to the Yorkist cause. Why would we not aid him against this Welsh pretender of the Lancasters?"

Emotions flashed across Aric's face—anger, guilt, resignation. Just as quickly, his expression became blank once more, no emotion visible in the narrowing of his flat gray eyes. Gwenyth frowned, wondering at all his sentiments and whence they had come.

"I am done raising my sword," Aric declared at length. "I have told you so again and again. Richard has other northern lords, like Northumberland, willing to aid his cause. But no one at Northwell will do so."

"'Tis treason you speak! He will send his soldiers here to cart you off to London and give us a traitor's execution."

"So be it." Aric looked as if he wanted to say more, but did not.

So be it? Gwenyth wondered in panic. Why did Aric dare defy the most powerful man in England? Certainly he didn't believe his relation to the deceased queen would save him, did he? Only a fool would think that. The king hadn't even been able to protect his nephews, though only the Lord knew what had happened to the young boys.

"You risk the death of us all!" Stephen ranted, throwing his hands in the air with great drama.

"Not true. The Duke of Northumberland will be looking for knights in his army for King Richard. Alnwick is a fine castle, and you are but months away from completing your training. Let the Percy family help you finish it. You may be loyal to Richard's cause there."

"Northumberland? He is not my brother."

"And I am not interested in raising an army."

Gwenyth wondered at Aric's unusual responses. He ignored a summons from the king upon risk of death and flung his brother's wishes back in his young face. Why? Whatever the reason, it clearly hurt him in some way, for a pained scowl tightened his features, and his gray eyes brewed like thunderclouds.

"This is because of Rowena," Stephen said finally, his voice accusing.

How could such an argument be about Aric's stepmother? Aye, she was younger than Gwenyth had expected and admittedly lovely, but what had she to do with the war? Gwenyth sent Aric a puzzled frown.

He, too, looked confused. "Rowena?"

"It unmans you that she chose to wed our father instead of you. I think it unmans you more that she now chooses to warm my bed instead of returning to yours."

Shock burst its way through Gwenyth in a numbing explosion. Aric had once shared a bed with his stepmother? Her memory reminded her of Rowena's pale, questing eyes drifting over Aric upon their arrival. At the time, she had thought the gaze that of a concerned mother figure. By the moon and the stars! Had the woman been longing for her former lover? Or did their reunion explain Aric's absence from the bedchamber she shared with him?

She turned to Aric for answers, knowing her shock lay evident upon her countenance. He sent her the briefest of glances, then turned his attention back to Stephen. Out of the corner of her eye, she saw Kieran grimace.

Though she wanted to demand an explanation, now, starting with the knowledge of whether or not Aric still wanted his former lover, she would not ask such before his brother and his friend. Nay, she would save that conversation for a moment alone in their chamber, one she prayed he had not shared with that pale wench in the past.

"I no longer find Rowena all that charming," Aric tossed out. "You are welcome to her."

Gwenyth found herself fervently hoping his words were the truth.

Stephen turned petulant, his brown eyes uncertain. "You were not so unruffled when Rowena ended your betrothal to marry our father."

Gwenyth felt her eyes widen again. The woman had broken her betrothal vows to wed Aric's own father? Though Gwenyth knew she would hate anyone who broke such faith with her, men were strange creatures of lust, or so Aunt Welsa had always said. Did Aric secretly want to reclaim the cool beauty he had thought of as his own? Or had he already done so?

Once they were alone, she intended to find out. As his wife, she had a right to know.

A real wife shares her husband's bed, said a pesky voice within her. Gwenyth pushed it aside. Hell would find its moat turned to ice before she would share the bed of a man who had another woman on his mind, even though she did not want him herself. Or did she?

Remembrances of his heated kisses upon the sensitive curve of her neck, his burning gaze raking her tingling breasts, his long fingers teasing her thighs, nudged her doubt—and her desire.

"Ask yourself, Stephen, why Rowena now warms your bed," Aric advised.

"Because her heart is mine, and she loves me well."

Aric raised a cynical tawny brow. "And why did she not love you well while she was my betrothed, or our father's wife?"

Fury stamped itself across Stephen's young face. "You imply something devious in her manner, and such insults me greatly. Apologize now!"

"For the truth?" Aric shrugged. "Nay."

Stephen approached, his fists raised. "This is your way of making me doubt her so she will come to your bed again."

Was such possible? Gwenyth did not want to believe her husband desired Rowena any longer, but the woman had once been his betrothed and his lover, and he had been gone from their chamber much of late. Nay! Gwenyth admitted she thought of Aric much during those long evenings, strangely yearning for his touch. Could he not know that? She bit her lip in uncertainty and waited for Aric's reaction.

"Think what you will," he said, irritation in his voice. Then he quit the room.

Unable to wait for the answers to her questions, Gwenyth followed.

* * * *

Gwenyth entered the solar to find Aric at a small window, a

mug of ale tightly clenched in his hands as he stared out at the crashing surf. What troubled him? Did he long to be elsewhere, as he claimed? Or did he find the truth of his lust for Rowena difficult to speak of with her current lover, his own brother?

As she approached, Gwenyth realized she did not know what she felt. Angered and justified. Uncertain and unwanted. Betrayed. Everything came at her so quickly.

She bit her lip, not knowing what to say. *Coward*, she railed at herself, then forced her feet a step closer.

She closed the distance between them, and Aric's gaze snapped around to her. His expression was again blank, as if he thought nothing, felt nothing. But as she peered into his eyes, the gray depths revealed something so mired with pain she nearly swallowed her accusations.

"You have come to ask me about Rowena," he said. It was not a question.

She wanted to say nay, to prove him wrong. But her stomach tightened with something terrible, and her heart beat too fast, tingling with everything she felt.

She needed the truth more.

"Aye," she admitted. "Why did you not tell me?"

"Because there is nothing more to say that you have not heard."

"She agreed to become your wife, then wed your father instead. Now she shares a bed with your brother."

Aric rose and set his mug aside. "I asked Rowena to wife because she has a quick mind, is efficient in the castle, and inspired obedience in the servants. With my father much gone, Northwell's running had become my responsibility. Rowena made a good helpmate."

The anger she had been feeling finally rose up above the other hazy emotions sliding around within her. "And now you make excuses for her behavior because she shares your bed and occupies your heart again. Is that not true? That is where you have been these past two eves, *my lord*," she sneered.

His countenance turned from indifferent to snarling. "I do not desire Rowena any longer, and I never pretended to love her, nor she me. I understand her motives. She nearly starved to death as a child and forever seeks money and power as security."

He understood Rowena, but he did not respect her. The

contempt in her husband's voice hit Gwenyth in the chest. Had she not sought to wed Sir Penley for many of the same reasons? Aye, but she had also sought a man to love her, one who would provide children's laughter as well as food. Her desires were not the same.

And as Aunt Welsa had told her more than once, a man's heart need not be engaged for his loins to be occupied.

So why could she not engage his loins?

"When my father returned from war," Aric continued, "he became lord of Northwell again, the one with authority. And so Rowena chose him. Once my father died and I left, Stephen became master here, so she chose him."

Fear gripped her. "And now you have returned." *And she will choose you.* The words hung between them, unspoken but understood.

Gwenyth knew she could not compete with the woman who knew the secrets of Aric's body, had lain with him before and would do so again without hesitation. The thought of Rowena wrapped in the strength and heat of her husband's sensual embrace made her chest ache in a way she did not understand and wanted to escape.

"Now you are my wife, and we will talk no more of Rowena."

Not completely your wife, Gwenyth wanted to argue. Since their marriage, she had done little but rail at Aric, refuse him access to her bed, and push him away. Nor for lack of desire, but for lack of courage, for lack of faith when he had vowed to always see her secure.

Now she felt like a fool and a child, even as part of her demanded one more show of faith.

"If I am your wife, I should be your chatelaine. Why does Rowena still direct the servants and carry the keys?"

Something in his face tightened. He paused a long time indeed before replying. "Rowena has been mistress here for six years. We have only just arrived. Give it time, Gwenyth."

His gaze evaded her, and she smelled something foul in his demeanor. "You will not make me mistress of your home, will you?"

"Not for some while," he admitted with reluctance.

Fury sparked and began to blaze within her. "So you would choose your whore over your wife."

"She is not my whore, Gwenyth!"

Aric had never yelled so loudly. 'Twas then Gwenyth feared he spared Rowena's feelings at the expense of her own, which surely meant he harbored some feeling for the woman.

She used every ounce of her dignity to square her shoulders and glare directly into his stormy gray eyes. "As you say."

Before he could see the tears threatening to fall, she whirled about and darted through the door. Kieran blocked her way, and she wondered how much of their conversation he had heard.

Her gaze tangled with his blueish one, which was full of empathy and pity. *Too much.* He had heard too much.

Before she could embarrass herself any more, Gwenyth shouldered her way past her husband's friend and slipped out the door.

* * * *

Aric heard Kieran's footsteps moments later and swore beneath his breath. Of the three, Kieran had ever been the best at ferreting out the secrets of others.

He wondered if Kieran would understand this hell of need, lust, pride, and something unfamiliar he now found himself in. 'Twas doubtful. Kieran bedded many and stayed with none.

Aric grimaced. Once he had been similar, though without Kieran's cheerful manner for leading a woman into dalliance. Now, Aric realized, he had wed one and bedded her not at all, despite a strong, disturbing longing to do so. 'Twould seem poor sport to Kieran, at the very least.

"Gwenyth is no passive wife," Kieran observed without judgment.

Aric knew what Kieran wanted. "You have never been one to mince words. Pray, do not start now."

"You are right. Now that we are alone, tell me how in the hell Gwenyth came to be your wife upon threat of death, my good friend."

Without ado, Aric explained. He expected many reactions—shock, dismay, anger at the injustice done Gwenyth. He never expected Kieran's laughter.

"You, a sorcerer? The clodpates at Penhurst know you not."

"Nor did they care to," Aric returned wryly.

"You can scarce accept the magic of your own warfare, much

less make a drought from your displeasure."

"It is not magic, Kieran. It is an odious talent."

"And someday again it will serve you well."

Aric shrugged. "For now, I must decide what to do."

"You will not support King Richard?"

Retrieving his mug of ale from a nearby table, Aric studied its contents. How could he explain to Kieran the atrocity he knew Richard capable of when he could hardly understand such brutality against children himself? He could not tell anyone—not without endangering their very lives, for good King Richard would not hesitate to kill anyone privy to such damaging facts.

"I've no wish to support anyone," he answered finally.

"Someday you will be forced to," Kieran advised.

Aric knew it to be the truth, but that day was in the distance. His trouble with his wife swirled about him now.

"Rowena seems unhappy that I have returned with a wife."

"Aye, though it would bring her comfort to know you have not yet lain with Gwenyth. Is that not right?"

Aric cursed the fact Kieran could see so much, often too much. He gave a bitter laugh. "Is it so obvious, then?"

"I guessed as much in part from the way Gwenyth looks at you, sometimes as if you are a riddle she seeks to solve but is afraid to try, other times like you are a bauble she covets."

"And the other part?"

"Do you truly want to know the manner in which you stare at her?"

Did he? Or would such force him to face whatever sentiment seemed to be growing inside him? "Nay. I am better off without such knowledge."

"But you want her. And you care for her." Neither was a question.

Again, Aric wanted to ask if that truth were so obvious, but he refrained, knowing it must be—at least to Kieran. Instead, he replied, "I cannot make her Northwell's mistress now. The feeling in my gut tells me Rowena would only make use her determination to hurt Gwenyth if I do."

"And so you protect your wife?" He paused, rubbing the back of his neck as if discomfited. "Have you considered telling her that, instead of letting her believe you're swiving Rowena again?"

"I have told her as much," he said glumly, knocking back the rest of his ale. It slid like a lump down his throat. "And still, she does not believe me."

Kieran sent him a rogue's smile. "Mayhap you ought to simply show her."

* * * *

"Lady Margaret Beaufort 'ere to see you, my lord," a maid said as she entered the great hall. "Shall I send 'er in?"

'Twas the eve before their departure to rescue Drake, and Aric felt ill prepared to deal with politics now, particularly Henry Tudor's mother. Aric's blood brother Drake and his own troublingly chaste marriage occupied all his thoughts.

Still, the woman had come a long way, and she certainly hadn't come to visit, despite a distant familial connection. His great-grandmother had been her great-aunt, but he had never met Lady Margaret in his life. Yet she clearly wanted something. Was she plotting treason?

"How big is her party?" he asked the young maid.

"Just 'er and two men, my lord."

He paused. What could she seek? "Admit them."

Within moments, a fashionable woman with shrewd eyes and a softly lined face appeared, her men behind her eager to take refreshment after a long journey.

"My Lady Beaufort?"

She nodded her graying auburn head. "The celebrated White Lion, I presume?"

He nodded in return, sizing up the small woman. She was determined, he decided, and clearly no fool.

"Please sit." He offered her a chair on the dais. "Wine?"

"Such would please me, aye."

Aric bade a servant to bring wine, cheese, and bread, then turned back to his unexpected visitor.

"To what do I owe this honor, my lady?"

She cast him a sharp gaze. "Have you not heard of my cause?"

He shrugged. "I am not a man who appreciates gossip."

"Of course not." She folded her hands primly in her lap and fixed him with a smile he felt certain had charmed many a man.

"There are those who would say Richard Plantagenet killed his nephews so he might gain the throne for himself."

Aric knew her speculation to be horrifyingly true. "And what would you say, my lady?"

"Like you, I am not much for gossip. However, for those people who believe Richard guilty, they cry he makes a mockery of the throne."

"I have heard that much," he conceded.

"And their numbers grow. Richard is not a popular man."

"Many kings are not."

She nodded. "My son, Henry Tudor, is the last grown man with Lancaster blood."

Here it was, the treason. The choice. Could he support a king who had come to power by foul means or support a usurper who would kill a king instead of two boys to gain such power?

"I have always been a Yorkist," he returned with care.

"That is the beauty of my...proposition to you, my lord. You can be both."

Aric frowned. The woman did not strike him as simple. How could she say something so baldly impossible?

"I see I have confused you. Let me be plain." She leaned forward, and her voice dropped to just above a whisper. "Help put my Henry on the throne. Once there, the dowager queen has agreed to wed her eldest daughter, Elizabeth of York, to Henry. The Lancasters and the Yorks will unite to form a new Tudor dynasty. No more war. No more need to choose sides, my lord. What say you?"

Aric's heartbeat drummed inside his head. His mind raced as he smelled a trace of the woman's floral scent and the fresh rushes upon the floor. Margaret Beaufort smiled smugly. 'Twas a good plan, to wed the dead princes' eldest sister to this Lancaster man, and well she knew it.

And Aric wanted to throw himself into the fire. Anything to end the bloody, ceaseless war.

Anything except endanger his friends, his family...and Gwenyth. Anything except return to battle himself.

"I think it sounds much like treason, my lady."

Margaret stood, her spine straight, her chin lifted with pride. "Perhaps you should think on it further, Lord Belford. I shall be in touch."

"When?" he barked.

She merely sent him another mysterious smile. "When the time is right."

CHAPTER TEN

Aric leaned against the cold stone wall, dragging air into his starved lungs.

An unconscious Drake lay at his feet.

Cursing the damp chill of the Scottish midnight air, Aric again lifted his friend, easing Drake's long, limp body over his aching shoulder. Drake groaned but did not awaken.

'Twas for the best, Aric felt certain. Drake's hair, hanging now between his shoulder blades, smelled as dirty and foul as the rest of him. Drake's normally tanned skin appeared a pallid imitation, making him look as if he might fade into oblivion. And he was so thin, Aric could feel Drake's ribs against his shoulder, poking each time he took a step toward Drake's freedom. Merciful God, let naught happen to risk it.

Aric did not think Drake would have survived much longer in that dungeon hell. If he survived at all.

The fresh, brutal scars on Drake's back pointed to nay.

Aric wanted to kill Murdoch MacDougall. No apologies would change his need; no explanations would soften his hate. Murdoch deserved to die like a dog, for he had treated Drake in that manner—and worse.

"*Pssst.* Aric!" Kieran whispered through an entrance to the now-empty wicket gate.

"'Tis clear?"

"Aye. I had but to knock a few heads together. Hurry! The roaming sentries will come this way again soon."

With a nod, Aric anchored Drake to his shoulder and stooped

down to make his way through the small tunnel. Mercifully, they encountered no resistance.

Bribing the jailer had not been difficult. But he and Kieran had been compelled to eliminate a host of other guards, either with fists or blades, in order to secure a clear path to the outside of Dunollie Castle, home of the MacDougall clan. 'Twas one time Aric welcomed the battle and blood—anything to save Drake.

As a stiff Scottish wind blasted over the wild crags of heather-dotted land, Aric made his way toward safety, carrying his blood brother—trying to push concern at bay. Kieran kept watch for interlopers in front and behind them.

Within minutes, the trio made their way to their waiting horses. Fearing for Drake's condition, Aric was suddenly glad he had had the foresight to procure a wagon of sorts to transport Drake. His friend could not otherwise endure the difficult trek back to Guilford's estate in England, where he would be blessedly safe.

Kieran and Aric tied their horses to the wagon. Kieran climbed in to drive the makeshift vehicle. The scents of rain and desperation tinged the empty night as Aric scrambled up beside his unconscious friend and prayed.

The three-hour ride south to an inn he and Kieran had deemed safe seemed an eternity. By moonlight, Aric had caught snatches of this gaunt, almost yellowed friend. He looked years older and wore tatters of the very clothes he had donned the day his father had been murdered, over seven months ago.

Aric knew then Murdoch MacDougall was a monster whose cruelty was only outmeasured by his hatred for his younger half brother.

Once at the inn, exhaustion tried to claim Aric. With ruthless control, he shoved it back. Beside him, Kieran worked with a grim, tired face as they carried Drake up the dark stairs, to a waiting room.

The fire inside the chamber burned brightly. A light repast of wine, bread, and cheese had been laid out, as they had requested before leaving for Dunollie. In the morn, the innkeepers would provide a heartier breakfast. Aric only hoped Drake would live long enough to eat it.

Heaving a worried sigh, Aric helped Kieran lay Drake on the room's lone bed.

"We'll need water," Aric said finally, trying to temper the anger he felt at seeing his friend's pitiful condition in full light.

With a tight-jawed scowl and fierce eyes, Kieran stared at Drake, seeing the damage done to their friend for the first time. "Bloody hell! That man is a savage."

Aric nodded, knowing the bleak expression in Kieran's eyes was reflected in his own. If Drake died, a part of him would die as well. The part that remembered laughter by the river when they had gone there as young men to spy on the village's bathing women— and saw an old crone instead. The part that remembered each of them taking a knife to their palm and sealing a pact to protect one another forever in blood.

Staring at Drake, Aric realized he had failed his friend miserably and vowed he would do everything possible to stave off death.

"Aye, Murdoch is savage," he said to Kieran. "Get the water."

With a tight nod, Kieran disappeared out the door and down the steps. Aric removed Drake's shirt, peeling away the ribbons of its back that clung to fresh lash marks in his skin. Working to control his fury, Aric moved to Drake's pants, noticing that everywhere he looked, his friend's skin was so browned by dirt and grunge, he wondered if it would ever come clean.

With a fresh blanket, Aric covered Drake's bare form and sank on the mattress beside him. "Live, my friend. We are here, Kieran and I."

A thick lump rose to his throat, and Aric worked to swallow it down. Drake must live. Murdoch could not deal in such treachery and win.

"The innkeeper's wife is heating water for a bath. We can start with this." Kieran entered and gestured to a clean bucket of water, lye soap, and a bundle of cloths in his arms.

"Quickly," Aric barked.

Side by side, the two men worked. Aric washed Drake's face, now covered with a crusty, misshapen black beard. Kieran soaped Drake's hands, arms, chest, and neck. By mutual consent, the men turned Drake over to his stomach.

Lash marks confronted them across nearly every inch of Drake's back. New wounds over fresh scars over older scars, all covered in thick grime. Aric shivered, while Kieran looked as though he were restraining the urge to hit someone or something.

"Not now," Aric whispered. "The time will come, my friend."

With a jerky nod, Kieran poured fresh water into the bowl and prepared a fresh soapy cloth for Drake's back. Aric placed the cloth on his friend's open wounds.

Drake came up screaming, dark eyes wild, glazed.

Gently, Aric and Kieran restrained Drake and lay him down upon the bed.

"You are gone from Dunollie, Drake. We are here to help you," Aric assured.

Drake looked about, then from Kieran to Aric. Sanity returned slowly to his haunted, thin features as Aric handed him a cup of wine.

"How?" he asked finally, voice slurred and scratchy from illness or disuse. Or both.

"Guilford tried for months," Kieran began as Drake sipped from the full cup. "Then he sent us for you."

"We will take you back to Hartwich Hall," said Aric as he passed Drake a hunk of bread and cheese and watched his friend take a hearty bite. "There you can recover—"

"Nay," Drake refused in a sharp, husky syllable.

"But—" Aric frowned. "Where would you go?"

"Dunollie." Drake bit into the dark bread.

"You cannot!" Aric blurted.

"Nay!" Kieran shouted.

Drake rolled bare, lean shoulders, grimacing against pain. "I can. I will. Murdoch must die."

"But—" both men began at once.

"The butcher killed my father and bloody near killed me. 'Tis by my hand he must die, and quickly," Drake insisted, then sipped again from his cup.

"Your ill health will not permit this vendetta." Aric frowned. "Return with us to Hartwich Hall. Guilford awaits you, and his soldiers can protect you until you are well."

"Or I should be happy indeed to kill the swine for you," Kieran offered with a nod.

Drake, usually the one to laugh at Kieran's ways, cracked not the slightest smile. "'Tis my duty to be done in a manner both swift and brutal."

Aric frowned, not liking the bleak determination in his friend's tone. "I do not believe you can survive such a mission."

His black gaze was full of…nothing. Only his voice showed disdain. "So?"

Kieran's alarmed gaze caught his a moment later. Aric sucked in a hard, dismayed breath. Drake had always been the cautious one, the planner, the most deft with strategy.

Was he so bitter that he would throw away his own life to obtain revenge by killing his half brother?

"My idea will gain you more," Aric offered in what he hoped was an intriguing, low voice.

Drake responded to it, instantly alert. "What speak you?"

"A carefully planned revenge, something to cost Murdoch more than his life."

"He holds nothing else sacred," Drake argued.

Nodding in sudden understanding, Kieran tossed out, "Do you not ache more for living amongst all you have lost in your home, your father, the respect of your clan?"

Running long, thin fingers through his beard, Drake seemed to peer off into the distance, considering.

Aric held his breath, sending Kieran a silent glance of thanks for assisting in his plan. Such would not keep Drake safe forever, but safe enough until his body and spirit might heal and reason might prevail.

"Murdoch loves Dunollie," Drake began. "And power. 'Tis as necessary to him as breathing."

"Then take those from him," Aric urged. "Make him walk alone, poor and unheard. Make others shun and heckle him."

Drake frowned, clearly impatient. "How? He and Duff have convinced the entire clan they witnessed me murder my father. I know of no one who can say nay to this falsehood."

Aric clapped a hand to Drake's shoulder. "You have ever been cunning and patient. Soon, you will see such a way. And we will help you if you have need."

With a reluctant nod, Drake addressed them both. "You have my thanks for saving me. I vow, even if I must die trying, Murdoch's life will become an earthly hell."

As Kieran and Aric cleansed the red, painful wounds on Drake's back, talk turned to politics, memories—and Aric's new hellion wife. But Aric was not fooled. Drake had emerged from Murdoch's dungeon a changed man—and not necessarily for the better. He kept a part of himself distant, remote, mired in hatred and dwelling on revenge.

Aric hoped such would not be the death of one of his dearest friends. But hope dwelt dim within him.

* * * *

Weeks later, though Drake's health had much improved and he resembled his self of old, his determination had not lessened, nor his demeanor cheered. Both were made of steel.

Cursing into his half-empty mug of ale, Aric looked about Guilford's clean keep. The foolish jesters made his head ache. The loud troubadours made his teeth hurt.

Before him, he watched Kieran toss back a long swallow of ale, then grab a passing kitchen maid to join him in dance. The young woman lifted her lips in a smile and her skirts above her ankles as she hopped and skipped to the merry lutes.

To his right, Aric found Drake watching the scene without emotion. The ale in front of him remained untouched.

Cursing, Aric wished he had never suggested Drake find a more sinister way to punish Murdoch. He and Kieran should have slaughtered the fiend while rescuing Drake and had done with it. Instead, Drake had thrown his mind and soul—what was left of it— into the strategy of revenge with cold abandon.

Aric tossed back another sip of ale and rubbed tired eyes with his thumb and finger. Glad he was that he had sent word to Northwell this morn that he would be coming home. Well, glad…yet uncertain. How would Gwenyth feel about his return? Would she welcome him into her arms—and bed—or would she be too busy about the castle she had always longed for to notice?

Ceasing such morose thoughts, Aric looked up to find Kieran, a mug of ale in each hand and a wench under each arm.

"I'm off to battle again, ladies. Send me away a happy man!" shouted Kieran as he climbed the stairs to his chamber with the laughing maids.

Grimacing, Aric shook his head, wishing the battles in Spain held no lure for his Irish friend.

Ever a scamp was Kieran. Aric doubted anything or anyone would change that. He also wondered if Kieran would ever realize he used the whirl of battle and the haze of pleasure to mask his pain.

A dew-cheeked kitchen maid cast a tentative smile his way—nay, he realized a moment later. 'Twas Drake she smiled at, and with good cause. If Kieran's charm drew women, Drake's dark face compelled them.

Beside him, Drake rose, gazing at the young dark-haired woman with purpose. When he paused at the bottom of the stairs and cocked a brow in question, the maid darted to his side and wrapped slender fingers around the thick of his arm. Together, they disappeared.

As the feast around him wound down, people found their beds for the night. Soon, Guilford approached and seated himself on the bench beside him.

"Thank you again for bringing my grandson back to me."

Aric glanced up at the old man, something of a father to him these past dozen or more years. "Drake is like my brother. I could do no less for him."

Guilford paused, rubbing his wiry white beard. "He is not the same."

So the old man had noticed. Aric knew such should not surprise him. Very little passed without Guilford's awareness.

"He needs time," Aric assured.

With a shake of his head, the old man's eyes turned bleak. "'Tis more than that he needs. It seems he feels nothing but hate."

Nodding uncomfortably, Aric acknowledged that truth.

"Well, lad, 'tis not like you to frown in your cups so," Guilford said, changing the subject.

"I am tired," he lied.

Guilford accepted the evasion with a nod. "Now that we are alone, tell me of this wife you have taken. Kieran says she is uncommon pretty and has a fiery temper to match."

In that moment, he tried not to miss Gwenyth, as he had for many days, but a flash of something—nay, a pang—jolted him in the gut. Why? Their last words had been harsh, and she had told him more than once she preferred that milksop Penley to him.

But he could not forget her sharp wit and sharper tongue—and the fact they masked a soft heart. Nor could he forget how she ignited in his arms when he touched her, how she arched toward his mouth when he claimed her breast, how her arousal had thickened in the air between them when he had but brushed the bud of her need...

He felt something clench again, this time lower. A glance around told him he could have a comely woman if he wanted one.

Damnation! For some blasted reason, he did not. He refused to examine why.

Aric sighed. "Gwenyth is…all Kieran says." *And more.*

"Bring her round to meet me, boy."

"Aye," he agreed with a dispirited nod into his cup.

A prolonged silence followed. Aric knew crafty old Guilford, knew the aged man sized him up, saw through his façade.

"There was a time you would have joined my grandson and that rogue Kieran in finding a wench or two to tumble."

True. Until recently, until Gwenyth, he had scarce missed an opportunity. Why?

Beside him, Guilford watched with wise blue eyes and the softness of an old man's smile.

"Ah lad, 'tis like that when you are in love."

In love? Did he love Gwenyth? How could he love an ill-tempered witch who sought castles of wealth and yearned for someone like Sir Penley to share them with? 'Twas simply lust.

"I do not love her."

Guilford rose with a hearty slap on the back. "'Tis something fierce you are feeling for her. Soon enough, you shall find out what it is."

Aric watched the old man walk away, then finished off his ale. Aye, he felt something fierce. Something needy, something that sought release. Something he feared only Gwenyth could assuage.

With a curse, he called for another ale. And another. And another.

A long hour later, Kieran's two wenches came fluttering down the stairs. One, a lanky girl with dark hair, giggled. The other, a plump blond, all but flittered into the great hall with rosy cheeks and a grin.

Aric smiled wryly. Kieran did love women—all women. All shapes, all sizes, from the shy to the brazen. And in return, they seemed to love him. But would he ever be able to love with his heart? Aric wondered.

Another dark hour passed before Drake's wench appeared on the stairs. She looked pale. Her dark hair tangled wildly about her shoulders. The woman's eyes were half-closed in weariness as she trudged down the stairs.

Frowning, Aric rose. Whether 'twas curiosity or foreboding that took him to the woman's side, he was not certain. Drake had indeed changed. Certainly not enough to hurt a woman, had he?

When he paused beside her, she looked up, stunned, as if she had not seen him approach.

"Are you well?" he asked, frowning.

"Tired," she murmured, lunging toward her bed on the straw floor.

His frown became a scowl that marred his brow as he helped her lie on her back. "Did Drake hurt you?"

She opened her hazel eyes slightly. "Hurt? Nay." Her eyes drifted closed again, and she yawned. "But yer friend, he 'as control of iron, the vigor of five men, and no heart at all."

The woman rolled to her side and fell into slumber almost instantly. With a puzzled frown, Aric rose and glanced up the stairs. What had the woman meant? She did not seem distressed or ill-treated, merely sated...overly so. Had Drake used her to forget his days at Dunollie? It seemed so, and Aric had a suspicion from the wench's words that his friend had not succeeded.

* * * *

May breezes had given way to June rains, then to the shimmer of July's heat. Gwenyth idly clasped the ruby pendant Aric had given her and wondered again when—or if—he would return to Northwell. Beside her, Dog whined despondently, seeming to echo something inside her.

With a sigh, she sat upon the garden's bench covered in chamomile and listened to the sound of the ocean behind the keep. The bench's cushioning fragrance rose up to blend with the mixture of mint, thyme, and perfect roses in the garden's air. Mandrake added a hint of spice.

Ah, she loved Northwell and its environs. Bessie, the cook, full of mischief and kindness, had made her feel welcome, as had Baswain, the porter, once he had recovered from the shock of Aric having taken a wife. She had been ensconced in the master's chambers since her arrival, and such fine luxuries she had never imagined. Penhurst paled in comparison. The wild, stark crags of this northern country, dotted with heather and gorse, captured her imagination. Everything here was so riotous, so alive—from the weather to the land itself and the surrounding vast ocean. She would never grow weary of life here.

It had been satisfying indeed to write to Nellwyn of her new home and her new fortune, to feel equal at last. Now she had a secure future, one that rivaled her cousin. Life should be nothing but pleasing.

So why did she feel...restless?

"My lady Gwenyth!" called Bessie, her large girth swaying beneath her coarse gown with each quick step. "My lady!"

"Aye, Bessie?" she answered, rising to her feet.

The panting cook paused before her, and only then did Gwenyth notice that a young, hearty wench stood behind her, eyes wide as she wrung raw, red hands.

"This 'ere is me daughter, Yetta. She works in the dye house."

The frightened girl dropped into a curtsy, gaze seemingly affixed to the ground.

Bessie thumped her on the shoulder with a flap of her hand, and the girl straightened but still refused to look up.

Gwenyth grimaced at the girl's obvious discomfort. "Hello, Yetta."

"Milady." Her high-pitched voice trembled.

"We was hopin' ye could 'elp us with a matter, since ye seen to stoppin' that crooked miller last month from sellin' his bad grain to all and sundry."

Knowing she'd done no more than confront a tradesman about a dishonest practice, Gwenyth shrugged. When he had refused to bow to her demands, Stephen had surprisingly—and shame-facedly—backed her up. He'd known such had been his duty, and the guilt for his remission had been clear. Since that time, he—and everyone in the castle—had begun to consult her in domestic matters, and she was glad of the diversion—and to be needed. She wondered if the servants did not involve Rowena, who by all rights was still chatelaine, because they feared her.

Still, Bessie had come to her now with a matter of some importance, Gwenyth assumed, smiling. She was more than willing to help.

"I shall try," Gwenyth said. "How can I help?"

"Thank ye. We be knowin' yer a good, kind lady since the day Lord Belford brought ye 'ere."

Gwenyth did not doubt the woman's sincerity. For in truth, the castlefolk had done much to make her welcome. Private baths from the maids, special pastries from Bessie, new dresses from the tailor—she had rarely ever had to request anything. A smile on each servant's face awaited her as she passed. It all pleased her greatly…except for Rowena's presence.

"Thank you. And what is the problem?"

Bessie lowered her voice. "'Tis Mistress Rowena. She has demanded a new dress in the color saffron by tomorrow eve."

At Gwenyth's frown, Yetta stuttered, "We… Ye see, milady…" She drew in a deep breath. "We've no-not enough crocus blooms for the…the saffron."

Many crocus blooms were needed to make saffron, which was a costly extravagance. Why would Rowena have need of such a dress by tomorrow eve?

Smoothing out the frown that had wrinkled her brow, Gwenyth asked, "Have you begun to dye the cloth, Yetta?"

The young girl shook her head, limp brown strands of her hair brushing her shoulders. "Nay, milady. Me mum said to come…well, that is to, ah, see ye first."

The poor girl. So shy and uncertain. Gwenyth's heart reached out, for she knew, as Yetta did, that Rowena's displeasure at not getting her way would be great indeed.

And though Gwenyth had done her best to steer clear of Rowena's path, sensing the woman's deep determination to protect her role here at Northwell, she suddenly relished the opportunity the cook and the dye maid had given her. The fear in young Yetta's eyes at the mere mention of Rowena's name, along with the various acts of displeasure she had witnessed recently, convinced her that the other woman rode the servants unnecessarily hard. Though Aric had not wished her to usurp Rowena, she would not allow the woman to terrorize the servants. Besides, she could hardly turn away such a distraught girl and her hardworking mother.

"Have you any saffron at all, Yetta?" Gwenyth asked.

"Aye, milady."

Mischief danced in her mind and made its way to her smile. "And corklit?"

"Plenty, milady." Yetta risked a peek at her.

"Mix them," she instructed.

"B-but, milady. That will make orange, and Mistress Rowena hates…"

"Orange?" Gwenyth finished with a nod.

Rowena, with her starkly pale hair and fair pink skin would look awful in orange. Gwenyth decided she rather liked that thought.

"I will tell Mistress Rowena 'twas the best that could be done with little saffron," Gwenyth promised.

Bessie, wise to Gwenyth's impish smile, winked at her with twinkling eyes. She turned to her daughter. "Well, go on wi' ye. Ye heard our lady speak."

Yetta sent her a fearful, uncertain stare.

Gwenyth reached out to pat the girl's hand. "'Twill be fine, I vow. You leave Mistress Rowena to me."

Reluctantly, the girl nodded. Gwenyth smiled softly.

"Aye, Mistress Rowena won't be lookin' so grand now fer our lord's return," added Bessie.

Shock bolted through Gwenyth as she whipped her gaze to the older woman. "He returns?"

Bessie frowned. "Aye, the mistress says 'e sent word just yestereve of his return."

Her heart skipped; her stomach danced. Finally, the man would be back at Northwell.

And he had not bothered to inform her.

Anger came next. So, Rowena had requested a new dress, no doubt to entice her former lover, now Gwenyth's husband, and the woman had chosen not to inform her of his return. Something fierce and possessive rose up within her. Rowena might have the look of an untouched angel, but the whore had a devious mind. The question was, did Aric still desire Rowena?

Given the fact he had sent the note to Rowena, she feared aye.

"Thank you," she said absently, then entered the keep, climbing the narrow, circular stone steps to their chamber. Dog trailed behind her, head hanging.

Once inside, she sat by a window and stared out over the blue-gray ocean crashing upon Northwell's lush green shore, all tinted with mist and seeming magic. Dog settled at her feet.

She had missed Aric, worried for his safety, waited for some

131

word of him, of his return. And he had sent word of his return to Rowena.

Before she could stop the memories, Gwenyth's mind flashed back to the morn she had sewn the red dress. His gaze of molten silver had traveled over her bare skin with desire, even as his mouth claimed her breast with a swirl of his tongue. And his large hands... Who would have thought they had enough finesse to beguile her, to bring her so close to a peak with a mere brush of his thumb? And the rest of him, rigid steel—from the ledges of muscle upon his chest to the rippled plains of his abdomen...and the length of shaft with which he sought to take her, which she had burned to receive.

Did he want only Rowena now?

Mayhap 'twas her fault if he did. She had lain naked beneath him and rebuffed him, despite the fact they were wed. He had tried to assure her that he would see to her needs always, ensure their children would never starve. Until she had looked upon Northwell's magnificence, she had refused to believe him. How many times had he made it plain that he did not want to return here or resume the life of his past?

And what had she done but push him to take up battle again? Feel utter delight when he had announced himself an earl?

Gazing away from the majesty of the ocean, Gwenyth realized she had been wrong so many times since their marriage. She should not have railed at him for wedding her to save her life. She should not have kept him from her bed. She should not have been so lost in her own joy upon coming to Northwell that she had failed to see his woe in returning.

She drew in a deep breath and crawled into Aric's big bed alone. Settling the sheets about her, she realized he had tried in every way to make a marriage between them. He had been nothing but kind and patient, things most men did not concern themselves with. Her stubborn temper had kept them apart.

But no more. When Aric returned, she would endeavor to be a better friend, a better helpmate—and the best wife possible.

CHAPTER ELEVEN

Clutching nervous fingers into fists, Gwenyth watched Aric arrive as the sun drifted behind the hill upon which Northwell sat. Dusk bathed the sparse green land and the castle stones about them in shades of honey. Aric sat tall upon his mount, in gray relief against the brilliant scene, the sky's fiery orb turning his hair a molten gold.

Gwenyth swallowed against the sudden flutter of anticipation and longing. She *had* missed him these past three months. Terribly. Had he missed her at all?

He dismounted, handing his reins over to a stable lad, and cast his gaze over the waiting party as they stood beside one another. With nary a pause, he glanced over Stephen, beyond Baswain. Then his gaze swept past Rowena, whose small pink smile of anticipation froze. Hiding a grin, Gwenyth hoped the witch disliked her orange gown. 'Twould explain why she wore blue now.

Finally, Aric's stare found her—and stayed—as he walked toward her. Around his feet, Dog leapt excitedly, wagging his shaggy gray-and-white tail.

Joyous, she grasped the pendant he had given her as he bent down to pet the mutt. "Welcome home, my lord."

He stilled, then stood upright, brow arching. "Gwenyth."

As he moved closer, his weariness was evident in his lean cheeks, the stubble dusting his jaw. Though tired, Aric still made her pulse leap. Despite his current mode of dress, the sculpted lines of his face and the breadth of his wide shoulders made him look something of a conquering Viking. She shivered.

"How good to have you home, Aric." Rowena approached silently beside her, laying a slender hand upon his arm.

Gwenyth gritted her teeth at the woman's use of her husband's Christian name. She needed no reminders Rowena had shared her husband's bed, for she could not forget it.

As Aric nodded in greeting, Rowena smiled, showing perfect white teeth. "I have prepared something of a feast in honor of your return. Come inside and let us sup."

Rolling her eyes, Gwenyth stared at the wench. Aye, as if Rowena had been slaving in the hot kitchens all day in an effort to please Aric. And pigs would fly tomorrow.

Still, Gwenyth had not thought to order a feast for Aric's return. In truth, she had believed he would not wish such. She cursed beneath her breath, certain Rowena knew something of Aric that she herself did not.

"Sup without me," Aric said suddenly, surprising—and pleasing—Gwenyth. "I seek only the comfort of my bed."

With that, he disentangled Rowena's hold upon him and walked into the keep, sending Gwenyth a long stare. What had she seen in his eyes? A question? An invitation?

Beside her, Rowena stiffened and lifted her chin, then made her way inside as well, directly to the great hall. Gwenyth followed and was just in time to see Aric ascend the stairs, Dog at his heels, to his chamber. *Their* chamber.

Biting her lip, Gwenyth held on to her resolve to be a better friend, a better helpmate. With that in mind, she dashed to the kitchens.

"My lady!" Bessie greeted. "What be ye doin' in 'ere, hot as it is?"

"I seek a light repast for myself and my husband. Could you prepare that for me?"

"I should be glad. Won't take more than a moment. I'll have it brought to yer chamber. 'Tis the least I can do after ye helped me recount the spices last week."

"I enjoy helping," she said with a satisfied smile, then left the yeasty warmth of the kitchen.

Retracing her path to the stairs, Gwenyth mounted them. Her thoughts shifted from her joy with the castle to Aric. Did he indeed want her by his side, or would he simply want her gone?

With a gentle nudge, she opened the door and started inside the wide room. Then she nearly stumbled.

Aric wore naught but his hose. He stood beside a pair of lit tapers, the warm glow of the flame illuminating the sun-swept plains and ripples of his bare back. Every lithe inch of him looked solid from hours of effort and mighty enough to be his own army. The thick columns of his thinly clad thighs led to a firm backside that flexed with corded muscle as he shifted his weight.

Gwenyth felt her mouth go dry.

Seemingly unaware of her presence, he dipped a cloth into a basin of water beside the candles and turned toward the window. She watched him in profile as he smoothed the dark cloth over his wide, golden shoulders and the unyielding breadth of his chest. Moments later, a droplet of water undulated its way between his flat brown nipples, to converge in the valley between the double ridges of muscle covering his abdomen.

Gwenyth struggled for her next breath.

He was beautiful…and kind, compassionate, intelligent, and brave—everything she had ever wanted in a husband.

Why had she ever refused to share his bed?

Where had she ever found the will?

True to her word, one of Bessie's kitchen maids entered through the open door a moment later and set their food down on a table by the fire with a clatter.

"The repast ye asked fer, my lady. My lord," she acknowledged with a bow of her head.

Aric looked up in surprise as the maid turned and left. Gwenyth noted he watched the woman's retreating figure, then turned his weighty gaze upon herself. A curious flutter disturbed her stomach.

When he said nothing, Gwenyth filled the silence, uncertain what else to do. Still, she could not pull her stare from him. "I thought you might be hungry after your journey."

Something in his eyes shifted, darkened. He turned back to the basin before she could discern anything in his look.

"I am. You have my thanks."

Again, silence, so awkward, so tense. Gwenyth worried her bottom lip with her teeth, then decided she should leave him be. He did not seem much in the mood for talk.

"Enjoy it. 'Tis glad I am you are returned," she admitted softly, then turned to leave.

Had she only mistaken that he wanted her near because she felt an urge to be by his side? To play the role of his wife?

"Gwenyth, wait."

His call spurred her to look at him again. With a greedy gaze, she took in the wide bulk of his ridged, browned chest that narrowed to a whittled waist and lean hips. Bristling braies, he would be like silken steel to the touch, warm and solid, enveloped in smooth, bronzed skin. Feeling heat flush to her cheeks, Gwenyth looked up into his face. She felt instantly contrite when she espied the weary expression pervading his eyes.

"Aric?" she whispered in answer to his call.

"There is food aplenty for two. Sup with me."

He had asked her to stay! Joy curved her mouth upward, though an unusually demure mood washed over her.

She nodded her assent. In return, Aric sent her a faint smile, then ordered Dog out of the chamber. The animal whined but left. Aric then shut the door.

They were well and truly alone.

Without words, they sat at the wooden chairs by the fire. Aric poured them both some spiced wine. Gwenyth realized her husband had no intent to don his tunic, and she would be tempted by his bare nearness through the meal. Lest she stare like a simpleton, she looked at the trencher they would share.

Haddock and mutton, served on a bed of cabbage, filled most of the plate. Various cakes and jellies filled the rest. Though it all looked delightful, Gwenyth found she did not hunger—at least not for the food.

Slicing off some of the boiled mutton, Aric offered her a piece from his knife. As she leaned forward to accept it, he placed a guiding hand behind her neck, fingers gentle, palms warm.

She felt herself flush and tingle at his touch. Though she accepted the bite and chewed it, she could not tear her gaze away from her husband. His rich musk distracted her. Gwenyth felt her palms turn damp and knew she must do something to break this thick silence.

"Where is Kieran?" Her voice came out husky.

"He returned to Spain."

"To battle?"

Aric nodded and grimaced. "'Tis what he likes best."

"But war is dangerous."

His smile looked truly sad. "'Tis why he likes it, little dragon."

Gwenyth sighed, wondering at the oddities of men. "Were you and Kieran able to save your friend Drake?"

He bit into the haddock and nodded. "Though he is a changed man. Bitter."

"And this troubles you." From the lines bracketing his full mouth with tension, she knew it to be so.

With a somber nod, he answered, "They both seem so anxious to die, Kieran for a moment's thrill, Drake for revenge."

Hearing Aric's sigh, Gwenyth abandoned the cabbage she'd been considering to stare at her husband. Worry lined the arch of his golden brow, turned down his wide mouth. In the face of his own disquiet, he still spared such concern for those he loved. His compassion humbled her.

Aric had wed her, a stranger, to save her life. She had been too absorbed in her own perplexity to take much note of his deed. Time and again, he had set his worries aside to dry her tears, encourage her, cheer her. And still, she had refused him the most important comfort a husband sought in a wife.

Unable to do aught else, Gwenyth rose and moved closer to Aric, then touched a tentative hand to his arm. He peered up at her in question, long tawny hair brushing his expansive shoulders.

"I know you are none too happy to have left your cottage to return here," she said.

Pain flickered in his eyes, turning them flat, stark, empty. "Aye."

He reached out without warning and settled his hands about her waist, then drew her closer, between the vee of his legs. Bowing, Aric buried his forehead against her abdomen, as if seeking her comfort and nearness.

Surprise vibrated within Gwenyth, even as desire curled through her belly and tenderness tugged at her heart. She wound her hands through the soft length of his hair, watching the fawn-colored strands curl around her fingers.

"Would that being here troubled you not, my husband."

Aric lifted his head, his gaze snapping to her face. He searched deep, probed her eyes, indeed her very soul, it seemed, with his intense gray perusal. She trembled with the weight of his stare.

Then Aric stood. His thighs seemed to bracket hers as he rose to his full height, more than half a head taller than herself. Still, his gaze drilled down to her, heating with each moment that passed.

"Husband?" His whisper demanded an answer.

Gwenyth flushed, realizing what she had implied. What she now wanted. "Husband."

"Gwenyth…" His raspy voice sizzled down her spine. "Having you near pleases me."

His water-woodsy scent, his body's heat, and that hot stare combined to scatter her thoughts. "It—it does?"

"I would show you how much."

With that silky-rough whisper, he took her face in his massive palms and tilted her mouth beneath his. Gwenyth felt her breathing shallow—then cease altogether. He drew closer, seemingly into her, as they touched at shoulder, chest, belly, thigh. She felt the hard length of his desire against her as he leaned in and possessed her mouth with a shimmering brush of a kiss.

Flashes of light bursting behind her eyes, Gwenyth grasped Aric's solid shoulders for support and opened her mouth at his silent urging.

The kiss was long, near endless, flowing like the meandering tides of a languid river. She tasted spiced wine on the tongue that swept her mouth with lazy abandon. A thick warmth slid through her veins when he nibbled gently on her sensitive lower lip, then indulged in another mating of their mouths.

His fingers wound through her hair as he cradled her head, keeping her at his gentle command. An ache formed inside her as she strained upward to receive more of his tender pleasure. And he gave it without restraint, without hurry, brushing his lips over hers again, before settling with a male moan of need on the curve of her neck.

"So soft," he murmured, then trailed a damp path down to the upper swells of her breasts, which began to ache for his touch.

As if Aric could hear her body call to him, he removed her stomach girdle after little more than a touch. With a *clink* it slid to the stone floor as his breaths mingled with her sighs and the sound of crashing surf outside. Her dress followed beneath his dexterous fingers, slipping off one shoulder in a silky caress, followed by the other, until the gown slithered to her feet. Until she stood clad in naught but her thin chemise and the pendant he had given her.

An instant later, his hands journeyed from her hips up, to cling to the front of her fluttering belly. Then up more he moved, ceasing only when he lifted the full weight of her receptive breasts in his hot palms. She gasped.

His stare was like thick liquid silver as his thumbs flicked across the hardened tips. A jagged sigh of pleasure, of need, escaped her lips. Fog swirled in her mind, leaving her deliciously dazed.

Restlessly, he dragged his hands down her back, to her buttocks, and pressed his hardness against her feminine mound. A current of desire bolted her, piercingly sweet between her thighs.

"Aric," she called, knowing full what she asked of him.

His stare fastened on hers in the next moment. He, too, knew what she asked of him. Something fierce and pounding lay visible in his gaze, gentled by the tapers' soft shadows and a surprising reverence that robbed her of breath.

"You, little dragon, I'll want always." His murmur skittered over her skin a moment before he lifted her to his chest, her knees supported in the crook of his arm, their faces inches apart.

He indulged in the taste of her mouth, savoring her with firm lips and an exploring tongue. Gwenyth felt her heart pound in rhythm with the fluid desire flowing in her body, pooling between her thighs.

As Aric reached the grand tester bed, he eased her down upon the soft mattress, palm lingering on the length of her thigh before he stood at her feet. Gwenyth propped herself up on her elbows and sent him a curious glance as he took a step back.

Then he removed his hose and stood before her in powerful, glorious nakedness.

Gwenyth swallowed at the smooth baring of his burnished skin, the solidity of his corded thighs, and between... God's nightgown. There he looked stiff and substantial, thick and ready. And large to her maiden's eyes. Her breath left her in an uneven sigh.

Aric lowered himself beside her and lay on his side, facing her. "Do not fear. I will do all I can not to hurt you."

Before she could speak, he took her in his arms again and eased her chemise up the length of her trembling thighs, over the fluttering curve of her belly, above the weight of her needy breasts. His palms trailed beneath the chemise, caressing her skin with a welcomed warmth, his hand alternately brushing and pressing into her flesh.

With a final tug, he freed her from the garment and tossed it to the floor. Now they both lay naked, and arousal was plain in his eyes.

Aric took her mouth again, tongue swirling, building more need. His fingers aided his quest to claim her, grazing over her sensitive skin where she least expected it, in the bend of her elbow, in the curve of her neck, about the indentation of her navel.

She began to feel heated, restless. "Aric…"

The smile he gave her was ripe with passion and gladness as his stare delved into her, seeming to seek possession of her very soul.

Then his mouth descended on the throbbing tip of her breast. She gasped, holding him prisoner with urgent hands in the softness of his hair. The fire of her need fanned to flame. She reeled at the sensations—the burning, the demanding torment of desire—all of which he created.

Her responses closed around her until she could feel nothing but his heated flesh pressed against her, his tongue taking her body hostage, his breath fanning like a whisper across her skin.

Then his hands began to move, like a musical accompaniment in a song of love. Fingertips made the merest brush across her abdomen, cradled her hip, clung to the inner softness of her thigh. Gwenyth began to anticipate the shooting pleasure that would come next with each caress. But even she was unprepared for his next stunning, intimate touch.

His fingers delved within her wet folds, knuckle stroking the crux of her desire in short, unhurried circles. She arched off the bed, silently demanding the completion her body screamed for. Still, he continued, adding to her agony with a maddening lack of haste and the heat of his mouth on her tight nipple. The need built between each caress, each swirl of his tongue.

He drew upon her breast again, sucking her skin, her very scent, into the heat of his mouth. Pleasure tingled in her breasts, then arched down to her belly—and lower, where her juices now flowed freely for him.

His palm cupped her feminine mound a moment later, engulfing it with the size of his hands. She melted at the sensation of warmth and possession, coupled with an odd sort of security, as if he would allow nothing to harm her.

Then he pressed the heel of his hand into her, kneading her eager flesh again and again. Sparks shot from the bud of her sensation to everywhere else in her body—her belly, her legs, her breasts. No part of her was immune to the tender persuasion of his touch.

When Gwenyth thought she could bear no more, one of his long, blunt fingers pressed the seam of her open and delved into her. Gwenyth felt her body close around his offering with greed, and she bucked against him. Pleasure spiraled to mindless heights.

Never had she imagined something so intimate between husband and wife. Aunt Welsa had always said that men stabbed at women greedily with their lances. Instead, Aric probed gently with the giving firmness of his finger.

He soon added another to the fray. Once inside her, he parted the two fingers, stretching her wider. The sensation was more uncommon than uncomfortable, and she understood its purpose.

"Worry not about hurting me," she croaked between deep breaths.

A rogue's smile flittered across his wide mouth as he continued his exploration. "The way I want you now, 'tis best if I have you well prepared."

Before she could do more than flush hotly at his words, his fingers plunged into her again, teasing her inner walls. More jolts of pleasure leapt within her, building on the others before it.

As she called his name, her need climbed to new pinnacles. The heel of one hand rubbing, the fingers of another pushing inside her, while his mouth devoured her tingling nipples… Suddenly 'twas too much. The building pressure became an ache that writhed for release. Something within her pulsed furiously, and a moan ripped from her throat as satisfaction began to wash over her.

Suddenly the pressure of his palm against her pleasure point eased, almost lifting away. Nay! 'Twas that pressure she most needed. Gwenyth moaned in protest and arched toward him, seeking surcease. Aric but gave her the lightest of rubs. Still, she convulsed within, gasping as her ache soared to breath-stealing pleasure that made her quiver. Then he returned his hand to her, massaging her center in firm strokes.

A long cry escaped her throat as she shattered in his arms. Wave after undulating wave of satisfaction tumbled through her trembling body. She struggled for one breath, then another, scarcely able to understand the magic of his touch. If she did not know better, she would accuse him of sorcery after all.

As the peaked pleasure became a glow, Gwenyth became aware of Aric's intent gaze upon her face—and her own unease. Had she been too free, too bold?

The heated gray stare that met her gaze said not.

Aric rolled toward her, above her, his face filled with impatience, with intent. He moved to settle the length of his great body over her. Gwenyth protested with a gentle hand to his shoulder.

"Wait," she called, voice breathy.

His gaze encompassed a question. His mouth tightened as if suppressing a groan.

She rushed to say, "I-I want to kiss you."

"Gwenyth, love, I vow we will kiss more."

She shook her head. "I speak not of your mouth."

His body stilled utterly. Lust charged into his eyes like a steed in a tourney. "Then where?"

Biting her lip at his whispered question, she gazed at him with expectant eyes. "You... I... Well, that is, your skin. Your body."

A wide, pleased smile overtook his features as he rolled to his back on the great soft bed. "I am yours, little dragon. And I've no intent to ask you to be gentle."

Despite the depth of her first passion, a giggle escaped her. Did desire and laughter fit together? Seeing the merriment dancing in his eyes, she supposed so.

"Shall I try to be rough, then?" she bantered in return.

"Whatever pleases you."

Aric curled a hand behind his head and propped his head up on it. And he waited, none too patiently. Gwenyth glanced at the expanse of his bronzed skin before her, the bulge of his arms, the ridges of his hard chest and abdomen. Though the landscape of his skin was by no means unmarred, the variety of scars intrigued her.

Curious, she ran her fingers down a particularly long scar, from ribs to belly, then another just beneath the brown of his taut nipple that stretched nearly to his hip. Both must have bled and hurt more than she had in the whole of her life. And he sat, smiling faintly at her ministrations. How?

Drawing in a deep breath for courage—and to still her quivering innards—Gwenyth leaned toward him. Aric held his breath, the flat brawn of his belly taut, as she placed her mouth on one of his scars, just below his chest.

He tasted like tangy silk, smooth with a bit of salt. To her tingling lips, he felt smoothly rough, like a textured stone. She flicked her tongue against him to retest the surface. Aric sucked in a harsh breath.

Gwenyth traced farther down the scar, toward his navel. She had never really seen one but her own, and his fascinated her. Deeply curved in with a light sprinkling of brownish hair, it invited her. She delved it with her finger, then traced it with her tongue. He groaned, and Gwenyth found herself well pleased. Could she, a woman with no experience in matters of the flesh, really pleasure a man such as this?

Emboldened by the thought, she brushed a thumb across the nubbin of his hard nipple. Aric rewarded her with another hiss. Indeed, their bodies had similarities, despite the vast differences. What delight!

Without further ado, she closed her mouth around the brown bud of his nipple and curled her hand around the length of his hard flesh. Again, he moaned. The sound sent tingles across her sensitive flesh.

God's nightgown, but he was hot and solid, with skin surprisingly silky. Wondering if the entire length felt thus, she slid her palm up and, with her thumb, tested the bulging tip, which now seemed a mottled blue.

He nearly came up off the bed.

"Gwenyth, love?" He sounded strained, as if he'd been training all day.

She smiled. "Aye, my husband."

"It seems an eternity I have waited for you. Mayhap you should not do that now."

Frowning, Gwenyth was reluctant to give up her exploration, but acknowledged that in matters of the marriage bed, he would know more.

"Later?"

"I shall look forward to it," he said, removing her hand from his length and kissing her fingertips.

The feel of his mouth on her hand made her heart race. When he leaned for her and covered her, a jolt of anticipation charged her stomach. His next words made her nearly faint.

"I want to be inside you. Open your legs for me."

Working to catch her next breath, Gwenyth parted her shaking appendages.

"Wider." As she moved to obey, he coaxed further with a voice of pure velvet. "Wider. More."

Suddenly he wrapped his hands around her thighs, taking control of the matter. His fingers curled into her, and she felt boneless, melting to her core.

Aric spread her wider then she might have thought possible, then finally settled his hips in the crook of her legs. Against the seam of her womanhood, she felt him, hard and unyielding, and not demanding—yet. Then he raised her legs up to his hips.

Leaning forward on his elbows, he took possession of her mouth again. Lower, she felt his probe. He quickly found her, and at the sensation of his mere tip within her, her desire returned with the force of a storm against a sea wall, tempestuous and unforgiving. He slid farther inside her as his tongue sought hers, swirling, engaging. Inundated by needs plaguing both ends of her body, she groaned.

His rough, hot breath fanned against her cheek as he eased his lance farther still within her. Then he stilled. 'Twas as if she could feel his heartbeat in the throbbing of his manhood. *Boom, boom.* The sensation made her draw in a ragged breath of anticipation.

Suddenly, Aric cursed. Before she could question him, he surged forward, severing her maidenhead. Gwenyth felt a tearing, then a sting as he settled himself more deeply within her. Then the pain was gone, replaced by the sensations of fullness and liquid pleasure.

He pushed forward, forward. More. Stopping to breathe, stopping to take in her expression with those eyes of magic silver. Then with a grunt and a final surge, he sheathed himself to the hilt within her.

Gwenyth gasped at the sensation. She felt filled in every way, somehow necessary and complete. 'Twas wondrous!

Then Aric began moving. Slowly at first, the length of him caressed her inside. Sensation gathered, like a weight pressing low into her belly.

He quickly gathered speed, each long, slow stroke a glide, a nudge, a subtle demand for more. Her own need urged her to meet his thrusts, one after the other, then again. A low moan tore from his throat that vibrated deep within her.

Yet still, she needed more.

Fingernails seeping into the skin of his shoulders, she dragged them down the length of his back, low, into his hips, as if she could take him entirely within her. A foolish wish, but somehow she needed it. She cried out.

He lifted his mouth from the damp crook of her neck. "You make it hard to be gentle."

At any other time, she would have smiled at his breathlessness. Now she ached too badly. "Don't."

His gaze flashed across her face for a single heart-stopping moment.

Then he ignited.

In long, powerful strokes, he claimed her. A continuous stream of fast surges, frictioned withdrawals, then the heat of his return, filling her, filling her—seeming to make her whole.

The clenching in her belly intensified until she lost her breath—her very mind—and shattered in his arms for a second time this night. As before, liquid satisfaction made a wondrous curl through her veins, only heightening when he cried out her name and, incredibly, stiffened further within her before finding his own pleasure.

Finally, Aric looked at her, eyes lazily half-closed, breathing still deep and hard. Her heart caught in her chest. She felt him still within her, smaller now but still warm, still a comfort.

"Damnation, little dragon."

Despite the curse, he seemed well pleased. The thought warmed her down to her toes. This part of the wifely role she would definitely relish in the nights to come.

Sweat dotted his brow, and she pushed away the tawny hair laying there, opening his flushed face up for her gaze.

He dropped a quick kiss on her mouth in return. "I should have known."

"Known?" Had she misread him? Had he not been pleased?

"Aye, that you would be a demanding minx." Then he smiled.

"And this is cause for complaint?" she asked saucily.

He laughed, then rolled to his side, taking her with him. "Never."

* * * *

Aric woke to sunlight bright in the chamber. He stretched and groaned, scenting Gwenyth's soft fragrance and the mingled smells of their passion. By the saints, he could scarce remember a night in which he had slept better. Peaceful dreamless sleep, too.

He had his wife to thank for that.

With a smile, he rolled over to find her in the bed. Aric found himself alone instead. He frowned. Aye, 'twas late, but certainly she didn't have so many duties that she must be up with the dawn.

Damnation! He wanted to possess her lush body again. Indeed, he had meant to during the night's small hours, but so sound had been his sleep, he had not awakened to take her in his arms again. Regret doured his mood. His sigh became a smile when he realized that Gwenyth was his to nibble, savor, or devour at will. No more nights of aching hell as he had endured back at the cottage, no more wondering if he would ever persuade her to warm his bed. Now that she had finally consented to become his wife in the most intimate of ways, well…

And why had she suddenly done that?

Why indeed? What had changed from their days together at the cottage?

Aric sat up in bed and stared at the tapestry-covered wall, as if it could provide the answers he sought. Well, Gwenyth had said she'd missed him.

Again, why? She had never wanted him when they first wed, and 'twasn't as if she had been afflicted by some notion of love inspired by song or poem. Even if he would engage in either of those activities, he had not been here to do so. Until last night, she had fought their marriage and denied him husbandly rights.

Would that being here troubled you not, my husband, his memory heard her say once more.

Suddenly, Aric felt certain he knew why.

Northwell and an earldom. Wealth, status, land. Those things she had sought from marriage. Aye, she had not wanted to share his sheets when she believed him a hermit and a sorcerer. Now that she

146

knew he was a man of consequence, a man with ample funds and ties to the throne... Now she was willing to lay with him and cloud his mind with her sensuality. Gwenyth would likely have offered herself to him sooner if she had not been so angry with him for keeping his title and his past with Rowena from her.

It seemed so clear now.

Damn her for lying and for making him crave the very essence of her.

Pressing his hand to the dull ache in his head, Aric cursed. He could not deny that women everywhere bedded down with men for power and protection. They had few other options. And though it made little sense, the realization Gwenyth had done the same pleased him not.

Rowena, at least, had childhood hunger and the starvation of her mother to account for her behavior. And he had been more relieved than angered when she had wed his father.

Gwenyth's mercenary ways and deception stabbed him like a knife in the gut. Why, he could not say, except that he had somehow expected more of her. Or mayhap his gnawing ache for her simply wanted more satisfaction. 'Twas all foolish. After all, Gwenyth knew that continuing to refuse him his rights as a husband made her position as his wife a weak one, even in the eyes of the Church.

Aric eased back the sheets and stood. He grabbed his hose from the chair beside his bed and donned them, nearly tripping over a sleeping Dog in the process. Gwenyth's reasons were common enough, and his foolish displeasure was of no consequence. If Gwenyth wanted to whore herself out to secure her position as his wife, why should he not oblige her? Often.

CHAPTER TWELVE

Gwenyth gasped in shock as Aric rolled her to her stomach in their big bed and covered her body with his. The breadth of his chest seared her shoulders, her back. The insistent length of his manhood glided down her buttocks, to her womanly portal. Did he mean to take her like this? Did he mean to take her yet again this night?

"Tilt up to me, Gwenyth." His instruction came in a low voice, raspy against her neck.

Despite the shock, anticipation slid through her. Three times he had taken her during the night, each time wringing such pleasurable completion from her that she nearly cried.

Still, this night seemed different than the last, when they had first shared this bed and their bodies. Last night there had been tenderness, even a bit of laughter. Tonight she sensed something different. He seemed remote and unyielding, as if a part of him were not there with her. Though his scent and voice remained the same, something in his touch, in his gaze bespoke an emotion that put her ill at ease. Displeasure? Nay, he had also found completion, and she could not mistake his groans and the passionate desperation in his hands. Anger? Gwenyth frowned. Aye, perhaps that. Aric was tight-lipped and more disinclined than normal to talk. Warmth seemed absent from his deliberate stare.

And he had yet to kiss her tonight.

Without a word, Aric fit his hand beneath her belly and tilted her up to him. An instant later, she felt his fingers clasp her pleasure center as he buried his length inside her.

Again, she gasped, this time in a wash of desire.

How could a mating that seemed something like a stallion and his mare excite her? Yet it did, his breath upon her neck, fanning her cheek. The tips of his fingers toying with the stiff bud of her need. And the thick length filling every bit of space within her until she felt near bursting.

But the desire filled more than her body. It seemed to reach somewhere into her heart, and she responded to him with all the joy in it, hoping he would let the warmth soothe him.

Then he began thrusting, sweeping her up into a mating dark and needy, strong and ravenous. Within minutes, she felt the crest breaking upon her, building, building.

"Aric…" she moaned, then cried out in satisfaction. "Aric!"

As she pulsed within, he, too, found release with a last hard thrust and a groan.

Suddenly, he was gone from her body. Gone from their bed. Startled, she rolled over and watched as he turned his back to her and quietly dressed.

Again, she frowned. What could be so wrong? Nay, he did not want to live here. And aye, he and Stephen had fought again yesterday over Northwell's raising of an army for King Richard. But whatever disturbed Aric tonight, whether displeasure or anger, seemed directed at her alone.

She covered herself with the sheet. "Aric, is all well?"

"Well enough," he said as he threw a tunic over his head and marched out of the chamber.

As he closed the door with a quiet click, Gwenyth frowned, then settled back against the bed. Had he really gone? Had he really taken her body so briskly, then left without a word?

Indeed.

Was such normal?

Uneasy, Gwenyth rose herself and dressed for the day. The sound of surf against the rocks outside Northwell's walls was a fine accompaniment to her uncertain mood.

What did you expect? she asked herself. Aric behaved much as Aunt Welsa had described a man would. Yet last night was the first time he had done so. Never once since their marriage had he seemed so unwilling to speak with her, so unwilling to share anything. Except flesh.

Still, she wanted more—his embrace, his tender gaze, his

149

concern and laughter. Where had they all gone?

Gwenyth crossed her arms over her chest, as if she could hold back the wistful ache that flooded her. It was impossible. She wanted the warmth in Aric's eyes once more, longed for their conversation. She needed to believe he shared a bed with her because he desired *her*. Last night, he had been a thorough lover, but somehow he left her with the feeling she might have been anyone, her identity of no consequence to him.

While a foolish part of her wanted to claim his heart.

Once, back at his cottage, he had eased her distress over her family's desertion, over Nellwyn's superior life. Now he caused her torment.

Aye, but those first days of their marriage were gone, replaced by politics, family, and daily duties. As an important earl, he had little time to spend at her side during the day. Such significance was a good part of what she had wanted in a husband, what she had wished of Aric when they wed. Indeed, Nellwyn had been much impressed by Aric's titles and holdings, based on the letter she had received that very morn. So why did she feel a sense of wretched melancholy?

Sighing, Gwenyth fled the chamber—and their rumpled bed—to break her fast. She felt no surprise to learn that her husband had left the castle to ride out for the day. He did that frequently enough.

She sat in the great hall, assuming her place in the chair beside Aric's empty one. Few milled about the fine room, Aric having taken several of the men with him. The others remained behind for training, led by Lord Stephen.

Without enthusiasm, she bit into a hunk of bread just delivered by a kitchen maid and washed it down with a thin wine.

The great hall pleased her. Warmed from the morning's chill by resplendent tapestries and the crackling roar of an orange-hot fire, Gwenyth settled into her chair and wished she knew what troubled Aric.

An instant later, Rowena sauntered into the room, looking deceptively waifish in a dress of delicate pink. Gwenyth would have ignored the other woman, who still played the mistress's role in the castle, but Rowena settled beside her. When Gwenyth made to leave, the other woman placed a hand over her arm to stay her.

"What do you seek, Rowena?"

The blond waif helped herself to a hunk of bread and a bit of cold duck before she spoke. "Though you are Aric's wife, Lady Gwenyth, do not believe you alone will share his bed."

Gwenyth gasped at such direct conversation. Rowena's tone held no spite or malice, no taunting. She'd spoken as if relating mere fact, like the sun rising in the east.

Blinking several times to clear the shock, Gwenyth was finally able to speak. "I assure you, I keep Aric much too busy to seek you out."

Rowena shrugged as if it were no consequence. "He will tire of you. Aric is a...vigorous man, and thankfully not one whose heart can be touched. Soon, he will harbor no tendency for you and demand you leave his chamber."

"And you believe he harbors a tendency for you, you mutton-eyed hoyden?" Gwenyth asked sharply.

The other woman paused thoughtfully. "Aric and I, we understand one another. I accommodate his healthy male drives, and in return, he allows me to remain here and in control."

"What of Stephen?"

"He is a child. You and I both know that."

Gwenyth gaped at the woman, almost feeling sorry for Aric's younger brother. "A child whose bed you have shared."

Rowena lifted a bony shoulder as if that fact had no bearing. "Aric has returned to become Earl of Belford once more."

She tried to remember Rowena's near starvation and find her Christian charity. She fell sadly short. "Rowena, I intend to become the mistress of my husband and his home. I will see that you do not starve, but you need not try to seduce my husband just to ensure your next meal comes."

With a faint smile, Rowena rose. "I intend to ensure my own fate. You shall forgive me if I choose not to believe the word of a rival."

Then Rowena was gone.

Gwenyth stared at the empty space after her and willed herself to calm the trembles in her belly. Could Rowena succeed? With Aric in his current state, as if the comfort of one woman over the other mattered not, she feared the woman could—and perhaps seduce Aric away from whatever fragile bond she had once shared with him.

* * * *

Aric lay next to a sleeping Gwenyth a week later, aching to touch her—yet loath to do so. 'Twas a bitter draught to swallow that his wife coveted his title enough to invite his touch. Aye, she had accepted him into her body, despite the many ways in which he had tried to take her, to shock her in the past six nights. He hardly knew whether he should be relieved or distressed that she responded to his lovemaking with such abandon.

More perplexing, why had every encounter with her—except that perfect first—left him with vague dissatisfaction? Because he took her but did not taste her. He lay with her but did not see her. He held himself away from her, bedding her without truly feeling her. He had swived her like he would any wench.

Such had led to a frustration he could scarce understand.

She did not turn him away—ever. Despite the fact he had longed for this very access to her body when they had lived at the cottage, now he found it bitter.

Even worse, Rowena had begun her onslaught, as he had dreaded. At least once a day, she found some reason to speak with him, in private. She invented reasons to touch him. Every day, she told him in her calm, intelligent voice that she desired his presence back in her bed. Nay, that she desired her own presence in his big tester bed while Gwenyth languished elsewhere.

For the woman he had almost wed, he felt not a stirring of desire. She inspired naught more than irritation. And all the while, he could think of little else but bedding Gwenyth until they neither could think nor breathe.

By the saints, what ailed him?

He glanced across the massive bed until his gaze rested on Gwenyth, the black tumble of her hair, the sooty lashes making delicate crescents upon her cheeks, the pert nose and wide mouth of sinful red, his mother's ruby glinting upon her perfect skin.

This must cease! He refused to disturb his pittance of harmony with this haunting disquiet her nearness brought. Soon enough, whatever troubled him would pass, and he would bed her again with satisfaction, forgetting peacefully that she wanted him only for his wealth and power. He would soon remember she did only what women must in a man's world to survive.

Until then, he was better off to leave her be.

He rolled away, seeking sleep that offered nothing but dreams of dead children and the tangled lure of Gwenyth's embrace.

* * * *

The next two weeks slid by slowly, as the shimmering heat drew closer to an oppressive August. Temperatures climbed, and the castlefolks' children took to frolicking about with Dog as dark neared.

And Aric no longer shared their bed.

After that last distant morn he had taken her in silence, then leapt from the bed as if she had scalded him, he had not touched her once. Indeed, he often slept in the great hall with the rest of his soldiers, and Gwenyth knew people were beginning to gossip.

Awakening again to an empty bed, Gwenyth donned her clothes with heavy hands and meandered downstairs.

Inside the great hall, Rowena chastised a kitchen maid for her idleness, then sent the sniveling girl on her way. Gwenyth resolved to check on the girl later. For even if her skills about the castle weren't needed, the servants had made it clear they appreciated her occasional kindness and advice. Knowing they liked her and needed her in their own way improved her spirits.

Rowena always dragged them back down.

Determined to ignore the other woman, Gwenyth made her way to the raised dais and sat, not looking at the remnants of the morning meal on the table before her.

The silence in the room deafened her. She knew Rowena watched her and wanted nothing more than to pretend the woman was of no matter, not worth her gaze.

Gwenyth had never been good at lying to herself.

She gazed up. The triumph on Rowena's pale face sent a shock of rage and denial through Gwenyth. Bristling braies! What should she do? Rowena's look said Aric now found his manly comfort between her skinny thighs. How could the coxcomb want a woman so lacking in heart?

The resulting vision of her husband and his former lover together made her want to shrink inside herself, even as she longed to punish Rowena, somehow humiliate her and force her to leave the castle.

Aye, she wanted to confront her wayward husband as well. But on the rare days he did linger within Northwell's walls, he spared no words for her—only disquieting stares that made her heart ache in a way she could scarce understand.

A moment later, Stephen entered the room. His forlorn gaze, full of pent-up longing, rested on Rowena and lingered. Gwenyth prayed she did not wear her sentiments so openly within her eyes.

"Rowena, my darling," Stephen begged. "Please sit with me—"

"I've no time. My duties await."

With that, the waspish waif swept from the room, head held at a regal angle upon her graceful neck.

Gwenyth turned her gaze on Stephen. His expression seemed nothing short of dejected. Unshed tears glittered in his brown eyes.

Unfortunately, she knew very much how the boy felt and couldn't resist making her way to his side to place a comforting hand upon his shoulder.

He jerked away from her. Gwenyth stared up at him in surprise.

"'Tis your fault! Why can you not keep Aric in your bed and out of Rowena's?"

Gwenyth's heart shattered at his question. She felt tears sting her own eyes. "I have tried! I vow I have, but any more…'tis as if he sees me not at all."

Stephen loosed a crude curse that made Gwenyth wince.

"You are certain they share a bed again?" she asked, not sure she wished to know the answer.

"She left my bed over a fortnight ago. Rowena is not a woman who enjoys being alone. To whom else would she go?"

Whom else, indeed? Gwenyth closed her eyes, absorbing the pain of Stephen's observations. God's nightgown, she hated to believe Aric would prefer the woman who had betrayed him with his own father, desire the woman who cared only for his power and position. But he did. For her familiarity? Her elegant aloofness?

Mayhap Rowena pleased Aric as a man in ways that Gwenyth, in her inexperience, could not. Though Gwenyth thought she had satisfied his needs, clearly she had been mistaken.

By damned, what was she to do?

Ideas raced through her, one discarded as quickly as the next. Seduce Aric? Gwenyth rolled her eyes. What did she know of that?

Next to naught. Perhaps confront him? 'Twas likely he would do no more than laugh at her. She sighed, determined to avoid such embarrassment. Well, then, debauch his naked person in sleep? By the moon and the stars, that reeked of desperation. She paced. No matter the means, Gwenyth knew she must make him see her as a woman, as his *wife*.

She turned to Stephen. "Tonight, after we sup, you must engage Rowena, occupy her."

He frowned, his boyish eyes reflecting confusion. How sad that his loins and heart should be so tangled with an icy wench, one who had bedded both his father and older brother—all to maintain her position, her existence.

"What will you do?" he asked finally.

What, indeed? "Pray for strength."

* * * *

Neither Aric nor Rowena appeared at supper. Gwenyth felt their absences acutely as a sharp pain embedded in her chest. She picked at her meal, as did Stephen farther down the lord's table. All around them, castle servants and Aric's knights sent her stares ranging from soft pity to hot suggestion.

All made her want to scream.

Enough! She would find them now in their lovers' glen and stop them...somehow.

Rising, Gwenyth leaned toward her brother-in-law and patted his shoulder. He looked up at her with sorrowful eyes, which quickly became hopeful pools of brown.

She let that—and her anger—fortify her as she left the great hall to find her husband and his wench of a lover.

Why his having a leman should disturb her, she did not know. Climbing the stairs to the solar, Gwenyth knew 'twas not as if she was devoted to him. Her heart did not pine for him. Did it? Nay. Such foolishness made her frown. She simply did not wish to be ignored, to be the object of servants' sympathy and knights' speculation.

As she approached the solar, which contained their bedchamber, Gwenyth found herself wishing with each beat of her heart that she would find it empty.

Such was not the case.

Seeing the door ajar, she entered the series of rooms without a sound. Thankfully, the bed lay empty.

But she heard the murmur of Rowena's voice, followed by the rumble of Aric's, behind the treasury door.

Damn them both!

Gwenyth clenched her fists as anger assailed her in hot waves that urged her to recklessness. The pain beneath prodded her as well. If they wished to fornicate, they would not do so in her rooms, so near her bed!

She marched past the large tester, past the cool, blackened hearth and trestle table, until she reached the door. Upon taking the latch in her hand, she yanked the heavy wooden door open.

Aric and Rowena stood inside alone. Together.

Nay, they were not taking a tumble at the moment, but Rowena's gown revealed enough breast to tempt a holy man. The wench had her hand upon Aric's shoulder. She leaned into him, inviting him. By the moon and stars, he did not look to be declining her enticement, not with his head bent toward her and some taut expression on his face.

The guilty pair looked up at her with surprise. Rowena sent her a faint smile and a shrug. Aric's expression showed nothing.

Gwenyth felt like exploding.

She stalked forward and grabbed Rowena by the arm. "Out!"

Rowena tried to break free. Gwenyth gripped tighter, refusing to let the bony bitch get the best of her.

"Aric and I are simply…talking," Rowena protested, though without much force.

Resisting the urge to put her hands around Rowena's neck and squeeze, Gwenyth gave the woman's arm a good yank and led her toward the door. "I should hardly care if you elected to lift your skirts and hump a butter churn, you milk-livered strumpet. But whatever you're about, you will not do it here!"

Though Rowena resisted being dragged out of the treasury and through the bedchamber, it did little good. Within moments, she gave the smaller woman a shove into the hall, slammed the door, and barred it against further entry.

Then she turned to her errant husband, hands on her hips, poised for battle.

He stood there with a smile.

Oh, how he must like this. He probably thought her jealous. The swine.

"A butter churn?" he asked. "'Twould hurt a mite, I fear."

"And 'tis clear you care, you pox-mettled rogue. Saints thunder upon us if Rowena should bruise the flesh you choose to plough."

Aric frowned, his face a fine imitation of confusion. She did not believe it for an instant. Hadn't Aunt Welsa always said men would lie to any woman for or about sex?

"What?" He glared at her.

Gwenyth cast her gaze upward, striving for patience. But she could find none this eve.

She let out a frustrated groan. "I see it suits you to pretend innocence, you urchin-snouted lewdster. Very well. What I cannot understand is why you sniff after her skirts. Have I lately denied you *any* husbandly demand you have made upon me? Nay. In sharing your bed, have I ever said nay to anything you have wished of me, of my body? Not once."

His silver eyes turned flat, icy. "As you say, not once."

A muscle worked at the side of his jaw, and his large body turned tense. What had he to be angry about? That she had broken up his tryst with the scrawny harlot, most like.

Her temper rose another notch, until she thought anger would burst from the top of her head.

"I scarce understand—" She broke off, too furious to find words. "If you wish to bed a wench who wants you only for your money and title, so be it, you ill-bred idlehead!"

With that, she turned for the door, determined to leave before he could see the tears threatening her eyes.

As she reached for the latch, one of Aric's huge hands clamped around her wrist and dragged her back to him, flush against the length of his massive body. His fingers twisted in her hair, and with them, he forced her gaze up to the tense lines and narrowed eyes in his face.

"Aye. So be it," he growled.

Then his mouth seized hers.

CHAPTER THIRTEEN

Aric could scarce believe Gwenyth accused Rowena of her own crime. Rowena, at least, had never pretended desire or affection for him. She had let it be known that she shared her delicate beauty in exchange for the security of shelter and food.

Fiery Gwenyth, on the other hand, pretended warmth and want and caring, so that a man felt betrayed by the truth she sought to veil in lust. 'Twas madness! The kind for which physicians bled men to cure them. Aric hardly knew whether to shout at Gwenyth or swive her senseless.

For the moment, he gripped her face between his hands and took her lips, even as he grappled to accept her brazenness.

Then her mouth parted beneath his. He hardened instantly.

Damnation. Like the veriest of witches, her sweet kiss cast a spell over his good sense. And he let it, for now he knew what she was about. Now he would not be tempted to believe that she actually cared for any comfort but her own.

But that did not stop him from wanting to believe it.

With a growl, Aric tore his mouth from hers, sides heaving with the effort to inhale air, clear his mind of her sweet female scent. 'Twas foolishness, she leading him to demise, him following so willingly!

Slowly, she opened her eyes, looking deliciously dazed.

"Aric," she called like a siren, her voice a breathy whisper.

She swayed toward him, and her breast brushed his palm. Her lush mouth had swollen tender and red from his kiss. Aric felt the tight ache for her pulse deep in his groin.

Why could he not want Rowena? Her exchange was simple, like a merchant's trade, as was his wife's. But Gwenyth inflamed him, seemed to ask for his soul, then have no notion why he should resist. He could not understand such himself.

Aric looked down into the bottomless blue depths of Gwenyth's passion-hazed eyes, the flush that pinkened her cheeks, her shoulders, the swells of her breasts. Her mouth seemed to beg the return of his.

Gnashing his teeth, he reached out and gripped her arms, searching within his mettle for restraint, praying for it.

His prayers were in vain.

Fury and lust twined inside him with an emotion so foreign he could not name it. Dark and irresistible, the feeling compelled him to touch her, taste her as he had not since the first night he had taken her.

With a groan, he gave in, need pounding, pounding mercilessly within him.

He swept her against his body, one large hand slipping beneath her buttocks to hoist her against him. With it, he lifted her from the carpet beneath and carried her to the big tester bed. When he sat her upon it, she stared up at him with enormous eyes, depths deepening with heavy-lidded expectation.

In that moment, he vowed she would feel desire—genuine and powerful—before he would give in to his own longing.

Grabbing fistfuls of his black woolen tunic in his hands, he jerked the garment over his head with a vicious yank. Her eyes widened as they made their way from his face, to his torso...and lower.

Needing surcease from his ache, he twined his fingers in her hair again and possessed her mouth in a single sweep, lips clinging, tongue claiming. She responded with a high-pitched catch of breath and a silent invitation into the honeyed depths of her mouth.

He plundered, hoping 'twould be enough. As he ended that kiss only to begin another, he wondered if he would ever have enough of her.

The thought angered him more.

Aric leaned into her, until she lay back on the mattress, looking temptingly muddled. His mouth made its way to the swells of her breasts, warm with a flush. For a moment, he paused to palm the weight of her flesh, test the hardness of their tips.

As she cried out, he tore into the embroidered belt about her small waist and flung it to one side with a grunt. About her, the purple outer gown fell to each side, revealing the silky white smock beneath. None too gently, he thrust the gown off her shoulders and tossed it to the far side of the bed.

He cast a quick glance at her face, only to find her breathing labored, her moist lips parted, and her eyes seductively watchful.

Upon stealing a quick kiss from her lush mouth, Aric moved down with determination to snare the rest of her treasures.

Quickly, he reached her feet and extracted her leather shoes, then threw them over his shoulder in haste. With both hands, he found the hem of her chemise and pushed it up from her ankles, past the garters holding up her woolen stockings, above milky thighs beginning to part in enticement.

Aric groaned and swept his palm across her flat belly as he exposed it. Farther up he went, cupping one breast as he gave the garment a final tug over her head.

Finally, with the exception of her stockings and the ruby pendant, she lay gloriously naked, from the pert button of her nose to the dark thatch of hair guarding her femininity. And for a moment, he did naught but stare. That mystery feeling churned within him as he considered all the different ways in which to give her blinding pleasure, to prove he would not be toyed with.

As wanton ideas tripped over one another in his head, begging for fruition, he began to sweat.

Gwenyth, who had been surprisingly silent for a time, finally spoke. "Aric?"

Did she think he would back away now? Aye, he realized as she held her arms up to him in invitation.

Passion and purpose mated in his stomach, and he whispered, "Not yet."

Without warning, he took hold of her beneath the knee and drew her down until her legs dangled over the mattress's edge.

"Aric?" Her curiosity almost masked her alarm. Almost.

"Not now."

Then he knelt beside the bed and took her thighs in his hands. He placed one on each shoulder. Gwenyth tensed as he leaned closer, and he exhaled so she might feel his breath upon her nether curls. She gasped and stiffened, the muscles of her thighs clenching in his hands.

"Aric, may-mayhap you should leave me be."

"Never," he croaked. "I intend for you to wonder if I've become a permanent part of you."

Before she could protest again, Aric parted her with a finger. Already she was wet with want, and her moan did naught to disguise her desire.

Which only inflamed his.

Fighting the vicious need tightening in his loins, Aric bent his head to her and sampled her honeyed musk. The scent of her surrounded him, the taste of her invaded him, as the tip of his tongue toyed with her pleasure center until it turned from firm to stiff and swollen. Whirling it about, he drew it into his mouth with a hard suck. Gwenyth bucked beneath him, grabbing handfuls of his sheets in her fists. With firm hands at her hips, he held her in place against his mouth.

"Aric!" she cried.

She neared a peak. He felt it in her tense body, heard such in her voice. He drew away, letting his mouth trail damp kisses upon her thighs.

"Nay," she protested as she lifted herself to him in offering, the musk of her arousal tingeing the air.

He smiled as he used a finger to beguile her flesh again.

Gwenyth's breath came hard. Her eyes squeezed shut as if she were fighting to control the hunger in her body. Aric intended she never have that chance.

Lowering his mouth to her once more, he dragged the rasp of his tongue over her pleasure center. She writhed against him desperately as he did it again, lapping her like a cat.

She let loose a throaty cry of satisfaction as she stiffened against his touch, splintered around him. Aric felt her hips, her very woman's flesh quiver as he drew out her release to the gasping end.

He moved to lie beside his wife and peer at her. For a long moment, she lay upon his sheets, eyes closed, face provocatively flushed, breath quick and jagged.

Then her eyes drifted open, shockingly blue, sexual, determined.

Gwenyth sat up and leaned over him with resolute motions. Aric swallowed as he tried to rise, but his stubborn bride held him in place and moved her hands over his chest, the flat of his belly...then lower. A moment later, she all but ripped off his hose and threw them to the stone floor.

Eyes glittering with challenge, Gwenyth claimed the aching length of him with a tight grip. Against his will, he groaned, needing her beneath him, needing to feel her desire. Aric sat up so he might ease her to the mattress and claim her body.

Instead, Gwenyth pushed him back down and closed her mouth around him.

Unbelievable sensation filled him. Her tongue played over his tip, and the fluid warmth of her mouth surrounded him.

"Dear God." The groan tore from his throat.

She suckled and laved him, nipped and kissed him with sweet lips. His desire tightened like a bowstring. Though he tried to fight it off, a wave of satisfaction rushed toward him as she swirled her tongue around him once more.

With a hissed curse, he gripped her arms and pushed her to her back. Aric stared at her—hard.

He was dangerously aroused, and judging from the wide-eyed look of her anxious blue gaze, she knew it. He took a deep breath, then smiled again. She swallowed nervously.

With a brush of his hand upon her thigh and a graze of his tongue upon her nipple, he mounted her. Gwenyth wrapped her arms around him hesitantly. Beneath him, she parted her legs so slowly Aric thought he would die waiting for her.

Once Gwenyth was open, waiting beneath him, Aric entered her in one smooth thrust. And stopped. Within moments, she wriggled beneath him, urging him on. He refused to be rushed.

"Aric..." she called to him.

Settling his lips against her neck, he whispered, "I want you to feel me deep inside you. I want you to wonder where I end and you begin."

He thrust. She cried out.

Then he settled in for a long, slow ride.

Deeply, he delved into her rhythmically and greedily, plunging, plundering, melding their bodies. Beneath him, she writhed, clutching at the tense length of his back, his buttocks, as provocative moans slipped from her throat, urging him on.

"More," she called on a jagged breath.

"In time," he answered, struggling to cage his teetering passion.

"Now!" she demanded.

And despite his ravenous, reckless pleasure, he held on, knowing slowly built pleasure always burst the brightest.

As if she could tolerate no more, she bucked hard beneath him as he filled her in hot, smooth strokes. Sweat dampened his temples, and he prayed he could last against the impossible pleasure rushing up to claim him. He held his breath, grinding against her, sheathed completely within her tight, hungry body.

Then Gwenyth turned rigid, and with a toss of her dark head, screamed her satisfaction. Aric had no time for triumph, as she pulsed around him in gripping contractions, violently stripping him of control.

He buried his face in her neck, breathing her in, as the arousal turned thick with sharp satisfaction. As if ripped from his body, the peak exploded within him, seeming to last a small eternity, staggering him. He felt as if he emptied all of himself into her: seed, blood, soul. It was both perfect and frightening.

Gwenyth's damp lush clung to him, limbs tangling, skin slick. He brushed a damp tress from her cheek and eased his mouth to hers on a sigh. He felt the wetness of her tears on his fingertips. His anger began to dissipate. A quick glance seemed to show she cried in release, not pain. Still, he could not stop his next words.

"I'm sorry."

She sent him a weary frown. "Why? For making me feel like hot butter?"

He smiled softly. "I meant not to hurt you."

Her slow, husky laugh dashed up his spine. "I should always be in such pain."

Nuzzling her ear, he whispered, "Aye, you should."

* * * *

Aric awoke to the feel of Gwenyth's soft lips upon his. He sent her a sleepy smile and stretched, pleased to hear her happy giggle. After brushing a long, glossy strand of hair from her face, he settled his hands on her face and smacked a kiss on her mouth. A new contentment, never before felt, curled through him in languid warmth. Aye, he could get used to this each morn.

163

Mayhap he had been wrong about Gwenyth and her greed. Last night, she had given him more than her body. 'Twas as if she had invited him into her very essence with each touch. Afterward, she'd cried in his arms and let him hold her while sleep overcame her. The openness of her actions made him feel contrite. He had judged her against his own experience with Rowena. And though he knew not what they were, he wondered if Gwenyth had motives other than avarice for sharing his bed. After all, 'twas only natural that she should want a home and a secure future.

She leaned over him, resting her chin upon his chest. "My, such a frown you wear. What could be so serious on this lovely morn?"

How should he answer? He chose evasion. "All manner of castle duties have to be done this day."

Gwenyth hesitated. "I am willing—and trained—to help you. I swear I would make a fine chatelaine, if you would but give me a chance."

Chatelaine. Aric felt his warm content evaporate, replaced by disbelief. He swallowed, trying to force suspicion down. Again and again, it came up, and with it a healthy dose of anger.

So Gwenyth, who lay warm and naked in his bed, chose this moment to ask for the command of the castle's household, when he was happy and well sated. What ironic timing.

Her scheming should not matter, given the fact women wed wealthy men for home and hearth. She did only what Rowena had, what his own mother probably had.

Still, he found her conduct disturbing for reasons he could not fathom.

Quickly, her plan became more clear: Goad him into sharing her bed, satisfy him until he felt near brainless, then seize the power she desired. Simple but clever. And nearly effective.

Rolling away, he set her aside and turned his back to her.

Why did he want to believe in her goodness, her caring so badly? Normally, he was no woman's fool. With Gwenyth, he seemed unable to see through her ploys until she broadsided him with demands. How had she so afflicted his mind? Mayhap he should accuse her of sorcery.

"Aric, I would be a good chatelaine," she said into his silence.

He told himself he did not care, but fury and mistrust railed at him. And something else within refused to believe her mercenary and urged him to give her what she sought.

What, and be her fool? Never. Caring too much for a woman who did naught but secure her position as his lady was unacceptable.

With short, economical motions, he rose and dressed, avoiding her hopeful, scheming face by watching Dog snore beside the hearth.

"Aric?"

"Nay." He risked a glance at her.

Her smiling face fell. "Your people seem to like and respect me. I enjoy tending to your home and helping you. Truly, I would do a fine job."

With her tenacity, he was certain of it. But he was not going to reward Gwenyth's whoring of her body with the very position she desired. He was not going to prove himself her personal jester, dimwitted and drugged by the feel of her.

"Rowena fills that role well enough. Leave it alone."

Gwenyth rose to her knees on the mattress, yanking the white sheet against her for covering. He tried not to notice her saucy dark curls brushing the white tips of her shoulders, nipping at the narrow curve of her waist.

Too late.

Aric turned away, only to have Gwenyth grab the back of his tunic and prevent his departure. Against his will, he sensed her light dewy-grassed scent. Something inside him stirred with a pain he wanted to deny. He glared over his shoulder at her.

"Rowena is not your wife, you buffoon. I am. I live with you, I share your bed, I bear your name. I am your wife in every respect but this one. Why? Do you think so lowly of me, or so highly of her?"

"Gwenyth," he growled in warning, crossing his arms over his chest. "I've no time to talk of this now. The castle is not suffering from her leadership."

"It is! She misuses resources and browbeats servants until they fear her."

He shot her a pointed glare. Her accusations were serious, but he had never heard the like from another. "You have made your displeasure with Rowena's presence here well known. And I—"

"And you, my lord, have made your appreciation of her presence quite known!"

With that, she wrapped the sheet around her and stumbled for the door.

165

He stopped her flight with a booted foot on the sheet. She cursed, maintaining her tentative hold on the white drape.

"What mean you by that?"

Gwenyth rolled her eyes. "As if you haven't a clue? Must I write you a poem? 'Ode to the Whore's Skinny Thighs.' How does that sound?"

"Bitter. You will not badger me into changing my mind. Leave it alone."

"Leave it alone? Nay, I shall leave you alone! Do not attempt to touch, kiss me, cajole me, smile at me, talk to me, share a room—or a bed—with me. If you choose Rowena as your chatelaine, you can choose her for those other things as well."

To Aric's shock, Gwenyth spat a vile oath at him and dropped the sheet shielding her nudity. He caught only a glimpse of her swinging hips and pale buttocks before she sauntered out of the room.

CHAPTER FOURTEEN

A fortnight passed before Gwenyth spoke a word to him. Aric minded not for the first day or two. His anger over her attempts to control him with his own lust kept his ire bubbling and his resolve bolstered.

Within a few days, Rowena realized he and Gwenyth not only shared no bed but no words, either. The woman's attempts to seduce him, often in the middle of the night, resulted in little more than sleepless irritation and a growl from Dog. Why did Rowena refuse to understand he did not desire her, particularly after he had consistently spurned her for more than a sennight?

Squinting into the bright sunlight glowing over the bailey, Aric grunted in disgust and sheathed his sword as the other knights did. The motley collection of men all took a step back and eyed him with caution. Had he been that short of temper recently?

Aye, he supposed he had. The thought annoyed him more.

Sweat ran in rivulets down the cords of his neck, down his bare back and chest. He grimaced, knowing he needed a bath something fierce and that Rowena, not his wife, would volunteer to assist him.

He raked a hand through the damp, overlong strands of his hair. Damn Gwenyth. Why could she not accept the duties he had given her? Why had the wench never learned obedience? Hell's fury, why had she never tried?

And why did he want to see a smile replace that tight-mouthed frown she now wore?

Could only be because he was a dimwit, longing for a woman who wanted only his wealth and title, a woman destined to question, challenge, and infuriate him at every turn.

Rowena's milder manner suited him more. So why could he muster no interest in his once-betrothed despite her numerous blatant invitations?

Handing the rest of his battle gear to his waiting squire, Aric marched into the castle, ordered an ale and a bath, then charged up the stairs to his chamber.

Inside the door stood something of a miracle—Gwenyth clothed in naught but her chemise. Aric smiled suddenly as his stare grazed the narrow plane of her thinly clad back.

With a toss of his head, he dismissed the wench who had been serving as Gwenyth's lady's maid of late. When the girl departed without a word, Gwenyth turned, wearing that constant bothersome frown. She stiffened when she saw him, then dived for the bed—and the clean dress awaiting her.

Aric wrested the dress from the bed before she could reach it. He tossed it into a corner behind him. "I need a bath."

She gave him a contemptuous once-over. "So take one."

Ah, words from his stubborn wife. Progress at last. "I will need assistance."

Gwenyth's expression iced over. "I shall find Rowena for you."

'Twas clear she toyed with him. That fact lit a fire of anger within him. "Can you put Rowena from your mind?"

The dark arch of her brow rose sharply. "Can you put her from yours?"

Had the woman been paying attention at all of late? Aric's patience gave way. "*You* are my wife."

"A fact that clearly holds no meaning here."

Aric took the jab in stride. "Beginning tonight, it does. A wife assists her husband with his bath."

"A wife is usually the castle's chatelaine, as well—so you see, nothing ordinary happens here at Northwell."

Aric clenched his fist to quell his urge to touch her, to soothe her suddenly vulnerable expression. Aye, a man's wife usually was his chatelaine. Of course, most lords knew their wives married and bedded them for their wealth and did not mind such. 'Twas common practice. Morosely, he wondered why he could not accept the same from Gwenyth.

And why did his refusal to make her chatelaine seem to make her sad and furious in equal measures?

Before he could form a reply, the tub and ale arrived, along with a fleet of kitchen maids holding kettles of boiling water. Gwenyth used the opportunity to try to escape through the chamber's open door. Aric clamped his hand about her wrist and held tight. She shot him a venomous glare but said naught.

A tense silence ensued while the maids finished pouring the water. Aric felt her pale softness beneath his fingers, smelled her spring-like skin, sensed her pulse beating too quickly at her wrist.

Suddenly they were alone, shut off from the rest of the castle by the muted scraping of the wooden door against its stone portal.

He wanted to be near her, inside her, so badly. A barbed ache bit into his gut.

"Bathe me."

"Release me." Her voice shook.

"Gwenyth..." His voice softened. "We must talk."

"Of what? You have made your preferences clear."

Her flippant tone did not fool him, and her assumption that he desired Rowena incensed him. Did she not realize that what they shared in their marriage bed had been like naught he had ever known?

"Nay, but I plan to make them perfectly clear tonight."

Something wary entered Gwenyth's blue eyes before she cast him a false smile and looked to the door. "By all means, go. I think you will find Rowena in the great hall."

"By the saints, woman! Do you ever listen?"

"I always listen," she tossed back, indignant.

"What with, your feet? I want you to bathe me, *wife*. We will discuss this no more."

"Bathe yourself."

"When you are here to perform your wifely role? Nay."

Before she could protest further, Aric took her wrist in his hand and dragged her to the tub. He felt resistance in her body. The fair face he knew too well held rebellion.

"When I get in this tub, I expect you to remain by my side until the bath is complete. If you do not, I will put you in the tub with me."

Gwenyth's mouth tightened in displeasure.

"Tell me you listened with something besides yon toes."

"I heard you, you mewling, pig-mouthed—"

Aric shed his hose and stood before her, his hands on hips, completely naked. Her eyes widened.

She might find him mewling and pig-mouthed, he reflected, but Gwenyth was not immune to the sight of him. A definite factor in his favor.

Smiling, he eased into the hot water and handed her the soap and a cloth one of the maids had left on the trestle table.

That wariness was back in her eyes as she took the proffered items.

"Go on. Bathe me."

Still, Gwenyth moved not. He could see her mind racing as she frantically sought to avoid this task. He frowned. Why would she do such a thing? Given the opportunity to incite his lust and possibly forward her position in the castle because of it, why did she not try?

Finally, she loosed a piqued sigh and dipped the cloth in the water, beside his hip. Aric felt her knuckles graze his skin. She jerked her hand out of the water, pulling it up to her chest. Her gaze flew to his.

For long moments, Gwenyth did not move. Aric met her wide-eyed stare, hoping his lust for her did not show in his eyes.

"This bath will take very long indeed if you do not start," he teased.

Gwenyth nodded, then appeared to collect her wits. She thrust the cloth back into the water, not flinching when she grazed his thigh. Within moments, she had soaped the cloth and applied it to his back.

He bent forward to aid her cleansing. Her rhythmic strokes across his skin were thorough and relaxing—until he realized she was taking great pains to keep the cloth between her and his skin.

So his little dragon was uneasy. He smiled, anticipating the feel of her in his arms again this night.

"Gwenyth." He put a complaining note in his voice and shrugged away from her ministrations. "That cloth. 'Tis rough."

He tossed a scowl over his shoulder for effect. She looked down at the suspect scrap of worn linen and frowned.

"Nay, it is soft."

"Not to my back," he protested. "Set it aside."

"But—"

"Does my request distress you? If it does, I can bear the discomfort."

Gwenyth looked torn between keeping her distance and admitting he affected her.

"Nay," she said finally.

With a last lingering look, she set the cloth aside.

She took the soap between her hands and lathered them. Aric eased back into position and let her palms and fingers curl their way around his neck, soothe his shoulders, meander down his back. He tensed, anticipating her touch elsewhere.

With the delicacy of a sprite, she trickled water from her hands and down his skin, rinsing it in warm refreshment.

Sighing, he leaned back against the tub and awaited her next move. It came quickly. Her bathing became brisk, almost impersonal. She stared at nothing more than the far wall as she washed the dirt and sweat from his chest.

"Ouch!" He grimaced for effect. When she shot him a questioning glare, he answered, "The men and I trained particularly hard today and I am sore. Slowly, please."

Gritting her teeth, she placed her palms on his chest once more and glided them across his torso in sweeping circles.

Aric fought for control of his breath as his heart picked up speed. To have Gwenyth touch him again after long weeks without her... She flattened her palm over his tense abdomen, then flicked a fingertip upward, over his male nipples. He hissed in a sharp breath. By the saints, he could think of naught else but holding the fire in her body and soul within his arms and possessing her completely.

He sent a covert glance from beneath his lashes to Gwenyth's face. She had flushed a pretty pink, and he doubted the cooling water had much to do with it.

Holding back a grin, he decided to throw a little kindling onto the growing fire. He propped his leg on the edge of the tub. His knee nudged her breast. Water seeped from his skin to her smock, and soon he could see her taut nipple through the garment. He smothered a moan and reached for Gwenyth.

She jerked out of his grasp and tossed the soap into the water with a plunk.

171

"Gwenyth…" he groaned.

She turned away for a moment, then whirled back. Before he knew what she was about, she had poured an entire bucket of cool water over his head.

Sputtering, he cursed roundly and cleared the water from his eyes in time to see Gwenyth's smirk.

Then she stomped toward the door.

Aric jumped up, water splashing all around, and sprinted from the tub. Uncaring that he wore not a stitch, he grabbed her arm and turned her to face him.

"We are not done," he gritted out, trying to control his fury.

"If it's a tumble you seek, I shall find Rowena for you."

He frowned. Her references to Rowena were becoming tiresome. "Are you blind? 'Tis not Rowena I desire."

His wife raised a skeptical black brow. "Have you tired of her already, my lord? Is that why you seek me now—at least until you are ready for her again? Or am I merely handy, being so close?"

"What?" His mind spun. Did she still believe he would take to his bed a woman who had betrayed him with his own father and bedded his brother? Did Gwenyth still think he preferred Rowena's pale personality over her?

Gwenyth's nose turned red and her eyes glossy with tears.

"Do not dare pretend you know naught of what I say!"

She swiped her palm across her cheek, then balled it into a fist at her side. "If 'twas Rowena you sought, why did you touch me? If you merely wanted a woman, why me? How could you make me believe you—"

Tears ended her sentence. Aric gathered her against him. As his wet skin dampened her chemise, he felt the warmth of her flesh flow to him. She smelled like a spring garden, earthy and alive, and he ached to possess her as much as he yearned to soothe her.

"I have not touched Rowena in two years, since before she wed my father. And I do not want to touch her now."

Suspicion clouded her blue eyes, now the shade of midnight. "But I found you together in the treasury with your head bent to her and her arm—"

"We spoke of the accounts, of missing grain and stray chickens."

"But your face… It looked so tense." Confusion colored her

voice into a shadow of its usually robust pitch.

He sighed and took her face between his palms. "Aye, because she had accused you of thieving. And she angered me. I cannot deny she has sought my bed since we came to Northwell, but I have refused her."

Gwenyth's brow furrowed. Tears welled in her eyes, then spilled to her cheeks in fat drops that slid warmly beneath his fingers. Her pain made him ache. He felt despicable for inciting such sorrow, even if unintended.

"I…" She shook her head and bit her lip, trying to hold more tears at bay. "Then why do you allow her to stay? If not to be your leman, then why?"

Aric smoothed a soothing hand over Gwenyth's glossy tresses, marveling at the black silk that slid through his fingers. "Rowena has nowhere else to call home. She is a distant cousin to Edward IV's queen Elizabeth Woodvylle. When the queen's oldest son, the boy who should have been king, disappeared, Elizabeth feared the worst."

She had been all too right, Aric thought mournfully. And he had played a hand in ensuring the death of her other son, young Richard. He closed his eyes in recrimination and let icy guilt slide through him.

"I do not understand how the dowager queen's troubles affect Rowena."

He nodded, returning to the present, to the feel of his distraught wife. "Rowena's family was poor but well connected. To improve their position, her parents tried to aid the queen in an ill-fated plot to overthrow King Richard. Elizabeth remained safely in Westminster, where Richard knew he could not touch her without appearing a perfect villain. And he is already an unpopular king."

"Aye," she said, but her frown clearly showed confusion.

"So King Richard stripped Rowena's family of their lands and executed her father for treason. We were betrothed by then, and I was responsible for her. I brought her to Northwell."

"Then she wed your father?"

"For a time, aye. But my father was a practical man, above all else. He knew I hesitated in speaking vows with Rowena, who was growing impatient to be wed. My father, who had been without a wife for nigh on five years, liked the order of the household, the

173

warm meals, the castle so well tended. And I'm sure he wanted a beauteous woman warming his bed. So he wed her."

"Why did you hesitate in wedding Rowena?"

Her breathless query and hopeful eyes tugged at something in his chest.

He shrugged in answer. "She does not…intrigue me. She is without passion. I never had to guess what Rowena would do next."

"Even when she married your father?"

"Especially then. When she moved out of my chamber, I knew it would not be long before she moved into his. She knew I regretted asking her to wife."

Gwenyth frowned. "Then why did you ask her?"

His laugh was without mirth. "For much the same reason my father did. The great hall at one time could easily have passed for our pigs' pen. A houseful of warring men can hardly be bothered with cleanliness. At the time, Stephen was merely ten and six." Aric laughed again at the irony of his thoughts. "I thought he needed something of a mother."

Grimacing, Gwenyth stepped away. "So why is she your chatelaine now?'

Aric crossed his arms over his chest, barely conscious of the cool air on his naked skin. Gwenyth's tears had been real, and his belief she had manipulated him with her body had kept him from treating her with the honor due any wife. Regret hammered him.

"Because I was a fool, Gwenyth. In the morning, I will see you receive the keys and instruct the servants that they will take direction from you."

Elation brightened Gwenyth's eyes. "Truly?"

The unease once knotted in his stomach unraveled when he saw the pure joy on Gwenyth's face. Aric took her hand in his and brought it to his mouth for a kiss.

Gwenyth smiled at him through her tears. "For eight years, I have waited to be a lady again." She sniffled, then continued, "Uncle Bardrick and Aunt Welsa treated me like a servant, though I had been born a baron's daughter. And they always said they treated me as well as I deserved. I began to fear they were right."

Her tears fell in earnest. Their power, coupled with that of her words, hit Aric in the chest with the force of a battering ram. She would believe such drivel? Why had he failed to understand her needs sooner?

"Nay. Never—"

"If you hear a thing often enough, 'tis all too easy to believe," she explained with a grimace. "But then we wed. Aye, I was angry, at first. But soon I did not feel such deep loss for my family anymore. And now you have accepted me as your wife and chatelaine." She drew in a shaky breath. "I am truly, truly happy! 'Twas nothing but foolishness to doubt that marrying you was best for me."

And he had doubted her motives, all but accused her of greed. Fighting off an urge to chasten himself, Aric wiped the tears from her heated cheeks. He felt a warmth within that had little to do with the temperature, a sentiment he could not explain. Fondness, affection even. Desire, certainly. He drew her into his embrace.

"So you like me better than Sir Penley?"

Gwenyth laughed, a trickle of a sound like a shallow brook on soft earth. "He is comely enough, but if he does not know how to use his sword as you do, what good is he?"

At her sly grin, he laughed. Then she stepped fully against his naked length, still damp from his aborted bath. Smiling, she looped her arms around his neck and drew his mouth down to hers.

Aric accepted her kiss with greed, possessing her mouth completely in one sweep. He had never wanted a woman this way, with more than his body. Something tender within urged him to be near her—always. Since he rarely ignored instinct, Aric pulled her even closer.

"I could demonstrate again my prowess with a sword," he offered between heavy breaths.

Her own breathing was no less labored. "Aye. I may have forgotten."

"Never do that," he growled, then captured her mouth again, sinking into the flavor of her, the feel of her, so more vibrant than any woman in his memory.

In response, she moaned, her lips pliant against his, her tongue driving him quickly insane with a sensuous slide. That chemise had to come off. Now.

With a yank, Aric tried to pull the garment down her body. It resisted, hanging on one milky slope of her shoulder. With a good jerk and a tear, her arm was free, and the silk slid quickly down her body to the wooden floor. Against him, she shivered and kissed him with greater urgency.

Needing to touch her, Aric slid his fingers down her spine, grazed the curve of her buttocks, then drew her against him with force. She wrapped her legs around him in response.

"Touch me," she demanded against his damp mouth.

Aric never thought of refusing. He peeked across the room.

The bed was too far away.

Beside the trestle table, he remembered a chair. That would do—for now.

Inching back until he felt the seat against his knees, he eased into the chair. Gwenyth gasped as his staff made intimate contact with her.

She sent him an uncertain glance. "I know not—"

"Shhh." He brushed a dark lock of hair from her ivory cheek "I know. Your body knows. 'Twill be good."

Gwenyth nodded, her eyes expectant. Aric vowed not to disappoint her.

Supporting the small of her back with his hands, he urged her to arch. She did, beautifully. He eyed the pale curve of her throat, her delicate shoulders—and her breasts, so tempting beneath his mouth. Had this been any wench, he would have used the moment to suckle her breasts while ignoring the rest. But for some reason he could not place, Aric wanted more. He wanted all.

He kissed her neck, his teeth grazing her sensitive earlobe. She moaned an encouragement and gripped his arms with tense fingers. As he breathed his way down her shoulders, placing tiny kisses on her arms, he thumbed her nipples, so pink and taut. But when she edged closer, seeming to place her breast within a breath of his lips, he succumbed.

She tasted light and sweet and of woman. She tasted as he remembered, yet something was different. That he could not deny. It made her all the sweeter as he swirled his tongue around her stiff bud, feeling it taut between his lips. She wriggled on his lap in invitation.

The feel of her against him, slick and open, nearly undid him. Not wanting to waste another second, he lifted her hips until he felt himself poised at her entrance. He captured her lips with his own at the moment he surged inside her. She sighed into his mouth.

With a steady, sure pace, Aric filled her again and again. Sweat dampened his forehead, and he closed his eyes in bliss at this blessed union.

By the saints, how he had missed her. She felt like a hearth to him, warm, snug, familiar, welcome. Aric wanted nothing more than to burn within her, then rise from the ashes into the comfort of her warmth.

Then she gasped and clung to his neck. Gwenyth cried out, her body throbbing around him. Aric drowned in her honeyed satisfaction, then quickly found his own in a bright burst of light and hope and wonder.

Minutes passed before either moved more than the bit required to breathe. Gwenyth's soft length curled around him, her cheek resting on the top of his head. Aric nestled her closer, spreading absent kisses on her velvet shoulders.

Suddenly, he felt her shoulders shake and heard a stifled sob. Alarm drilled through him.

"What ails you, wife?"

No answer.

He set her back until he could see into her flushed, damp face. "Gwenyth, did I hurt you?"

She shook her head and drew in a deep breath. "You have made me happy, more than I would have believed. In every way. Not even Nellwyn could be happier."

She sank her fingers into his hair, brushing it away from his face. And she stared into his eyes, truly looked at him in a way he doubted any woman ever had.

"I am glad." His voice broke as he tried to decipher that look in her eyes.

"I love you," she whispered.

Aric stopped breathing.

Three words. Gwenyth needed no more than three words to stagger him completely.

In that moment, joy soared in his gut. His hands tightened on her waist, as if ensuring she would stay every day and prove those three words.

But what did she expect in return?

Worse, what if she learned what had driven him to the forest where they had met?

His joy became fear. How could he make her happy in the days to come?

"Gwenyth—"

"Say nothing now," she broke in, her face clouded with something he disliked. Regret? Uncertainty? "What I feel for you can be nothing else, and I merely wanted...you to know."

She tried to leave his lap. He held her tightly against him, keeping himself intimately entwined.

"You are like no other," he said, staring up into those hopeful blue eyes. Something tightened in his belly. "I am glad to have you as my wife. But..." He shook his head, looking for the words he needed. "Love comes when you know each other completely."

"I know your heart!"

Aric wished it were that simple, wished he had not spent most of his life warring and killing. Wished there were not a dead ten-year-old prince whom he'd helped to see slaughtered.

"Nay."

She had not seen the greed and ambition that had beat in his chest for nearly fourteen years since his uncle Warwick's death and the crown's seizure of Warwick Castle, a Neville holding for generations. She knew not how badly he wanted the family honor restored, that for a time he would have done—and had done—*anything* to have it all back.

"You are a good, kind man," she protested.

He tried not to laugh at the bitter irony. "If I told you of my past, you would shrink from me in horror, Gwenyth."

"Aric, all men make war on the battlefield—"

"The battle cannot be helped. 'Tis a matter of survival. The rest...I have no excuse."

"I am certain you speak false. Tell me what happened."

Shaking his head, Aric refused. Aye, he wanted to unburden his soul. But at what cost? The information he held could be twisted into treason in the blink of an eye if the wrong ears heard it fall from Gwenyth's mouth. He must protect her from the knowledge, from himself.

"I can tell no one. Not Drake or Kieran. Not the Earl of Rothgate. Not my brother. Not you."

He lifted her from his lap and set her aside. After rising to his feet, he dressed quickly in a simple gray tunic and black hose. He tried not to notice Gwenyth's stunned, hurt face.

"We will never speak of this again," he vowed.

And before Gwenyth could lure him into breaking his word, he left the room.

CHAPTER FIFTEEN

Aric endured a frosty confrontation with Rowena the next morning. The woman bristled, pleaded, cajoled, and screamed, the likes of which he had never heard from his once-betrothed. But it was done; Gwenyth would now be chatelaine. Aric did not relish the fury Rowena had unleashed upon him, but 'twas worth the tongue-lashing, for he had done well by his wife.

He had entered the great hall to break his fast and imbibe a large cup of ale when a pair of guests arrived. One was a page of Margaret Beaufort's, bearing a letter from his mistress which more than likely contained cryptic plans regarding Henry Tudor's invasion.

The other was Henry Percy, the Earl of Northumberland—one of King Richard's staunchest supporters.

Anxiety prickled along his skin. Aye, he'd known it would not be long before he would have to choose sides in this upcoming war. He had not known that moment would be now.

With a whispered word, he instructed a servant to keep Lady Beaufort's page waiting in the barbican and usher Northumberland to the great hall.

Scarce minutes passed before the duke sauntered into the huge room and greeted Aric with caution.

"Belford. How does this summer see you?"

Aric choose his words with care. "Well enough. And you?"

"I cannot complain. King Richard keeps me busy, but he keeps me wealthy as well."

With a forced smile, Aric bade the man to sit and called for ale. Northumberland said nothing until ale and bread had been put before him.

"His majesty has tried most frequently to reach you, Belford," the man said between bites.

"I journeyed to Bedfordshire and stayed for some months."

"You have holdings there?" Northumberland looked alarmed by that prospect, as if he feared the king had given Aric some concession he had not received himself.

"Nay." How could he explain that he'd given up on ambition and politics—and most notably on King Richard? "I—"

To his left, Aric saw Gwenyth enter the great hall, looking more beautiful than ever in soft yellow silk. Her nearly black hair hung down her back in a truss of glossy curls.

She paused when she saw Northumberland. "My apologies, Aric. I can eat later."

"Nonsense," said the other man with an amiable smile. He turned back to Aric. "Who is this lovely lady?"

He hesitated. King Richard would view his marriage to Gwenyth as politically unfavorable. Hell, he had no notion if Lord Capshaw's sympathies lay with the Yorks or if they had converted to the Lancaster cause.

Seeing no choice but the truth, Aric said, "This is my wife, Lady Gwenyth, late Penhurst Castle."

Shock flared across Northumberland's smooth features before he schooled it. "Was she, by chance, the reason for your journey to the southern country?"

Aric sent a quick glance to Gwenyth and prayed she would not dispute him. "Aye."

Northumberland's dark gaze raked Gwenyth with a familiarity that sent Aric chafing. "I see why. Does His Majesty know of your union?"

"Nay. I had planned to advise him this week," Aric lied.

Northumberland patted him on the back as if he were a friend. Aric had never liked the man. "She is a beauty. But such a hasty union will make your loyalty to King Richard seem...questionable."

Gritting his teeth, Aric said nothing. He also ignored Gwenyth's gasp from the edge of the room.

Henry Percy could make trouble for Northwell and its inhabitants. Aric knew well that ambition could be a powerful motivator for greed. His neighbor possessed enough ambition for an army. And King Richard, feeling insecure upon his throne, would listen to the hearsay of one of his closest supporters.

"Of course," Northumberland went on, "having ignored all four of his summons has cast a certain amount of suspicion upon you as well. The king is most displeased."

"I have nothing to hide," Aric said, knowing it would not save him from doubt. But he had nothing else to offer except a pledge of support...one he did not want to give.

"Not even Margaret Beaufort's page?" Northumberland asked shrewdly.

Aric forced himself not to flinch. Northumberland was baiting him, wanting to unnerve him into confessing treasonous activities. If Northumberland could brand him a traitor, Richard would most likely give his sly neighbor control of Northwell for his devotion, making him the most powerful lord in the north.

"I know what the woman wants, but I have not encouraged her," Aric answered finally.

Nodding his dark head, Northumberland appeared to consider Aric's words. "Perhaps, but King Richard may not see it that way. You must admit, it all looks suspicious. No reply to his most urgent summons for help. A sudden bride with uncertain loyalties to the crown. And now a rival's personal page beneath your very roof..."

"Lady Beaufort's page is not here at my invitation, and my wife has naught to do with my loyalties."

"Are you certain? Your uncle Warwick likely started his treason in just such a manner."

Pushed beyond bearing by Northumberland's intimations, Aric stood suddenly.

"Have a care. You imply something where naught exists."

With a nod, Northumberland said, "I'm merely making certain. So I can tell King Richard he has Northwell's support?"

Aric wanted to throw the odious Northumberland out of his home. But if he did not do so carefully, he would ensure a traitor's death not only for himself but perhaps Stephen, as well.

"My men have grown soft in my absence and look not to be fit enough to battle one another, much less Henry Tudor's army."

Aric had little hope that would deter Northumberland, but he had to try. Lives other than his own depended upon this. Aye, he felt aversion for King Richard's tactics in obtaining the throne, but

Stephen knew nothing of such ugliness and should not be punished for Aric's beliefs. His brother did not deserve to be half hanged, to have his entrails cut out before his eyes, be torn into pieces by horses, and to have his head hung on a pike for all of London to see. Stephen's only crime was in possessing a lamentable lack of foresight and responsibility.

"Soft men are better than no men," Northumberland returned, his voice soft, deadly. "You have no hesitation in supporting your king, I hope?"

Damn! He had much hesitation but could do little to prevent lending aid. Besides Stephen, Northwell's people would suffer if Aric were branded a traitor. Richard would seize the demesne and give it to Northumberland—or someone equally loathsome—who had naught on his mind but making more money and obtaining more power. The villagers, the hard-working men and their families, the widows and children—all would suffer if he allowed Northwell to be branded a traitor's haven.

And then there was Gwenyth, who could easily suffer, too. At the least, Richard could annul their marriage. Or he might wait until Aric's execution to force Gwenyth to take another husband, one who would covet Northwell for its wealth and not its people. One who might mistreat Gwenyth. One who would expect her sweet presence in his bed each night.

The possibilities were limitless and unthinkable.

Aric drew in a deep, resigned breath. "I will write to King Richard today. What does he expect?"

Northumberland smiled, as if he knew exactly how reluctantly Aric's answer had been given. "His majesty expects you and Northwell's army to support him. Henry Tudor has finally left France and landed in Wales, in a place called Milford Haven. But I'm sure Margaret Beaufort's page would have been pleased to tell you such—if he has not already."

Aric clenched his teeth at the man's repeated inferences to treason. He could prove nothing, yet better men had been executed with less evidence. If any should wonder, they had only to ask the widow of Lord Hastings, whom King Richard had cut down as a traitor to the crown without a jury of his peers and without benefit of a last meal.

He bellowed for his squire, noticing Gwenyth still standing at the edge of the room, her eyes wide with terror. He looked away.

"My lord?" the young boy asked.

"Send Lady Beaufort's page away with the message that we have no interest in her information."

The squire nodded before he walked away to do as he had been bid. Aric ignored his own regret. Henry Tudor would most surely make a better king.

"I hope, for the sake of your neck, you meant that." Northumberland sent him a tight smile.

Before he could reply, Rowena swept past a stock-still Gwenyth and into the great hall. "My lord Northumberland."

Rowena's smile was beauty and warmth itself, and his neighbor looked most transfixed by it. Aric smiled cynically.

"How wonderful it is to see you," Rowena went on.

"My lady Rowena, you are a fine, fetching sight early this morn."

She laughed like an innocent girl, as if she had not shared the bed of the late lord and both of his sons.

Northumberland looked blinded by lust.

"The morn is much brighter now you are arrived at Northwell." Rowena smiled wider than Aric remembered. Clearly, she wanted his neighbor's attention.

"Nay, sweet lady, 'tis you who brightens the morn. I but bask in your rays."

Aric rolled his eyes, even as he prayed something would come of this flirtation. Although Northumberland was wed to one of Aric's Neville cousins, Eleanor chose life in London.

Rowena cast a glance at Aric that he might have thought annoyed, had she really let it show, before she returned back to Northumberland. "Sit in the garden with me, my lord. What a fine day to be out of doors, and your company would be fair pleasing."

Once more, she smiled in a hollow flash of small white teeth, leaning slightly forward so her bosoms were closer to the other man's rapt gaze.

"Indeed, my lady. I should like nothing more."

Without a word, the pair departed.

Aric saw them not for hours. He was not surprised when, at day's end, Stephen entered the great hall with a mournful wail.

"She is leaving!" he cried.

He could not pretend to misunderstand. "Then I will wish her well with Northumberland."

"How can you care so little?" Stephen's brown eyes were wide with distress. "Her leaving will rip the very heart from my chest. How shall I go on?"

With a sigh, Aric regarded his brother, wondering when he would finally become a man. "It will pass, and another will replace her in your bed. It is the way of women."

"You must stop her!" Stephen said, as if he had not heard Aric's advice.

"Let her go, Stephen." He put a comforting hand upon his brother's shoulder. "She loves you not. 'Tis better for you to know this now."

Agitated and infuriated, Stephen jerked away from Aric's touch and fled the hall.

Rowena appeared moments later, dressed for travel. She looked serene, at peace in a way she had not been for some weeks.

"I go with Northumberland," she informed him.

He nodded. "I wish you well."

"You have cared for me for many years, though you did not have to. For that, I thank you." Rowena stood on the tips of her toes and pressed her cool lips to his cheek.

"You did my father a service in running Northwell when he had no other. You were welcome here."

With a soft smile, she was gone, leaving a sulking Stephen behind.

Now Aric knew what he must do next in order to keep his honor and spare his family.

But his next conversation with Stephen proved difficult. Politics clearly overwhelmed the young man, and Aric could not provide all the information Stephen might have liked about the reasons for his decisions. But the necessary was done. Now—soon—he had to find the right moment to tell Gwenyth.

* * * *

By the moon and the stars, how busy she had been these two days past! Gwenyth lay in her bed with a weary sigh, satisfied with her efforts. She had directed a thorough cleaning of the kitchen and pantry, as well as taken a complete inventory. The linens for every bed in the castle had been washed and hung to dry. Every tapestry had been taken down and beaten free of dust. Fresh rushes lay upon the floor, strewn with sprigs of lavender for a pleasant smell each time someone took a step. Eager maids had been hired, lazy ones released. Visiting the crofters would take more time but could be done soon. The dye house would be replenished by week's end, and servants were collecting herbs from her garden.

Hectic though they had been, she had enjoyed each minute of these two days.

This was the very position she had been born to, and she had to admit grudgingly that Rowena had done a fair job here at Northwell, even if she had been a bit harsh. Still, Gwenyth knew she could do better because she wanted this so badly, had wanted this for so long, and loved her husband so well.

Finally, happiness shimmered in her sight, brushing her each day. As time passed here, Aric's contentment with her presence and abilities would grow. Then they would know naught but joy in their surroundings, in their love, and someday in their children.

Around her, reminders of Aric abounded. His understanding, his passion coupled with great gentleness... 'Twas no wonder she loved him—and had for some while. The expression in his silvery gaze of late bespoke great tenderness. Even if he had not told her of his love, she felt certain it was but a matter of time before he realized such.

Yet he had spoken little since the morn they had last made love, and had not been back to their bed since.

Frowning, she burrowed into her pillow and drifted off to a fitful sleep.

Later, hours before dawn, she awakened to find Aric sitting beside the bed, staring out the room's window, Dog at his side. She sat up and allowed her gaze to follow his over the vast inky-blue ocean lit by a sparkling gold moon. Gwenyth frowned. What had been troubling him so of late?

Rising, Gwenyth made her way to Aric's side and placed gentle hands upon the back of his chair. In no way did he acknowledge her presence. Still, she knew he was aware of her just behind him.

"What troubles you, Aric?"

"Naught you must worry over, little dragon. Return to sleep."

His voice carried an unmistakable note of weariness and

resignation. Her heart ached for him, and she smoothed her hand over the golden strands of his hair.

"If you worry, I will also. Share your troubles."

Aric hesitated, then finally looked her way. Exhaustion claimed his features, as if he had not slept in days.

"It is Rowena's leaving that disturbs you?" she whispered.

A smile softened his features as he wrapped an arm about her waist and rested his cheek against her belly. "Nay. If anything, I wish Northumberland well with her. Perhaps he will please her as no Neville ever did."

Shrugging, Gwenyth took Aric's hand in hers, giving him the comfort she sensed he needed. "Then it is the war, the choosing of sides you dislike."

Beside her, Aric stiffened. He sighed, raking a hand through the long strands of his tawny hair. "Aye."

"And Northumberland's accusing you of treason sits no better with you, I think."

"He is an ass."

"Aye." She smiled wryly. "And fen-sucked as well."

The quiet rumble of Aric's laughter set her at ease.

"Come to bed," she whispered.

Aric looked up at her from the chair, his gray gaze a tangle of appreciation, lust, and something warm. She drank it in as he rose and followed her to the bed, his hand still clutched in hers.

They lay side by side as Aric touched her face and kissed her mouth. With welcome, she urged him to a deeper joining. He loved her well and with care but with urgency. After, they lay together in perfect silence. By morn, she hoped his trouble had found succor and that she had helped ease his burden.

When she rose with the sun, it was to the sight of Aric staring out over the crashing ocean once again, his expression distraught. Panic nudged her. Would nothing relieve his mind?

"Aric?" she called from the bed, holding the sheet above her naked breasts.

He hesitated, then looked at her with bleak eyes. That he had not slept all night was clear. Gray eyes rimmed in red met her gaze in the predawn light. The set of his wide, proud shoulders seemed stooped and weary. Concern needled her as he rose slowly and made his way to her, his sharp features inexplicably heavy.

"I must ask you something," he said as he sat on the bed beside her.

'Twas important—deeply, though his words did not say so. She reached out to place a comforting hand upon his arm. "Of course."

With a seemingly grateful nod, he sighed. "As you heard the other day from Northumberland, war is on its way. Within weeks. I have been called to choose sides. My conscience will not allow me to fight for King Richard."

"But why—"

"Do not ask me the one question I cannot answer."

If anything, Aric's face became bleaker, more remote, until it resembled the roughhewn stones protecting Northwell from the sea behind it. Concern and a strange anxiety formed a hard knot in her stomach.

"Will you fight for Henry Tudor, then?" The very idea of open treason frightened her. What would become of Aric if the Tudor man did not emerge the victor?

He would die a traitor.

Gwenyth's knot of fear grew to the size of a boulder and threatened to crush her with its weight.

Aric's reply cut into her trepidation. "Nay. I fight for no one."

No one? "Are you not likely to be branded a traitor anyway?"

"It is certain."

His words were like a blow to her belly. Gwenyth felt herself lose air as something cold and terrified exploded within her. Panic began to claw at her belly.

"King Richard will see you dead," she argued.

He nodded slowly. "'Tis no less than I deserve."

Deserve? "You cannot mean this. Any of this! 'Tis foolishness to do nothing and see yourself die. Pick up a sword. Close your eyes and choose a side."

His eyes slid shut, and a furrow of pain wrinkled his wide brow. "I cannot. That is why I must ask you a question."

Confusion, concern, and alarm all raced through her with each heartbeat. Aric planned to allow himself a traitor's execution and his most pressing concern was to ask her a question?

"Nay. I will not have this! You are my husband."

He cupped her cheek with a tender hand. "And I will be until I am dead, but you must listen to me.

"I must think of Northwell's interest. The people here are my responsibility. Stephen wants to support King Richard, so I have given him back the run of the castle. He will raise an army to meet Henry Tudor's. Northwell itself remains loyal to the crown, as does my brother. None of them suffer for my allegiances."

"*What?* This is our home! You cannot give it away—"

"I must and I did. And if you remain here, King Richard will find you when he comes looking for me. I believe he may take you prisoner or harm you to draw me out, and I cannot allow that. You are my responsibility, too."

Gwenyth felt herself frowning. Aric spoke too quietly, was thrusting information on her too quickly. She felt numb and uncertain, despite the cloying fear that pervaded her.

"I do not understand."

"I am asking you to return with me to the cottage. If King Richard's soldiers find me there, I can argue your innocence or send you back to your uncle. He will take you in again now that you are a Neville and can add to his consequence."

"Leave Northwell? Leave being a lady for dirt floors and a cruel family?" At his nod, she cried. "Do I mean nothing to you?"

Though Aric's plight weighed upon her, certainly there must be another solution, one that would see him safe and keep her from the poverty and neglect that had marred most of her life. And because he refused to tell her why he would not pick up a sword for King Richard or Henry Tudor, she was expected to change her life, to return to the poor cottage and be happy?

Apparently, she meant little to him at all.

"Gwenyth—"

"I will not return there." Tears stung her eyes. "You cannot give me everything my heart desires, then rip it away from me as if it meant nothing! Just fight. You can keep Northwell and your life. We can stay here and all will be well."

Shaking his head, Aric rose from the bed slowly. "I have told you I cannot."

"What reason can be worth your life and mine?"

"Honor. If a man has none, he is worth nothing."

"What is honorable about refusing to fight? It shall look nothing less than cowardly and cost us everything. Everything! I will not go back to the cottage."

"Then I shall take you elsewhere. Be ready to leave come morn."

Before she could sputter an objection, Aric left the room.

Her mouth gaping open, she followed him out the chamber door into the narrow hall. "What mean you, elsewhere? Where do you think to take me?"

Her stubborn husband said naught. He simply kept walking toward the stairs.

"I asked you a question, you boil-brained beast!"

Still not a word from the man.

"I will not go!"

As her words echoed off the stones about her, Aric disappeared down the stairs, not to return to her that night.

* * * *

Dawn broke a bleak gray over the foggy shore behind Northwell. Aric looked at Gwenyth, mounted on the horse beside him. Between them, Dog wagged his gray tail.

Fury described his wife's look well. Those blue eyes that so intrigued him flashed like bolts of lightning that would as soon strike him dead.

Aye, and why not? He now took her from Northwell and wealth and her role as chatelaine—the things she had long sought.

But he could do naught else to protect Gwenyth in the wake of his decision to stay away from the battlefield.

"I do not wish to leave here, you simple-witted buffoon," she snapped. "Let me stay!"

He sighed, weary after a long eve of nightmares filled with children screaming for help in the night. "I have already said that is not possible. Danger will soon come to Northwell."

"Did you have to tell the servants I was no longer welcome here?" The fists at her side seemed strangely in keeping with the tears shimmering in her eyes.

"Would you have come if I had not?"

Nay. And that was the point.

Aric knew she had long coveted the very things her cousin Nellwyn had in marriage to Sir Rankin—a fine home, a bevy of servants at her call, and money aplenty. And these things he had given to her of late. 'Twas little surprise she resisted parting with them, even though he, her lord husband, had asked her to come with him. Had even given her a choice!

Nay, she did not surprise him. Yet somehow her decision hurt in places he could not comprehend, in ways he did not want to understand.

"Why can you not stay and fight? Why rip our lives asunder over honor that no one will care for but you?"

A new wave of anger hit him, even as he told himself she could not possibly understand the underhanded politics that had led to this inevitable war. Nor could she see that a man's honor was all he had once the trappings of castle, title, and money were stripped away. Aric knew he had done wrong in chasing ambition. It had cost a ten-year-old boy his life. From now on, the only death he would be responsible for was his own—even if it was as a traitor.

"Gwenyth, I will not fight, and that is all."

As they left Northwell's outer walls and headed south and west, toward Yorkshire dales, he wondered if, after journey's end, he would ever see her again.

The thought he might not saddened and angered him at once.

They broke their journey that night at a small inn. Silence reigned. It did not escape his notice that she asked not where they journeyed.

As he lay beside her in the small bed, feeling her sleeping form curl up to him for warmth, he wrestled with himself. He wanted her; his body could never lie about that. Something within him craved her touch, her taste. Yet he held back. Touching her would be like a sweet, sharp pain. He would enjoy it even as it hurt him. He was a fool for hoping women everywhere didn't want their husbands to battle for power and wealth and the king's favor.

What a useless wishing!

Several afternoons later, Hartwich Hall came into view. From the inn, he had sent Guilford word to await them. 'Twas no surprise when he rode into the outer bailey to find his mentor, along with Drake and Kieran.

"Aric, my boy." Guilford stepped forward in greeting, then cast his rheumy gaze toward Gwenyth. "Is this lovely woman your lady wife?"

She sent the older man a direct stare. "Not by choice, my lord."

Holding a groan, Aric saw Guilford's brow rise in speculation. Kieran laughed. Drake followed.

Grimacing, Aric dismounted and turned to help Gwenyth down. She ignored him and slid down under her own power, sparing a pat on the head to a panting Dog but not a glance for him.

A feeling he could scarce understand churned inside him, loud like a drumbeat. "Gwenyth, this is Guilford, Earl of Rothgate."

She sent him a brief curtsy. "'Twould be a pleasure, my lord, under better circumstances."

Gwenyth stretched after such a grueling ride, trying to gain her footing on wobbling legs, then approached Kieran. "How fare you, sir? I thought you in battle."

"Aye, I should have liked such, but Guilford has called me here."

"To fight for King Richard?" The acidic note in her voice did not escape Aric's notice.

"What else?" He shrugged. "It shall be as good a fight as any."

Gwenyth shook her head, then settled a concerning gaze on his dark, tight-jawed friend. "I presume you are Drake MacDougall."

He fixed her with a stare that had intimidated many a man. Gwenyth flinched not an inch. "I presume you are Aric's wife."

She raised her chin proudly. "I am Gwenyth, not merely the dimwit's chattel."

Drake's frown deepened. "Clearly not."

Kieran chuckled once more. "I told you she was no demure maid."

With a tilt of her head, Gwenyth regarded the dark man's solemn face with seeming regret. "I am sorry. I meant only to inquire as to your health. Are you faring well?"

His tormented friend's gaze rose in question. Aric met the stare. With a silent nod, he confirmed Gwenyth knew all.

"I-I thank you for your concern." Drake stumbled over the words, as if he had not expected them. I am nearly mended now."

For a mended man, his eyes looked haunted.

"I wish you well," she said softly.

Though Drake nodded, the granite of his expression changed not. Aric wondered if anything, anyone, would ever reach the man's iron heart again.

"We all wish the brigand well," said Kieran, coming toward

Gwenyth. "'Tis a pleasure to see you again, sweet lady."

As Kieran took Gwenyth's hand and raised it to his lips, Aric stepped beside them and glared at his friend with annoyance.

Kieran merely lingered over Gwenyth's palm, then sent him a jaunty smile.

The noise in his head grew louder. Aric knew he should not feel a churning or charging in his gut at the thought of another man's touching Gwenyth. She cared for her future, her position at a fine castle, as all women did. 'Twas not the man who mattered, only what he could provide.

He was twice the fool for wishing otherwise.

Behind him, Guilford cleared his throat, and Aric turned to face his mentor.

"Aric, I am sure your bride would like to see her temporary home when you are able to pull these two swains from her."

Gwenyth's gaze flew to Aric, prickly with anger. "You mean to leave me here?"

"Aye." He nodded.

"While the war goes on about you?"

Aric gritted his teeth. "Aye."

"While people are dying, you mean to do no more than hide in your cottage?"

"Gwenyth…" he warned, his ire rising.

"And leave me, your wife, in the care of strangers?"

"Enough! You had no wish to return to the cottage—"

"Who possessing sanity would?" she interrupted.

"Nor did you want to return to Penhurst." He went on as if she had said naught. "Northwell is too dangerous. Guilford can protect you whilst you stay and enjoy the castle life you—" *want more than your own husband,* he started to say. Then he stopped himself, conscious that Guilford, Drake, and Kieran all watched with great interest.

The noise in his head grew so loud he wondered if it would burst from his ears. He wanted it to cease, to leave him in peace. It continued until he thought he might lose his mind.

He took a deep breath and willed his voice to something toneless. "Here you will stay."

With that, he made his way into the keep without looking to see if Gwenyth or the others followed.

CHAPTER SIXTEEN

Late that night, Gwenyth lay abed in the comfortable chambers she had been assigned, waiting for her husband. Searching for the moon, she rolled toward the tall, thin window, the crunch of straw and the smell of fresh moss from the mattress blooming in the crisp air. She saw nothing and surmised the moon must be beyond its zenith, the night nearly morn.

Still no sign of Aric, just of Dog sleeping across the room.

After the greeting in the bailey had become an argument between the two of them, she had not seen him until the evening meal. There, he had been distant, sharing no more than the necessary trencher. Certainly no words, no lingering looks.

How could he simply leave her? He knew she loved him. How could that mean so little to him?

Listless, Gwenyth rose and dressed, then left the chamber in search of her husband. Down the spiraling stone steps she trod, conscious of Aric's ruby pendant between her breasts.

Dim lighting pressed weakly against the darkness. When she encountered a wall sconce, she took it, grateful to have a lighted path.

But once she reached the great hall, Gwenyth was not sure she wanted to see the sight before her.

Aric sat slouched over a mug of ale that was clearly not his first. Drake and Kieran sat beside him, also nursing tankards. A pair of servant women sat on the massive table in front of them, their flimsy bodices pulled low.

Drake stared moodily into his cup, eyeing the two women with little more than passing interest. Kieran nibbled on one's ankle until she tossed back her red hair and laughed. The other, a blond wench, eyed Aric in blatant invitation as she pulled her skirts up to her knees before his gaze.

Jealousy plunged into Gwenyth's chest, as if Aric himself had thrust it there with the force of his sword. Tears pricked her eyes.

As if sensing her presence, Aric glanced up. His face held nothing.

Gone was the tenderness she had oft seen. Gone, too, was the desire. 'Twas as if he had never held her while she felt ecstasy, joy, or sorrow. 'Twas as if he had never heard her words of love or felt her attempts to comfort him.

Gwenyth swallowed against the pain and forced herself to step forward into the circle of light provided by the blaze in the great hearth.

Quickly, Drake and Kieran caught sight of her. The latter released the redhead and ceased his amorous activities. Drake returned his brooding stare to his cup. And though Aric had not touched the blond woman—yet—Gwenyth had a terrible fear he would not have resisted such enticement for long.

With a whisper, Drake sent the women away. The redhead left Kieran with a giggle and a promise. The blond cast her hungry gaze at Aric and lingered as if she hoped he would call her back.

His gaze never left Gwenyth.

A scream of fury clawed its way up her throat. She pursed her mouth tightly to hold it in. Later, he would feel the force of her anger—not when they had an audience.

"Aric," she forced out. Hearing the quiver in her voice, she cleared her throat and started again. "I would speak with you. Alone, please."

He looked as if he might object, and Gwenyth prepared her next argument. But Aric rose and made his way toward her slowly, his eyes the gray of a stone.

Without a word, he followed her up the stairs and shut the door to her chamber behind them.

"We have no more to say, my lady."

His formality stunned her. She felt as if he had cut her from his life—and without much struggle.

The thought hurt and infuriated her.

She let herself rail at him, fist clenched. "We have plenty to say, you slimy, pig-sucking—"

"Name calling will change naught." His face held all the warmth of the sea in winter. "I leave come morn."

"This morn?" Shock numbed her before panic set in. So soon?

He nodded and turned for the door.

"Wait! Why must we part? I— I…it seems foolish to—"

"You want to reside in a castle. Here you are." He gestured around him with open arms. "Guilford's wife is long dead, and he can use a good chatelaine."

"But I do not want to be without a husband. If Northwell is dangerous, can we not stay here?"

"If I stay here, I must fight. And I will not."

"Why?"

Gwenyth knew as she asked the question that he would not answer. Still, his refusal disappointed her.

"We have discussed this."

She shook her head. "Your refusal to make your reasons known is not a discussion, you stubborn man!"

He grunted, nostrils flaring. "Stubborn? Can you, for once, heed your husband and believe me when I tell you that you do not want to know why?"

"Nay, our very lives are at stake! Your reasoning makes little sense."

The anger brimming beneath the surface of his distance finally boiled to the top. "Nor does yours."

"Mine? 'Tis perfectly logical, you mewling lout. We should continue with the same life. You fight a battle or two, as you have done the whole of your life, then return home to my side. Why can you not do that?"

"And you would have me disregard my honor so you might live in wealth and luxury? You would have me turn my back on what I know to be right so you may surround yourself with servants hired to cater to your whims? I will not ignore my beliefs so you may enjoy the fineness of the master's chambers and continue writing your cousin Nellwyn of your good fortune."

Her mouth dropped open at his barbs. Did he really know so little of her? Hurt panged inside her chest. "Do you think me so mercenary?"

His stare was nothing short of incredulous. "By every word and deed, you have proven how badly you wish to secure your place as my countess. Would you consummate our marriage in the cottage? Nay, but once you learned of my title, of Northwell, well…you fell willingly into my bed, even seduced me to it."

She gasped in ire and disbelief. "How could you think—"

"Did you not?"

"Nay, you mean-mouthed coxcomb. I did not!" Gwenyth came at him, her fists clenched and aimed for his chest.

Aric grabbed her wrists to ward off the blows.

"Let me go!" she shouted, lashing out at his shin with her foot.

She caught him with her heel. He loosed an ugly curse at the contact.

He gritted his teeth. "Kick me, if you like, but you wanted your place so badly at Northwell, you shared my bed every night, every way I wanted you. And why I expected you to be any different than any other woman seeing to her future, I will never know."

She gasped. "Do you compare me to Rowena?"

Something dangerous flashed in his eyes. "Nay, for her excuse is one of survival. Yours is much less noble."

The swine! The varlet! She yanked free of him and picked up a pitcher beside her. She threw it at him, but the heavy clay piece missed his head by inches before crashing to the floor and splashing water everywhere.

"Do not liken me to that scrawny whore!"

"At least she never lied to me about what was in her heart. You, my lady, merely seek to compete with your braggart cousin, Nellwyn, and lied about your love to keep all you wedded into."

Tears stung her eyes, and she closed them, lest he see. Bristling braies! Why did he think such? How could he? The words repeated themselves like a chant deep within her. How could the man be so half-brained as to think she would bed down with him for any reason other than the fact he had touched her heart? Had he not seen her feelings in her eyes?

Gwenyth swallowed her bitterness. "I wanted to be a lady again, damn you. I wanted the return of all I was born to, which Uncle Bardrick stole from me when my father died! You seemed to understand that once."

"Aye, before I saw all you would do to obtain and keep it."

That he had called her nearly everything but a whore did not escape her. Pain ripped through her chest, but fury eclipsed that—at the moment. Later, she knew, his words would hurt in a way no one's ever had.

"You qualling bum-bailey! If you think I would swive any man simply for such gains, you know me not at all." She lifted her leg and stomped on his toes, then prepared to storm out of the room and slam the door in his face.

He shouted and hobbled in pain but seized her wrists in a tight grip. With a yank, he dragged her closer, against the length of his hard, massive body. The sharp rasp of his breath fanned her mouth as his chest rose and fell against her own.

Time seemed to stop. Every moment she had spent in his embrace, in his life, flashed in her mind. His confusion after their marriage, his tenderness after Nellwyn's visits, his struggle to tell her of his true identity, his desire when he claimed her body. Would he remember, too, and kiss her? Stay with her? Understand her?

She held her breath, willing him closer. *Please kiss me...* If he could but feel her love in her touch, 'twas certain he would comprehend her feelings.

Aric stepped away.

Pain sliced into her, shredding her heart and her belly. Her eyes teared more.

He would not believe.

By the moon and stars, the man was a fool. She had told him she loved him. He had chosen to believe she lied for the sake of some mercenary nature he believed she had.

Looking furious—and more remote than she had ever seen him—Aric released her abruptly, a challenge in his gaze. "Unless you choose life at the cottage, I bid you farewell."

His flat tone chafed her. Did he not understand she could not live with a man who thought her so heartless, share a bed and the rest of her days with someone who had naught but mistrust and contempt for her?

'Twas impossible.

Aric watched her intently, seeming to await her reply. When she gave him naught but silence, he bit out a curse. And with a final hot glare in her direction, he slammed out of the room.

As she sank to the bed, her tears began to fall, one after the other. She could not go to the cottage again. Nor should he. Whatever he sought to avoid would only find him again. Why was he blind to that fact?

Duty often meant unpleasant things. Certainly the White Lion knew his share of battle and should not be repelled by such.

She frowned. Then why did he insist upon leaving her and hiding in the forest once more with people who feared and loathed him?

Worse, if he abandoned her now, would she ever see him again?

* * * *

At dawn, Aric sat in Hartwich's great hall, waiting for the sun to fully emerge from behind the hills. He lingered over his ale, waiting. Aye, he was twice the fool for hoping Gwenyth would appear and tell him she wanted to be by his side, no matter where they called home.

He cast another glance at the stairway, his tenth in as many minutes. The only figure emerging was that of an old man.

Guilford.

His mentor wore something brown this morn that made his white-gray beard and his watery blue eyes appear paler. But nothing could ever erase the shrewd intelligence in those keen eyes.

With a disapproving glance, Guilford glanced at the empty chair beside his own. "Where is your wife?"

"Abed, I presume."

"You mean to leave without a proper farewell? And do not try to tell me you cared for that last night, for my guard saw you down here from nearly dusk until dawn."

"Mind your own affairs, old man."

"A sensitive subject, I see."

Aric gritted his teeth, doing his best to ignore the old earl. "I would ask that you care for Gwenyth in my absence."

"She will always be protected beneath my roof, no matter where you go. Have no concern about that. But Drake, Kieran, and I spoke this morn. We all agree you must fight."

Aric closed his eyes wearily in disappointment. If his brothers by choice and the man who had been like his own father could not understand, he would truly leave this earth not only a traitor, but alone.

"I cannot."

"So you have said. I would hear why."

The urge to tell Guilford rode him hard, but he refrained. The dangerous knowledge could mean a traitor's death for his dear mentor. "'Tis not for you to know."

Guilford was silent for so long that Aric glanced up to make certain the man had heard. His wily expression told Aric he had and was scheming something.

"Nothing you say will change my mind," Aric said.

The man merely nodded, stroking the length of his white beard.

"I have thrown down my sword, and I will not pick it up so more innocent people will die."

Aric might have thought his argument fell on deaf ears except for Guilford's murmured, "Hmm."

Anger mounted within him. "This is about honor, damn you!"

"Aye, honor," he mumbled.

"Without it, a man is naught," Aric returned.

"True."

Aric waited, sensing the old man had more to say. But the silence continued, cutting into him.

"Out with it!"

With a shrug, Guilford said, "Honor indeed makes a man. You have learned that well."

"As you taught me."

Still, the old man continued to stroke his beard. "But do you think to keep your honor by refusing to kill other warriors when doing so means everyone you care for will likely die?"

"*What?* 'Tis why I've left Northwell and Gwenyth, to protect them—"

"You are not so innocent, Aric, that you believe such. You refuse to fight because you've grown tired of battle. You left Northwell so it does not encumber you. You abandoned Gwenyth so you can deny she means aught to you. And as you turn your back on these duties, the crown will seize Northwell and give it to a more loyal lord. Gwenyth will be branded a traitor beside you, to die as well."

"Nay!"

"Aye. If King Richard wants to give your land to a devoted

subject, do you think he will leave alive the widow who can claim it?"

"Gwenyth had naught to do with my decision."

"Think you King Richard will care? And what of your brother?"

"Stephen is loyal."

"But ineptly so. The king will demand a lord with skill and power to oversee such important land."

Guilford's words hit Aric like a blow to the stomach. He had merely sought to protect those in his life, had he not? Stephen and Gwenyth could not die for his honor. Resisting the urge to pound his fist upon the table, he turned to Guilford with a troubled gaze.

"And if Henry Tudor takes the day," his mentor went on, "naught will be different. He will assume your loyalties remained with King Richard, even if you do not fight. Again, he will want to seize your land and give it to one of his supporters. Again, it is less tiresome to have your brother or your widow around to demand their claim…"

Aric swallowed against the truth. His heart bear like a drum in his head. *Boom, boom, boom*—the insistent drone made him quickly feel unsound of mind. Thoughts flew through his head, but he could latch onto only one: He could not be the death of Gwenyth.

Breathing deeply, he willed his heart to slow, his head to silence. Neither heeded him.

Suddenly, Guilford rose at his side. "I have said enough. Drake and Kieran left earlier this morn to find the battle. Now you must go wherever your conscience takes you."

The old man left the great hall and disappeared up the stairs, barely visible in the dawning morn. Aric cast his gaze into the mug of ale before him. Where should he go? What should he do now?

But his heavy heart already knew the answer.

* * * *

Gwenyth awoke near midday. A serving woman, Kieran's redhead from the night before, brought her fresh water to sponge with and a light repast to break her fast. She stared at the cheese and fine white bread and frowned. The smell of mead and the hard cheese left her stomach unsettled.

That and the fact Aric had gone.

201

With a shake of her head, Gwenyth refused the meal and wandered to the window. As she sank into the chair beside it and stared out onto the inner bailey below, the rolling pasture of green hills and the saffron-dotted dales beyond, she held in fresh tears.

After their argument the past night, Gwenyth had hoped to find oblivion from her heart's pain in sleep. But the comfort of slumber had not come. From this very window, she had watched her husband depart while Dog whined beside her. Aric's rigid body had looked full of anger, the face he turned up to her window without emotion.

The foolish part of her heart that loved him wanted to run after him and follow him to the cottage. Her mind stayed her with reminders of his ugly words, his poor opinion of her. The dark, drafty cottage rife with insects and the dirt floor that quickly became mud after a good rain made her shiver as well. Nay, life in such a place, with such a stubborn, unfeeling man, was not for her. No one needed her there, least of all Aric.

Of its own will, her hand rose to the ruby sundial Aric had given her at the cottage. The trinket held little value in the face of his total wealth, yet he had cared for it at one time, as he had seemed to care about her.

Now he thought her nothing more than a mercenary bitch. The mewling, jester-brained varlet.

Mewling though he might be, Gwenyth missed him already. She bit her lip to stop the stinging moisture in her eyes.

A knock on the door behind her brought her to her feet and whirling about. At the command, the Earl of Rothgate entered, cautious in his old steps, his gray beard framing a gentle smile.

"Good morn, Gwenyth. I will not ask if you slept well, for your face tells me you did not."

Frowning, Gwenyth stared at the man. What did he want here? Had not Aric told his mentor of her "faults"?

"The chamber is most comfortable," she began. "I simply was not..."

"At ease?" When she would have rebutted him, Guilford put up a wrinkled hand to stay her. "Nay, I see your heart's distress upon your lovely face."

"It will pass." The old man's intrusion into her feelings puzzled her greatly. Why did he care about her heart?

"Will it? That is a pity, for I do not think Aric can say the

202

same."

Gwenyth stiffened. Not certain what her husband had told the older man, she refused to provide details he might be lacking. "He is gone."

"Aye, to battle."

She signed impatiently. "Nay, to his cottage near my home of Penhurst in Bedfordshire."

Guilford's kind smile deepened. "We spoke this morn. He goes to battle. He goes for you."

For me? What a seductive thought. If only she could believe it. "You are mistaken, I am certain."

"Sit, child, and I will tell you some truths."

Skeptical, Gwenyth sat. For all she knew, the old earl might be as hen-brained as any village idiot. Still, Aric would not afford him such deference were that the case.

Nodding, Guilford settled on the sill of the window, his height still substantial, despite his age. "Aric loves you—"

"Nay!" Gwenyth protested, even as her heart leaped.

"Aye, and this I know because he is ready to fight for you. For himself, he would rather have died."

"That puzzles me greatly," she admitted.

"As it does all of us, child. Aric's heritage is steeped in ambition, always wielding power in court circles with the authority of a master over his vassals. He was no exception to his father and uncle, as well as his grandfather before that. He has ties to England's most powerful families, including the Plantagenets…and the Tudors.

"He was ever a shrewd child. As a young man at court, he found ways to make others capitulate happily to his wishes. Together with his skills on the battlefield, 'twas long thought Aric could have more influence over the crown than even his uncle, the kingmaker."

Such hardly fit her image of the sorcerer living in a hovel. Why would he abandon such a life of his own will?

"What changed?" she asked, wearing a puzzled frown.

The old man lifted his shoulders. "We would all like to know. Aric has chosen to keep his reasons in the matter a secret."

That same reason was why he resisted battle; Gwenyth felt that deep down.

Yet Guilford thought he had gone to battle for her.

Impossible. Why would he fight to protect the wife he thought ignoble? The wife he had abandoned?

"It is of no consequence now," she murmured. "He is gone."

The old man hesitated, then rose to his full height before her. "But your heart has not given up on him. Perhaps you should not, either." When she might have protested, Guilford ploughed into the silence. "For now, rest comfortably and know you are always welcome at Hartwich Hall."

Gwenyth watched the old man in silence as he slipped past her, wearing a strangely satisfied smile, then left the room.

CHAPTER SEVENTEEN

Aric rode south and west between Kieran and Drake through the foggy English morning. Conversation had been sparse, except for his Irish friend's attempts to wheedle a smile or two out of him and Drake.

Nothing made him want to smile now.

Without a doubt, he should have held his tongue with Gwenyth. She did only as other women in laying with a husband to secure a future. 'Twas his foolishness for wishing more of her, of their marriage. Mayhap he could have borne it if not for her lie of love. He abhorred lies. Worse, he foolishly wanted to believe she truly cared, and evidence to the contrary had roused his anger—and something that felt suspiciously like hurt or betrayal.

He frowned. Mayhap marriage had made him soft, made mush of his mind. Or mayhap Gwenyth held the kind of dark powers the people of Penhurst had once believed he possessed—the power to bewitch.

Or perhaps he loved her.

Aric drew in a sharp breath as the truth sank into him. He had hit upon his trouble. Somewhere in the past few months, he had given his heart to the irksome, ill-tempered, warm, wonderful minx he called wife.

God help him.

No wonder he had been unable to accept the barter of her body for his wealth. He loved her and had for some time.

Would Gwenyth ever really love him in turn if he survived this battle? By the saints, he hated to consider living out his days with a woman who sought naught from him but money and position. He could easily see himself falling deeper and deeper under her spell, drawn by her sparring mouth and unique spirit, until he might do anything to truly win her.

Nay—not that such mattered. Love her though he might, they were better off parted. With Guilford, she could have the castle and position she craved. He would seek peace in the cottage once this foolish battle ended, for he would not endure ruthless politics and senseless death again. He could not gladden his heart by hastening the death of his soul.

With a sigh, he studied the gentle rising of the slope before him. The misty green landscape was familiar and not unpleasant. Still, he did not wish to make this journey.

How ironic that he had once wed Gwenyth to spare her life. Now she might die because he had. Aric shook his head in disgust.

Politics, which had once fascinated him, now reeked of inhumanity and dishonor. King Richard, for him, symbolized all that was wrong with England's affairs of state and morality.

And in order to spare the life of the woman he could not banish from his mind, he had to fight to uphold the very regime that sickened him. Another irony.

And a definite sign of love.

"You look puzzled, my friend." Drake spoke quietly beside him.

Aric smoothed the frown from his face. "Merely thinking of the battle to come."

Drake nodded but said naught.

Kieran smiled. "A little sport is good for the soul."

Sport? Death and blood and battle made for more than sport. Why could the young fool not see his careless beliefs would likely lead to his death?

He held in a sigh, knowing from years past any attempt to convince Kieran that war was not amusement would be met with disbelief or disdain.

With a chiding glance at his Irish friend, Aric kicked his horse's sides and rode ahead. He knew Kieran and Drake would silently question his odd behavior, but he cared not.

Rarely had he wanted more to be alone.

Miles upon miles fell away. The morning turned into one day, then the next, punctuated by warm, humid nights of fitful sleep. Aric willed his thoughts away from Gwenyth, but his mind rebelled. And the one thought he could not escape taunted him each hour: He loved a woman who would never accept the simple life he needed to keep his sanity.

* * * *

The trio of men encountered King Richard's forces in Nottingham and followed them south to Leicester, where they camped. Aric shared a tent with Drake and Kieran and prayed for some miracle, that God might end this foolish war before it came to a bloody climax. Henry Tudor's forces had marched westward from Wales and now awaited the clash mere miles away.

Sleep would not come that night, except for scattered crimson dreams of the dead boys and their cries for help. Aric rose to another hot, damp dawn, knowing how badly he had failed the princes, the younger in particular, and how badly he had judged the king's intent and shamed his own honor, all because of ambition.

More than anything, he wanted not to fight this useless war, but he must—for Gwenyth. Hopeless fury ate into his gut. Still, naught could be changed or avoided. The moment of his truth—indeed, of England's truth—had arrived.

The thought made him ill.

Restless, he strode out of his tent, leaving a drowsy Drake and Kieran behind to rise at will. His agitated gait took him past rows upon rows of tents, all housing men loyal to King Richard, all harboring men willing to keep a heinous killer upon the throne.

Such a realization made him grit his teeth—until he passed the Duke of Norfolk's tent and happened upon a note pinned to its canvas.

Jockey of Norfolk:
Be not too bold, for Dickon thy master is bought and sold.

Frowning, Aric read it again, trying to decipher the riddle. Over and over, he turned the puzzle in his mind and could reach only one conclusion: King Richard had been betrayed by one of his supporters, bought to the enemy's side by Henry Tudor. But who?

Many northern lords had withdrawn the better part of their support over the past two years. The Duke of Buckingham had been caught in open revolt and been executed for his treason right in

Salisbury's market. Though his neighbor Northumberland was still supportive, Aric had heard rumblings that the earl resented the king's tightfisted nature. Lord Stanley, well known for his uncertain loyalties, seemed even more in question than usual now that he had become the third husband of Margaret Beaufort, Henry Tudor's mother. Only Lord Howard could be counted upon for certain, Aric mused, and his army would not be enough to sway the whole battle.

God help them all, for many this day would find death. And for what?

"Know you what this means?"

Aric froze, recognizing that sharp, authoritative voice in an instant.

Bracing himself for the loathing and schooling it from his features, he turned to face his king and gave a slight bow. "Your Highness, I do not."

King Richard cursed, his wiry body still with tension. "Can no one's loyalties be trusted anymore?"

Fury reared up, and Aric wanted to let loose his angry tongue, to tell the foolish man he would not fight, not for a child killer. Here was his chance, as they stood alone and he had the king's ear.

But to do so would resign him—and, more important, Gwenyth—to a traitor's death.

Aric choose his words carefully. "There are ambitious men everywhere who would seek power for themselves at the expense of others."

Ambitious men like the king, who had sacrificed his nephews to capture the throne.

Richard's dark eyes narrowed. "A smart man knows when to cleave to others in order to preserve his domain and when to seize power for himself."

Apparently, Aric mused, the king considered himself a smart man. Any why not? 'Twas nearly unheard of for a third son to become king. How neatly he had arranged for the deaths of his nephews and supported his grieving eldest brother, Edward, who, as king, had been forced to execute their other brother. How neatly such maneuvering left the door to power open to a man such as King Richard.

And how little he appeared to regret his murdering ways.

Aric forced a tight smile. "Many a foolish man has thought

himself clever in the past. I see naught that bespeaks change."

The king's dark eyes sparked, but he paused uncertainly. Aye, he thought he had been insulted, only he could not say for certain.

"I will see any traitors dead!"

"I would expect no less of you, sire."

Giving a cold glance and a stomp of his foot, the king ripped the note from the tent, turned his back on Aric, and marched into Norfolk's shelter.

With a sober bearing, Aric turned away to prepare for the coming battle.

Within the hour, the procession was underway, Drake and Kieran riding beside him. In silence, he followed the king's knights south and west. They encountered the River Soar, where a massive bridge spanned the broad, blue stream, and the men began to cross it.

King Richard rode in the middle of the procession, his head held high, the summer morning sun glinting off his dark hair and the crown representing his power.

"Richard Plantagenet," yelled an old crone upon the bridge.

The men turned to stare at the poorly dressed peasant woman who would speak so boldly to a king.

With no heed for the soldiers' stares, she brushed long gray strands of hair from her aged face and said, "Before this day is done, your head will strike where your spur now hits yon fence."

As the woman pointed to the sidewall of the bridge, some of the men gasped, whether in fear or outrage, Aric knew not. Others crossed themselves, bemoaning the fact the woman looked to be a witch. Aric knew how easily one could be accused of having such powers, but a shiver passed over him, and he wondered if the crone spoke true.

"Cheeky old woman," Kieran muttered in Aric's ear.

King Richard, eager to appear brave, laughed at the aged dame and rode on. But his arrogance seemed to make the men more ill at ease. Their disquiet hanging in the air like an English mist, his army rode on.

In the tangle of bodies, horses, and armor, Aric spotted Northumberland. Stephen rode beside him, looking uncertain.

Gritting his teeth, Aric prayed this day would not see the death of his young brother.

With clatter and much pomp, the army made its way south

through Market Bosworth. Peddlers hawked wares to the soldiers, while playing children stopped to stare. Farmers and their wives shouted their thanks to the king for not marching through their crops.

Aric tried to ignore it all, but the smells of hay, horses, and manure stung his nostrils, keeping him alert—that and his apprehension, which chewed into him like a beggar into a hunk of fresh bread.

Finally, they came to an open field, punctuated by a gentle hill, where a flat plain claimed all the eye could see.

At least until the eye saw Henry Tudor and his army.

Once the combatants spotted one another, forward progress ceased. Each army lined up, one man beside the next, in a long show of power. Purposely, Aric took his place just beside Stephen, who sat his steed sullenly beside Northumberland. They were situated slightly behind the hill. If his brother was surprised to see him, Aric couldn't see it on his young, nervous face. Still, here he could protect his brother, if need be, and stay as far from the fighting as possible.

Grimly, Aric glanced across the plain he'd heard someone call Ambien to see Henry Tudor's smaller army lined up along an old Roman road.

Anticipation hung heavy in the air. Warriors checked their weapons as their horses pranced nervously, neighing for release. Though the morn was still young, the sun inched up in the sky.

How many men would not live to see it set?

"You there, MacDougall and Broderick." Northumberland pointed at Drake and Kieran. "Take two of my men and scout behind enemy lines. When you have learned their secrets, return to the fight."

The ornery earl's gaze challenged Aric, as if he thought removing his friends from his side might anger or discomfit him. To prove Northumberland had accomplished neither, Aric merely nodded to his friends as they rode away, then turned his gaze back to the battlefield.

The distant sound of a trumpeter and the clank of armor brought Aric back to the present. As he drew his sword and made to charge, Northumberland held up a hand to stay him.

To the near one hundred men positioned behind the hill he shouted, "We wait for the signal to charge and surprise our Welsh enemy."

Aric sighed and clutched his sword, waiting. Far in the distance, Henry Tudor's small army advanced to meet the king's, a slow march complete with archers beyond the marshy field at the base of the plain.

Then came the clash of steel ringing in the air, along with the shouts of urgency, the cries of agony, the dash of arrows across the sky to land in human flesh. Horses whinnied and pawed the earth, and the scent of blood rose.

Nay, Aric did not want to fight this battle, but waiting chafed him. By the saints, he wanted this over, but he did not want a coward's reprieve, either.

Soon, the Tudor army ceased its advance, straying not more than ten feet from their standard. Had the king's army overpowered them so quickly and easily?

"What can you see, Belford?" the shorter Northumberland demanded, straining in vain from his saddle for a view.

"It looks as though Tudor's army advances no more. I cannot see much of the king's men," he advised.

Northumberland scowled with impatience. "Ride to the hilltop and tell me more."

"Will that not give our position away to Tudor's scouts?"

His neighbor sent him a nasty glare. "The king himself put me in charge of this part of the attack. That is an order, Belford."

Shrugging, Aric nudged his mount to the hilltop, only to find Tudor's army seeming to struggle for is last breath.

In the midst of the royal army, King Richard attacked his horse's flanks with his heels and charged forward, past his soldiers, into the open field. Shock zinged through Aric in a cold blast. By the saints, what could Richard be thinking?

Then he spotted Henry Tudor standing beside his standard-bearer slightly to the north of the battle. Richard saw his enemy alone and meant to take him.

Dear God.

With a vicious thrust, King Richard cut down the standard-bearer in a gush of blood and cries. Another man rushed to Tudor's side to take up the flag, but Aric doubted the Welsh contender noticed.

Henry and King Richard fought hand to hand, with all the

desperation and determination of two men fighting for a nation.

Each lashed his sword at the other. The clang of steel rang in the air as the soiled metal glinted in the wicked August sun. Around them, the king's army advanced on Tudor's, winning by sheer numbers.

But not for long.

Lord Stanley's formidable forces, sitting to the side of King Richard's, made a sudden flanking maneuver and began a surprising attack on the royal forces. Fresh into the battle, Stanley's men charged the king's knights, engaging them in a deadly struggle.

The match now appeared even.

Aric knew Lord Stanley's army might—or might not—possess the strength to remove the crown's true traitor from its throne. The fighting looked fierce indeed. But what if Lord Stanley should lose? What if King Richard punished the man as a traitor for doing what every God-fearing warrior with a conscience would do?

How would the senseless killings of the two princes ever be avenged?

He must not leave the future of the nation to the whims of fate and the might of another's army. Aric wanted Henry Tudor on the throne. Nearly any man had to be more fit to bear the title of king than Richard.

And if he wanted Henry on the throne, he would have to fight for the cause, consequences be damned.

A feeling of peace settled in his belly, along with a surge of excitement. Aye, he should have decided this long ago, to cast his lot in with another man, one who had not learned the evil lessons the Plantagenet family had taught one another over the decades.

"What see you now?" Northumberland shouted.

Aric hesitated. Should he tell the odious earl the truth, the man would charge Lord Stanley's forces with all haste.

Holding up a hand to stay the small contingent of warriors behind him, he said, "I must ride closer. I cannot say what transpires from here."

Northumberland hesitated.

Aric began sweating beneath his armor and feared the earl would challenge him. "Unless you should like to ride into the melee yourself."

Hoping the task would sound beneath Northumberland, Aric

waited for his answer.

"I should not be seen." His mouth pinched with displeasure, and Aric could not help but think he and Rowena would understand each other. "Go, but be careful who sees you."

With a nod, Aric charged down the hill, circling the heart of the battle, before his neighbor could change his mind.

Around the side of the warring, he rode, skirting the muddy marsh, until he approached the rutted Roman road at the back.

He joined the army at Lord Stanley's side, his sword raised.

Upon his approach, Lord Stanley turned to stare at him, shock visible in his blue eyes, which showed through his helmet.

"Be you friend or foe, White Lion?"

"Your friend, though I should have seen such sooner."

"It matters not," shouted Stanley, fighting off one of King Richard's knights, then skewering the man. "Join us now!"

Retrieving his helmet, Aric secured it on his head, then raised his sword with a cry.

Into the fray, he charged, cutting down the king's men in his path. His arm was strengthened by his resolve, by the certainty he did right.

Richard's cruel reign would come to an end today.

Before him, Lord Oxford, the leader of Tudor's frontal attack, charged King Richard's van and set them on the run. As Aric thrust his blade into his enemy's belly and pulled it free, he saw Northumberland's troops in the distance making a frantic dash over the top of the hill toward the melee.

Nay! Those men could sway the battle to Richard's favor.

Evil could not carry the day.

Aric charged toward Northumberland, determination to rid the battle of this new threat biting into his belly. The hot wind swept around him, dripping sweat into his face. Retreating opponents engaged his blade. With brutal efficiency, he dispatched each, feeling only his higher purpose—to stop the odious earl and save Henry Tudor's cause.

Before he could reach the encroaching group, Northumberland, Stephen, and the other men stopped suddenly on the marshy plain. His brow furrowed in puzzlement, Aric watched as the earl shouted to one of his men, who quickly jumped off his horse and tried to guide Northumberland's forward.

Naught happened.

Even from this distance, Aric could see Northumberland shouting, wildly cursing the man at his horse's feet, all but jumping out of his saddle as he kicked the animal's sides.

They were stuck!

Aric laughed, relieved that Northumberland and his men were tangled in the mire created by recent rains and the warfare. The earl continued to run, swinging his blade and cursing all roundly. He watched Stephen struggling to free himself and join the fray. Aric could only feel gladness at Stephen's predicament, for here, away from the battle's heat, his brother would be safe.

A commotion to Aric's left caught his attention. Lord Stanley and his men now surrounded the king. Most of Richard's army had retreated to its original position at the base of the hill, many suffering Northumberland's piteous dilemma in the marshy soil.

The king stood alone amongst his enemies.

Stillness fell across the plain as all began to witness the unfolding drama.

"Bring me my battle-axe, and fix my crown upon my head," cried Richard into the sudden silence. "For by him who shaped both sea and land, King of England this day will I die. And if none follow me, I will try the cause alone."

No answering cry came from his army. No one came to the king's aid.

Stanley and his men raised their swords and axes as one and hacked the life from the resourceful, conniving Richard, who made not a sound. The crown fell from his head.

The battle was done.

Relief and weariness seeped through Aric's blood. Justice had been done, aye. But as he looked about the carnage on the Ambien plain, 'twas clear this new peace had come at an awful price. Bodies lay strewn everywhere, and some, still uncertain or uncaring that the battle was done, continued to make carnage on one another.

Once Lord Stanley made certain of the king's demise, he sought the crown, the symbol of England's power, and found it had rolled beneath a hawthorn bush beside a well.

With great flourish, he retrieved it and placed it upon Henry Tudor's head.

Tudor, a plain, dark-haired man, accepted it with a hearty smile.

"This is the true judgment of God, and I claim the throne of England by my right as victor!"

A cheer went up among the new king's army. Aric joined in, shouting until his throat felt raw.

There was a rightness in this victory. Only time would tell Henry Tudor's ability as king. But he would end this bloody war as one of the last Lancastrian men in the taking of Elizabeth of York as his bride.

He prayed that prosperity and peace would heal the land torn asunder by turmoil and strife for more than thirty years. He prayed that the souls of the slain princes would find peace and never be forgotten by England. And he prayed for his own future.

Now that the very man who had ordered the princes slain had met his own end this day, perhaps, Aric mused, he might be able to assemble his own happiness. Now that he had fought for the right and just, mayhap he could find absolution in that knowledge, along with Gwenyth's embrace. For he had no doubt he loved his sweetly temperamental wife.

He wanted naught but to spend the rest of his days with her at Northwell, making laughter, babies, and love.

He wanted to leave the butchery now and return to her side, but the ugly business of war was not yet behind them. The new king would want all to swear fealty to him, something Aric was heartily glad to do.

In the aftermath, Drake and Kieran returned to Aric's side, looking little worse for the battle. The trio watched as Tudor's men stripped Richard's body and tossed it over the saddle of his horse.

Drake placed a hand on his shoulder. "Here is your new king. Will you follow him?"

"'Tis for him I fought," Aric answered.

"And damned good you did!" added Kieran. "You smile at last."

With a wry grin, Aric said, "Aye. Well, do you leave now?"

Drake nodded. "We have done our duty to Guilford. This Henry is your king, not ours."

"Where will you go?" he asked both his friends.

The determined glint in Drake's eyes gave Aric pause. "To see to my revenge. 'Tis past time Murdoch pays for what he did to my father and to me."

Aric nodded, trying to hide his concern. Now was not the time to dissuade Drake from such a foolhardy scheme, but soon…

"I shall return to Spain," interjected Kieran. "There the *senoritas* are lovely, and Spaniards pay well for wicked sport!"

Biting back an admonition that would only fall on deaf ears, Aric patted his Irish friend on the back. "God go with you. Both of you."

"And you," said Drake.

"Keep you well, and Gwenyth, too," instructed Kieran, his expression surprisingly sober.

With a hearty handshake and a final farewell, the men disappeared, one riding north to Scotland, the other south to London and the sea beyond.

He hoped somehow, someway, each could bury his demons and find happiness. But his hope looked bleak indeed.

With a sigh, Aric faced the present and followed Henry's contingent as they headed northward with the fallen king's corpse. Passerby stabbed or kicked the body as it passed the rest of the soldiers, then wound its way through Market Bosworth.

Aric turned away from the sight, supposing the crone on the bridge had been right; Richard's head might well strike the sidewall his spurs had hit that very morn.

Before him, he witnessed Northumberland being arrested by Tudor's soldiers. Though he felt no surprise at the act, for such was the way of new kings eager to secure their position, he wondered at the fate of his neighbor. Would the man be given leniency, as he never truly participated in the fighting? Or would he simply be executed as a traitor for supporting Richard all these years?

Stephen was nowhere in sight, and Aric could only pray he had managed to extricate himself from the marsh before the new king's wrath descended on the old king's army.

After traveling through Market Bosworth and beyond, the army arrived in Leicester. The victorious men stopped at a friary. Its old, gray stone walls, dotted with ivy and moss, rose majestically against the humid August noon.

The new king instructed that Richard's near-naked body should be strung up where all could see. Northumberland and Richard's other supporters had been taken away, presumably to the Tower of London. Again, Aric hoped Stephen had escaped.

As the remaining knights gathered on the friary's grounds,

Henry Tudor took his place at the front and demanded, "Kneel ye down, all who would call me king!"

Eager to serve a righteous sovereign and begin anew with his own lovely Gwenyth, Aric knelt in the soft grass, as did the others about him.

Tudor began making his way through the crowd, praising some men for their bravery, thanking the rest with a silent tap on the head. The sun belted down upon him. Not a breeze stirred, and he began to sweat anew beneath his armor.

Suddenly, Aric saw Henry's boots before his very gaze, planted in the dirt and smeared with mud, reeds, and blood.

"Lord Belford, the White Lion?"

Aric looked up. "Aye, sire."

"And do you now swear fealty to me as well?"

Nodding, Aric cast his gaze down respectfully once more. "I do, Your Highness."

"After you refused my mother?"

"Forgive my error in judgment."

Silence fell upon him. Aric fought the urge to look up into the king's face, see if he might indeed be forgiven. But appearing so eager would only bespeak impertinence on his part, which he could ill afford.

"You long supported that Plantagenet prick. I do not think I shall forgive you. Arrest him!"

CHAPTER EIGHTEEN

After a rough, rushed journey to London, Aric found himself locked in the dark isolation of the Tower of London. In fact, locked in what had come to be known as the Bloody Tower—the very tower that once housed England's slain princes.

When he'd first entered the infamous prison, he'd been haunted by remembrances of his last trip here—the last time he had seen the young princes alive. As he paced the curiously luxurious lodgings he occupied, he wondered if he would meet the same fate as the boys, be condemned by the echo of the children's cries during his stay—or both.

To his relief, Aric felt no lingering guilt, no ghosts, within the Tower walls. The boys' young souls had been avenged now in battle and with King Richard's death. He wondered if the children and their mother had truly blamed him for their murders, or if he had merely blamed himself.

Two weeks later, he still had no clear answers about his guilt or his fate.

A sudden clatter at his door brought Aric's attention to the front of the room. He looked up from his pillowy bed in time to see a pair of guards stride into the small space. Fear and expectation mingled thickly in him, threatening to steal his voice. Their faces revealed nothing, but Aric knew somehow the moment that would decide his very future had come.

He missed Gwenyth each day. His love for her grew as he yearned for her smile, her saucy mouth, her kiss. He hoped his future was with her, not Lady Death.

"To yer feet, prisoner. The king calls fer ye."

Without waiting for a reply, the burly pair hauled him to his feet and thrust him through the door, into a dank stone hall, then down a flight of narrow, circular stairs.

Before another door he stood, waiting as the guards knocked. Soon, an armed man opened the door and pulled Aric into the room.

There, upon a large chair, holding a mug of frothing ale, sat England's new king, Henry.

Aric shrugged from the guard's hold and approached the king, who nodded his assent. When Aric stood before the sovereign, he bowed.

"Stand, Aric Neville, and face me."

Without hesitation, Aric did as he was bid.

King Henry studied him with unabashed thoroughness. "No wonder men fear you throughout the land. You're tall enough to scare most away."

Out of the corners of his memory came a vision of his Gwenyth on the day they wed. She had feared him not. In fact, she had never feared him, even at his worst. Always, she had shown more courage—and more spirit—than most men. Her keen mind ever took turns he scarce understood but were at times sublimely accurate. He loved her all the more for it. Her lovely face and extraordinary curves only added to his pleasure.

"Something amuses you?" asked the king, jerking Aric's attention back to the present.

Aric cleared his throat. "Thinking of my wife, your highness."

Henry nodded, a crooked smile emerging on the flat cheeks of his plain face. "Women. May they always amuse us, eh?"

"Always," Aric replied as the king lifted his mug in toast and took a deep swallow.

Long moments passed. Henry wiped his mouth with his sleeve, then looked back to Aric. "Well, Lord Stanley tells me I have been much wrong about your loyalties. Did you, in fact, fight for my cause during the battle?"

"Aye."

"Then why did you refuse my mother your support when asked?"

He barked the question, so Aric chose his answer carefully. "I had to consider needs other than my own, sire. I sought the safety of my wife and younger brother, should King Richard have proven victorious."

"And do you not fear my wrath now?"

Aric nodded, his palms beginning to sweat. "I am most hopeful you will show the mercy Richard did not. 'Tis why I ultimately chose to fight for you. I want goodness for this land."

The king's dark brow shot up. "You think I will prove myself merciful and release you for your very late show of allegiance?"

Given his tone, Aric doubted it, but had little choice except to answer. As he considered a safe reply, blood roared in his ears. "I think nothing, but simply place myself upon your mercy."

"Lord Stanley did mention you have a very careful way with your tongue."

Aric studied the king's face but could not discern if the man was irritated or amused.

"Very well," King Henry said at length, then took another sip of his ale. "You are free to go, so long as you do here and now swear fealty to me."

With a nod, Aric dropped to his knees. "I do, sire. And it pleases my heart and soul."

"Rise," he commanded, frowning. "If you cross me again, I shall have you executed."

As any king would, Aric reasoned. That he would be allowed to live now was nearly more than he had hoped for. He could return to Gwenyth, and they could make Northwell their home. He would tell her of his guilt in the young princes' deaths. Perhaps she could begin to forgive him, as he began to forgive himself. Together, they could live peacefully, happily with one another, and he could spend the rest of his days trying to understand her, thankful marriage would never tame her…

"However, I am most displeased you did not come to my aid upon my mother's request."

Aric's heart ceased beating. He sensed the king had a point in this speech, and if it began with his displeasure, Aric doubted he would like it.

"Had I not had my duty to my wife and brother to consider, sire, I would have chosen differently," Aric offered.

"And did your brother fight for Richard?"

"He fought for no one," Aric hedged. Henry need not know

Stephen had been mired in the mud with Northumberland and had only managed to escape moments before the king's men arrested their odious neighbor.

"Well." Henry waved his hand in the air as if Aric's information was of no consequence. "For your defiance, I have decided to seize your lands and titles. You may go." The king waved him out.

Aric stood, stunned and staring, a hum of shock ringing in his ears. His lands? His titles? His very heritage?

"I said you may go," Henry repeated and motioned to one of his guards.

A pair of rough hands wrapped about his arm and thrust him out the door, into an empty stone hall.

From memory, he found his way outside, where the blinding late-summer sun cascaded upon him, portending the coming autumn.

He was free of imprisonment, and the land was free from war. He was free to return home.

But he had no home now.

Where would he live? Where would he live out his days with Gwenyth?

Oh, by the saints! Gwenyth, his lovely, needful bride. His wife who needed a castle to feel whole. The beloved vixen who sought the trappings of wealth and power to secure her happiness.

Now he had naught to give her.

He wandered outside the Tower's walls, along the banks of the Thames, stumbling upon a rock. Righting himself before he fell, Aric walked on blindly.

Nothing to give her. Nothing at all. Not a castle. Not a title. No money. No power.

The future he had envisioned with Gwenyth began to dissolve before his eyes. He frowned as pain lanced his chest and speared its way through his entire body. A deafening clatter began in his head. He began to run.

He had nothing to give Gwenyth. Nothing she wanted. Aye, he had given her pleasure. That meant naught in the midst of an insecure future.

Panting, he stopped running and found himself miles from the Tower, along a deserted section of the river. Somehow its isolation reminded him of his life.

Just as he had reached out to love and believed he had a worthy future, Fate took it from him.

Sliding tense fingers through his long, damp hair, he stared out over the murky green river. Such irony. His attempt to fight in the name of King Richard and thus protect his wife had resulted in the one consequence that would drive them apart forever.

Leave being a lady for dirt floors? Gwenyth had asked. Nor could he forget her saying, *You cannot give me everything my heart desires, then rip it away from me as if it meant nothing!*

A sick, sliding nausea sloped from his chest to his belly.

His marriage to Gwenyth was over.

She would never be happy by the side of a landless pauper. How many times, through words and deeds, had she made clear her need for wealth and status? More than he cared to recall, Aric thought, shutting his eyes as if that could shut out the agony ripping through him.

He wanted her happiness. More than anything, he could not bear her tears, to know he was the cause of them.

Opening his eyes once more to lofty green trees swaying against a blue sky, Aric knew he must leave Gwenyth. He must give her leave to find happiness.

Even if it shattered his heart.

* * * *

August nudged into September and a bit of cooler weather. At dawn, Gwenyth stood about one of Hartwich's battlements, Dog at her side, as always. The sun rose off to her left, a magnificent display of nature's wonderment, to be sure, but her gaze remained to the south.

The direction in which Aric had ridden over a month ago and from which he had yet to return.

Wrapping a blanket about her shoulders to ward off the autumn breeze, she wondered why he had not come back. News of King Richard's final battle had reached them nearly a fortnight past.

A few days later, Aric's brother, Stephen, had come to Hartwich, contrite and haggard, seeking his brother. His eyes told her the boy had somehow become a man since she had left him last. Mayhap war had done that. Who knew?

Gwenyth would have feared for Aric's life, except Stephen had seen him leave the battlefield with the triumphant new king. And though Guilford, bless his kind heart, had sent many letters of inquiry to London, thus far no news had reached them.

She missed Aric so deeply, wanted him back with her so badly…regretted their terrible parting so much.

The approach of a rider from the south interrupted Gwenyth's musings. Within moments, she could hear the faint sound of the horse's hooves upon the soft soil below, urgent, matching the sudden rhythm of her heart.

Dog barked. She peered closely at the rider as he approached. Disappointment stabbed her when she realized he possessed neither the size nor hair color to be her Aric. But mayhap he came bearing news!

"Come, Dog!" she called as she rushed from the battlements.

Gwenyth and the mutt made haste to the great hall, where she found Guilford dispatching the man with a shiny coin. In his wrinkled hands, he held two rolled parchments.

With a grim set to his jaw, Guilford held one in her direction.

"'Tis from Aric," the older man said needlessly. She'd known somehow that was so.

But from Guilford's expression, Gwenyth felt certain the news was anything but good.

With trembling fingers, she tore into the missive and began reading with greedy eyes.

Gwenyth,
Now that England has a new king, I have chosen to return to my cottage. Stay with Guilford. He can provide what you seek.
God keep you,
Aric

Again, Gwenyth read the words. Aric had chosen to return to the cottage, even after fighting? With King Richard dead, he no longer posed any threat of branding himself or her traitors to the crown. Certainly if the new king were of a mind to accuse them of the same crime, Aric would not be free now, and the royal soldiers would be pounding upon her door. Confusion swirling inside her head, she frowned.

And what did Aric mean in saying Guilford could provide what she sought?

She turned a pained gaze to Guilford. "I do not understand."

"Nor do I," he said, sitting upon a nearby bench with a heavy sigh.

The scents of yeast and ale combined with her sorrow until her stomach near revolted.

"He does not return to me?"

His note made that much clear. Nor did he give any indication he wanted her with him.

Guilford scanned the missive in his hand, disappointment deep in the lines of his old face. "Apparently not. I had hoped you could help him find his way once more." A sad smile played at his mouth for a moment. "When Aric was with you, I saw more fire on his face than I had yet seen."

"'Twas no doubt how angry I made him." she said.

For the hundredth time since Aric's departure, Gwenyth recalled their parting argument. He had asked her to leave castle life behind to return to the cottage. The idea was still abhorrent to her. Yet her reaction shamed her in ways she did not understand. Certainly Aric was in the wrong, wanting to discard the very comforts most could only yearn to know.

Why, then, did she feel as mercenary as he had once accused her of being?

"Blame yourself not, child." Guilford patted her shoulder. "You are most certainly welcome to stay. I don't think Hartwich has had this much shine since my Matilde was a new bride."

Tears clogged Gwenyth's throat. "You are too kind."

Guilford rose and patted her shoulder. "At least we know he is safe."

Aye. That should have been some consolation. Instead, Gwenyth felt she was dying inside, as if Aric's abrupt missive had torn the heart from her with its very lack of warmth, its intimated farewell.

Had he ceased caring?

Had her dreams of being a lady once more chased him away forever?

Crushing the missive in her palm, Gwenyth lifted her head and marched from the great hall, Dog at her heels. Only when she was in her room, safely alone, did she give in to the tears clawing their way up from her vanquished heart.

* * * *

A fortnight later, Gwenyth settled down to the needlework at hand with a sigh. In the past, she had found comfort in the quiet ritual of mending, the necessity of the peaceful work. Today—in fact, all the days since she had received Aric's missive—she had found comfort in naught.

Aric had left her to the life of a lady, and as such, she would see to this duty, even if her fingers bled in the process.

But she could scarce see to her task for the tears blurring her vision.

How could that man simply abandon her? He had always been a surly coxcomb, to be sure, but this... Gwenyth stabbed her needle into the pale fabric in her hand. Aric was naught but a selfish, churlish varlet. What was so wrong with living in a castle, surrounded by wealth? Why had he chosen that irksome cottage over her?

Gwenyth thrust the needle back up through the cloth in her hand—and straight into her palm. With an unladylike curse, she threw her needlework down in disgust.

It was all Aric's fault. She could be skilled with a needle if she could concentrate on the work at hand, as opposed to the ridiculous accusations he had made at their parting. She did not want him for his castle and title alone!

Gwenyth paced the room. Why couldn't the lout see she could not give up life as a lady? After eight long years of sleeping on dusty floors, fighting off the advances of her uncle's soldiers, working in the heat of the kitchens, and wearing her cousins' cast-off clothing, she simply wanted the life she'd been born to, the life that would have been hers had her parents lived.

A pox on him, for she was living that life! And would continue to live it until she drew her last breath, damn him!

With an angry swipe of her hand, Gwenyth brushed an annoying dampness from her face. Then she realized her cheeks were wet with tears.

Tears? She was not crying again. She was not!

She enjoyed castle life and did not need Aric by her side to do so, even if she loved him so much she ached more than a dungeon-dweller just pulled from the rack.

Behind her, Gwenyth heard someone clear his throat. She turned to find Guilford standing within the sunny solar, wearing a curious expression.

"Tears? That is a bad sign."

"I but pricked my finger with my needle," she lied.

He nodded as if that explained everything, but his knowing eyes looked anything but convinced.

"Gwenyth, I had not thought to mention this, but I do not believe I have seen you smile in near a month."

"It has naught to do with Aric's being gone, so do not think that."

"Of course not." The furrow in his gray brow was all seriousness.

Then why did she have a suspicion he was playing her for a fool?

"Hear me now, my lord. Aric chose to leave me here."

"He did, and we shall talk no more of the ill-mannered brute. We need him not anyway. My army is sufficient without his help, and I am still spry enough to lead them. And you"—he made a sweeping gesture with his arms to her—"you are a fine chatelaine. Certainly you take great pleasure in your abilities."

She did. Didn't she?

Frowning, Gwenyth recounted her day, her week, and snatches of the last month. Odd, she could not recall a single moment of pure enjoyment between organizing the kitchen staff, taking stock of the herbs, ensuring the castle's cleanliness, not to mention planning a festival for St. Crispin's Day a week hence. True, she had enjoyed such activities at Northwell. But since arriving at Hartwich... Nay, that was not quite right either.

Since Aric had left, nothing in her life had felt right.

Knowing not what to say, Gwenyth merely smiled.

"Milady?" called a servant girl softly from the door. "There is a Lady Brinkley here to see ye."

Nellwyn? She frowned. Why had her cousin come here?

"Send her in," she told the servant finally.

"Lady Brinkley?" Guilford questioned beside her.

Her brow furrowed, Gwenyth nodded. "My cousin, wed to Sir

Rankin."

Something resembling distaste flitted across the old man's bearded face before it disappeared. "You are surprised by her presence?"

"We have maintained correspondence since she wed Sir Rankin and left Penhurst, my home. I would not say we have always been close, however."

Guilford nodded as if he understood. Gwenyth was glad he did, for certainly she did not.

Within moments, Nellwyn entered the room, carrying a blanket-wrapped bundle in one arm and wearing a hooded cloak.

"Hello, Gwenyth. I-I journeyed to Northwell, but…was told you had come here. I"—she shifted the bundle from one arm to the other—"I hope you do not mind that I have come for a visit. You did not expect me, certainly."

Her cousin fidgeted from one foot to another, her face still behind the cloak. How unlike the usually assured Nellwyn.

Guilford spoke before Gwenyth could. "My land, I am Guilford, Earl of Rothgate. You are welcome to visit your cousin here at Hartwich."

Nellwyn gasped and turned her head to gaze at the old earl. "My lord, I did not see you—that is—"

When her cousin grasped the bundle in her arms closer to her chest, Gwenyth frowned anew.

Then the bundle began to wail.

Nellwyn's babe!

Her cousin began to cry as well.

Concern brought Gwenyth to her feet and over to Nellwyn's side. "You have traveled a long way with your babe, who cannot be more than three months."

"Just over two," she croaked.

Beneath the shadow of the hood, Gwenyth ushered Nellwyn to her seat, then pushed the hood from her face.

The remnants of bruises circled both her eyes and streaked from her temple to her cheek. Gwenyth gasped.

Nellwyn squeezed her eyes shut in shame.

"I'm afraid I displeased Sir Rankin. His son was born a daughter." Nellwyn held up the blanket-wrapped bundle.

Gwenyth looked at her cousin in disbelief. Nellwyn looked

exhausted from her long journey. Strands of dark hair hung limply about her pale face. Worse, her eyes seemed bleak and pain-filled, spent emotionally.

A quiet mewling brought Gwenyth's attention down to the babe wrapped in the soft gray blanket. Her heart softening, Gwenyth lifted the child from Nellwyn's arms and held her close.

"Her name is Mary," Nellwyn whispered.

"'Tis a lovely name." Gwenyth peered at the pink-cheeked infant, her little mouth bowed, her eyes closed. Gwenyth felt her heart swell. "She is perfect."

A sad smile, full of pride and anguish, lifted the corners of Nellwyn's mouth. "I love her so dearly. But after she came and Sir Rankin...made his displeasure known, I-I knew I must leave. He wanted me to give Mary to the Church to raise. I wanted to please my husband, but..."

Nellwyn dissolved into tears. Gwenyth held the babe with one arm and soothed her distraught cousin with the other.

"I came to you," Nellwyn continued, "because I knew not where else to turn. My father cannot help. He does all he can to win our new king's favor. And Sir Penley, well... He has always feared Sir Rankin. But your husband—I mean the White Lion—he fears no one. And since he is an earl, I hoped he could—well, of course he *can*, but that he *would*—protect me."

Biting her lip, Gwenyth looked at Guilford. She wanted to beat Sir Rankin senseless. She wanted to help her cousin. But she knew not how, not when Aric resolved to live apart from her.

Bristling braies, now the man disappointed not only herself but her desperate cousin as well!

"Lord Belford has not returned from battle as yet," Guilford said smoothly, "but I should be glad to help you, dear lady, in every way I can."

Nellwyn turned her red-rimmed eyes up to the older man. "Bless you, my lord. A thousand times, bless you!"

Against Gwenyth's chest, Mary squirmed, and Nellwyn accepted the infant back into her arms. Gwenyth kissed the child's tiny forehead as she released the babe, nearly moved to tears herself. Nellwyn's every dream had been shattered, and now she had a daughter who relied solely upon her.

No longer, for Gwenyth resolved to ease her cousin's burden in whatever way she could. For now, she patted Nellwyn's thin shoulder.

But how awful to lose one's happiness so quickly. Nellwyn, who had seemed perfectly wed, now had naught—no husband to keep her warm at night, no security for her future. Always, her cousin's life had seemed flawless. Gwenyth had been envious that Nellwyn had wed such a handsome, wealthy man, possessed of such a prestigious reputation and luxurious home.

Now she pitied her cousin more than she ever had another.

This sad state of affairs, all because Nellwyn had coveted Sir Rankin's rank, money, and castle.

Gwenyth shook her head at the sadness of it.

Then she froze.

Had she not assumed the same reasoning Nellwyn once had? Had she not believed marriage to a wealthy, well-landed lord would ease her aches and heal her heart?

Nellwyn wept noisily beside her, interrupting her thoughts. Guilford soothed her cousin with a soft whisper of comfort. Beside the two, Gwenyth stood stunned by realization, as if the sun had sent a blast of summer's heat upon her during January snows.

Aye, she had been mistaken in thinking a wealthy husband would make a good one. Sir Rankin had proven that quite wrong.

In fact, she had been wrong about happiness needing a home to flourish. It merely needed a heart within which to grow. 'Twas so clear now. Gwenyth wished she had seen such sooner. Then she frowned. For all that Aric had been at times difficult and uncommunicative, he had understood what she had not.

But he did not understand everything. For instance, he did not understand running from his home would not bring him happiness. He failed to realize that lying to her about his identity, accusing her of bedding down with him simply for his title, then abandoning her when she finally admitted she loved him, were churlish and despicable. The wretched coxcomb.

Gwenyth muttered a curse. By the moon and the stars, she had cried for him, yearned and pined like the most foolish of maidens! And what had he done, beyond leave her to the care of a stranger, fight a battle after swearing he would not, then never return for her?

Aric Neville was a fen-sucked lout, just as she had always suspected.

Did the rotten codpiece actually believe she would let him loose so easily, without feeling the edge of her angry tongue?

If he did, he was twice the fool!

One last time, she would see Aric and tell him exactly what she thought of his mangy, ill-mannered hide.

Jumping to her feet, Gwenyth began to leave, then remembered her distraught cousin and her husband's aging mentor.

Gwenyth bit her lip, her mind racing. She could not simply leave them, Nellwyn during her most unhappy time of need and Guilford without a chatelaine.

The old man must have seen something in her eyes, for they sparkled as he smiled. "For a moment, your step seemed suddenly vigorous. Think you of going somewhere?"

If Gwenyth had not known better, she would swear the man had gypsy blood and could read minds. "I— Well…I had thought… I must see Aric."

The old man's mouth curled up into a grin. "Indeed, you must."

"But—" She gestured to Nellwyn, who still sat quietly, clutching her daughter to her chest, weeping.

"I will care for her," he whispered for her ears alone.

"But—" She waved a hand to indicate her surroundings.

"Nellwyn is well qualified to take over a chatelaine's duties whilst you are gone, is she not?" At Gwenyth's hopeful nod, Guilford continued. "You see, all will be well here. Such duties may relieve her mind of her troubles. For now, you go."

Gwenyth clutched the earl's hands. "Thank you, Guilford. I know the words are not much…"

"Nonsense," the old man insisted, smiling. "I have had the pleasure of a lovely lady's company for some months now. You have no need to thank me."

Stopping the smile creeping across her mouth seemed impossible. "You are incorrigible."

"Nay, I leave that to your husband. And by the way, you may tell him when next you see him that—"

"Believe me, my lord, when I tell you I will fill his rogue's ears until they bleed, if need be."

CHAPTER NINETEEN

Aric stood inside the Tower's outer walls but still exposed to London's gray and biting late September chill as he waited for the summons.

By the saints, he had not wished to return. The royal missive he had received just a week past crinkled within his grip. But it could not be ignored.

Cursing, Aric stared at the door of the king's temporary chambers within the Bloody Tower, the same room in which King Henry had stripped him of his future and doomed his marriage only a month ago.

Why, when he had barely returned to the cottage and begun his existence of lifeless isolation, was the king forcing him back to London? Why, when he had nearly blocked out the exact blue of Gwenyth's eyes, had Henry chosen to summon him now?

To further degrade his rank?

To throw him back in the Tower?

He gritted his teeth at the thought of either.

After Aric had spent an hour impatiently pacing, the door swung open and a guard bade Aric to enter the king's domain.

Little had changed in the past month, except that King Henry had been officially coroneted, and the crown now sat upon his head. His clothing and apartments were a bit more opulent, and a small court crowd surrounded him, but the king still had mystery dancing in his dark eyes.

"So, Aric Neville, you have finally arrived?" he said by way of greeting.

Executing a respectful bow, Aric murmured, "Sire."

The king dismissed his court followers with a wave. Most, fugitives from the crown under Richard's reign, stared at Aric with speculation as they left.

Once they had gone, King Henry leaned back in his deep chair and regarded Aric with a watchful gaze. "Know you what the most difficult part of being a new king is?"

Aric tried not to allow his resentment or puzzlement to show. Purposely, he lowered his gaze to the stone floor, hoping the king would take it as a sign of respect. Damnation, he could not fathom why the king would utter such a question to him, a question that seemed to invite confidences of Aric—a man in whom the king had little faith—and why Henry had dragged him all the way to London to ask it.

"I confess, Your Highness, I do not."

"'Tis knowing who to trust, Neville." The king rose and paused before settling his weighty gaze upon Aric once more. "Many of the men who fought for me were French and have returned home. I must find trustworthy Englishmen and reward them for stabilizing the country to a new reign, loyal men strong enough to hold land in my name. And I know not always who is friend and who is foe."

With a nod, Aric indicated he understood the king's logic. But he had no notion why King Henry disclosed this fact to him when he had all but made his displeasure clear upon their last meeting.

"The Tower is filled with such men," the king went on. "Take your neighbor Northumberland, for instance."

Northumberland? Aric frowned. The man's loyalties should not be in question. He, no doubt, would accept Richard back on the throne this day were such possible. Henry would never view such a strong supporter of the previous king as a true ally.

"Your face bespeaks confusion. I would have you tell me why," Henry barked.

Aric grappled with the truth. Would he, in speaking his knowledge, consign Northumberland to death? If he said naught and Northumberland thought to aid the revolt said to be under plan even now, what would happen to England?

Was this question some royal trap, well plotted?

"Sire, why ask me of Northumberland's loyalties if you do not even trust mine?"

"I know your reasoning for lining up beneath Richard's standard, Neville, just as I know you stood beside Northumberland before the battle began. What I do not know is the man's mind."

Muttering a curse, Aric regarded the king with wary eyes.

"Do not hesitate!" King Henry roared. "I would have the truth and have it now!"

Sighing, Aric knew he had little choice. Better to see Northumberland executed than an entire nation possibly plunged into death and disorder once more.

"'Tis doubtful Northumberland can be counted among your friends, sire."

The king nodded thoughtfully. "For whom did he fight?"

He hesitated but again knew he must speak. "For Richard Plantagenet."

Furrowing his brow, King Henry regarded him with uncertainty. "How did he fight?"

"He was to await further orders behind the hill. I believe he could not see the battle in progress from behind the slope, so—"

"Did he never move to attack?" The king's face reflected disbelief.

"He did, Your Highness, but 'twas much later. He, along with his men, became stuck in the marshy soil before they could engage your forces in battle."

The king nodded. "'Twould explain his position on the plain when my men arrested him. That is all. You may go."

Familiar with King Henry's abrupt dismissals, Aric knew he should leave, but his conscience made him linger. Aye, he had never liked Northumberland but did not wish to see another die, particularly because of his words.

"Sire, I know I am in no position to request favors, but I must beg one now."

King Henry raised an imperious dark brow. "That is presumptuous of you, Neville."

Aric cleared his throat and forged ahead while he had the king's ear. "Do not brand Northumberland a traitor because of my words. If you deem him one, like many of the others in the Tower, execute him for his service to King Richard alone."

"I have heard you are a man of great honor. And you have shown me thus today." He paused, as if in thought. "Very well, I will

233

consider your request."

Aric wished he had the daring to ask for the return of his home and title so that he might be with Gwenyth now.

Someday, perhaps with continued service to England's new king, he might receive some scrap of land, mayhap even a tiny barony.

And perhaps not.

What irony that the very importance he had once fled in misery was now the one thing he needed to bring him lifelong joy.

"Thank you, sire." Aric bowed his farewell, then turned to leave.

He would return to the cottage, where he would spend endless days dreaming of the times he had held Gwenyth, wondering what their lives would have been like had war not intervened, imagining the faces of the children they would never share. He would go on enduring the torture of sleepless nights, no longer haunted by the screams of dead princes but the silent death of his heart instead, wilting, withering, wasting away.

Still, he had seen to Gwenyth's happiness, and for the rest of his life, he must take comfort in that.

As Aric reached the door, the guard pulled it open, and the gray afternoon swept in with the wind.

"Wait, Neville!" the king called.

The guard shut the door in Aric's face.

Given no choice but to face his new sovereign again, Aric wondered what the king might want now. Suddenly, he felt too tired to stay a moment longer. A dismal future awaited.

"There is more on your mind. I see that upon your face."

Aric swallowed, uncertain how to respond. He could not tell the king that he craved the return of the possessions he had seized. The impertinence alone would likely get him killed.

Still, without Gwenyth, he had only misery to lose and a bright love to regain.

Despite his knotted stomach, he forged ahead. "Twice I have sworn fealty to you. I answered your summons with all haste and told you a truth about an old neighbor, which brings me great unrest."

Cynicism settled over the king's face. "And now you wish a reward for your valiant service?"

Aric curled his damp palms into fists, wondering what had plagued him to take such a risk. Love, he knew. Only love. As only love gave him strength now.

"Nay, sire. I wish only the return of what was mine."

Henry raised a dark brow. "Do you assume what is yours includes the lands and titles once belonging to your uncle, Warwick?

Aric recoiled from the thought. Once, he had sought nothing more than the power associated with Warwick. Now he hoped the entire earldom rotted for all the grief it had caused his family for generations.

He cleared his throat. "Nay, sire. If you feel inclined to confer it upon someone, you should consider my uncle's widow. Her claims were long ignored by Richard Plantagenet."

Astonishment changed the king's features. "Again, you surprise me, Neville."

"I no longer seek the benefit of Warwick for myself, but that which will benefit England and her people."

"Of what benefit do you speak?" Henry frowned.

"Limiting the power of noble families to prevent further wars over succession. Having a good, fair man upon the throne. And I will serve you loyally as long as you serve England thus."

King Henry studied him. "I hear you resisted serving Richard with your battle prowess some time ago and that he all but forced you to Ambien plain in August. Be that true, Neville?"

He swallowed again, his heart pounding faster than a charging steed's hooves. "Aye. He had ceased serving England well."

"You know this for certain?"

Instead of the familiar pain he had lived with for nearly a year, only a deep sadness settled in his gut. "I know more than I would like."

King Henry raised a brow, seemingly intrigued. "If I asked you today, would you take up a blade in defense of me?"

"I already have, sire," he answered in all truth.

"So you have." King Henry nodded thoughtfully. "So you have."

"I would do so again if need be."

"Do you swear this?" Henry demanded.

Churning with uncertainty, with hope, Aric nodded.

"Very well. I grant the return of your lands and titles, Lord

Belford."

His heart leaped as relief infused him. Already he wanted to be gone from London. To Hartwich he would ride tomorrow—nay, tonight. Already he could picture Gwenyth, taste her, feel the love in her touch—

"I believe you will serve me well when I need you," said the king suddenly.

Aric heard the confidence in the king's voice, and gladness bloomed within him. "I believe you will serve England well, sire."

With that, Aric bowed and left, his stomach dancing with anticipation for a blessed and beloved future.

* * * *

A grueling six days later, Aric arrived at Hartwich as the sun rose above the sleeping brown-and-rust-hued countryside. He scarcely noticed nature's display of the autumn as he vaulted off his horse and strode toward the great hall. Dog barked in greeting, then bounded toward him.

Stooping to pet the gray mutt, whose wildly wagging tail hit the earth with repeated thumps, Aric greeted Dog.

When he looked up, Guilford stood before him.

The old man did not often show his disapproval. Today, he did. His scowl showed all the subtlety of a thunderclap. Aric flinched.

"So you've returned?" the old man asked sharply.

Despite his pounding heart, Guilford would no doubt make him earn his place by Gwenyth's side once more. "Aye. I've come for my wife. Where is she?"

The old man shrugged then turned for the great hall.

"Why should you believe she would stay here with strangers after you abandoned her?"

As he followed his mentor inside, Aric's stomach plummeted to his knees. *Gwenyth gone?* "I did not abandon her."

"You left her to my care with no intent to return."

"Damnation, Guilford, much has changed, and I confess my error. That I know well. Do not make me spar with you, for I shall have to beg well enough to my wife as it is."

"You have learned to stay by her side, no matter what?"

"Aye."

"And *if* she will have you, what of politics and battle? Any life you choose will most certainly contain both, unless you plan to return Gwenyth to your hovel."

"I would not do such to her," Aric vowed, then hesitated. "'Tis why I did not come sooner. On the battlefield, as I fought for King Henry—"

"You switched sides?"

Aric nodded. "'Twas the only fight my conscience would allow." At Guilford's frown, he went on. "During the battle, I realized I did not hate the war as much as I hated my own ambition and the way King Richard had used it."

"I do not—"

"I know you do not understand me now. Soon, I will explain. Now I must be with my wife."

Guilford paused, and Aric feared the old earl would say naught. Damnation, if Gwenyth had indeed left, he would tear apart the countryside, look in every forest and shire until—

"She has gone to your cottage."

Aric's mouth dropped open in shock. "The cottage? But she... I do not—"

"I know you do not understand me now," Guilford mimicked Aric's earlier statement. "Go be with your wife. She will tell you all—and more, I feel certain."

Scowling, Aric resisted leaving Hartwich until he understood Gwenyth's actions. Had she gone to be with him? Had she gone to show him the sharp side of her anger? Had she gone to tell him he needed never return to her side?

"My lord Belford?" called a quiet, unfamiliar female voice from the corner.

Aric looked beyond his mentor's shoulder, until his gaze fixed on a wan, dark-haired lady.

Nellwyn? "Lady Brinkley."

Why was she here at Hartwich?

"I know you realize I wasn't always kind to Gwenyth. She always had so much beauty. My own father asked me why I could not be more like her..." She trailed off, her tone full of apology.

"She understands," Aric said, making his way to the door.

"Wait, please."

Aric turned back to her, impatient to be away. "Aye?"

237

"If she resists you, tell her…tell her I said if I had a man who loved me so, I would sacrifice nearly anything to keep him." Slow tears ran down the woman's face.

"Sir Rankin beat her for birthing a girl," Guilford whispered to Aric.

Gritting his teeth against an unexpected surge of anger, Aric vowed to seek the sorry bastard out and pummel his face blue.

"Beat him, if you wish," said Guilford, seeming to read his thought, "but we received word just yestereve that King Henry stripped Sir Rankin of all his lands. 'Tis fitting, I think."

"It is, but I still plan to beat him," whispered Aric. To Nellwyn, he called, "I will tell Gwenyth exactly what you said, good lady."

Now he only hoped Gwenyth still felt the love she had once confessed, the love he had yet to tell her he returned with the whole of his body and heart.

* * * *

Gwenyth meandered about the empty cottage, wishing she had brought Dog with her, but she hadn't wanted reminders of Aric, and sad Nellwyn seemed to favor the animal. Mayhap she should not have released Guilford's escort to return to Hartwich Hall so quickly, but she had not wanted the dubious comfort of strangers, either.

Unfortunately, such a solitary situation left her with nothing to do but wonder where on earth her errant husband had gone. The wretch.

Though Aric had lived here recently, according to the whispers of the wary villagers, no one knew for certain when he had departed the area or where he had gone. They only hoped he never returned.

And she had no way to tell him what a cowardly, mealy-mouthed bounder she thought him.

After pacing to the other side of the room, she fluffed the pillow lying upon the cot, then hung the kettle above the hearth and restacked the kindling.

Where had the man gone? Had his ridiculously brief missive announcing his intent to live here been a lie? If it had, she would search him down to the ends of the realm and show him the full heat of her fury. The swine!

Drawing in a deep breath, Gwenyth walked around the cottage once more, taking in the dirt floor and less than stout roof. But her traitorous mind saw only happy times within these walls—her lively exchanges of words with Aric, their intimate kisses on the cot, their cozy meals at the hearth. The rest of the dwelling faded into the background, leaving a vision of her perfect, solemn husband.

She frowned, for she knew not why Aric resisted castle life so completely. But resist it he did. Damn the churlish mucker! She at least deserved an explanation. And when she saw him, she would drag the words from him, even if she had to do it with her teeth.

Gwenyth trudged back to the cot and flung herself down upon the blankets. Despite the fact she had slept upon them for three nights now, they still kept the earthy, woodsy scent that reminded her so fiercely of Aric and brought back their intimate couplings deep in the night.

Forcing her mind elsewhere, Gwenyth propelled herself off of the cot and fingered the pendant at her neck.

Where could the moldwarp of a scoundrel be?

And what would she do with her life once she fed him a healthy dose of her fury? What was left but accepting the fact he was gone forever?

Stubbornly, she clung to her anger. She did not yearn for him in a way that made her soul ache. It pleased her well not to have to live beside him always. It did!

With a sigh, she forced herself to acknowledge she had no reason to remain here. If Aric had truly fled the cottage, never to return, lingering would not bring him back so he might hear her opinions of his desertion.

Nor did Gwenyth have a reason to stay in Bedfordshire. She had no further ties to the village. Everyone here still thought her a black sorcerer's wife, and so they avoided her or whispered behind her back.

Even Uncle Bardrick was gone now. Apparently he had displeased King Henry, who had seized Penhurst and its lands. Gwenyth knew not where her aunt and uncle had gone. Moreover, she did not care.

The day before, she had walked about the nearly deserted castle of her girlhood, only to find it held naught for her—not loathing or pain, not anguish or longing. Naught at all.

Somehow that relieved her nearly as much as the note she had received that very morn from Nellwyn saying all was well with both Guilford and the babe, Mary.

In general, life pleased her.

If, deep in the night, she thought of Aric, 'twas only lack of sleep playing games with her head. Her dazed mind foolishly feared she would never be whole again without him. She could scarce imagine whence such feeble-witted thoughts arose.

But in those dark hours, the thought of living the rest of her life, watching seasons come and go, observing the people about her live and die, all without Aric's arms around her... She shook her head, unable to avoid the truth any longer. Worry that unhappiness would slowly drain the very life from her soul plagued her day and night.

Had the man become crucial to her happiness? Nay.

Aye, whispered her heart.

When?

How?

And now he was gone.

Gwenyth scarce knew whether to scream or cry.

Sinking to the cot, she did both.

CHAPTER TWENTY

Aric's heart raced as he rode up to the cottage in the dead of night. He cared not that all but the moon slept or that he made an easy target for the thieves who might be lining the roads.

He cared only about reaching Gwenyth.

Finally, their little cottage came into view, backlit by the brilliance of a hopeful golden moon. Night's chill put a nip into the wind, and Aric tethered his mount and rushed inside away from the cold—toward his wife.

Complete darkness greeted Aric, and he struggled to see inside the small dwelling. Cursing, he felt about for a candle and flint, then cursed repeatedly until he finally had the thing lit.

Flame in hand, he turned to seek out his wife, only to find her rising from the cot, pushing strands of midnight-hues hair from her sleepy, beloved face. She wore naught but a thin white shift.

He swallowed then started toward her with love and purpose in his heart.

"You!" her voice rang with fury and accusation as she ignored his approach. "I've waited here three days to tell you— What are you doing?" she screeched as he pulled her against his aching body.

Without a reply, he captured her soft mouth beneath his, sinking into the taste and texture of Gwenyth. She smelled of green nature and life, felt perfect and solid in his arms. Pleasure exploded across his senses as he coaxed her mouth open beneath his and began exploring her recesses with his tongue, taking her in completely.

Suddenly, she tore her lips from his and backed away with a hard shove. "Have you gone mad?"

She was angry. His abrupt missive to her, written after King Henry had taken his lands, must have annoyed her more than a trifle.

And it would not have done so had she not cared for him at least a little.

Aric smiled. "Quite the opposite, my lady wife."

"Do not think to charm or kiss me from my anger, you sapless knave. You cannot send me a weak-headed message that you are forsaking me forever whilst you squall away your life in poverty, offer no explanation, then kiss me as if your vexatious, scurvy actions are of no import—"

Aric took her mouth again, then laughed. Aye, his Gwenyth had never lost her fire, and he was going to enjoy trying to tame her for a lifetime.

Her heel mashed his toes to the ground. Pain shot up his legs, and he backed away from her in disbelief.

"Do not touch me, you troublesome jackass. I came here to tell you what I think of your cowardly desertion, not to be mauled."

Holding his abused toes in one hand, Aric hopped to keep his balance and glared at his wife. She had more fire than even he remembered.

"You have made your point amply, and I will not touch you until we have spoken."

"You will not touch me at all, ever! 'Tis you who left—"

"So you have repeatedly reminded me. You also said you wished to know why. If you will sit and close your mouth for a moment, I will tell you."

Gwenyth's look was surly and rebellious, but sit she did on the edge of the cot, then looked at him with cool, regal expectation. In every way, she would make him a fine countess.

Easing down beside her, Aric wondered where to start this convoluted tale. He felt his palms sweating as doubt crept in. What if he could not persuade Gwenyth to stay with him always? He loved her, and he must convince her of that. Aye, but he must also choose his next words carefully, else she would never stay long enough to hear his declaration and believe his devotion. Damnation, how to begin…

"I grow old waiting," Gwenyth prodded.

Aric stared at his impatient wife and sighed. "I fought the battle."

"So I gathered from Guilford and Stephen. Do you plan to tell me that such a battle, so like every other you ever fought, made you want to part from me forever?"

"Nay. I could not fight for King Richard."

"So you fought for King Henry?" Surprise sounded in her voice.

He nodded, realizing suddenly that he should—indeed, must— tell her all. "My conscience would allow naught else. You see, I knew…well, I have known for nigh on a year now that Richard ordered the deaths of his nephews, the princes."

Gwenyth gasped, shock transforming her expression to one of horror. "'Tis certain?"

Aric gave her a bleak nod. "He had them suffocated in the Tower two years past. And my refusal to fight had as much to do with my own horrific actions in the matter as his."

Shock became confusion on Gwenyth's sweet face. "What say you? Such makes little sense."

"I know," he said, sighing. "But in the spring following King Edward IV's death, King Richard, then the Duke of Gloucester, had been named protector of his brother's two sons."

"This I know."

"And you probably know as well that Richard intercepted young Edward and his maternal uncle, Earl Rivers, on their way to London following the king's death. Once Richard had the boy in custody, he sent the lad off to the Tower under the guise of keeping him well until his coronation. Rivers he beheaded for some false charge.

"Richard set a coronation date for young Edward but complained privately that having a minor on the throne would bring naught but unrest to England. In truth, I think he had always wanted the throne for himself. Though he had ever been a competent manager of his northern estates and well liked for it, 'twas never enough, in his mind."

"How do you know this?" Gwenyth breathed.

"I was ever at his side. We spent part of our youth together at my uncle's castle, Middleham. We battled together many a time. As you know, he even wed my cousin, Anne."

"You were friends with a king?"

Aric shrugged off the awe in her tone. "Of a sort, aye. Anyway, at some point, I must assume that Richard plotted to seize the throne for himself. Accordingly, he came to me and asked for my help in mending the rift between himself and the dowager queen, Elizabeth Woodville. They had been enemies since the day she wed King Edward and the dolt began giving the Woodvilles land and titles."

Gwenyth nodded her understanding. "Go on."

"Richard convinced me that were young Edward's brother to stay with him in the Tower to await the coronation, Elizabeth and all of England would see he supported his nephew and ultimately his mother's family."

"But that was not the case."

"It was not, and I knew naught of his true intentions for months. That is the truth."

The overwhelming information sat like shock upon her pale face. "What happened then?"

"As I said, Richard asked for my help. Ever since my Uncle Warwick had been killed in battle supporting Henry VI, his lands and titles had been divided between Richard himself and his older brother, the Duke of Clarence, who was executed for treason. I had once imagined King Edward might restore Clarence's share to me, including the earldom of Warwick, but he feared the power of the Warwick title returning to my family, especially to me."

"You had the prowess in battle and the power in court to be of harm if you chose."

"Aye, so when Richard asked me to assist him in mending this rift, I thought the boy, when he became king, might be grateful enough to grant my request. I wanted Warwick back so badly. Its taste teased my tongue daily. I wanted to be the next powerful Earl Warwick and command politics, as was my family heritage." He couldn't stop his bitter laugh.

"You *wanted* money and power?" Shock vibrated in her voice.

"More than anything." His self-deprecating tone hung in the air between them. "So Richard asked me to go to Elizabeth Woodville in sanctuary with her other children in Westminster Abbey and convince her to release Edward's younger brother to me so he might wait with Edward for the coronation. I thought it a simple enough task to lead me back to power. I did as he requested."

She gasped. "Elizabeth released the boy to you."

He nodded. "And I delivered him to the Tower myself."

Gwenyth closed her eyes as dismay overtook her face.

"Now I see you understand," he whispered. "I assure you, you cannot revile me any more for my greed than I did myself."

Her blue eyes snapped open, and she touched a soft hand to his arm. "You could not have known Richard's plans."

"I did not," he admitted. "But I should have at least suspected."

"How could you conceive of such evil from a friend?"

Aric shrugged. "Elizabeth Woodville feared for her life and the lives of her children. 'Tis why she was in sanctuary. She pleaded with me to leave the young boy be. I vowed to the woman nothing bad would befall the prince. In the end, I made his death possible by giving him over to Richard and his dastardly plan."

"Oh, Aric…" She took his hand in hers.

"Once I realized what Richard, then the king, had done, I was horrified by his actions—and my own. My grief and my guilt constantly plagued me. I could not sleep or eat. Battle sickened me, to know I was the cause of so much death…"

"Battle is the way of a warrior's life."

"I could tolerate it no more. So I left all behind and came here."

Gwenyth sat tensely, staring. Aric could see the thoughts churning in her head.

"That is why you did not want to tell me your identity after we first wed."

"I was ashamed," he said with a nod. "I had planned never to return to that life."

"And later, when I knew the truth of who you were, why did you not tell me all of this?"

"And put your very life in jeopardy? Nay." He rose and paced. "I told no one, not Guilford or Drake or Kieran. I refused to risk having anyone else die because of me."

Gwenyth stood, her eyes wet with tears. "Why did you not return to me after King Richard died in battle? Did you really mean never to see me again?"

"I knew not what to do. You must believe that." Aric seized her shoulders in desperate hands. "King Henry imprisoned me in the Tower for a fortnight."

Gwenyth gasped.

Aric went on. "When he released me, I thought of naught but retuning to you." He swore, willing her to see the truth in his eyes. "Then Henry took away my lands and my title. I had naught to offer you. You had made it clear that life as a pauper's wife held no appeal, and that you hated this cottage was in no doubt."

"And you left me at Hartwich because you thought life in a castle—any castle—would please me?"

Aric nodded uncertainly. She had said as much many times over. Why did her question make the concept sound ludicrous?

"You thick-skulled clod! I waited for you. I cried for you."

"Cried? For me?"

"Do not distract me with stupid questions—"

"Stupid?" he began to grin, hope tripping his heart.

She sighed in annoyance. "Vexing man! Would you stop flapping your lips long enough to let me tell you that I do not require a castle or title for my happiness?"

"You do not?"

Gwenyth shook her head. Her dark tresses, glossy even by candlelight, slid over her shoulders. "Whilst you were gone, I realized many things, mostly that I was not pleased without you. Then Nellwyn came to Hartwich."

"I heard of Sir Rankin's despicable actions."

Impatiently, she nodded. "Despicable, indeed, but they made me realize that such a man, no matter his worth, could only make a wife miserable. One cannot make love to money, nor will it warm your heart. And Hartwich, for all its glory, held no appeal in your absence. I knew with certainty that Northwell would be no different without you."

"What?" he breathed, hardly daring to believe his ears.

"'Tis not so hard to comprehend. A place alone cannot make one happy. If that were true, I would have been well pleased to remain at Penhurst, no matter how badly Uncle Bardrick and Aunt Welsa treated me. But after my parents' deaths, I hated every moment of life there."

"And you came here to tell me that?"

"Nay." Irritation flitted across her features. "I came to tell you I thought you a sniveling scapegrace for leaving me."

Aric laughed and walked toward her. "Aye, but now that you are here and I am here…"

He curled his arms about her small waist and drew her against his body. Gwenyth felt perfect in his arms, and every part of him responded to that certainty.

"Now that we are here?" she breathed as her deep blue gaze

fastened upon his face.

Smiling, he whispered, "Now that we are together, I will tell you I could not stay away from you."

Her eyes lit up with bliss. "You need not stay away—ever. I do not require a castle or a title to please me." She pressed her sweet lips to his, and Aric's heart soared with gladness. "I require only you."

"And I require you." He captured her face in his palms and let his gaze delve into her blue eyes. "I love you."

At her soft gasp and dampening eyes, Aric kissed her mouth with tender joy, forging a renewed union between them. With quiet need, he savored her mouth, releasing her when passion began to override his need to hear of her love for him.

"Gwenyth—"

"I never thought to hear you say you loved me." Gwenyth's voice trembled. Her hands tightened about his neck as she smiled. "I have loved you for so long...and I felt like a simpleton when you accused me of wanting you only for your wealth."

He grimaced. "I was an idiot. I yearned so badly to believe you wanted me as a man, but feared you wanted me only as an earl with a grand castle."

"I know." She hugged, holding him close. "But now that we are here together, should we not go about life as husband and wife?"

Aric could not miss her meaningful glance to the cot. He smiled. "We could, but I fear Northwell will rot with neglect if we don't tend it soon."

"Northwell? But I thought—that is, you said..."

"Oh, did I not tell you?" he feigned confusion. "Let me think." He tapped a finger to his chin as if deep in thought. "Nay, I suppose I did not. I have just arrived from London and King Henry's audience."

"*That* is where you have been?"

Nodding, Aric swept Gwenyth into his arms and pulled them both down to the cot.

Though laughing, she protested. "Aric, you must tell me what happened. He cannot be angry with you. You fought for him!"

"Indeed, he knows this and knows me to be a loyal subject as well."

She sighed with relief. "My heart near stopped for thinking of you in the Tower, along with all the others he has branded traitor."

"I feel fair certain we will have no more of that."

"Good." She nuzzled his neck with kisses—kisses that distracted him from his purpose.

"Gwenyth, Northwell?" he prompted, nearly choking on his growing desire to have her.

She feathered kisses along his cheek, toward his mouth. Aric swallowed a groan.

"What of it?"

"Naught...except 'tis ours again."

"It is?" her voice held no more than passing interest.

"Aye, we can journey there today—"

"I am in no hurry, my lord, for I like the privacy here."

With that, her mouth brushed softly against his own before settling over his lips for a kiss that heated his innards to a blaze.

"Privacy?" he whispered.

"Much of it," she confirmed.

The idea held appeal for him as well. "We can wait a day or two."

Her mouth formed an impish grin beneath his own. "Or a week or two."

"My, you are a greedy wench," he chided, laughing.

"Only where you are concerned, and only because I love you."

The teasing left his face as he beheld his wife in his arms, her soft features open and welcoming. His heart expanded in his chest with happiness until he thought he might explode. Always he would remember this moment, just as he would always keep her by his side, no matter where politics led, no matter where they made their home.

"Gwenyth, my wife, I love you, too."

He ended his whisper with a kiss that sealed their union in devotion and rapture, knowing she would forever be his lady bride.

Author's Note

Though we will never know for certain what exact sequence of events led to the tragic deaths of Edward V and his younger brother Richard, Duke of York, Alison Weir paints a vivid and terrible picture of the political intrigues and murders in her book *The Princes in the Tower*. I have borrowed Ms. Weir's interpretation of the actions leading up to and directly following the disappearances and deaths of the two royal children. Sir Thomas More wrote some graphic accounts of the tragedy, almost entirely corroborated by physical evidence. It is from this account and others that Ms. Weir drew her theory. Any misunderstanding of these events is purely my own. My apologies to the Richard III Society, for I know you disagree with this analysis.

What we do know is the boys disappeared from public view during the late summer of 1483 and that the inhabitants of London surmised them dead by January of the next year. Although no hard evidence existed linking Richard III to the murders of his nephews, most of England believed him guilty. For this, he was an unpopular king.

The boys' skeletons were finally recovered, buried in rocks and rubble at the base of a staircase within the Tower of London in 1674. At that time, King Charles II gave them a proper burial, befitting their station, in Westminster Abbey, where they can still be seen today.

King Richard fared no better. After his near-naked body was displayed at the friary in Leicester for two days, it was buried without ceremony. Today, the friary does not exist, thanks to Henry VIII and his dissolution of the monasteries in the 1530s. At that time, Richard's grave was dug up and his body thrown out. According to local lore, his coffin found its way to a nearby manor, where it was used to build a horse trough and some cellar steps. Richard III was the only king since the Norman invasion of 1066 to have no burial place. In September 2012, Richard III's body was found buried under a parking lot in the Grayfriar's area of Leister. After some court battles, he was again buried at the cathedral in Leister in July 2014.

As for the battle that came to be known as Bosworth, history was not kind in preserving accurate information, and to this day, controversy stirs over the exact location and participants' loyalties, including the Earl of Northumberland. In my telling, I blended several accounts and hope I have done such a momentous occasion justice.

Though no one knows the potential of England's loss in the two princes who might have been king, the Tudor dynasty established England as the world's supreme nation for some time. But England never stopped mourning the children cut down cruelly in youth.

I sincerely hope you enjoyed *His Lady Bride*.

HIS STOLEN BRIDE

Brothers in Arms, BOOK 2
By Shayla Black writing as Shelley Bradley
Coming August 18, 2014!

Captives of Love…

Wrongly accused of murdering his father, Drake Thornton MacDougall wanted nothing more than to strike back at his guilty, duplicitous half-brother. So he made the fiend pay by abducting his bride-to-be. But as Drake carried his captive off to a windswept Scottish isle, he soon found that vengeance wasn't the only thing on his mind. Lady Averyl Campbell proved herself no biddable maiden, but an alluring, strong-willed beauty who could tame his dark moods with her touch. When danger and treachery threatened to part them, Drake realized that only she could heal his tormented soul, for she had won his love.

No Prince Charming
The Secrets of Stone, Book 1
By *USA Today Bestseller* Angel Payne and Victoria Blue
Available Now!

Excerpt

<u>Prologue</u>

April

Claire

Oh my God.

The words sprinted through my head, over and over, as I prodded at my lips in assurance I wasn't dreaming. Or hopping dimensions. Or remembering the last half hour in a *really* crazy way. Or had hours passed, instead? I didn't know anymore. Time was suddenly contorted.

Oh. My. God.

What the hell had just happened?

Forget my lips. My whole mouth felt like I'd just had dental work done, tingling in all the places his lips had touched moments ago—which had been everywhere.

My mind raced, trying to match the erratic beat of my heart. "Christ," I whispered. My voice shook like a damn teenager, so I repeated myself. Because *that* helped, right?

Wrong. So wrong.

It was all because of that man. That dictatorial, demanding…

Nerve-numbing, bone melting…

Man.

Who really knew how to deliver a kiss.

Hell. That kiss.

Okay, by this age, I'd been kissed before. I'd been *everything* before. But after what we'd just done, I'd be awake for long hours tonight. *Long* hours. Shaking with need…shivering with fear.

I pressed the call button for the elevator with trembling fingers. Turning back to face the door I'd just emerged from, I reconsidered pushing the buzzer next to it, instead. The black lacquer panel around the button was still smudged by the angry fingerprints I'd left when arriving here not more than thirty minutes ago—answering his damn summons.

Yeah. He'd "summoned" me. And like a breathless backstage groupie, I'd dropped everything and come. Why? He was my hemlock. He could be nothing else.

I was even more pissed now. At him. At me. At the thoughts that wouldn't leave me alone now, all in answer to one tormenting question.

If Killian Stone kissed like that, what could he do to the rest of my body?

No. That kind of thinking was dangerous. The tiny hairs on the back of my neck stood up as if the air conditioner just kicked on at full power.

It had been a while since I'd been with a man. At least like…that.

Okay, it had been a long while.

For the last three years, career had come before all else. After the disaster I simply called The Nick Years, Dad had fought hard to help rebuild my spirit, including the doors he finagled open for me. Wasting those opportunities in favor of relationships wasn't an option. My focus had paid off, leading to a coveted position at Asher and Associates PR, where I'd quickly advanced to the elite field team for Andrea Asher herself. The six of us, including Andrea and her daughter, Margaux, were called corporate America's "miracle cover stick." We were brought in when the blemishes were too big and horrid for in-house PR specialists, hired on a project-by-project basis for our thoroughness and objectivity. That also meant the assignments were intense, ruthless, and very temporary.

The gig at Stone Global was exactly such a job. And things were going well. Better than well. People were cooperating. The press was moving on to new prey. The job was actually ahead of schedule, and thank God for it. Soon, I'd be back in my rightful place at the home office in San Diego and what just happened in Killian Stone's penthouse would remain no more than a blip in my memory. A very secret blip.

I shook my head in defiance. What was wrong with having lived a little? At twenty-six, I was due for at least one heart-stopping kiss with a man who looked like dark sin, was built like a Navy SEAL, and kissed like a fantasy. *Sweet God, what a fantasy.*

"You didn't do anything wrong," I muttered. "You didn't break any rules...technically. He consented. And you sure as *hell* consented. So you're—"

Having an argument with yourself in the middle of a hallway in the Lincoln Park 2550 building, waiting on the world's slowest damn elevator.

I leaned on the call button again.

While *still* trying to talk myself out of pouncing on Killian's buzzer, too. Or perhaps back into it. If I could concoct an excuse to ring his doorbell before the elevator arrived...

No. This is dangerous, remember? He's dangerous. You know all the sordid reasons why, his and yours.

Maybe I could just say I accidentally left my purse inside.

And that'll fly...how? One glance down at my oversized Michael Kors clutch had me cursing the fashion trend gods, along with their penchant for large handbags.

I leaned against the wall, closing my eyes and hoping for a light bulb. I was bombarded with Killian's smell, instead. Armani Code. The cologne was still strong in my head, its rich bergamot and lemon mingling with the spice of his shampoo and the scotch on his breath, like he'd scent-marked me through the intimacy of our skin...

My fingers roamed to my cheek, tracing the abrasion from where he'd rubbed me with his stubble. My head fell back from the impact of the recollection.

In an instant, my mind conjured an image of him again, standing in front of me. Commanding. Looming. Hot...and hard. I felt his breath on my face again as he yanked me close. The press of his wool pants against my legs. The metallic scrape of his cufflinks on the wood of his desk as he shoved everything away to make room for our bodies. Then the wild throb of my heart as he tangled his hands in my hair, lifted my face toward his, and...

Yes.

The memory was so vivid, so good. I used the flat of my palm on my face now, thinking I could save the magic if I covered it. Protecting it from the outside world. Our perfect, shared moment in the middle of all this chaos.

Whoa.

"Get a grip." I dropped my hand along with the furious whisper. It was one kiss. Incredible, yes, but I guaranteed *he* wasn't still thinking about it like this. Behind that majestic door, Killian Stone moved again in his world, already focused on the next of his hundred priorities, none of them bearing my name. And he expected me to get back to mine: cushioning his company from that big, bad outside world I'd just been brooding over. *You've been hired to help clean up the Stone family's mess, not add to it.*

The elevator finally dinged.

At the same time, Killian's condo door opened behind me.

I locked a smile on my face, trying to look like I had been patiently waiting for the elevator the entire time.

"Miss Montgomery?"

Not Killian. I didn't know whether to curse or laugh.

"Yes?" I managed a Girl Scout-sweet reply.

A kind face was waiting when I turned around. The man wore such a warm expression, I was tempted to call him Fred. *Not* Alfred. Just Fred. The man was too handsome for a full "Alfred."

Fred handed me a small ivory envelope, then stepped over into the elevator. He held the doors open while I got into the car with him. We rode in silence down to the lobby. I squirmed while Fred smiled as if it were Saturday in the park. Did he know what his boss had just done with me?

I winced toward the wall. Technically, Killian was *my* boss right now, too.

Mr. Stone. Mr. Stone. Mr. Stone.

He can never be "Killian" again.

The sooner you remember that, the better.

I was dying to open that little envelope, but carefully slipped it into my queen-size clutch for when I was alone again in the cab on my way back to the hotel.

"I'll call the car 'round for you." Like his employer, Fred made it obvious the subject wasn't up for debate, so I forced a smile and followed him across the gleaming lobby to the building's front awning. In less than a minute, the black town car with the Stone Global logo on its doors appeared. I climbed in, all the while yearning for the anonymity of a city cab instead.

255

Chicago was a great city, but the traffic was insane, even as evening officially blended into nighttime. Nevertheless, Killian's building was swiftly swallowed by the lush trees of the neighborhood. I was on my way back to the hotel. Back to real life—and all the dangers that waited if anyone on the team ever learned where I'd just been.

For just a few more seconds, I yearned to remember the fantasy, instead. Perhaps the treasure in my purse would help.

I pulled it out, running reverent fingers over it again. Nothing was written on the outside. Killian—Mr. Stone—had simply expected it would be delivered straight to me.

The elegant handwriting inside, dedicated to just one sentence, dried out my throat upon impact.

I must see you again.

He left no signature. No phone number. Not even an email address. But the strangest part about it all? I wasn't surprised. He was Killian Jamison Stone. And he kissed like *that*. Things—and people—came to him, not the other way around.

But did I have the strength to be one of those people, knowing I'd never see him again after three months?

About The Author

Shayla Black (aka Shelley Bradley) is the New York Times and USA Today bestselling author of over forty sizzling contemporary, erotic, paranormal, and historical romances produced via traditional, small press, independent, and audio publishing. She lives in Texas with her husband, munchkin, and one very spoiled cat. In her "free" time, she enjoys reality TV, reading and listening to an eclectic blend of music.

Shayla's books have been translated in about a dozen languages. She has been nominated for career achievement in erotic romance by RT Bookclub, as well as twice nominated for Best Erotic Romance of the year. Additionally, she's either won or been nominated for the Passionate Plume, the Holt Medallion, Colorado Romance Writers Award of Excellence, and the National Reader's Choice Awards.

A writing risk-taker, Shayla enjoys tackling writing challenges with every new book.

Connect with me online:
Facebook: https://www.facebook.com/ShaylaBlackAuthor
Twitter: http://twitter.com/Shayla_Black
Website: http://shaylablack.com/

Visit Shayla's website to join her newsletter!

If you enjoyed this book, I would appreciate your help so others can enjoy it, too. You can:
Recommend it. Please help other readers find this book by recommending it to friends, readers' groups, and discussion boards.
Review it. Please tell other readers why you liked this book by reviewing it wherever you purchased your book or on Goodreads. If you do write a review, please send me an e-mail at interact @ shaylablack.com so I can thank you with a personal e-mail.

Other Books by Shayla Black

EROTIC ROMANCE
THE WICKED LOVERS
Wicked Ties
Decadent
Delicious
Surrender To Me
Belong To Me
"Wicked to Love" (e-novella)
Mine To Hold
"Wicked All The Way" (e-novella)
Ours To Love
Wicked and Dangerous
Forever Wicked
Theirs To Cherish
Coming Soon:
His to Take (March 2015)

SEXY CAPERS
Bound And Determined
Strip Search
"Arresting Desire" – Hot In Handcuffs Anthology

MASTERS OF MÉNAGE (by Shayla Black and Lexi Blake)
Their Virgin Captive
Their Virgin's Secret
Their Virgin Concubine
Their Virgin Princess
Their Virgin Hostage
Their Virgin Secretary
Coming Soon:
Their Virgin Mistress (April 2015)

DOMS OF HER LIFE (by Shayla Black, Jenna Jacob, and Isabella LaPearl)
One Dom To Love
The Young And The Submissive
Coming Soon:
The Bold and The Dominant (Late 2014/early 2015)

STAND ALONE TITLES
Naughty Little Secret (Shayla Black writing as Shelley Bradley)
"Watch Me" – Sneak Peek Anthology (as Shelley Bradley)
Dangerous Boys And Their Toy
"Her Fantasy Men" – Four Play Anthology

PARANORMAL ROMANCE
THE DOOMSDAY BRETHREN
Tempt Me With Darkness
"Fated" (e-novella)
Seduce Me In Shadow
Possess Me At Midnight
"Mated" – Haunted By Your Touch Anthology
Entice Me At Twilight
Embrace Me At Dawn

HISTORICAL ROMANCE (Shayla Black writing as Shelley Bradley)
The Lady And The Dragon
One Wicked Night
Strictly Seduction
Strictly Forbidden

Coming Soon:
BROTHERS IN ARMS
His Lady Bride, Brothers in Arms (July 2014)
His Stolen Bride, Brothers in Arms (August 2014)
His Rebel Bride, Brothers in Arms (September 2014)

CONTEMPORARY ROMANCE (as Shelley Bradley)
A Perfect Match

CPSIA information can be obtained at www.ICGtesting.com
Printed in the USA
LVOW13s0903180814

399674LV00001B/187/P